LETTERS
FROM
ELSINORE

CHRISTOPHER RUSH

LETTERS FROM ELSINORE © 2024 CHRISTOPHER RUSH

Christopher Rush asserts the moral right to be identified as the author of this work in accordance with the Copyright, Designs and Patents Act 1988.

This is a work of fiction. Names, characters, places and incidents are either the result of the author's imagination or are used fictitiously. Any resemblance to actual persons, living or dead, business establishments, events or locales is entirely coincidental.

All rights reserved. No part of this publication may be reproduced, stored in or introduced into a retrieval system or transmitted in any form or by any means (electronic, mechanical, photocopying, recording or otherwise) without the prior written permission of the author.

ISBN: 978-1-914399-62-6

This book is sold subject to the condition that it shall not be resold, lent, hired out or otherwise circulated without the express prior consent of the author.

Printed and bound in Great Britain by Clays Ltd, Elcograf S.P.A.

Cover Design main image © Artur Braginzski, 'Zima', additional images courtesy of Dreamstime, layout by Mercat Design All Rights Reserved

To Helena Bonham Carter and her spirited Ophelia

And let me speak to the yet unknowing world
How these things came about: so shall you hear
Of carnal, bloody and unnatural acts,
Of accidental judgements, casual slaughters,
Of deaths put on by cunning and forced cause;
And, in this upshot, purposes mistook
Fall'n on the inventors' heads: all this can I
Truly deliver.

Contents

PART ONE

To Whom It May Concern 11
My First Night 15
My First Morning 21
An Account of My First Meeting with Hamlet 28
My Second Night 40
Hamlet's Account of His Meeting with the Ghost 46
An Account of How Marcellus and Myself Saw Hamlet Following His Meeting with the Ghost 55
Two Notes to Posterity: 60
On the Antic Disposition 63

PART TWO

A Pause for Thought 67
The Real Ophelia 69
Ophelia in Distress 78
My Thoughts on What Happened in Ophelia's Closet 80
A Note on Fork and Knife 87
A Note on the Chamber-Pot 93
Hamlet's Account to Me:
Of How he Ran Rings Round the Chamber-Pot 101
Hamlet's Account of How he Rattled Fork and Knife 109
The Players Arrive At Elsinore 118
What Hamlet Thought About 130

PART THREE.

Enter Osric with Information and a Flourish 135
Hamlet and the Sea of Troubles 137
Ophelia's Confession—and Country Matters 142
Before the Play 148
The Mouse-Trap 151
A Short Note on Hot Blood 168
Osric Overhears What God Did Not 170
Hamlet's Last Chance 172
A Note on The Above 174

In Gertrude's Bedchamber	175
A Few Notes on The Above	184

PART FOUR.

Hamlet on the Loose	187
The Council Meeting: Claudius in the Chair, Osric Taking the Minutes	189
Hamlet Meets the Fortinbras Army	193
Ophelia's Insanity	196
A Sea-Breeze	211
A Letter From Hamlet	212
The Poison Plot	213
Ophelia's Muddy Melodious Death—And Dreams	218

PART FIVE.

Grave Matters	227
Sound and Silence	246

Epilogue

A Gallery Of Ghosts	266
Enter the Ghost of Hamlet	267
Enter the Ghost of Claudius	271
Enter the Ghost of Gertrude	273
Enter the Ghost of Ophelia	276
Enter the Ghost of Polonius	281
Enter the Ghost of Laertes	282
Enter the Ghost of Fortinbras	282
Enter the Ghosts of Rosencrantz and Guildenstern	283
Enter the Ghost of Osric	284
Enter the Ghost of the Gravedigger	284
Enter the Ghost of Yorick	286
Enter the Ghost of Sigmund Freud	287
Enter the Ghost of Old King Hamlet	288
Enter the Ghost of Horatio	291
Re-enter the Ghost of Ophelia	293
Re-enter the Ghost of Horatio	298
A note on anachronism and language	300
Acknowledgements	301

PART ONE

To Whom It May Concern

Where to begin? At the beginning is the good old adage, and how this story starts off is dramatic enough to capture anyone's attention. Being a pedant by nature—and some training—my first inclination therefore is to follow the prescript. On reflection, however, I won't. You see, for me it was the actual ending that was also a sort of beginning, and is precisely why I am now putting pen to paper, as I was asked to do. Or again, in the interests of accuracy, as I was ordered to do—commanded would be an even better word—by a dying man, a friend. And no breath has such potency as the last breath, especially the last breath of a close friend. One other thing: I was asked to tell it, not to write it. But here again the pedant prevails—and the need for permanence. To whom should I tell it? And to how many, so many of those who were involved now being dead? And how many could I tell before I die too and can speak no more? Ears are mere shells, hollow in the end, where only a child can hear the sea, and its mystery. And what are words after all but mere breath, melted into the wind, into thin air? Unless they're written down.

I appear to have convinced myself, so let's waste no more time and get to the quick of it. Picture a cup of wine. Not difficult to do, is it? But this is no ordinary cup: it's a substantial one, expensive, bejewelled and made of gold, a goblet in fact, the kind of cup a king would bring to his lips. Or a queen. Except for one thing: it's a poisoned cup, the wine is deadly, it has already done its work on both king and queen, and the king didn't bring the cup to his lips, it was forced between his teeth and the contents poured down his throat. Being more of an old Roman than a Dane, I'd have joined them with the dregs—but for the fact that the dying man I have referred to summoned up his last ounce of energy and wrested it from me, sending it clattering across the castle flagstones. I could have fallen on my sword instead of course, and joined all those old Romans, and my friend too, in the silence that was about to fall on him, to deafen him, but that's when he came out with it. He was gasping and the words were hard to catch, but the message was clear enough. It was dramatic, like the end of a play, an old tragedy, and if it had been acted out in a theatre, which was exactly how it felt—let me give you the words—it might have gone something like this:

Give me the cup: let go: by heaven, I'll have it!
O God, Horatio, what a wounded name,
Things standing thus unknown, shall live behind me!
If thou didst ever hold me in thy heart,
Absent thee from felicity awhile,
And in this harsh world draw thy breath in pain,
To tell my story...

To tell my story. *My* story. The man was surrounded by corpses! The place was like a battlefield. Yes, he was about to be a corpse himself and he knew it, but apart from the corpses littering the floor—I'd never seen so many on a stage, even at the catastrophe—there were others he'd left behind, already dead and buried, people who'd have been alive and well if he'd acted differently. Or if he'd acted at all. And only one of them really deserved to die. Even a hardened soldier who happened to arrive on cue to bustle in and view the blood, the sheer carnage, was almost lost for words. He wasn't a man of words anyway, action was his thing, but I could see what went through his head. So again, I'll drop some words of my own into his mouth:

This quarry cries on havoc. O proud Death!
What feast is toward in thine eternal cell,
That thou so many princes at a shot
So bloodily hast struck?

And so, unknown reader of these letters, what do you think? Could I have been a writer, do you suppose? There's a lot more where that came from, let me assure you. There has to be, especially as the hardened soldier I referred to is another reason I'm putting pen to paper so assiduously. He was just passing through, of course, on the way back from his special operation against the Poles, but he stopped off to find himself all of a sudden King of Denmark, and decided to put in his bit. In fact he took charge on the spot, entrusting me with the job of providing him with a thorough report on everything that had taken place—the multiple casualties, and what exactly had led up to such a royal slaughter.

'A bloodbath? That's all in the day's work for me, generally speaking. But not this one, not with all these loose ends lying about.'

He glanced at the corpses littering the hall.

'No disrespect intended, none at all. But I want everything tied up and accounted for, understood? Names, minutes of meetings, decisions taken, nothing left out. And after that a clean sheet.'

It made sense. A new regime, none of the old innuendo and intrigue. That was his way. And it suited me too. I was ready to follow his brief. But I was also more than willing to give my version of events, for posterity—from the inside. I was no mere observer. I knew a thing or two. And in that respect it didn't do any harm that I'd been around for quite some time, and I'd known the old king since I was a young boy at court, before his son, the prince, was born. I could have been a courtier if I'd chosen that path. But I opted instead not for Elsinore but for the university, and the life of the eternal student. So I was still sucking the nectar of academe when the prince turned up at Wittenberg, and we got drunk on it together, and became close friends. He was an only child. And in some ways I think he saw me as an older brother. Something like that.

But to return to my remit. I won't go so far as to say I picture myself as a playwright. I repeat, I'm too pedantic for that. But

I shall dramatize these letters to the best of my ability, I shall go for atmosphere, and you shall be the judge of poor Horatio's efforts. Now at least you know my name. And be advised, I do not intend to restrain myself, except where necessary, and I shall give you the whole story, which concerns and contains lecherous behaviour, murders, monstrous acts, retributions, executions, deaths by chance and desperate contrivance, and in the end, plots gone all to pieces, blown to the moon, and come back down to crush the skulls of the plotters.

That's a lot of ground to cover, then, so let me at the outset say this much: my friend was a man who'd been landed with a hard task, one he found impossible to fulfil, and accomplished it only by pure chance. But he landed me with an even harder charge: to tell the truth. And what's harder, do you think: to kill a man, or to say what truth is? However you see it, this is my mission, and although I shall respect his last wish and tell his story, I have a duty to tell the other stories too, stories that are much caught up in his, their lives heavily involved, including one which was all but forgotten in the end, and in the general slaughter. And if he hears any of this in the silence that surrounds him now, or against the choirs of angels I hired at short notice in a valedictory little prayer, I ask him to forgive me.

I'll not be holding my breath. Forgiveness wasn't in his nature; it didn't come easily to him, if it came at all. The truth is he found it hard even to forgive himself. At times. But let me say again: among the tangle of tales in that bloody toll, there is one which means more to me than I care to say, not at this moment. Perhaps I will—if the pen permits. What I can say here and now is that she will not go into the dark so hopelessly, so irreversibly, as fate intended. I mean to retrieve her. Tell *my* story? Yes, my friend, I can, I will. But I shall also tell hers. And where she can, she will tell her own. It goes back a long way. And suddenly it seems a very long way...

My First Night

Elsinore. The Battlements. Darkness. Silence. Bitter cold. Everybody is asleep. Even the whores are sleeping now, on their semen-stained pallets. The king and queen are sleeping soundly in their perfumed chamber, their meanest subjects sleeping too, pillowed on rough straw, and hushed by buzzing night-flies to their slumber. The medieval knight is sleeping inside his armour, but you can still hear his snores. Snoring bones—enough to keep you awake all night. Oh, and the date—I'd better record that before I get too carried away in my effort to achieve the atmosphere I promised. I'm more the scholar than the scribbler, as you will quickly discern, all the way down to my feet of clay. The date, then, and the time of year.

Time of year... time of year? No time of year. Elsinore was its own time of year, its own time of night, though I knew it had just struck twelve when Marcellus and I approached the platform, where Francisco was on guard duty, about to end his shift. We heard Bernardo ahead of us, challenging the challenger with his 'Who's there?' On edge, obviously, to make such a mistake, though he'd come dead on the hour to relieve a man who clearly didn't want to be left on his own a second longer than was necessary. Seconds are important to a sentry. Not that he'd seen what the other officers had seen—he wasn't in the know. But he was a man sick at heart—for a simple soldier. I heard him say so, his words carried by the silence and the quiet bitter wind. Jumpy. Same as his relief. And glad to get off duty and get to bed.

I chucked in my tuppenceworth of scepticism right away, partly to ease the tension. Easy for me. I've already admitted it, I'm a pedant. I have no imagination. Not that anybody needed an ounce of imagination to be nervous that night. Denmark stood demoralised and in danger, its brilliant warrior-king still green in earth, and with a portlier posterior now sitting on the throne, an altogether flabbier set of flanks. It was embarrassingly obvious—not much muscle there. And an attack was imminent.

Everybody knew why, understood the background. Far from being a secret, it was a matter of national pride. It had been thirty years since old King Fortinbras of Norway had lost land and life in a duel fought with our old king, Hamlet, deceased, and now young Fortinbras wanted the lost land back. He hadn't inherited the throne – his uncle was king, but not in great shape, and the nephew, being a hothead and a young man of mettle, had gone his own way and sharked up a band of desperadoes to make a dash for the lost territory. They were men who'd do anything in return for a square meal, and they'd kill between courses—the more courses, the quicker they'd kill. So Denmark was preparing for war: arms imported from abroad, shipwrights pressed into forced labour, the forges churning out newly-cast cannon—and extra guard duties. The whole country was jittery and dead beat, especially the army, our best defence. The officers of the watch were understandably on edge.

But that's not what was troubling the sentries that night. They'd seen something, something scary, and it had put the fear of God into them. I should rephrase that—the fear of the devil. Or, if you're not into either, let's just say they'd had the hot stool shot out of them—that's real enough for anybody, whether you go in for God or Old Nick. And they'd asked me along for an opinion on the 'thing' that had appeared to them, or just 'appeared', if you like, these past two nights on the trot. I was the right man to invite, I suppose, as I don't believe in ghosts. Or perhaps I should say, I didn't believe in ghosts, not until that night. Even then I was sceptical, as is my wont. But not for long. That was the night that changed everything. For everyone. No-one escaped. Not even me, as I'm left with all this, to unburden myself, to the best of my ability, as I was asked, directed to do. I don't recall promising. But then there was hardly time. And the flights of angels were suddenly dispersed by a Norwegian drum.

Cut to the chase, lad. The squaddies were busy assaulting my ears with their spook-stuff—this dreaded sight, apparition, portentous figure—and I was playing my sceptic's part, the one expected of me, only a piece of me present, there in body, not in brain, and all prepared to dismiss it as an illusion, to laugh it off and settle their nerves, when without any kind of warning, right out of the silence and the cold and the dark... it came! I say 'came' without knowing what that means. Came from where exactly? All I do know is that quite suddenly it was there, in front of us. And I say 'it' because at that point I didn't know what else to call it.

Bernardo was in no doubt.

'In the same figure, like the king that's dead.'

And I had to admit it was a dead ringer—pardon the pun, I wasn't laughing at the time—for the old king, whose corpse right now was rotting in its tomb, two months into putrefaction and stench. There was nothing imaginary about that part of it. We'd all seen the body—briefly because it was in such bad condition, horribly disfigured after the attack by a deadly snake, so it was supposed, whose venom had caused an eruption of the entire skin and left it looking ghastly, worse than any ghost you would have said. But now it had come back from the crypt to stalk the parapets of Elsinore and scare the shit out of me too—excuse my French. No point in pretending. I was petrified.

Paranormal? The word scarcely did it justice. I'd always assumed ghosts to be diaphanous entities, essences rather than organisms, but this particular spook was no astral body, that's for sure. Disembodied or not, it was fully weaponised and in complete steel, carrying a truncheon and with all its accoutrements on show, sword and axe and dagger, as if ready to take the field and defend Denmark from the expected attack. I wondered just how Fortinbras's freebooters would have reacted if they'd seen it coming at them in the front line. It could have reached out and scattered your brains on the spot, as was its wont.

And its identity? It was no corrupted corpse either, that was clear enough, not something that had just burst out of its graveclothes after two months of decomposition and decay, and donned a spanking suit of armour instead. Only Jesus could have done that—and did. And the still blindly bandaged Lazarus stumbled out like a mummy from the tomb only because Christ called him, and in spite of the onlookers protesting that by this time he'd be stinking. So was this thing some sort of embodied memory of the old king? The thing's identity had to be questioned, naturally, and was questionable enough even though it wore its visor up. Of course it was the old king all right, visually—old Hamlet—except for its expression, the look on the face. I'd never seen an aspect so afflicted, so sorrowful, so utterly woebegone, not on any human being.

But clearly it wasn't a human being, not now. So what was it then? Whatever it was, it looked as if it was waiting to be addressed. Spooks won't speak unless they're spoken to, and even then only in Latin. That's where I came in, Marcellus having begged me to do the needful. I did, but I'll spare you the Latin. Who are you? What are you? I put the questions and got no answer. The thing—I don't know what the best word is—evaporated, leaving me to face the inevitable ribbing. Well, what do you think then, Horatio? What do you make of it? What would your clever schoolmen make of it? An illusion? A figment of the imagination? A long way from Wittenberg, eh? And I had to admit it was more than an illusion, not a figment but the spitting image of the old king. Young as I was, I'd been one of those present at the famous fight, the duel, when he killed his man, old Norway. And I was there again at a summit meeting, when he suddenly tired of talking, broke up the conference, and smote the sledded Polacks on the ice. That's putting it poetically. He was a skull-splitter and he knew no fear. And that was him all right, no question about it. Or it was his fetch, or spirit double, or God knows what it was. It was philosophy I'd studied at the University of Wittenberg. I didn't take classes in necromancy.

Whatever it was, it gave us a second chance to make up our minds. Bernardo advanced the not unreasonable theory that the apparition was on account of the current threat of war. Ghosts can be raised for all sorts of reasons, but especially if those they loved in life are in danger. That's the theory, at any rate. And in the case of a king whose country is under threat, it stands to reason it would be a troubled ghost. Exactly the same thing happened long ago, I told them, in ancient Rome, just before the assassination in the Capitol, didn't they know that?

They did now. I laid it on for them, parading my learning a bit, but also taking their minds off what we'd just seen. One solitary ghost? It's a speck of dust, that's all, a mere dot on the horizon of history. In the high and palmy state of Rome, just before Julius Caesar fell—or was pushed—the graves stood tenantless, and the sheeted dead stood up and walked towards the city walls, to squeak and gibber in the Roman streets...

Brrr!

The sentries gaped.

'You mean graveyards opened?'

'Yawned. Wide open. Wide as your mouths. And shrouded corpses stalked the walkways, not to mention blood-red comets, both moon and sun sick with eclipses, as if doomsday had dawned. As if. As if...'

'But look! Horatio, look! Look there! It's come again!'

Come again. Came again. Appeared. Materialised. Was there. Freezing us with fear where we stood. Only this time I determined to take the necessary steps, to unfreeze myself. I not only gave it the sign of the cross, but I stepped out and crossed its actual path: a fatal thing to do if you believe in fables from the world of ghosts. I don't and didn't expect to be blasted on the spot, struck dead, or whatever the powers of darkness are supposed to do to you. I wasn't. Otherwise I wouldn't be writing this. And I gave it the works, the full formula: what did it want with us? Was it troubled? Were we in trouble? Was there anything it could tell us that might help avoid a catastrophe? Or was it the old story—had it come back for the cash it had stashed away in its lifetime? We all know we can't take it with us, but that doesn't stop some of us from piling it up and packing it away for other people to spend. And if it's hidden in the bowels of the earth, that can make a ghost walk the globe forever, or until it's found, and does some good to someone, and lets the restless spirit rest in peace. And so on.

I thought I was beginning to get somewhere with it. I weep to say it, as both instinct and instruction, my entire experience, still told me it was to some extent at least an illusion, something apparent, beguiling, not entirely real, and yet I felt in my blood some sort of answer about to take shape, or sound, out of the dark.

And then the cock crew—and the thing was all over the place, peripatetic, flexible, fluid, the darkness fizzed with its presence, now here, now there, everywhere, and the men panicked and struck out at it with their spears, and it was swallowed up and gone, leaving us shaken and uncertain what to do, or even think.

Except to acknowledge what we all know: that cockcrow is our reveille but it's a ghost's last post—back to your bed, old mole, back to the clay covers and the fretting worm, all that fireside stuff our grannies told us when we were nippers shaking in our nightshifts, like the cock crowing all night long on Christmas Eve and after, putting a stop to all wicked spirits wanting to roam the earth like tigers and spread harm abroad. No, no fear of that, the old gammers crooned, reassuring us—they're confined to barracks along with the grim witches and the bad fairies; and the nights are wholesome and sound, and you can walk till dawn and not be moon-struck, or Saturn-struck, or rooted to the spot by any sprite or goblin on the prowl...

Ah yes, the faces in the firelight, and the winter tales. Well, granny would have wet herself and serve her right if she'd seen what we saw that night. And it was with whacking great relief that we got to the end of our watch with no further visitations, only the apparition of the dawn, all done up in rustic russet colours, like some sleepy labourer, blinking and brushing the dews with his boots and making his way afield. A lovely sight. Morning. And the sanity and safety of work, and the business of the day. Things always feel better at 8.20 a.m. than at 3.20 a.m., in the middle of the night. As for us, we knew exactly where our own business lay: to seek out the young prince Hamlet and tell him what we'd seen.

My First Morning

We couldn't see Hamlet straight away as I had to attend the great gathering that morning. It was a state occasion: the new king's opening address to his court after the coronation, with important business to be got though, parliamentary and personal. And apart from all that he had to break the ice...

I must say he handled it well, for a man who wasn't an ice-breaker in the sense that his all too recently deceased brother had been. But Claudius was made for the part. He was an actor whose role was, like any actor's, to impress, to please everybody. And he succeeded—except for the one spectator he knew would never applaud: the young prince from whom he'd not only pocketed the crown, following his father's death, but whose widowed mother he'd married, making her a wife again, and making Hamlet into his son, or nephew-son, himself into his uncle-father, and Gertrude into his aunt-mother, as Hamlet used to say, spitting out each word, each awkward relationship, like a piece of poison.

Leaving aside the double relationships with which Hamlet was understandably uncomfortable, there were other awkward obstacles for Claudius which needed to be addressed. The new sovereign had some explaining to do.

First off, the crown. His father having died, young Hamlet had strong reason to presume he'd ascend the throne as the next king of Denmark, and morally this is what he had every right to expect. Politically, however, that's not how it worked. Denmark was an electoral constitution, and it was for the court to decide who their next king would be. They went for Claudius. Or rather they went *with* Claudius. And while that was statutorily in order, it didn't mean that Hamlet would not feel aggrieved, a fact of which Claudius was all too aware. The drums sounded, dutifully documenting the death, the sea tolled like a bell at Elsinore. The black flags were unfurled, and dropped down, draping the old grey castle walls. They didn't hide Hamlet's hurt, his savage indignation.

Second, the marriage, and the date of the wedding. Here I'd best elucidate for you the sequence of events and their precise timing. It's an important part of my remit, if I'm to fulfil the obligation properly. So: here is what happened. The old king died—suddenly. Very suddenly. The circumstances were distressing enough in themselves—and we'll be coming to that anon. Suffice it to say that there could be no question of a lying-in-state for the king's stiff lips to receive the cold kisses of the entire country, filing up in a long reverent line to pay its peck of respect. The corpse was too far gone for that and the funeral was held right away. Nothing improper there—everybody accepted it was the only course of action, and the right one too. Some bodies just have to be shifted at once and got below the sod, lapped in lead, sent up in smoke, burned in a boat, turned into a fistful of ash, or in the old king's case, inurned in the marble that masks all ugly sights and stifles all unpleasant stenches.

But then what happened? Gertrude, his loving queen, the grieving widow, married again—within a month. A month. Unseemly haste would be a kind and generous way to express it. Her son put it rather differently. And I'll be coming to that too. Or rather he will. I am no omniscient narrator and have had to rely on testimonies wherever I could find a fly on the wall, and believe me, there are many walls in Elsinore and no lack of flies. Apart from which, others must have their say, whoever and wherever involved. And that's just about everybody, everywhere. Including the flies. For now though, let's just say that people talk. And people did talk. And were it not for her matronly years, you could have been forgiven for wondering—some people did wonder—if she wasn't pregnant, given the unladylike lick at which she went for it, for him.

And he was her brother-in-law. The unkindest cut of all, you could say. And again, some did say. They said it was not only unnatural but unscriptural too. *Thou shalt not uncover the nakedness of thy brother's wife*. Ambiguous or not, you didn't have to be a purist like young Hamlet to call it incest. I know a churlish priest who'd sooner have buried them than married them. And in unconsecrated ground too. That was another item that needed a lot of glossing over.

But as I've said, the new king acquitted himself well, if you consider that he was on trial on these counts, and on the question of foreign policy. First, the dead king, his departed sibling. After wiping away a brotherly tear, a verbal one at least, he got straight to the point, as had the lady. Last month she was my sister—if you insist. But that was last month. Now it's this month—and this month she's my wife. After all, whatever she is, she's a queen, and you can't have a queen without a partner, the ship of state left rudderless, not when we're at war, which we sadly but most certainly are. And so, yes, I stepped up, I did the decent, the necessary balancing act, with gladness in one eye and grief in the other, with mirth in funeral and with dirge in marriage—(these were his very words)—in equal scale weighing delight and distress, I took her to wife!

But not before I'd sounded all of you out on the subject, naturally, and relied in the end—dare I say it—on your better wisdoms, your statesmanlike enlightenment, superior, after all, to mine.

Here I noticed that he winked at Polonius, the Lord Chamberlain, and Polonius smirked back, though the smirk and the wink might have been the other way about, or a bit of both from each, the lobbyist and the lickspittle eyeing each other up, subservience and self-seeking hanging in the air. What did it matter? He'd got there, and for good reasons, and the good reasons were dripping off the end of his tongue, showing where it had been.

He hadn't exactly touched on the uncle-father aspect—that was scarcely state business and would be left till later. Nor was there a whiff of incest in anything he said—the sister bit was swept into history. Our 'sometime' sister was what he called her. But what matters now, says he, is not the past—who cares for history, after all?—but the future for Denmark, and the pressing present, with that young shaver Fortinbras thinking he can tramp all over us now that we're in pieces following our late dear brother's death (dear brother for the second time, I noticed, and not the last of the loving epithets by any means). Well, Claudius had news for Fortinbras—and this is where the master-stroke came in. He was this very morning sending ambassadors to Norway, not to the young squirt but to his uncle, the bed-ridden sovereign, a sickly king, scarcely aware of what his nephew was up to, his subjects being marched off unlawfully to war, and asking the old man very politely to put a stop to the young dog and his pestiferous demands for the surrender of territories lost perfectly legally by his father. That too was history. And the ambassadors, Voltimand and Cornelius, were handed the commission and dispatched on the spot to broker peace.

An impressive performance. You couldn't fault it. And the subtext was poking its nose like a snake through the slime and honey of every syllable, each artfully balanced phrase: the head-splitter is no longer in charge, a diplomat is now on the throne—never mind the fat cheeks—and we'll have no more wars. That suit all of you?

Every one. Down to the ground. And on your knees. And now, Laertes, what's the news with you?

Laertes was the Lord Chamberlain's son. He'd come from Paris a month ago for the coronation and was now anxious to get back to his studies. Or so he said. The University of Paris, if that's what he was implying, was never even mentioned, and that didn't surprise me then, and doesn't now. I'd met him once or twice and felt no inclination to meet him a third time. There wasn't a book in that boy's brain. You'd squeeze more learning out of a lizard if you asked it the Latin for 'lady', or the Greek for a giglet. But Claudius buttered him up. And now, Laertes? What is it, Laertes? What do you want, Laertes? What can I do for you, Laertes? Caressing him over and over with his name, and not forgetting to bend over for his old man. Have you your father's leave? What says Polonius? And Polonius says to let him go, so that's all right then, off you trot—Laertes—and have a whale of a time. I will, Your Majesty, no fear of that, Your Majesty. *Absolument*. French tarts, hold on to your knickers. I'm out of here.

And so he was. With business concluded. And each man happy. Well, almost. Except for one.

'And now, my cousin Hamlet, and my son...'

Another masterstroke? Or so he thought. He'd broken another piece of the ice, no bumbling: he'd spoken smoothly and directly up till now, delivered the goods, bussed the backsides of those who mattered and kicked the ones that didn't—and now, the really delicate part he'd left until last. Hamlet, dear boy, what's with all this black? Your choice of costume—it's unfriendly, it's inappropriate, disproportionate. Your father's been dead these two months, your mother and I have been married a month, it's a month since the coronation, and this is the big day, the day of celebration, the affairs of state, human affairs too, time to move on, to get out of that black garb of yours and stop your mourning, let the sun shine on you again, at last. And so on.

A cryptic comment was all he got, muttered under his breath. I doubt if Claudius even heard it. But if he had, this is what he would have heard.

'A little more than kin and less than kind.'

Hamlet had a habit, if he didn't like you, or was suspicious of you, of talking in riddles. I was used to it, and didn't have to be a lip-reader to work out what he was saying. Kin? Don't talk to me about kinship. I'm too much related to you now, and less than naturally disposed to you, certainly not close to you. The meaning would have been lost on Claudius, as would the next laconic line—something about being too much in the *sun*, meaning, I suppose, in the unseemly glamour of the court, and an atmosphere of celebration instead of mourning. Or, if you like: I'm too much the subject of your attention as it is, too much in your royal presence, and if I'm a *son*, I'm a son twice over, once too much for me, and I reject the second sonship, all the more so since I'm a son, a prince, when I should be a king. Or unspoken words to that effect. Wordplay was Hamlet's favourite weapon: attack and defence.

So his mother had a go. Gertrude begged him gently to get himself out of his black clothes and black mood and be more sociable. Look up, can't you? Instead of looking down at the dust? Are you going to be downcast forever? Forever. She said forever. His father had been dead two months. Is that the allotted time for mourning? And is dust all that's left, after a loved one has died? Hamlet had something to say about that, as you will hear.

Claudius meanwhile had more to say: about mourning and how long it should sensibly last. About fathers—all fathers lose fathers, and their fathers before them lost fathers. About obstinacy and impiety and unmanliness. About wimpishness and irritability and intolerance. About naivete and lack of common-sense—worse, about blasphemy and disrespect for the dead, and sheer stupidity; about fruitless, inane and unavailing grief. Oh yes, he fairly laid it on. The kindly king had switched to the role of the stern but solicitous stepfather, who must firmly but gently guide his erring child, and who wants to be accepted as a father. And as proof of his fatherly affection he had two further things to say: one, that Hamlet was now to be regarded as heir to the throne—none of that electoral nonsense, he'd be his successor, it was official; and two, that being the case, he didn't want him going back to Wittenberg to take up his studies again. Yes, Laertes had just been granted leave to return to Paris, but no—that is not what I want for you, and I beseech you, beg you to remain with us, here where I can offer you cheer and comfort. You after all are the first man of the court after myself, and you are my dear kinsman—and my son!

God, he could talk, could Claudius! He had the gift of the gab. It got him nowhere, and the entire court could see that he'd tried his best but that this character in black was inflexible, determined to be a dog in the Danish manger and a gooseberry to the love-struck new king and queen, who'd scarcely completed their courting. He just wouldn't let them get on with it, get on with life. Everybody felt for Claudius. And for Gertrude too, who now came in with a simpler and more succinct approach.

'Don't let your mother's prayers go unanswered, dear boy. I beg you, forget Wittenberg—stay here with us.'

The gentle touch, coloured with a mother's love, and tender entreaty. Did it work?

'If that's an order, then very well—I'll obey you as best I can.'

Stiff and still unbending, you'd have to say, and a pretty dry reply, containing the hint perhaps that he'd be obeying her, not him. But he'd given in at least, and Claudius fastened on it fast as you'd like, with a quick grin and a twist of the truth.

'A loving answer!' And a gentle and unforced concession.'

Hardly. But he was so tickled, he said, that there would be an extra celebration, and he'd mark it with what was to turn out to be one of his pet larks. Each time he bent his elbow to drink a toast to the new order, drums and trumpets would sound the signal to the cannoneers, and a burst of ordnance from the castle walls would echo to the skies, thundering out the king's carouse.

Quite a treat for the ears. And as Claudius was never short of an excuse to bend his elbow, the day was unlikely to pass off quietly. Festivity was afoot, revelry in the air, and a right royal rave-up on the cards. Enormous applause. And the whole court swept from the hall of state in high spirits to get on with the shindig.

All except Hamlet.

An Account of My First Meeting with Hamlet

All except Hamlet.

And myself, of course. I stayed behind and kept to the shadows. No shortage of shadows at Elsinore, no difficulty there. The only question you had to ask yourself was: who else might be sharing them? At that moment there were only the two of us. I waited a respectful interval. He was deep in thought. It was a large hall, spacious, and gone so quiet following all the commotion of the court. You could hear him brooding, cut his thoughts with a knife. Almost as if he'd overheard my own ruminations, he unsheathed his dagger and stared at it. Or was he thinking of—something else? I came quickly forward and startled him, the dagger suddenly defensive. Then his eyes flashed recognition.

'Horatio!'

'That's me.'

'Where the fuck did you spring from?'

'Out of the shadows. Back there.'

'And before then? Where have you been hiding? How long have you been here?'

'How long? Do you want my exact date of birth?'

He grinned. For the first time. Sheathed the knife and gave me a bear-hug.

'Aha! Old Horatio still! And still thinking Wittenberg, I see.'

'Still the pedant, you mean?'

'I mean still the logician, old chum, the Socratic questioner. But when did you leave Witters? How long have you been skulking at Elsinore?'

I told him I'd come for the funeral.

'Ah, you mean the wedding?'

'Not long between them it has to be said.'

'Not much. But it made sense. You know the custom: cold fare for a funeral, and they didn't even take the time to warm up the pies for the wedding breakfast. We have a thrifty king on the throne now.'

A sudden burst of cannon-fire from the battlements. I gave a rueful grin.

'Not so thrifty after all?'

'He's more into drink than thrift. And into my mother. Can you picture her being screwed by that satyr, that horny little goat? Can you just imagine those dreadful dewlaps dangling over her—and that fat stinking gut? But seriously, where have you been all this time? I didn't see you at the funeral.'

'You didn't look like you wanted to be seen. And you weren't at the wedding.'

Misery. Stamped on his face again. I didn't know what to say next.

'I'm surprised you even showed up for this morning's performance. But I saw you making your point. In black.'

'Black garb for a black day. And you? What did you think of it—the performance?'

'Polished.'

'Seriously?'

'You've got to admit he has a flair for it.'

'A flair for flannel. And fanny. Oh yes. And for flattering old farts.'

'That's true too. But what do you think, then? I mean right now, what are you really thinking?'

Big sigh. Huge shrug of the shoulders.

'Well, for starters, as you've just heard, I was thinking of going back to Wittenberg.'

'And you still can. Except you've just told your mother you'll stay. And your uncle's busy celebrating the fact—and toasting your health.'

'I can change my mind, can't I?'

'You can, old lad. And you should!'

I shed ten years and some gravitas and did the student reunion bit.

'My God, yes, live it up a little, why don't you? Live again. Do you remember that night, with Greta and Griselda, the four of us, the chimes at midnight and all that? Griselda's still around, by the way, and if you come south, she'll see you as far south as you care to go. You know she—'

'No!'

He grabbed me, held me tight, bent and buried his head in my chest. I'm a small man. He was trembling with emotion. I wished I'd kept my mouth shut.

'No, Horatio, not to be, I'm sorry. Thanks for trying, old fellow, but I can't do it any more, the days that we have seen stuff, I just can't.'

'So why then—?'

'Oh, I thought I'd take a course, go back to the old studies for a while. There's nothing for me here, you can see that well enough. Unless…'

'Unless? Aha!'

A bit of grinning and rib-digging here.

'I smell a woman. I knew it!'

Hamlet shook his head.

'Again, thanks for trying, but no, never mind that. But what about you? You stayed on.'

'Sort of. I haunt the lecture halls. Professional student, if you like. I couldn't face the church or the law, any more than you can face the court. But tell me seriously, I mean seriously, what are you really thinking? I mean about everything?'

That's when it all came pouring out of him, when he first admitted that he was feeling suicidal, his hand stopped only by the strict injunction against self-murder, and that he'd been feeling that way not on account of his father's death alone—Claudius was right about that, fathers die, that's what they do—but he'd chosen to ignore, or had failed to see into the real reason for his stepson's state of mind. It wasn't frustrated ambition, the loss of the crown, wasn't grief for his father so much as the shock he'd suffered because of his mother's behaviour. He'd thought she'd go to pieces: her husband had loved her so much he wouldn't let the wind blow on her, she was still his little girl, the one he'd fallen in love with more than thirty years ago, and she—she'd hang on him, hang on his every word, hang on his arm, her arms around his neck, like a newly-wedded bride, desperate to get to bed, as if she just couldn't get enough of him, needed to gorge on him till she was sick with love, not like the shepherdess in Solomon's Song, the Shulamite, but a biblically terrible tart, a scriptural shocker, a Jezebel who'd eat him up like apples, by the bushel, drink flagons of him to satisfy her lust, her love for him being strong, strong as death… until death came, that is unexpectedly, and the love melted like the morning dew, melted in a month, a mere month. Even a year would have stretched decorum, but a month, imagine, a little month—and then she married, married again, barely able to stand up in her new black shoes, let alone follow the body—the detail of the shoes stuck so sharply in the eye, you see, drooping and downcast as the eye is in the cortege, fixed on the feet of the one in front of you, and she went first in line, the grieving widow, crazed out of her wits and spouting tears like blood, like Pompey's statue, like Niobe, yes, all too like Niobe, she was turned to stone, but the tears were summer tears and ceased within a month, all dried up. O Jesus, even a dumb beast would have mourned longer for its mate, but no, the heart of stone dried up, the month was up, her month, her period of weeds and weeping, her period, yes, by God, she looked like she was ready to menstruate again, menstruate for marriage, bleed again, roll back the years, roll back the bedcovers, the sheets, the incestuous sheets, hurry now, scurry, scutter, shake a leg, two legs, four legs, and fuck four times and four times four, fuck till the cows come home, fuck till there's no tomorrow, fuck, I've heard them at it, fucking heard them at it all night long, heard them at it…

'Hamlet!'

It wasn't enough to put my hand over his mouth, I had to take his head in both hands and shake and squeeze hard to stem the stream of thoughts, dam up the consciousness. He'd lost control. Anybody could see he was in deep trouble, and I told myself that for me to speak a single word about what we'd seen the previous night would be unwise. He was half-mad and half a straw could tip him over the brink, there was so much going on in his head. But he stopped as suddenly as he'd started and calmed down. The outpouring was over. He spoke quietly

'But let me ask you, Horatio, what do you think of it?'

'Think of what?'

'The pair of them, the circumstances, the situation, everything.'

What I did think was that this had clearly gone beyond mere mourning. It was clear too that the crown did not rank high on his register of grief and grievances. Partly it was the sheer speed of it that had acted on him so badly, causing such a shock to the system, to both mind and heart. I admitted that even to me, an outsider essentially, it seemed pretty, well, pretty low.

'Deplorable?'

'Deplorable.'

'Ignominious?'

'You could go so far.'

'And sinful?'

'I had to admit the incest was also an unfortunate angle, and though it was more a line to be toed by a strict church than a king's court, I could see how uneasy it would feel to watch an uncle sitting in the shadow of his much superior brother one month, and the next month wearing his crown and presenting himself as father to a bereaved son.

'And sharing her bed.'

That was what was really getting to him and he couldn't let it go, his mother's sexuality. She still had the appetite, the need, the libido to get laid. And she was a fine-looking female with years of sex ahead of her.

Hamlet read my eyes. As students we'd been close. We were still close.

'Yes, I know. But with him. With that—that *thing*.'

Thing. Yes, that was it, the other thing. The difference between the two brothers, the soldier and sybarite. God knows what old Hamlet thought of him, the prehistoric fish-grin, the snake-smirk, fixed, primordial, impossible, post-Edenic. He had never joined the king in any of his military enterprises. He was, let's face it, fatty, gone to seed long before his prime. Bloated was Hamlet's usual word, a fat little athlete of the sheets, he said, all fuck and no figure. And once when Hamlet and I were out in the streets, Claudius happened to pass by, heading a string of useless-looking courtiers, and you could see the commoners making funny faces at each other, mocking his looks, taking him off, showing their contempt. One young lad even did a shambling act, like an ape. He turned pale when he spotted Hamlet striding up to him. He thought he'd be cut down on the spot. The prince tossed him a coin, winked at me, and we laughed and went on our way.

That was then. But this was now. It was no laughing matter. Nothing was any laughing matter, not any more, not for Hamlet. He'd lost faith in everyone.

'Present company excepted, old friend.'

And the disquieting thing for me was that the sickness that had entered his soul seemed to have spread out of control. It was indiscriminate. All women were guilty. They were all the same, all tarred with the brush of the lickerish queen. Even... I hardly dared think her name to myself in case he read that also in my eyes. But at that point I feared for Ophelia. And when he came out with that sweepingly antique scriptural thing, *Frailty, thy name is woman*, the overarching abstraction, so typical of him, I was in no doubt what I should do next. Nothing. My lips were sealed. I'd sing dumb about the thing that had happened up on the battlements. Even now, well away from the darkness and silence, the bitter cold of the small hours and the phantasmagorical atmosphere, I was starting to tell myself that it had never happened. I could have dreamed it all. And Hamlet need never know. Best forgotten then. Let it go.

And that's the way it would have gone. And if it had gone as I'd intended, you will understand in due course that I would not be writing these letters as none of the events that followed would have ever occurred. And I can tell you, I have often thought long and hard about this, the extent to which I hold myself responsible for these casual slaughters, deaths intended and unintended, plans gone to pieces, and the whole bloody train of events. But if you start to think along those lines you can end up blaming yourself for every disaster under and including the sun. And moon. And all of a sudden the stars—the buggers—are not buggers after all, but innocent, and you're the spanner in the cosmic works and the turd in the teeth of justice; and you're the spade in the hand of the gravedigger, shovelling in the corpses in the last act of any tragic drama you care to mention. No, you can't go there, and you shouldn't. And I wouldn't have gone there myself had it not been for the bloody squaddies.

No offence, but there they suddenly were, in the open doorway, hovering. You know how it is when somebody hovers. They're clearly desperate to speak to you but they want you to speak first.

And here I had two hoverers, Marcellus and Bernardo, doubling the expectation. Hamlet caught sight of them and beckoned them to come forward, shook hands with each of them.

'Marcellus? Bernardo? Good evening—I mean good morning. It doesn't matter, I'm very glad to see you.'

Whatever you say about Hamlet, he was no snob. On the contrary he'd sooner talk to a trooper than to a nob. A nob himself, but no snob. And he put people at their ease—unless they were insufferable pricks and deserved to be kept on edge, without the benefit of detumescence. So the officers were relaxed, and eager to get to the point, as we had—to be fair—previously agreed.

And so.

'Marcellus? Bernardo?'

'My good lord.'

I saved them the embarrassment, the awkwardness.

'It's about your father.'

'My father?'

'Yes, they'd like to talk to you about your father.'

Of course Hamlet misunderstood. How could he not? He had absolutely no idea, and probably thought they wanted to say a few kind words about their old leader, and how they missed him, especially in the—well, the present circumstances. Hamlet took them up on the unspoken sentiments.

'Ah yes, my father. I know, he was like you gentlemen, he was a soldier, not like that—never mind, you know what I mean. You men, you know what it is to face the enemy. I'd rather have seen my worst enemy in heaven than have lived to see this day.'

He went over to one of the high windows and looked out.

'My father—I think I see my father.'

The officers shot a glance at each other, and at me. They were all eyes, all ears, all on edge. I came to their rescue again.

'You see your father? Where, my lord?'

I called him 'my lord' out of formality. If the officers hadn't been present I'd have called him anything I liked, including an old scholastic voluptuary, the loosest fish in Wittenberg. Which he wasn't, but former students like to recall what jolly dogs they once were.

Hamlet was distracted now. I repeated the question.

'Where?'

'What do you mean?'

'I mean where do you see him—your father?'

The soldiers were having kittens by this time. Hamlet smiled a sad smile.

'Where do you think? In my mind's eye, Horatio.'

'Ah yes, of course. Not a man you'd easily forget, especially if he was your father. He was a great king.'

'He was a man. Take him as he was, or not at all—I'll never look upon his like again.'

'No, never.'

A deep breath here, the officers' eyes boring into me, begging me to speak.

'My lord, I think I saw him last night.'

'Saw? Who?'

'The king, your father.'

'The king my father!'

Yes, I know. What was he supposed to think? What the hell was I talking about? I wasn't even sure myself.

'Hang on here—these men are witnesses to what I saw last night, up on the battlements.'

'The battlements!'

'They were on duty. And they asked me along to see what they had seen.'

'For the love of God, tell me, let me hear!'

And so I did: how on two consecutive nights the men on watch had encountered—an apparition, a figure like his father, the dead king, wearing full armour, stalking the parapets, and turning them to jelly in their terror, with never a word spoken on either side.

'And the figure, the apparition—it said nothing?'

Dumb as a stone it stayed, and the men on watch had no idea how to address a ghost—if that's what it was. In any case they lacked the Latin. So they sought me out, a scholar, and on the third night I kept the watch with them, and just as they'd said, the thing appeared.

'No doubt about it—it was your father. At least it was his exact image.'

'But where was this exactly? Marcellus?'

'Up on the platform, my lord, where we had the watch.'

'And didn't you speak to it, Horatio?'

'I did.'

I told him what I'd said, and how I'd got no answer, except for that one moment when it lifted up its head and looked as if it was about to speak.

'But right there and then the morning cock crew out loud, and at the sound it simply disappeared, melted away into the air.'

Hamlet stared at us, stared away again, into space.

'It's very strange.'

'I know,' I said. 'Strange but true. As they say.'

'Of course, of course, I don't doubt it. It's just so—so unsettling.'

'That's for sure.'

'You say it faded on the crowing of the cock?'

'It seemed to shrink at the sound. And then—then it was gone.'

'And what did that tell you? What did you think?'

'Nothing. Nothing rational. Or everything. Everything irrational. What can I say? Anything you want to believe.'

'Cockcrow.'

Cockcrow, yes. What does it conjure up? All sorts of associations: betrayal, forgiveness—possibly; the limpid Christian code, as opposed to the angry old Elsinore revenge code, for example; spiritual alertness; the light of moral law, resurrection, dispelling the darkness and its black thoughts, banishing ghosts back to their graves, back to the chiding worms again, all that stuff, all that guff.

Hamlet smiled at me.

'I know what you're thinking.'

'Ah, so you're a mind-reader now.'

'I don't have to be.'

He took the two officers together, apart, a hand on each shoulder, and bored into them.

'Are you on watch tonight?'

'We are.'

'Was he armed, did you say?'

'Armed.'

'From top to toe?'

'From head to foot.'

'So you didn't see his face?'

'Oh yes, we did, my lord, he wore his visor up.'

The two officers were speaking together.

'What did he look like?'

'What do you mean, my lord?'

'I mean, what was his expression—angry?'

'More sad than angry.'

'And his face—pale? Or as he was in life—you know, ruddy, healthy?'

'No—pale. Very pale.'

'I see. And he fixed his eyes on you—kept looking at you?'

'Constantly. Never took them off us. It was fearsome.'

'I wish to God I'd been there.'

'You'd have been astounded.'

'I'm sure I would. Did it stay long?'

I came in at this point in the interrogation.

'I reckon I could have counted to a hundred.'

The officers protested.

'Longer, longer.'

'Not when I saw it.'

'Doesn't matter, Horatio. You have a scholar's clock in your head. We all know you're not prone to exaggeration.'

He pressed on with the grilling.

'How did he appear to you?'

'How do you mean? He just appeared.'

'No, no, I mean how did he look? Did he seem familiar? How was his beard, for example?'

'His beard?'

'Yes, was it grizzled, or what?'

I came in again.

'It was exactly as I'd seen it in his lifetime.'

'How was that?'

'A sable silvered—dark, but streaked with white.'

'Right. Did you say you're on watch again tonight?'

The officers nodded.

'I'll watch with you.'

He looked at me, meaning—you too. I nodded.

'It may walk again.'

'I think it will,' I said. 'I'm sure it will.'

I don't know what made me so sure, but I felt it in the air around us, something life-changing, time-changing. Hamlet was alive again. He paced up and down, turned and looked at us.

'God knows what it is, what you saw, but if it does come again, if it assumes my father's person, I'll speak to it, by God, though all hell's let loose to silence me.'

He came close and gathered us into a ring.

'And on the subject of silence—say nothing to anyone about this, tell no-one, give nothing away, this is between ourselves. And so enough. I'll meet you on the platform, between eleven and twelve. Tonight. Wait for me there.'

We left him to his thoughts. And I knew exactly what they were. The old king's spirit in arms. All was not well. Foul play? Foul deeds? They can't be hidden, can't be contained, no matter how deep you've dug them in, under the earth's crust, they steam right through, like the ghosts that come in their wake, bringing the stench of sin up into the air. Darkness would reveal all. I could hear him thinking it.

'Would the night were come!'

My Second Night

It was colder than before, with a shrewd nip in the air, the silence bitter as ice. The three of us there, high up on the platform, huddling close together, waiting—for the hour. The hour of what? We didn't know, not exactly. Not at all, if truth were told. I thought we'd arrived early to the watch, but Marcellus said no, it had gone midnight. A sentry's ear, attuned to time, to routine, a bell in his brain. Down in the stables we could hear the horses moving about. I pictured the twitching ears, the bristling manes, the hooves shifting nervously on the flagstones, sifting the straw.

'They say beasts know things that we don't.'

Marcellus's eyes burned beneath his helmet. There was a glimpse of moon on the metal—a sliver had slid out between the crenellations, higher up. He was looking at me for confirmation, something casual but comforting, perhaps. Talk about the hour, talk about the weather, talk about horses. Talk about anything to make the time go by, to take the mind off what we'd come for, whatever that was.

'They say lots of things,' I said. 'Do you think animals are psychic?'

'They could be closer to God.'

'Or to the devil?'

Not what Marcellus needed to hear. It hardly took the edge off his nervousness, whetted it all the more. We all had the jitters. We waited. And waited.

'How's the hour?' asked Hamlet.

Marcellus didn't get the chance to answer. The silence was split apart—a sudden blast of trumpets from down below that made all of us jump and sent us clutching at each other like frightened kids. My heart nearly came off the stalk.

'What the fuck was that?'

I got my answer. The flourish was followed by a burst of ordnance, the cannon booming out from the battlements on the landward side of the castle, and from the great hall beneath us flickerings of lights and faint cries and laughter, and hellish merry music. We released each other and breathed again.

'What does it mean?' I asked.

Hamlet scowled.

'What it means, my friend, is that his Fat Majesty down there is as good as his word. You heard him, didn't you? He'll not knock it back now without the whole world knowing about it. Down his neck and up he struts, carousing out of his boot, the burst-bellied sot. A peacock on the piss. It breaks its brothers' eggs and swallows its own dung.'

Marcellus grimaced. He looked away in the direction of the banqueting hall.

'I'd sooner be down there than up here.'

A friendly fist from Hamlet.

'No you wouldn't. You're an honest soldier. You stood with my father against the Poles, remember?'

'I remember. But I fought geezers, not ghosts. Down there at least—'

'Down there nothing.'

If there was a frown on the princely brow it turned into a thundercloud.

'No, Marcellus, no, no, you're a better man than that down there. I know it and you know it. He'll be at it all night long now, you'll see, quaffing and cackling and swaggering at the dancing like the bloated toad he is—a pathetic spectacle. God knows how he stays on his feet with that belly on him, and his fine Rhine wines and his up-spring reels, drowning his soul in a gallon-pot.'

The battlements boomed again and the smoke from the guns billowed up like a sea, scattering the stars, it seemed. Nothing looked real, felt real. Hamlet snorted his contempt.

'There's another bucketful gone down the gullet. You can keep a tally of his tipple. Go on, you drunkard, slug it down your gut! And each time he swills it away, you'll hear the drummers and trumpeters and gunners booming out, and braying all his triumphs—his glorious achievements.'

'What achievements are those?' I asked. 'As a drinker, you mean.'

'What more is there? He's got fuck-all else to celebrate—apart from pocketing the crown and poking the queen—getting his dirty Danish dick into my mother—'

'My lord.'

I could see that Marcellus was looking embarrassed, and the last thing I wanted was for Hamlet to get going on this uncomfortable topic and working himself up again. I quickly changed the subject—back to the drinking.

'But this carousing—it's not exactly a Claudius invention, is it, to be fair?'

'Not entirely, no. The difference is, my father could hold his drink. And he fought first and drank after—when there was something to celebrate. Even the best of men suffer sometimes from a particular fault, picked up in the blood perhaps, at birth, or maybe they were ill-starred, who knows, you know how it goes, you can't pick your parents, you can't choose your stars—'

'My lord.'

'And if you can't command yourself, if you can't control the— you know—the general corruption—'

'My lord!'

We were in a semicircle. Marcellus was facing us, his eyes, like lamps, burning in his skull, fixed on the embrasures behind us, high above our heads. We turned and followed his stare. The temperature suddenly plunged.

'Here it comes!'

Here it comes? What had Marcellus seen? I could see nothing, not a thing. But I felt something all right. A freezing wind hit us without warning, blasting from the parapets. I looked aside at Hamlet. His blond hair was blown back by the sudden squall, and he was staring like me into the nothingness up there, nothing but the battlements etched against the sky, and that slice of moon brightening the streaks of cloud that swirled like smoke among the stars, moving strangely somehow, moving, yes, something was moving, something on the move, something up there, or was it...?

And yes, yes, there it was—the figure! But it was different, it was not like the figure we'd seen last night. That had been scary enough, but still it had approximated to something human, or once human, the image of a man, ghastly yet grounded, on a level with us, almost approachable, as you could approach a wild beast if you had to, and beard it with a spear, or a leprous beggar, and offer alms, thrown at the feet, or as close as you dared come. But this thing pacing the parapets looked to be twenty feet high, a giant in glinting armour, striding in slow profile. Was it some sort of vista-trick, a distortion of perspective, an optical illusion? The blast was no illusion. It was a hurricane now, whistling shrilly from the walls, where the thing continued to waft across our field of vision, encased in steel, like the figure we'd seen the night before, its helmet high up, passing slowly through the stars, as calm as the steadfast constellations.

'How can it walk?' roared Marcellus.

We had to scream at each other to be heard above the blast.

'In all this—this howler? Where did that spring from? Why doesn't the thing get blown over?'

'Because it's not real!' I yelled back at him. 'It can't be.'

Hamlet was yelling at us too.

'It looks real enough to me! Let's follow it!'

His shout was almost drowned out by the next burst of cannon fire, and the faint sounds of the laughter and the dancing floated up to us and were carried off by the blast. Even at that terrifying time I somehow found the leisure to reflect on how surreal it seemed: normal life, if that is what it was, going on down there, the drinking and dancing and living it up, giving it all they'd got, while up here, only feet away, we were in the throes of something paranormal, metaphysical, occult, call it whatever, and about to be in touch with something from another world. One king was down beneath our feet, junketing and jarring as if there were no tomorrow, and another king, once a king, a dead king, was walking on another plane entirely, up above. He'd left his tomb to tell us things we couldn't even guess at, and didn't want to, not particularly, apart from Hamlet, naturally. The rest was unnatural.

We came to the end of the seaward wall and the figure stopped in its slow stride.

'It doesn't want to come inland!'

Hamlet still had to shout to be heard. We all did.

'It wants to be…to stay close to the sea!'

'What does that mean?'

'God only knows! But I need to speak to it! I'm going to hear what it has to say!'

And Hamlet shouted up at the now static figure, looming high above our heads, still silhouetted against the stars.

That was when I heard the horses down below go mad. Somehow with flailing legs they'd beaten down the stable doors and broken loose, their hooves clattering on the courtyard flags, the sound of iron on stone. And amid the din Hamlet kept shouting at the thing in the sky.

'What is it you want with me? What are you? Where have you come from—heaven or hell? How can I know? And how can I know to trust you? Are you the dead? Are you my father? Are you his spirit? We saw you in the crypt. I saw you myself. The burial rites were observed, due formality, finality, hearsed in death, canonized, quietly inurned, no violation. Your bones were all bound up. How did you burst out? Where are the winding-sheets? They shut you up in there—it was meant to be forever, for all eternity. Why has the sepulchre spewed you up again? Vomited you out like a piece of undigested meat? It's horrible! It's against nature! And why the armour? Where did it come from? You were like a bandaged mummy when I last saw you. How am I to believe who you are? What you are? What am I meant to think? To do? What do you want me to do?'

As an honest recorder I have to state now that this is my general impression only of Hamlet's address to the ghost. The confusion of the moment, the sheer terror of it, the whinnying and screeching of the horses gone wild down there, the clattering hooves, the sounds of debauchery still going on in the banqueting-hall, still that wind screaming in our ears, drowning our words. It was madness, sheer hysteria, for what might have been minutes or moments, it's impossible to know. But I do remember that the effect on the apparition of Hamlet's desperate plea was immediate. It lifted up a moonlit arm and beckoned, clearly asking the prince to follow it, as if it wanted to say something to him alone, in secret.

'Don't follow it!' shouted Marcellus. 'Don't be deceived!'

'Why? If it won't speak to the three of us then I'll go after it on my own.'

'No you won't!'

I signalled to Marcellus and we both seized him, an arm each, keeping him pinned to the spot. He was livid.

'Get the fuck off me!'

'No! You're not going off after that thing!'

'Why? What's there to fear? It's a spirit, isn't it? Can a spirit wield an axe? Can a ghost kill the soul? And what have I to live for anyway? Look, it keeps on asking—entreating me.'

'And what if it's tempting you? I yelled at him. 'What if it's some sort of devil? A demon. What if it should lure you to the brink, right off the walls, and to the cliff edge, and there assume some other form, not your father's—how do you know it's your father anyway?—some shape, God knows what, that could drive you stark raving mad—and then what? You know what's out there—it's the edge of Elsinore, it's empty space. And beneath it the sea, fathoms deep. Listen to it roaring. That's not just the edge of Elsinore, it's the edge of reason, the end of existence. It could be the end of you!'

We struggled to hold him but he got his sword out and we sprang apart. He pointed the weapon at us.

'I'll tell you what, ghost or no ghost, whatever it is I'm going to hear it, and if either of you gets in the way, there will be one more ghost up here to reckon with, maybe two. Do you understand me?'

And with unsheathed sword he ran from us and was swallowed up by the dark.

'He's crazy, Marcellus! He's lost it!'

'Completely. We can't leave it like this.'

'I know. Let's go after him. God only knows what's to come of it.'

'I know one thing, though!'

'What's that?'

'Something is rotten in the state of Denmark.'

Hamlet's Account of His Meeting with the Ghost

(My Record Of The Above Following Our Conversation Later That Morning)

Something is rotten in the state of Denmark.

I heard Marcellus say it as I went up from the platform, as high as I dared go, and the comment stuck in my head. They were the words of an honest soldier—accurate, unvarnished, astute beyond reason. And prophetic, as I now know. But what was it that was rotten? Some would say the thing itself. Others, whatever it had come to uncover. I didn't have long to wait to find out.

The visitant facing me from the battlements proved capable of speech. The sea still surged as the ghost spoke, broke on the rocks behind it and below, rose like white brides, billowed and died down, as brides do, in time, in the same sad dusk that shrouds old queens when they sleep. That was the ambience it had brought with it, or created, unearthly and unreal. It stretched out an arm and the screaming wind died down, gave way to a dense silence and a wide expanse of greyness. I listened, barely breathing. I could hear every word it uttered, though spoken so quietly. It was my father's voice all night, but I'd never heard him speak like that in his life. If the thing really was my father, the tone was so sorrowful, so desperately sad, the expression of a creature in pain. My heart cried out to it, but there was no need for me to speak—it knew exactly what I was thinking, feeling.

'No—no pity. None. Only your attention, my son. Look at me, listen to me.'

That was my father: authoritative, commanding, magisterial. I was a little boy again. 'I'm listening, father. What is it that you need to say?'

'One word—'

One word. I waited.

'Revenge!'

'Revenge! Revenge what?'

Revenge the torment, that's what. Avenge the agony, the purgatorial pains doomed to be endured by unshriven spirits, until the deadly sins done in their days of nature are burnt out of them by fires as fierce as hell. I sensed the unimaginable suffering, the precise nature of it not even admissible to ears of flesh and blood, it was so blood-curdling, soul-harrowing, so excruciating.

'But why? Why?'

'No questions—no time. Say nothing. Not a word. But listen, listen, listen…'

'Tell me, tell!'

'My son, if you ever held me in your heart…'

'You know I did.'

'If you ever loved your dear father…'

'O God!'

'Revenge his foul and most unnatural murder.'

'Murder!'

Murder as grim as hell. Murder that would have been thought brutal and hideous even at the best of times, but in this case no-one could begin to picture the circumstances or to assess the enormity of the crime, it was so inhuman, so utterly grotesque.

Rage rose up in me, and a whirlwind of other emotions—revulsion, execration, grieving, anger, even a kind of wild excitement.

'The name! Tell me his name! He's a dead man! Dead within the hour! The moment I know it, I'll swoop to my revenge!'

A long slow sigh out of the darkness.

'Good. Good.'

Good? Yes, good. Of course, good. What would I be otherwise? Other than a gross weed, rooted in the river of oblivion, forgetfulness. And how could I forget the story that was now unfolded to me by a dead father, his body rotting in its vault, but his spirit alive and suffering in eternity?

And this is the story. Not the story that was given out at the time—that the king had been asleep in his orchard in the afternoon, and had been stung by a reptile so venomously that he died where he lay—no, not that spurious story, but the truth behind the fabrication that had been passed off as the cause of death, and deceived all Denmark. A snakebite? Metaphorically, yes, and if the image answers the event, then by all means call it a snake in the garden, a serpent, if you will.

'A serpent.'

'A serpent. But know this for a truth, my son, know this, and act on it: the serpent that pierced me with its poison that afternoon—now wears my crown.'

'The crown?'
'I have said so.'
'The crown!'
'The crown of Denmark.'
'O my prophetic soul! My uncle!'

I'd always harboured the uneasy dread that something did not sit right, even before I heard about the apparition, after which I did fear some foul play. But not before, or even afterwards, had I suspected something like this, something so monstrous you couldn't dream it up. Or had I? Could I? It didn't matter now, now that I knew. Now all that mattered was the terrible truth, but just how terrible—let me say it again—I could never have imagined, no, not the story that now came groaning out of those ghostly lips, hissing like flames to set my whole soul on fire.

This is what happened.

My father, when at home, had an unbreakable habit of taking an afternoon cat-nap, a routine he'd picked up on his campaigns. Being accustomed to a soldier's life, he also loved to sleep outdoors, and his favourite spot was the orchard on the landward side, where he'd doze off, free from care and from all suspicion. He was a much-loved monarch, and it didn't matter to him that everyone knew where he'd be and at what hour. He refused a guard. There was a sort of safety in it, the homely familiarity of it. Or so he thought. Sudden snoozes, thick deep sleeps, sweet impromptu afternoon naps. And so there was, until that particular day, when the snake slid through the grass, stole close to the sleeping king, and kneeled down at his head.

My uncle.

He was carrying poison in a vial: hebenon, henbane, the juice of the yew, that sombre tree from the dark arbours of graveyards. Its roots are wrapped around bones, its fibres net the skulls, the dreamless heads of the dead.

It was lethal. And poured into the porches of the ears, the leprous distilment did its work, quick as quicksilver on the quick of the flesh, to render it dead, but not before the entire skin-covering was splintered, breaking out all over into a vile and loathsome crust, an agonizing death, following on from a disfigurement like leprosy, the entire body wrecked before its existence was ended. And so as he slept, my father was deprived, at one fell swoop, of life, of crown, of queen. By his own brother. That was the manner of it. That was how he was murdered.

It's not how it should have been. It should have been the soldier's way, the man of action's exit. He could have fallen on his sword, or somebody else's, could have walked into the blast of a murdering-piece, or under a bomb. Could have sailed into the sunset, or into fin-infested waters, and ended up as shark-shit, floating in the ocean. Even that would have been better. Or he could have meandered into eternity, almost unnoticed, another antique hero, killed in action. Instead he got bitten by a reptile, the king of snakes.

Horrible? Horrible, yes, horrible! And worse, much worse. The murderer's action had deprived the victim not only of his life but of what all mortals fear most to be taken from them, the time and chance to square their account with God before life ends: extreme unction, the last rites, and the contrition and conversion that absolves sinners of their crimes and equips them for heaven and the life everlasting. But the unction my uncle gave his brother was not the holy oil of redemption but the unholy ointment of that hebenon, which sent him to his reckoning with all his imperfections on his head. Horrible? It meant that he was sentenced to an unimaginable stretch of suffering: the scorching flames of purgatory by day, and doomed to walk the earth by night, searching for satisfaction, retribution, and lamenting his lot, and all that he had lost.

Which was everything, all that he held dear, his queen above all, so much more than his crown she was to him, my mother, my much-loved mother. But O, God! God! The worst wound had yet to be exposed, the wound that should have killed all over again and caused a double murder, but festered instead as it festers in me now, in mind and soul, beneath my skin, filling me with filial hatred where once there had been so much love. My mother, yes, my dear mother, who married within a month of my father's burial, and married incestuously too, her husband's brother, yes, my lovely mother was guilty of the unthinkable, and this was the foulest and ugliest of the ghost's revelations, this is what my father had returned from purgatory to the parapets of Elsinore to tell me—my adored and adorable mother, my father's companion, his queen and consort, had not even waited for her husband to die before getting into bed with that incestuous beast. She'd been sleeping with him all along! He'd won her over with his filthy gifts and lingo, his lewd tongue, he'd won her to his lust; and she, lustful in turn, was more than willing to be so seduced, and lay with him in secret. Couldn't keep his cod in the piece, and neither could she. She wanted to gobble him whole.

When did it first start? How did it happen? How often did it happen? When my father was in the field, risking his life? Or when he was taking his sleeps on all those afternoons that preceded the fatal one? Is that when she first reached down and clutched his genitals? I wanted to know the squalid details. It wasn't enough that she'd fallen from grace, disgraced her marriage vows, broken them for a brother who was as nauseating as my father was noble. She desecrated the temple of her body. She let in an adulterate animal. She left a celestial bed to prey on garbage. She was sated, but still greedy for more of the sordid sort—his sort. And it was for him that she spread her queenly legs, as liberally as to the midwife, opening her cunt wide, taking his cock in her gob, all the way down to the balls, gagging on his bigness to make him feel bigger still, taking it up her arse, right up to the root, giving him the reach-around, taking it across her swinging tits, in between, sucking the hot spunk down her gullet, swallowing to the last drop, and with foam-flecked lips licking the glistening tip before doing it all over again, thrilling to his thrust and the shudder of his nuts. I can't shift it, the picture of it in my head—while she bucked and groaned, the dirty bitch, the filthy whore, and while her lover broke the sixth commandment, she broke the seventh to keep him company—she committed adultery, and might as well have committed murder…

And that's when I began to ask myself… Had she? Had she been an accomplice to the actual murder? Had the two of them planned it, whispering homicide, fratricide, while they were busy making the beast with four legs and two backs and joined-up genitals? While he fucked her and she fucked him? There were so many things I could have asked that poor, suffering spirit. But a ghastly dawn was about to break and it felt its hour slipping away and needed to tell me one more thing. What was it? Vengeance was already the word burned into my brain, and needed no repetition for me to go out and kill the adulterate pair with one cut, even while they were at it together, in the very act, and so rid the royal bed of Denmark of the couple who'd turned it into a couch for lust and filthy incest…

And so the way was clear. The ghost was a thing of darkness, outside the laws of man, but it was justified by another law: revenge. Vengeance is mine, echoed an ominous voice from scripture. But another voice argued that blood will have blood, and an eye for an eye, and revenge was written into the code of the old Elsinore society, the code of honour. Nothing therefore stood in the ghost's way. Nothing stood in *my* way.

Except for the last dire ghostly command, one which froze my blood and turned my avenging hand to stone…

Your mother. Take no action against your mother. Do not hurt her in any way. Leave her to heaven, and to those thorns of conscience lodged in her still, sufficient to sting her into shame when the time comes.

So: the murdered brother, the betrayed husband, my poor father—he still loved her, in spite of everything. And wished her no harm. I felt his deep grief rise up in me, turning to anger, abhorrence and blood. But how could I proceed against the guilty king without implicating her, or at least involving her in some measure? It seemed an almost impossible order to carry out with this loving injunction laid on it to leave her out of it. My mind whirled.

And the whirling mind remembered one more thing which the ghost had whispered, seconds before it faded into the morning air. It was a strange injunction, lost on me in the surrounding shocks into which it was slipped, almost as an afterthought. *Do not taint your brain.* Those few short words. What did they mean? Avoid ignoble passion? Be detached and objective in your execution? As impartial as the axe which punishes the murderer, the traitor, the regicide? You are not to indulge in personal vindictiveness? You are God's even-handed agent, heaven's minister. And your natural feelings as your father's son must also embrace your mother. You are neither to cherish any animosity against her, nor take any action against her. Was that it? Or was the tainting merely a monition against madness? And if so what mental corruption did the spirit fear, or foresee? My brain was tainted already. I was reeling. And I was only dimly aware that the thing was dissolving in front of me as the glow-worm's fire died down, and dawn broke over the hushed roar of the ocean. All night long it seemed the sea had been running urgently every which way, trashing its tides, travestying its salt gods, surging up high into the sky in sudden thunders, blinding white, the whole scene explosive and conflicted and ear-splittingly, eye-dazzlingly strident, chaotic, loud. Now it had all died down into a great greyness, so wide, so lofty, so serene, like the sound of peace after war, and in that strangely spurious quietness I felt suddenly anonymous, weirdly non-existent, and I heard that last lugubrious adieu: Hamlet, Hamlet, remember me…

Remember. Never forget. I'd already been advised to forget, to move on, to let go of the dead, advised by the murdering uncle and the adulterate mother, whose funereal platitudes included urging on me all the consolations of oblivion. I should be like them, they'd said, like the fat cankered weed on Lethe wharf, sunk in apathy, laxity and sloth. And the sordid stew of sex, no doubt, what they called life. No, I would never take their vile advice. I would follow the ghost, and its last lingering words. I am alive for you. My face is to the south wind and my eye inhabits eternity. Adieu, adieu, adieu. Hamlet, do not forget. Hamlet, Hamlet, remember me...

When I regained consciousness, I was lying flat on my back. I was looking up at the sky. I could clearly see the last faint constellations, the fading host of heaven. I realised I must have fallen backwards in my blackout. If heaven was all up there, hell was just beneath me, never so close as now, and I lay there between the two with my brain beating and everything I'd ever done or known or felt wiped out, as easily as you'd erase impressions in wax. There was nothing there, nothing except those impossible orders: to kill the murderer, to let my mother be, and not to taint my brain. How? They cancelled each other out and left me in a limbo of uncertainty and yet certainty. That pernicious false-hearted woman! That dissembling grinning villain! I had to write it down, to tell my friend Horatio, to record this eighth wonder of the world that sent the other seven sliding into the sea and left Denmark alone possessed of the greatest phenomenon in history: that a man like that can smile and smile and be a villain. And so now it's written down. And so I've sworn. Remember? Remember you? Oh yes, by heaven and hell, I will. I will remember. And now adieu, poor ghost, dear father. Adieu. But not forever. And not for long. I've sworn it. As for the other king, I have you in my eye.

And so, uncle, *there you are*.

After which, prolonging the awful effect of the apparition, an eerie aftermath.

An Account of How Marcellus and Myself Saw Hamlet Following His Meeting with the Ghost

The previous account is not verbatim but represents my best attempt to convey the essence and atmosphere of Hamlet's 'interview' with the ghost—if that formal threadbare term can be taken to apply to what must have been the strangest of encounters. I have to stress that in composing this record I have had to rely on Hamlet's word alone for what took place, and although I had no reason to doubt that word, I asked myself then, and have since asked myself, if he was entirely in his right mind at the time, or if the tainting of the brain—to employ the ghost's expression—might account for a corrupted version of what went on. I can write only what I know. Certainly when Marcellus and I tried to locate Hamlet with the falconer's cry following the ghost's departure, he responded and came running out of the first grey light like a man caught up in a maelstrom of madness. I do not imply actual insanity, but he both acted and sounded as if he'd been sucked deep into the vortex of another world, far removed from reality. Marcellus couldn't contain his own excitement and curiosity.

'What happened, my lord?'

He didn't answer and I repeated the question.

'What is it? What news?'

He seemed elated.

'Wonderful! Wonderful news!'

'Tell us!'

'No! You'll reveal it!'

Marcellus and I looked at each other. He shook his head.

'He won't,' I said. 'Nor will I. Our lips are sealed.'

A wild grin. He glanced round furtively.

'You're sure? You'll keep it a secret? Give nothing away—to anybody?'

He was laughing hysterically now and we both yelled back at him.

'You have our word!'

'In God's name we'll say nothing!'

'Well then—'

And he held us close to him, an arm around each shoulder, looked about him as if we were in danger of being overheard, and lowered his voice to a crafty conspiratorial whisper.

'Right you are, here it is. Would you believe it—if there ever was a villain, alive and kicking right here and now—you know what I'm saying—the worst crook in the whole of Denmark?'

'Yes? Yes?'

'Then let me tell you...he's a downright scoundrel. An absolute bastard!'

Said triumphantly, and with a sly wink. Apart from fearing for his sanity, I was at a loss, and didn't know what to say. I said the obvious.

'It scarcely needed a ghost to come from its grave to tell us that much, did it?'

'Right! You're absolutely right!'

And he pushed us apart, shook hands with each of us ceremoniously, raised both palms in the air dismissively, and turned on his heel. I shouted after him.

'Come back!'

He turned.

'Why? Why come back? We're done here. There's no more to be said. And so, if you've got better things to do, business or pleasure to see to, then don't let me keep you.'

I'm a patient, placid sort of man, some would say bovine, a bit frigid. I've been told as much and I wouldn't deny it. Phlegmatic is the word I'd use myself. But at that moment I felt even my own cold blood hotting up.

'This is crazy! You're spouting like Charybdis! You're drowning us! You're violating your friends!'

The effect on him was immediate.

'I'm sorry, Marcellus. And Horatio, old friend—I've offended you.'

'There's no offence,' I said.

'Oh yes, but there is.'

Calm again, and speaking quietly.

'I can tell you right here and now that as sure as St Patrick got rid of snakes from Ireland, and banished one to Denmark—as sure as that I can say that there's not only an offence that has been committed, but it's a huge one. Enormous. And more than one offence too.'

Calm, but still talking in riddles—though thinking about it afterwards, I realised he was hinting to me something which he didn't want Marcellus to know about. St Patrick was the keeper of purgatory, I knew that much. Was he telling me that the ghost was a purgatory ghost, the spirit of his father, and no demon? And the snake in Denmark made sense in the light of everything he told me afterwards. For now though, on the face of it, he treated us as equals, and asked each of us to swear an oath.

'What is it?' I asked.

'Never make known what you've seen tonight!'

'We won't.'

'Not enough. I need you to swear it!'

'We swear.'

'No, still not enough. I want you to swear it on my sword.'

Even the respectful Marcellus was bewildered and becoming increasingly edgy.

'But we've sworn already!'

'Not on my sword. Do it now!'

And he unsheathed the sword and held it up so that the hilts and the blade formed the shape and sign of the cross. We were reaching out to clasp the handle together when he suddenly put up his other hand.

'Wait! Do you hear him? Down there? He's asking you to swear.'

'Who is?'

'Him! Him!'

'You mean—?'

Marcellus looked frightened. I tried to bring it to a conclusion.

'So propose the oath.'

'Never to speak of what you've seen and heard.'

We reached out again for the sword and again he raised an arm.

'Swear, did you say?'

He appeared to be listening intently again, hearing something, talking to it.

'*Hic et ubique*? Here and everywhere? Let's shift our ground then, try another spot. It's a dangerous business, you know, dealing with demons.'

'Demons!'

Marcellus almost choked on the word. His hand reacted instinctively for his own sword.

'No panic, Marcellus, just follow me.'

We followed, and Hamlet listened again. We could hear nothing.

'Swear? Yes, yes! Swear! But hold on, he's right under us now, right beneath our feet. Quick—relocate! Change of ground once more! Follow me!'

And again we went after him, Marcellus terrified, and me wondering if he really was deranged.

'Stop! Stop here, friends!'

Marcellus clutched at me.

'This is too much! I can't cope with it!'

'He's right,' I said. 'It's altogether too strange.'

Again Hamlet fell quiet, became contemplative.

'Strange, yes, I know, strange. But there are even stranger things, Horatio, and more things in heaven and earth than are dreamt of in your philosophy. *Our* philosophy. All we've ever thought and known. We're a long way from Wittenberg, old friend. And you'll see stranger things yet. And you too, Marcellus. They all will.'

And that's when he came out with the plan for what he called the antic disposition: in plain terms a mad act. He intended, he said, from now on to play the part of a lunatic. Marcellus glanced at me and I could see him thinking that the plan had already been put into effect, except for the fact that it was no act. Clearly the man was half off his head as it was. I gave Marcellus a slight nod, as if to say: let's humour him, and at the same time let's play safe. At that point I had no way of knowing if Hamlet might enlighten me later, or if he really had taken leave of his senses and would never remember what had taken place between us. But for now he was clear about what we were to expect. He'd be putting on a performance—he didn't explain why—and we were to go along with it and give no indication to anyone that we knew better, that his lunatic behaviour was all an act, a clever piece of theatre.

'And I need you to swear to that too.'

The sword went up again.

'Swear.'

We placed our hands on the hilts, as if we were all three holding the cross, Hamlet still listening anxiously, intently, away from us, hearing something that we didn't, couldn't.'

'Quiet now, quiet. It's time to rest.'

And we swore the oath of secrecy. We'd been sworn to silence three times, concerning what we'd seen, what we'd heard, and what we knew about Hamlet. And we all knew that threefold oaths have a particularly binding force, and that this one would possess a still stronger solemnity, from seeming to be sworn at the behest not just of Hamlet, but also of a powerful supernatural agent. At any rate we'd sworn. And Hamlet embraced us both briefly.

'Let's go now.'

We came back down to the platform, from where we'd started, and we were headed for inside when he suddenly stopped and gave us a look of—what was it, panic, doubt, despair? And whispered some words, half to himself.

'Things. Things are… they've come apart. They're broken, dislocated, all in pieces. Everything. And me too. How can I… ? How can I put it all together again, make everything right? It's not like mending a broken arm, is it? Or a leg? Am I a barber? Is it the surgeon I'm expected to be now? Is that what I'm meant to be? Whatever I am, it's… it's the wrong time for me. I'm out of joint. Worse than that. Cut to the brains. You could say that, couldn't you?'

We looked at each other, and nodded. Not knowing what he meant. Or if he knew himself. And we followed him inside.

Two Notes to Posterity:

1) On Demonology

2) On The Antic Disposition

On Demonology

Before I proceed with the story which I have been asked to tell, there is one aspect of it which I am bound to explain: all the more so as you, my unknown readers, may inhabit a time and place in which your traditions, superstitions and beliefs are likely to have changed, even to the degree that you would find parts of my narrative entirely incomprehensible in the absence of explication, and in this case a whole history of the occult. In spite of which—brief let me be.

My friend Hamlet was given a difficult task, what I shall refer to as the revenge task. Additionally this duty, or burden, was laid on him not by a fellow creature but by what we initially spoke of as a 'thing', a 'fearful sight', an 'apparition', possibly a fantasy, an illusion, and which we subsequently accepted, as far as we were able, as a spirit. It appeared to be the spirit of Hamlet's father, lamenting its lot in the torments of purgatory, and demanding vengeance for its sufferings, the vengeance to take the form of killing the murderer, the guilty king. Scarcely the easiest of exercises, you could say. How would you have acted—reacted?

And there was a further complication, which I have already hinted at, but which I must fully explain. The difficulty for our time lay in distinguishing between genuinely tortured souls, imploring human help, and ingenious demons, eager for evil, loosed from hell to worm their way into human affairs, and in particular into trusting souls, by pretending that they themselves were souls in pain, when in reality they were players of a sort, putting on an act to deceive the living and lure them to their damnation.

Some scholars have even argued that *all* apparent apparitions and ghosts of departed persons are not the wandering souls of men that they appear to be, but the unquiet walks of devils, suggesting and prompting us to mischief, blood and villainy, all the more effectively if the apparition takes the shape of a father, mother or kinsman in order that his victim shall all the sooner swallow his lies and commit atrocities such as unjustified vengeance. And I have read other scholars who say that such spirits are eager to appear to melancholy minds—such as Hamlet's. They say, moreover, that when the fuming melancholy of our spleen enfeebles and distempers our faculties, the Devil will be at his busiest, to disturb and torment us.

A blood-curdling business, then, but one which was lent unintended comic relief in those hammy theatrical representations of spooks at which Hamlet and I used to laugh our heads off when we were students in Wittenberg: spooks straight out of Seneca, rearing up their ugly heads from Tartarus with smoke-and-squib tricks all laid on, and then some filthy whining thing wrapped in a foul sheet or a leather pilch came on stage screaming like a pig half stuck, and shrieking *Vindicta! Revenge! Revenge!* All very different from the apparition we witnessed at Elsinore—a sad apparition, yet dignified, with its military bearing and its solid armour. Absolutely real. This was no Jack-in-the-box botched up mockery of a man's shade. And it was also real in the sense that it was seen by four witnesses, two of them honest hard-headed soldiers who didn't frighten easily, at least not in normal circumstances, and the former scholars of a university renowned for its theology and philosophy and associated disciplines. None of the four of us was a fool.

But what were we to think? Hamlet clearly had his own doubts about the nature of the thing if not about its reality as some sort of spirit. The major question: was it really the spirit of his father, or some evil entity that had assumed the likeness of his dead father's person? Was it a macabre masquerade, a spirit of health or goblin damned? What was it bringing—airs from heaven or blasts from hell? And were its intents wicked or charitable, or what? But unlike the other three, Hamlet met with it alone, and the audience he had with it, however harrowing, convinced him of its authenticity, its honesty, if you like, and dispelled all his doubts.

It left him, however, with one more difficulty: the need for secrecy on the part of the sentries. Imagine it, just imagine. One word breathed about a ghost haunting the battlements of Elsinore and the whole court would be in a fizz of fear and excitement. Not Claudius. He was made of sterner stuff, not the type to believe in men returning from the dead. But he had a good nose for danger, not a soldier's nose, a politician's; and happy ghosts don't walk the earth, let alone stalk the parapets of castles. He'd be alerted to something going on, the last thing Hamlet wanted, and this was the reason for his bizarre behaviour after coming from meeting the ghost—the shifting of the ground, and the hinting at something lurking just beneath our feet, the insistence on swearing an oath on the cross-hilts of the sword, and so on.

Putting it simply, Marcellus's lips had to be sealed, and the surest way of achieving this was to make him think that there really was a devil down below us, a malevolent mole, a foul and ugly collier—Hamlet laid it on—and that we were swearing an oath to silence in its presence. If Marcellus were to break that oath he'd be blasted in this life and face eternal penalties in the next. For myself, I felt that Hamlet trusted me, and hoped he would confide in me later, when we were alone, as indeed he did, informing me of everything that the ghost had said, and the position in which he had now been placed. Even during this bewildering episode he had given me that scholar's hint with the reference to Saint Patrick, that the ghost was a purgatory ghost and no demon, a reference that was lost on Marcellus. And so, although Hamlet's mental state at that time was precarious, he had still managed to act with great presence of mind, and the ruse worked. It was only later that he began to entertain doubts about the character of the ghost. But that is a matter which lies outside the scope of this note.

On the Antic Disposition

This, as I have explained earlier in my narrative, is the term coined by Hamlet to describe his plan to feign madness as a first step on his road to avenge his father's murder. As to the matter of Hamlet's *un*feigned madness, if that is what it was, I shall return to this later. For now I confine myself to the assumed madness, which he first suggested to us back down on the platform, after listening to the ghost, and without explaining the reason for it. Clearly it was not a contrived plan but an instinctive and instantaneous decision, immediately following that momentous meeting, and the revenge task imposed on him. In other words it was, I would say, an idea arrived at on impulse rather than after careful thought, and in that respect it resembled other actions by Hamlet that were to follow.

But why? Why act mad? What was to be gained by such a pretence? There are two answers, one of which Hamlet offered me himself in private conversation, following the events I have described.

After the traumatic encounter with his father's spirit, Hamlet suddenly remembered, so he said, one of the stories his father had told him when he was a very young child. Such story-telling occasions were rare, it seems, which is why he remembered this one so vividly. As you would expect, it was no charming fairy story to fill a young boy's head with sweet dreams, but a piece of brutal family history, part fact, no doubt, part perhaps ancestral legend, deriving from old Norse myth.

At any rate Hamlet had been named, apparently, after a remote ancestor, or mythical ancestor, Amleth, whose royal father had been murdered by his brother, Amleth's uncle. Amleth planned to avenge his father, and his first move was to pretend that he had gone out of his mind and turned into a harmless idiot, a witless imbecile. He seemed to think that by practising this subterfuge he would be able to proceed against the murderer unwatched, and with impunity.

Hamlet's own unconscious aim must remain an imponderable. What I do know is that the story his father had told him sprang up in his agitated mind, and he saw a parallel and decided to act on it, and to play the fool.

But why? Still you will ask why? Why pretend to be mad? The reason given in the old Nordic story was to deflect suspicion from Amleth, and allow the prince free rein to proceed against his uncle. If this really was Hamlet's plan then the ruse turned out to be a failure—as it had to. Consider: if you uncover a hidden crime against you or your family, a crime committed by a member of the family, and if you wish to punish the criminal by taking revenge, the obvious course of action will be to behave normally, to grieve for the lost loved one, as would be natural, but to conceal any resentment and give no indication of any emotional disturbance; to assume instead a healthy acceptance of things as they are, while plotting the opposite. What Hamlet did was surely contrary to what ought to have been a sensible approach. His antics, as I shall describe these to you in the course of my story—*his* story, if you like—simply aroused his uncle's wary interest, later to turn into suspicion, and finally deep distrust and fear for his life. Amleth's antic disposition was more of a shield, and even then it did not fully protect him. Hamlet's behaviour did not act as a shield; it rang an alarm bell.

Thinking about all of this afterwards, I have long concluded that Hamlet assumed madness partly at least because he felt that he really was going mad, and thought it best to conceal his breakdown behind a mask of madness which he could put on or take off depending on his state of mind, allowing him to give way to his fits or fancies whenever he felt them coming on. In other words he pretended to be mad because he genuinely felt that from now on he'd be struggling at times to retain even a shred of self-control. The antic disposition, I reckon, was a safety device.

PART TWO

A Pause for Thought

At this point in my report I have to ask myself: what will you make of the story so far? It's not too hard for me to speculate what you must be thinking, anonymous to me though you are, and must remain. I've asked myself the same question and I can tell you exactly what I'd be likely to say if I happened to be wearing your shoes, whatever their style or era. And what would my own reaction be?

Let me give you an easy one-word answer: improbable. Highly improbable, if you'd care for two words. Remove the ghost from the sequence of events and it would be a different story entirely: adultery, incest, usurpation, murder—now where have you heard all that before? And the answer to that one is: throughout history, throughout life itself. You may even have encountered similar circumstances in your own backyard, or in your own family, and you will know that these things happen. We all know it. But—return the ghost to the bloody but banal train of events, and this is where the improbability comes in.

And yet and yet. There are two inescapable facts concerning the ghost, one of which I suspect you will also know about already from your own experience, and one is this: the dead will not stay dead, and they don't need murders and moonlit battlements and nervous sentries as an excuse for their appearance. They crowd into our thoughts and invade our dreams, and there are many occasions when you must have wondered whether they are really altogether gone, even if the only afterlife they know is their enduring existence inside the heads of you who knew them and survived them. There is nothing unnatural about the influence of the dead on the living.

And the second simple fact of the matter is that in this particular case it was the ghost that inspired the initial action, and all the action that followed. The ghost is the mainspring of my narrative. Without it there would be little else beyond the story of a bitterly unhappy and angry young man and a perfectly contented if corrupt court, and a society turned in on its own affairs, a society oblivious to everything except the everyday, with no ghosts on the go.

But the ghost walked! And those affairs took an entirely different turn, leading to events all the more improbable as they accumulated, converging in the catastrophe which I will describe in due course. It is not my task to make the story more believable but to state what happened. And if it were fiction, there would be no problem of credibility. Ask yourself, after all, what are the world's greatest invented stories? Think of Hercules, think of Faust, of Baldur the Beautiful, and Ragnarok. Think of Odysseus and Penelope, Paris and Helen, Tristan and Isolde, Orpheus and Eurydice. What is it that these stories have in common? Surely the fact that they are all fundamentally improbable. That is precisely why they are such fine and unforgettable fables. Their improbability is the price of their effectiveness. Such fantastic and fruitful situations—I think you will agree—life itself simply does not afford. On that basis, if I were an accomplished narrator, and not the inept pedant that I am, I would turn this tale into a play fit for the immortal stage. As it is I must confine myself to my account of what took place.

It is at this point, therefore, that I take up a strand in the story that became somehow unwound, sadly unravelled, all the more distressing since the person concerned was not an intrinsic part of these events, and should not have been part of them at all, but in her innocence and unprotectedness was dragged into them—and destroyed. I have referred already to Ophelia, with whom I spoke on more than one occasion, and what I have to say is based on our private talk. She left no record of her own, no letters, no diaries, nor any other accounts in her own hand. Nor could she have done, even had she wanted to. Ophelia was illiterate. And intelligent. But like many of her sort, she was taught to dance, to sing, and to sew. And that was it. Embroidery was the ultimate art to which she was encouraged to aspire. Beyond that would have lain only child-bearing and obedience. Like other young ladies, therefore, if she had received a love-letter, its contents would have been spelled out to her by a lettered person in her household, by a go-between, or by her parents, had they been sympathetic. Ophelia however, was motherless. Her father was the Lord Chamberlain, Polonius, and her brother Laertes left like a flash for Paris, as I have said. What follows next is a record of this, and of what happened subsequently. It has passed through my pen without embellishment, and is essentially therefore Ophelia's own account.

In it you will see revealed the real Ophelia, not the docile doll that was the part she was made to play at Elsinore, the only part she was accorded, and here I shall speak plainly and openly—to have been enabled to play this part myself in telling her story, is the greatest honour of my life. Had things been different, I could tell you… But I won't go there, not yet. Suffice it for me to say that, apart from being intelligent, Ophelia was a lovely girl and a beautiful human being, both in her actions and in her appearance. She was innocent but astute, amusing but not frivolous, and she was no sweet nothing. She could see through a millstone. She could see, for example, right through her perfectly uncomplicated and unprincipled brother.

The Real Ophelia

My brother was out of here as soon as he could get his clothes back on after a few weeks of philandering with the court fillies. He hadn't come for the old king's funeral four months earlier. He didn't come for the marriage either, a month later, when the queen managed to find the time to doff her mourning togs and slip quickly into wedding-weeds instead. But our father sent Reynaldo to Paris with a letter, insisting he turn up for the coronation in good time and not the night before. Reynaldo brought him back practically in shackles. I didn't see much of him, not until the morning of his exit lickety-split back to the French wenches, when he had the gall to do his brotherly duty, as he saw it, and give me the benefit of his advice on my love life and how to conduct it—speaking from wide experience, naturally, if not too deep. I could have asked what love life was that exactly, compared with his, but I let him press his point.

He's good at that and got straight to it, as he usually does with his *fillettes* and his little bits of fluff. In my case, though, the point was Hamlet. A point not to be pushed too far, apparently. Or not at all, according to big brother.

'Now then, little sister. What's this I hear about your being played around by the prince?'

'I've no idea, you'll have to tell me what you've heard.'

And so he did—what he'd heard and what he thought about it. I got the works, the full 'take heed' speech. And it out-fathered father. There's nothing worse than a chip off the old block, especially when the chip doesn't have the maturity to know when to stop, or to stop listening to the sound of his own voice. Our father stopped listening to himself long ago. He's a prattler, an old windbag, but I love him all the same, he means well in his own devious way, he's all I've got, after all, and as far as I'm concerned he has to act as father and mother too. If I said I forgive him for all that it would sound self-righteous, so I won't. He cares for me and does his best. But oh, big brother, spare me your sermons!

He didn't. First it seems I should acknowledge and accept what I am: a shrinking violet, that's me, an innocent, a doll without intellect, an angel with good legs but no wings, no pinions to protect me and fly me out of harm's way.

'But what harm can you possibly mean? Am I not safe?'

I asked the question with wide eyes, playing the part expected of me. It allowed him the luxury of laying down the law on the ways of men where women are concerned, and judging Hamlet by himself and his own shallow habits and dubious standards. But in Hamlet's case there was a particular problem. He was an intellectual. My brother pronounced it *in-too-lectual*, thinking himself witty, and piling on the platitudes and puns. Obviously Hamlet was not too intellectual to be into *me*. Time for me to wise up then, catch on—he was merely trifling with me for his own *end*. I had to stop myself laughing at that point, as dear brother's serious face showed me that he didn't even spot his own unintentional *double-entendre*. He pressed on with the lecture.

'They're not lasting, you know, these amorous impulses.'

Amorous impulses. Good phrase—he must have picked it up from father when he was giving him the same lecture about French flirts and flibbertigibbets. I gave him the saucer eyes again.

'Really?'

'Yes, really, believe me, Ophelia. Nothing he says or does has any permanence.'

'None?'

'None whatsoever.'

'Oh dear.'

He stroked my frowning brow, doing the brotherly bit to smooth away my troubles.

'Don't judge him too harshly, though. After all you must remember that he's not a free man. That's the real problem. The woman he is to marry is a matter of concern to the whole state. He can't just help himself to any dish he happens to take a fancy to, not even a tiny tit-bit. And he knows it. So if he says he loves you, you have every right to ask yourself: what does that really mean, in practical political terms? Does Denmark love you? Does Parliament approve of you? Are you considered a fit consort for a man who may one day be king? Think about it.'

I thought about it. And while I was thinking, he came out with the next on his list of one-liners.

'You're safest when you're afraid, you know.'

I thought about that too, thought about the insecure outworks of Elsinore, looking out to sea, where oddly enough I never feel afraid, whereas down below, deep in our apparently unassailable interiors, there I do feel fear, even in my own room, where I should feel safe. But the rooms somehow are not secure...

'Ophelia, are you listening to me?'

Listening? Yes of course I'm listening. I'm always listening. What else is there to do but listen—listen to men and their advice on vice and life. And so on it went, every word a warning, every line a lesson. Don't be gullible, don't let your heart rule your head, and above all be on your guard. Love is war. Men are the enemy. And their best shot—(another phallic alert!)—can prove deadly for you if it hits the target—you take my meaning? In case I didn't he employed the usual euphemism: that I might lose not only my heart, but even open my 'chaste treasure' to him, and yield to his unmastered importunity. My chaste treasure was his fig-leaf term for my vagina. I could have told him that my vagina was my own internal affair and had nothing to do with foreign affairs, or with him for that matter, but he got in ahead of me with more figurative tips about the grub that bores into a fresh young flower and infects it, and just to ensure I understood the image, he kindly explained that it was a sort of worm that penetrates the female blossom when it's still an unopened bud, and makes it very sick.

After that he got on to the contagious blasts that attack the genitals, hinting at venereal disease, in case I hadn't heard of that either. Obviously he had. And the best way to avoid such a shocking scenario would be not to show myself off even to the moon, let alone strip to the waist and expose my other two buds—which might lead to fondling, and other inappropriate actions. He waved at me vaguely, and again I could have told him that there was no need for sign language and that I knew he meant my nipples. But I expect he'd have been shocked to hear me say the word, even if I do have one on each breast, or did last time I looked. Maybe I'm not supposed to know. Maybe I'm meant to sleep in my bodice. Or in a suit of armour, with a chastity belt for a crotch. Love being war.

Anyway I assured him I'd be on my best behaviour, but suggested he should do the same and practise what he preached, not like those unholy priests who spout about celibacy and self-restraint and salvation while shagging their way as hard as they can to hell. I didn't say that last bit aloud, and in any case we were interrupted by our father, who'd breezed in to tell him the boat was waiting and he'd better get on board for France—though not before he'd given him the same sort of send-off as sonny-boy had just given me: how young people should conduct themselves, especially in Paris. I noticed he omitted any reference to sexual conduct but assumed that was partly to spare my blushes, and also because he'd be sending out Reynaldo again in due course to do some digging and find out what the lad was up to, as he's done often enough before. Father is an incorrigible meddler, and a mole. I don't blame him for that. He's a politician. It comes with the territory and keeps him happy, and he's an affable enough old buffer, if a little strict with his strictures and his stratagems.

Laertes probably didn't see it that way, now that he was on the receiving end and had to sit through the sermon: think before you speak, before you act, especially if you've got anything reckless in mind. Be easy in your manners but don't cheapen yourself in company. Keep a good grip of good friends but don't waste your time on newcomers. Avoid fights, but if you do get into one, be sure to give a good account of yourself. Listen to what people have to say but don't you be shooting your mouth off and accept criticism but keep your own complaints clamped behind your teeth. As for clothes, buy what you can afford; dress well but don't be a show-off—no ostentation; you can tell a man's character by what he wears. You're not nobly born, remember, but remember too that you're in France, where they take pride in their apparel, so don't be afraid to be as fastidious as the next man—you can be an aristocrat in your rig-out if not in your blood. And in the matter of money, remember—no borrowing, and no lending either, because as soon as you make a loan to a friend, you're sure to lose that friend, and the cash into the bargain; and by the way, borrowing is not good economy, so be thrifty, and above all else be true to yourself—that way you'll be true to all and false to none.

Something of a non-sequitur at the end there, I thought, but big brother was fast asleep on his feet by that time, dreaming of French cuisine, or courtesans, and wouldn't have spotted a fallacy if it had dropped in his flute of plonk or his tart's lap.

'Right, that's it, son. Good luck, take care, take my blessing with you too—and I hope it bears fruit.'

As you can see—or hear—my father's approach to ethics is business-like and practical. I couldn't honestly describe him as a deeply moral man, not with his cynical take on human nature, springing, I'm afraid, from his own low-mindedness. After listening to his lecture on good living, I thought I'd got off lightly by comparison, but on his way out my brother let slip that he'd been having a quiet word with me, and urged me to keep in mind what he'd said. I said I'd keep it locked up in my little brain-cells and he'd be keeper of the key. Wrong thing to say. There's no such thing as a quiet word in our family and no lock that my father wouldn't pick. It was like tossing a crumb of cheese straight into the path of a scampering mouse. The mouse pounced on it at once—only a cat would have been faster. What's that, what's that? What had he been saying to me? I tried to play it down—'Oh, nothing much, just something about Prince Hamlet.' Aha. Now the mouse's nostrils were twitching and the cheese had no chance.

'Indeed! And your brother did very well indeed to bring this up!'

That's when he really got going on me. It had come to his attention, he said, that the prince and I had been seeing a lot of each other lately, and that I'd been encouraging him openly. Of course I understood that when he said it had come to his attention, this was court-speak for the spying game, and he'd been employing his flunkeys to keep an eye on me. I'd seen Reynaldo loitering, and that ridiculous courtier Osric skulking about hiding his silly face in his even sillier hat, as if it weren't perfectly obvious he was on the mooch. And now I knew I was in for a second lecture.

'So: let me tell you here and now that this is no way for a daughter of mine to behave. There's your reputation to consider. Is it at stake? You'd better tell me now. Come on, spit it out! What's between you? What exactly is going on? Let's have it all out in the open!'

Hell. There was no way out of it. I made it sound as respectable as I could. I said Hamlet had confessed his affection for me and had spoken quite fondly, that he'd been very tender. That set father off.

'Tender! Tender do you say? Oh yes, I know all about tender affection when a man's after a woman! Do you believe this sudden tenderness of his?'

I went wide-eyed again, as I'd just done with brother boy, hoping it would take the heat off.

'I'm sure I really don't know. I don't know what I should believe.'

As I'm such a little innocent after all. It didn't work, though.

"Yes, you're a tenderfoot all right. A green girl—just as green as he'd like you to be!'

He'd taken the green bait but he wasn't letting Hamlet off the hook.

'Tender indeed!'

Once father gets hold of a word he works it to death.

'I know precisely what his tenders mean. He's tendering you up. He's the prince, don't you know! He's trying to buy his way into you—and I mean literally. Keep those iron gates locked and shut. You've got no idea about these things, you're in untried territory and he wants into the virgin forest. Tender? You'd better tender yourself more carefully in future, and put your price up, to put no finer a point on it, so that you can't be bought, do you hear? Otherwise I can tell you exactly what the outcome will be—you'll be presenting me next with a princely little bastard, I'll be the laughing stock of Denmark, don't you know, and you'll tender your poor old father a fool! But it won't happen, I tell you, you're not going to tender me up on this one, no my lady. And you too. Tender? You're going to have to toughen up, and sit up, and send this hot prince packing, tenderiser and all! Have you got that?'

You get it twenty times over when father's on a word-roll. But I wasn't going to let him write Hamlet off as a lecherous opportunist. Normally I'm the obedient daughter, the door-mat, but I spoke back.

'Hamlet's approaches to me have been impeccable. He's expressed his love for me over and over, and in a perfectly honourable and upright fashion.'

That produced a cross between a snigger and a snort.

'Upright? You bet your sweet life he's upright—and he wants you to take him down. Well, not while I'm Lord Chamberlain— and your father. Upright fashion? Aye, that's all it is, a fashion, a passing fancy, fancy for your nancy, more like, and once he's had his wicked way with you, you won't see him for your big belly and all the dust in Denmark.'

'Father!'

'Enough!'

'But father, he's dedicated to me, he's devoted, consecrated. He's sent me letters.'

'Letters? You can't even read! Surely he knows that. Bloody hell! Has someone read them to you? Come on, out with it, every detail!'

'An intermediary, he sent them by a lettered messenger. But he was going to read them to me himself—along with the poems.'

'Poems? What poems?'

'His own verses—the ones he composed for me.'

'Verses? Verses indeed! I want to see them! At once! Hand them over! I'll give him verses! Or his uncle will. He'll verse him in what's right and proper! Sniffing around and about, after my daughter…'

'And vows.'

I brought in the vows as a hopeful red herring to draw him off the track of the verses, but it made him all the more apoplectic.

'Vows? Vows! So he's made vows now! And you believe them, these vows? You must be more stupid than you look! Are you bird-brained or what? Vows do you call them? I call them snares, pitfalls, traps, vows to catch virgins, tricks, that's what they are. And if you fall for them—it's a valediction to virginity. Oh, and talk's cheap, don't you forget that, especially a man's when he's playing the bull and he feels the cow on heat, then he'll say anything to get you between the sheets, then you'll find out how upright he is, all right. Don't believe a word of his vows, they're false fire, that's all, nothing more, they're pimps, procurers, every word a bawd to beguile you, to make a whore out of you, and a brothel out of my house—no! He can find another floosie down at the docks if it's coupling he's after, no, no, no, no daughter of mind's a dolly-mop for his lust, and you're the only daughter I've got, so I'm going to look after you, and that means I'm telling you once and for all to keep your door closed in future, to lettered messengers and to him, no whispering in chambers, he can roam wherever he likes, he has the freedom, but he won't be taking you for a ride, either literally or metaphorically, and from now on your apartment and your presence are out of bounds to him, so no more vows, and no more chatter, no words of any kind, understand? This little affair is over.'

Over. That one little word, so easy for him to say. Over. He meant well for me, my father, but he had no idea what 'over' meant for me. I see little enough of him, ensconced as he is in his nest of politics and affairs of state. I've said it, I have no mother, no sister, my brother is back in Paris, doing what he does. And it's true, I was never taught letters, Hamlet had offered to show me, starting with his own precious letter to me. He said it would be a great joy to him, a privilege. I was so much counting on it, on him. He was the one thing in my life that kept the loneliness and pointlessness at bay, and scattered the shadows. There are so many shadows at Elsinore. Now they can gather again, now that it's over. Over.

Ophelia in Distress

Is it over, then? Is it really over? This morning the question appears to have been asked—and answered. Something is over, that's for sure. Or so it seems, in an Elsinore where everything seems and nothing is certain, and where nothing is but what is not. It's been two months since my father pronounced the Hamlet affair over, and in a whirling world that one fixed point has ceased to be a certainty. During this time I've been forbidden to see him, he sent more letters but father had them intercepted and refused to reveal their contents. I can only suppose he was asking to see me, but I've no way of knowing. I wasn't even allowed to send back word to him, protesting that I'm being kept a virtual prisoner here, and that it's because of father's orders that he's being denied access to me. No chance of that, no opportunity for explanation, not in Elsinore, where the shadows are in charge. They crowd round me, they push me to the side of my life. They have their way.

I can scarcely imagine what he must have been thinking all this time. It's no secret here that he reacted badly to his mother's precipitate affair with her dead husband's brother, and the rash marriage that fell so hard on the heels of the funeral. Can you blame him for that? Who is a man closer to than his mother? And she let him down—painfully, shamefully, and shamelessly, that at least is how he saw it. No wonder he suddenly felt so disillusioned, so dismayed and depressed. Because of one woman. And because of one woman he lost faith in all women. Except me. We had something precious. We had each other. And then what happened? I let him down. I rejected him. For no reason. And without a word of explanation or apology. Or farewell. Nothing but a door shut in his face. And behind it a woman as shallow and inconstant as his mother.

That's how it must have looked to him, that's how it's been. And today he must have decided he couldn't bear it any longer, the silence and separation, the not knowing. He needed desperately to discover what kind of woman was hiding, or was being kept hidden, on the other side of that door. He needed to find out, to see for himself. And so this morning he burst in…

I was sewing in my closet when he appeared. Standing there holding the suddenly swung open door. And in a shocking state. I'm neither a giggler nor a screamer, but I'd have shrieked if I'd had the voice for it. I didn't. I couldn't take a breath. His doublet was unbraced—the laces looked like he'd gnawed them to shreds. His chest was bare, his face white as his shirt—and this too was hanging open, all the buttons ripped off. His hair was a bloodless shambles, a tangle of knotted strands and snags. His legs were trembling, violently—he looked ready to collapse on the spot and expire.

All that was nothing to the expression he wore. I've never seen anything like it on any human being—on anything. I don't know how to describe it. He looked as if he had just been let loose from hell, to tell me of the horrors he'd seen, he looked so ghastly. I was terrified. I stood up and all my needlework fell to the floor. I waited. At that moment I asked myself: has he come to murder me? I really thought he had, and I didn't have the power to move, didn't have the breath or strength to call for help. Then he came into the room.

I thought the moment had come. I closed my eyes. Then I felt his hand on me. He took hold of my wrist, gripped it so hard—I still have the marks—and pushed me slowly, so slowly away from him, so that I was at arm's length, but still he kept holding on to me tightly, by the wrist. Then he took his other hand and lifted it to his forehead, shading his eyes and looking into mine, as if he were finding it hard to make me out, as if he were studying my portrait, but simply couldn't see what he needed to see, whatever it was. His eyes bored into me. They were the eyes of a man who wasn't really seeing me, he was seeing someone else, something else, something inside me, behind me, I don't know. I don't know what he was looking at, looking for, probing into, scrutinising, sifting. It wasn't the man I loved, it was someone else standing there, staring through me, past me.

How long he stayed like that—it could have been a minute, it could have been an hour. It felt like an hour. And still holding me by the wrist, he shook my arm ever so gently. I don't know what it meant. Then, weirdly, his head started to rotate, sideways, up and down, and he held on to it, hard. It was as if he really feared it was about to fall off. Finally there was a great long sigh. I've never been at a death-bed, not even at my mother's, unless it was so long ago I've forgotten it, but it was the sort of sound I could have imagined coming from someone who was breathing his last. It was pitiful, profound, it was as if he were being split in two, ripped apart. It seemed to shatter his entire body and end his being.

At last he released my wrist and let me go, retreating through the still open doorway. But the strange thing was that as he left he never took his eyes off me, but kept his head turned back over his shoulder. He went out like that, blindly, as if he were being drawn through the doorway by some sort of guiding force, and to the last possible moment he bent his eyes only on me. It was almost as if he couldn't bear to see the last of me, as if he couldn't bring himself to say goodbye.

My Thoughts on What Happened in Ophelia's Closet

Ophelia was not the first to realise that something had happened to Hamlet, something other than the distress of his father's death and his mother's remarriage. The whole court, including the guilty king, knew that something was up. But other than Marcellus, who'd been sworn to secrecy under the most terrifying circumstances, I was the only one who knew that Hamlet had followed his father's spirit up onto the castle battlements, and had come down into the dawn a changed man, never to be the same again. Marcellus too shared the secret of the antic disposition, but again only I was privy to what had taken place that night, to what had been said by lips that were stiff and still and rotting in the tomb, and yet had spoken…words unimaginable to any listener, let alone the son of the dead speaker. And if I am to fulfil my assignment, it's not enough for me merely to deliver an account of these events, I must also try as best I can to interpret them. I need you to be my audience. I need to bring both actions and actors before you, the who and the when, so that you can as far as possible see them for yourselves, as if on a stage.

To recap therefore. Hamlet had suffered a series of shocks: his father's unexpected demise, followed by his mother's dishonourable marriage, tainted both by incest and by unseemly haste, which a complaisant court had not only condoned, but had bent over even further by electing the dead king's brother to the throne instead of the prince, his only son. That was enough, more than enough, to put the prince into black, publicly proclaiming his mourning in defiance of the new sovereign, and shaming the mother who had abandoned black within a month and slipped blithely into a wedding dress, thrown on, if you like, to cover her matronly age. Then came the coronation, and Hamlet stood aloof from all of it, from all of them, with the sole exception of Ophelia. In spite of his misogynistic mutterings, she remained. She was there for him. He still loved her. Or so he believed.

That was the point at which she was forbidden by her father to receive both Hamlet and his letters, and this was followed immediately by Hamlet's meeting with the ghost and the revelations of adultery and murder—murder by a brother, and poisoning in the most devious and sickening circumstances. It eclipsed imagination.

It was gruesome. The prince's uncle, a murderous usurper, now wore the crown, while his father's spirit suffered in Purgatory, having been denied the crucial sacrament of confession, which could have allowed him extreme unction and hence salvation—all because of the underhand and unscrupulous manner of the murder. Hamlet couldn't even be certain in his own mind that his mother hadn't acted as the murdering brother's adulterous accomplice. Horrible, was the ghost's word: horrible, horrible, most horrible.

And enough to crush anyone? Yes, but even that wasn't the end of it. On top of all this came the imposition of the revenge task: kill the killer! And Hamlet's first impulse was that he'd fall like a hawk, like an avenging eagle, on whoever it was—and swoop to his revenge. It was a murderous surge of the blood, honest and instinctive at the time, and heartfelt. He was even exhilarated by it. Until something came in its way and slewed the swoop: the spirit's strict instruction to his son not to harm his mother, to leave her out of it, to leave her to heaven, and to the thorns of conscience. It was a devastatingly difficult stipulation: to kill the killer without implicating the killer's queen. Everyone would have asked the same question: had she been an accessory after the fact, or even, God forbid, before the fact and to the fact? Whatever the fact, the facts were black against her, so it seemed to her son, so much so that he not only suspected her complicity but considered exacting vengeance on her too. In any event, any public attempt to expose Claudius would have reflected inevitably on the woman who had married her husband's murderer. She'd be seen as his accomplice. In the end therefore there seemed no other way to deal with his uncle except by chopping him down.

So, imagine: put yourself in Hamlet's position. Here you are walking around with a corpse for a companion, a corpse come back to some sort of life, to take over your own life. Not a loving and forgiving spirit but an angry, grieving and vengeful one—except that the murdered king still loves his adulterous queen, she who was so quick to forget, and who had urged her son to forget, to forget the dead. Look up, not down, contemplate the sky not the dust, go forward, not backward to what's past—and live, don't die. We all die, so let's live while we're waiting, and forget the rest.

Good advice—if you haven't got a ghost in your head, and if you're allowed to forget, if forgetfulness is an option. Forgetfulness—it might have drowsed Hamlet with the poppy of peace, the dull opium of oblivion, and an ecstatic exit from the obligation and the charge. But the dead father wasn't a forgetful father, he was a fertilising father all over again, siring the same son for the second time, only this time with a difference, bringing to birth a sickness in his soul, feeding a death, a darkness. It suited him, you could say. The son had been too much in the sun. He'd said so himself. It was time to say goodbye to the light. Only—the ghost's goodbye wasn't a valediction at all. Three consecutive farewells: adieu, adieu, adieu, it sounded terminal, conclusive. But they weren't the last words. The last words were: *do not forget. Remember me.* Not—remember life, but remember death, and hell, and the ghost from the grave. Not—look after yourself, dear boy, but concentrate your mind on me and my unforgiving mission. Not—forget me and be glad, but remember me and be sad, and angry, and bitter, and disillusioned, and on edge for revenge, on edge for death. And don't taint your brain…

But the brain was already tainted. And so a sick soul was ordered to heal, jangled nerves commanded to produce harmony, and out of the sewers of hell had to come some sort of cleansing. I think he knew it was mission impossible, and that the demons of insanity and despair would prove too strong for him. Knowing this, knowing that sanity and stability were under attack, he remembered the old ancestral saga of Amleth, the antic disposition, and he reached out to it as a device, a defence stratagem, a shield. It helped, but in itself it could never have been more than that. There was only one thing left that might have saved him, that he might have held on to and survived, and that was Ophelia, and his stated love for her, and hers for him. And when that too was taken from him, when she rejected him and even returned his letters, or so he was made to believe, it was the last hammer-blow to the tainted brain.

That at least is how I saw it at first, made sense of what happened in Ophelia's closet. Before that he was playing the part he'd invented for himself, the part he'd taken on from an old story. He could be seen walking for hours along the lobbies, unseeing, unspeaking, staring, dangerous, the human traffic parting to let him go by. He looked through them as if they weren't there. Or he lay stretched on the stone floors in empty rooms all day long, scowling into space. Or he leaned dangerously far over the parapets, scrutinising the sea, the long skylines, sharing some secret with them. Or he occupied the king's throne at the end of the long conference table, addressing the empty places with nods and grins and frowns, as if chairing a meeting. Sometimes he sat on window-seats, smiling at sitters that only he could see. Sometimes he talked to walls. Sometimes he appeared at state meetings with drawn sword, scattering the gathering, freezing the guards, who didn't know how to react when the danger to the throne was the Prince of Denmark himself. Courtiers avoided him, shrinking into the shadows when they saw him coming. Even the castle hounds snarled and flattened their long ears, slinking out of sight, growling quietly, uneasily.

All that was play-acting. It was part-playing on an unstable stage, as he confronted himself as best he could, and took a bow to his alter ego. But what happened with Ophelia was an altogether different matter. What she saw was no mock-madness. She said he looked as if he had been loosed out of hell to speak about the horrors he had seen…and she little knew how close to the mark she'd come. During his encounter with the ghost he'd entered hell, vicariously, and he'd been let out only to be imprisoned again in Elsinore, and in the prison of the impossible, in the cell of mental death: a triple lock-up. So yes, he did simulate insanity in front of the court, but when he appeared in Ophelia's chamber he was a man who really had lost his mind. He'd faced hell and was now facing hell on earth. His mental state had clearly deteriorated during these two months, and in this desperate condition he turned to the girl he'd said he loved. For help? For strength? For consolation? She offered him none of these, nothing. And she couldn't be blamed. She was dumbstruck, wordless, terrified. What could she have said or done? So after waiting in vain for the help that never came, that could never have come, after sending her the speechless appeal that could never be answered, he left—and his long shattering sigh in leaving expressed his realisation of her failure, the inevitable failure to respond to an insanely inarticulate plea. She had now rejected not only his love but his desperate entreaty. She had failed him. That is not how it was, but it was how he saw it, in his hopelessly muddled mind. It's a pitiable picture I bring before you, of two people who once were close and were now totally unable to make contact.

And yet at the same time he was saying so much, or attempting to, if his actions can be explained in any rational way, which I believe they can. The keeping her at arm's length and the intense scrutiny of her face—did these gestures express his uncertainty about her, his hurt and frustration and regret at her rejection? Or something of his misogynistic suspicions? Perhaps, perhaps. But still she was the one he remained attached to, expressed so dramatically in the manner of his departure—going slowly through the door while fixing his eyes on her to the last, to the bitter end. What did it mean? Was he saying 'I love you, only you, and I'll love you always, but I have to leave you'? And if it really was a parting of the ways, was it because he knew there could never be a future for the two of them together—not now, not now that things had changed for each of them, irrevocably?

Perhaps. But I ask myself another question: if his behaviour in the closet had nothing to do with her returning his letters, or her apparent rejection of him, then did his actions signify something else? The clues, if I am correct, lie in the perusal of the face, and the parting with eyes turned back upon the woman parted from. It flashed into my scholar's mind that the eyes that bended their light on her echo Ovid's description of Orpheus, *flexit amans oculos,* at the moment of his losing Eurydice when coming back from hell. Like Orpheus his eyes were wedded not to her, but to the darkness, to his dedication to revenge and his oath to heaven to wipe all past memories and emotions from his brain and purge himself of his past, including Ophelia. His appearance in the closet was not only his despairing farewell to her, but also emblematically to all hopes of love and marriage, a silent anticipation of what was to come.

An answer to the unanswerable? But it was with such unanswerable questions in her bewildered mind that she came first to me, and I urged her to go to her father and inform him of the consequences of his orders. So she ran to him and told him what had happened. And Polonius's logic was simple and impeccable, as he saw it. She'd obeyed his instructions, she'd repelled her lover's letters and refused to see him—and the lover had gone mad. Yes, of course he had. That's what lovers do. Men do go mad for love, and even old Polonius could see now that the prince really did love his daughter, and had not been out simply to seduce her. He acknowledged his error of judgement, and decided that as this concerned no less a person than the Prince of Denmark, whose recent behaviour had been a cause for such concern, the king would have to be immediately informed. Polonius was in his element. Apart from the inadvisability of keeping this family matter secret, he had something of great consequence to report. He had a diagnosis. He had discovered the reason for Hamlet's madness. Or so he thought.

A Note on Fork and Knife

If you had breath left for just a hundred words before you died, what do you think you'd want to say? With only that much left to him, Hamlet asked me to report him and his cause correctly, to provide a satisfactory account that would explain things to the uninformed—and that is precisely what I am trying to do. As I hinted earlier, if this were a stage-play instead of a report—and as I've said at times it feels that way—I would at this point make a stage direction: enter Rosencrantz and Guildenstern.

Quite a mouthful, isn't it? *Ro-s-en-crantz* and *Gu-i-ld-en-stern*: a six-syllable pair, seven if you add the conjunction, the polysyllabic weight of the appellation augmented by the fact of the names always being spoken together. You could never address one without the other. They sounded almost as impressive as Voltimand and Cornelius, except that the ambassadors beat them by a syllable, and Rosencrantz and Guildenstern didn't have the status of ambassadors. In fact they didn't have any status at all. They never did.

Looking back to our university days, as students we called them fork and knife. Or knife and fork. They belonged together and they fed on their friends. At Elsinore they fed Hamlet his lines, like minor characters in a play. I'm back to drama again, forgive me. But yes, I knew them well enough, if you can know people about whom there is not really much to know. They were our fellow pupils at Wittenberg and that's essentially all that can be said about them. As companions they were amenable enough, I suppose, and conversable—if the talk didn't turn to Aristotle, or anything educational. They were friendly flies and fliers by night. Other than that they were nonentities, and like many of their kind they hunted in couples, each trying to compensate for a complete lack of individuality by an alliance with the other. Together they bowed themselves in and out of company, they bandied tittle-tattle and shallow compliments, they whored and wheedled, smirked and insinuated. They were general fetchers and carriers. They were the indispensable quidnuncs, the gossipers and hangers-on of the obliging world, which they always sought to oblige.

As I've said, they were nobodies. But nobodies can be somebodies, if somebody has a use for them. And King Claudius had a use for them. He had decided at this point that as nobodies they could pretty well blend in. He'd made enquiries. There were several of our former fellows still in Wittenberg and Claudius was crafty enough to select the perfect candidates. They too were still living there, still bowing and scraping and fiddling and fetching, and he'd sent for them—to blend in and draw out, according to their natures. I was present when they arrived, and not just by chance. The king kept me close in to the swing of things at first, hoping that as a friend of Hamlet I might fulfil the function of a Rosencrantz or a Guildenstern—if I can split them for a second—and keep him informed of his nephew's mental state and his potential menace. It didn't take him long to decide that as far as Hamlet was concerned, I was more a friend than an informer, and not to be trusted too far, certainly not to be counted on to divulge anything useful. And that's where Rosencrantz and Guildenstern came in.

'Welcome, dear Rosencrantz and Guildenstern!'

Well spoken, Claudius. Dear Rosencrantz and Guildenstern. He'd never set eyes on either of them in his life, and if you'd set an eye on one, you'd have seen the other half in the other eye. But the master butterer-up was only just getting started with the lashings of the churn, to be shared between the fork and the knife. Or would that be the knife and the fork? It was obvious he didn't actually know which was which. Never mind. On with the motley. And they were too beslobbered with the butter to discern the jest, or to see through King Cook. If only they'd known, if only they'd had the power to see ahead, to the day when their goose would be cooked, and not a knob of butter to help it go down, and ease what they were made to swallow in the end. But this morning it was a different story. Things are often better in the morning, though night must always fall.

So, 'Welcome, dear Rosencrantz and Guildenstern! It's worth repeating isn't it—as you're a couple! A warm welcome, to each of you, then. And quite apart from the fact that I need to use you—let me rephrase—that I need your help, I have of course been longing to see you—both!'

The pair he'd never even heard of until quite some time ago, but he couldn't wait to see them—and so he'd been a-wearying, just for them, and in any case he had a use for them—and so he got to the point. Their old friend Hamlet was a changed man, sadly changed, badly changed, and to put no finer a point on it, quite possibly dangerously changed.

'And I can't think what it could be that's troubling him, other than his father's death.'

No? Can't think of anything else? Even by trying hard? Can't think of the cursory courtship, the winged wedding, the nifty election? Can't think of incest, adultery, murder, purgatory, poison...? And why indeed should he even dream of those last three or four on the list of possible griefs and grievances? Hamlet, after all, knew nothing of them. Nobody knew anything about them. Only Gertrude knew about the adultery. And the only other one who knew about the crime itself and the nature of it was the victim, the dead king himself, and dead men don't come out of their graves, they don't come back from the dead to blab about it. Dead men don't tell tales...

Ah, but they do, you see—and we did see. We saw what scholars saw, and lore-learned commentators, and even priests and Plato, that murderers were pursued by the souls of their victims, so certainly does the vengeance of God or Nemesis pursue the abominated assassin, to the extent that when witnesses are wanting of the fact, the very ghosts of the murdered parties can't rest quiet in their graves until they have made the detection themselves. And although Claudius didn't see the dead, didn't know what the dead knew, and what we knew, and was never to know, not even in the unseeing seconds of his death, even so his comment about being unable to imagine what it could be that was disturbing Hamlet, what could possibly be at the back of it—that showed clearly the working of the guilty king's mind. Because: if you have a guilty secret, you know that your secret is safe, don't you, since no-one else knows? Yes—but *you* know! And you yourself can never be safe from that knowledge. It's always with you, like another self, a wicked self, like a secret agent, a double-agent, spying on you, informing on you, wanting to whisper to the world what you really are: an adulterer and a murderer, a killer got up as a king. A brother-killer. A Cain king.

'So find out, please, I beg you both, find out if you can what it is that's eating away at him. There are no two men better placed to get to the bottom of it.'

He'd got to the bottom of them, certainly, he'd got the measure of them, and hearing that I understood that I was now out of the equation, ironically enough, as I was much better placed than the two of them, or ten of them for that matter, to know Hamlet's mind, and to know Claudius's guilty secret.

'After all you were practically brought up with him.'

That too made me wince—and nearly snigger. He made it sound as if they'd shared cribs and wet-nurses, not wine and women and lessons on logic, and the May days of adolescence. But he finally got to the nub of the thing.

'Stay with us for a little while, why don't you, shake the dust of Wittenberg from your weary feet, get settled in, drink deep in Denmark. I myself shall be your cup-bearer—and see if you can draw him on a jot to some sort of entertainment, some healthy activity, you know, so as to bring him out of himself.'

And that was closer to what he really meant. Not—draw him on, but draw him out, gather, glean, uncover, dig up, dig deep. He wanted them to be the drawers and tapsters and the wheedlers that they were. He wanted them to suck at the bung that stemmed the secret grey cells of the brain. And he wanted them to be surgeons of the mind. A little blood-letting, after all, is a healthy thing, it's good for the tainted brain, so be blood-letters by all means, but be blood-suckers too, and see if you can discover what it is I don't know that runs in his blood and lies along his heart and corrupts his soul, what exactly his affliction consists of, so that I can help him, bring him back to his old self, make him well again, that's all I want to do, you understand?'

They understood exactly what he wanted.

'Open the vein then, lads, see what comes out, and I'll be his doctor, and apply the remedy.'

As consummate a Claudius performance as always. But to my surprise the queen came in and bettered it.

'Let me assure you, gentlemen, he's just longing to see you. He's talked of nothing else but you two since he heard you were coming. He'll deny it, naturally, as he won't want to embarrass you with his enormous affection, still strong in him for you since his student days, but believe me there aren't two men alive to whom he more adheres. So if you will indeed be good enough to grace us with your presence for a while, and help us to help Hamlet, your efforts will be well-rewarded. In fact, if I may speak on behalf of my dear husband—royally rewarded.'

Astonishing. Hamlet not only had no idea they'd arrived at Elsinore, he didn't even know they'd been sent for. And as for itching to see them, and talking of nothing else, and the two of them being the best boon companions he ever had, or could hope to have, all I can say is that at that moment I found myself wondering if Gertrude really had been her second husband's accomplice all along. She had certainly been put up to delivering this little speech, that much was obvious. Hamlet had never uttered a word about these two, certainly not in my hearing. It's not hard to see why these two flies from the past would be the last thing on his troubled mind. Once only, some years ago, when I was at Elsinore and we were reminiscing, they came up in conversation, and only then because I happened to ask him if he remembered fork and knife.

'You mean right tit and left tit? So perfectly paired you couldn't tell one personality from the other. Fine form in a female, matching breasts, but in their case as I remember, best covered up.'

After they'd turned up at Elsinore he gave them a grosser image.

'Rosencrantz and Guildenstern. Why waste breath on such long names? Life's too short. How about left bollock and right bollock? Two testicles sharing the same ball-sack—the king's scrotum. The French call them waltzers, don't they, Horatio? Suits their slightness and legerity, don't you think?'

'Too good for them, I'd say.'

'You're right. Not exactly the dog's bollocks. St Augustine has a better term: *inter urinas et faeces*. Yes that's them pinpointed, right between the excrement and the urine. Ugh!'

But right now left tit and right tit were spouting out the milk of meekness in a crushingly door-matting and spineless little speech—each. Rosencrantz: oh, please, both Your Majesties, no need to entreat us, you have the power to command us, and if it so please you, to crush us. We're insects, that's all. And Guildenstern: insects indeed, insects at your feet, not even worth the crushing, but if you choose not to, we'll bend over and do your bidding. As insects after all, we have the snouts to sniff out cash—cash for information. Leave it to us—we're already on the trail.

Had the speeches been written down and you did a word-count, I do believe you'd find they used the exact same number of syllables in their respective replies. They knew exactly what was being asked of them, and the 'use' to which they were being put, and they thought and spoke as one, without collaboration or rehearsal. They were joined at the hip. And as Hamlet was later to add—at the genitals. One foreskin between the two.

Claudius made out he was charmed.

'Thanks, Rosencrantz and Guildenstern.'

Said with a grin that took them in.

And the queen, spotting his error of identification, put it right for him with a sly nudge and a little joke,

'Thanks, Guildenstern—and Rosencrantz!'

Ah!

Attendants were then appointed to conduct the pair of utensils to Hamlet.

That's if you can find him—I thought to myself. And the queen almost read my mind.

'You'll find him—much changed.'

'But God willing, our company will prove a great blessing to him.'

'And—let's pray for it—a great pleasure too,'

Suddenly the tone had turned religious. Amen, said the queen. And fork and knife went off to dig into Hamlet.

A Note on the Chamber-Pot

So: exit fork and knife—and enter the chamber-pot! That was the Lord Chamberlain's sniggeringly whispered nickname among the lower echelons of Elsinore, and even more quietly among the courtiers. The wordplay was palpable, though if you asked around in the right quarters, you'd be offered explanations that were apparent afterthoughts to the immediately obvious: he could sniff you out, he always needed to be emptied, he was so awash with whiffy intel; he was the Lord of Bumf, he was kept close to the throne—just below it—to answer the king's needs and be shat into with a smile; he was the chamber-pot because he was perfectly placed to spy up your posterior (he had an eye for arse) and tell you what you'd had for breakfast; or, quite simply, he was full of piss and wind, or just an old windbag. And so on.

Less crudely, Hamlet once called him Corambis. I asked why.

'A punning derivation, old lad. Back to your Latin, fellow-fresher! *Crambe bis posit mors est:* cabbage served up twice is death, and apt for one who regales us with stale and tedious wisdom. You know how he witters on.'

'Witters. Is that another pun?'

'Hardly.'

But on cue and on form he came bustling in at the heels of Rosy-pants and Gilded-stern (they'd earned themselves suitable nicknames right from the start) to raise the tone, as he thought, to the loftier level of affairs of state.

'Your Majesty, the ambassadors have just returned from Norway—and they have good news!'

Claudius patted the chamber-pot and gave it its much-handled handle.

'Dear old Polonius, what else do I expect from you but good news? You're its founding father, the bringer of joy, and if I may say so, the gospel of good news.'

But the pot was too busy for the butter. He couldn't wait to spill his latest discovery.

'There's good news—and even greater news! And what would you say if I told you I'd found out the actual cause of your nephew's lunacy?'

Suddenly the political news was second-class gossip. You could see the Claudius feelers twitching with curiosity.

'The cause? You've found the cause? What is it, for God's sake? Tell me—tell all!'

But the chamber-pot wanted its big moment.

'Affairs of state first, Your Majesty? Surely? It's a feast of information. And I'll provide the last course. I promise you, Your Majesty, you won't go hungry!'

Polonius scurried out on his spindles to admit the ambassadors and Claudius muttered some comforting words to the queen.

'Apparently our indefatigable Lord Chamberlain had discovered exactly what's disturbing your son.'

You couldn't help noticing that when Hamlet was causing a problem he was always *your* son, never *our* son. Gertrude didn't much care about the maternity and paternity business, and showed not much interest in Polonius's perceptible pleasure in having solved the present enigma of Elsinore.

'I'm sure it's nothing else but the old story: his father's death, and our rushing into marriage so soon.'

At that point Polonius ushered in the ambassadors and Voltimand and Cornelius reported on their mission. When he'd realised that his nephew intended to attack not Poland but Denmark, the Norwegian king, old, ill and feeble, and much grieved that young Fortinbras had deliberately deceived him, suppressed his conscripts and summoned him home. The fiery youngster took his dressing-down on the jaw and promised to desist in his quest to recover the lost lands. He was rewarded with quite an incentive: three thousand crowns a year and permission to employ his dogs of war to launch an attack against Poland instead. Clearly the young adventurer didn't much care which country he was attacking so long as he could go into action and have a good war.

Only one small request from old Norway: that the Danish king would consider allowing Fortinbras and his army to pass peacefully through Denmark's dominions en route to attack the Poles. Claudius announced that he would take that request very seriously and would let Norway have an answer. The ambassadors were thanked for their efforts and dismissed, with the promise of a celebratory feast to round off the evening—more drums and trumpets to be expected, and loads of cannoneering. By which time the chamber-pot was brimming over and couldn't wait to slosh out its steaming contents.

Let me spare you the bulk of those contents, the usual wind mostly—Polonius could never use six words where sixty would do—and let him come to the heart of his revelations: Hamlet had gone mad for love. Nothing unusual there, as men have lost their minds to women throughout history. And in Hamlet's case the female in question was the Lord Chamberlain's own daughter, who had dutifully and obediently shown her father a love-letter from the prince—and not the only one. This one began with the conventional enough approach, high-flown and formal, which men of a certain rank and level of breeding use to address well-bred women:

To the celestial and my soul's idol, the most beautified Ophelia.

Nothing much wrong with that, if a touch artificial and overdone—but men in love aren't inclined to be practical and prosaic. The Chamberlain, however, didn't approve of one particular word which had dropped in his pot. It was Hamlet's use of the word 'beautified' which had offended him. He thought it a vile phrase, God knows why. Maybe he thought there was an implication that his daughter was not naturally beautiful and had to rely on cosmetics to enhance where nature had come short, but the word carries no such insinuation and I've heard of its being used often enough in a complimentary context.

Claudius was all ears but the queen clearly had had enough of the Polonius prolixity, and the wallowing in the big moment.

'Keep going, man, cut it short or get to the point. What comes next?'

Next came the words: *In her excellent white bosom, these...*

Whatever phrases were to be received into Ophelia's splendid and spotless bosom we never got to hear. At the breast reference the queen came in with a mother's question.

'How can you be sure my son wrote this?'

After all, love-letters were frequently penned and sent anonymously, which adds to the excitement and the intrigue. Polonius neglected to answer the question, however, and begged leave to continue, promising to report in full. He was allowing nothing to interrupt his performance. He was happy to drag it out. And so, with much throat-clearing, he recited the next portion of the letter, a poem written by Hamlet:

Doubt thou the stars are fire,
Doubt that the sun doth move,
Doubt truth to be a liar—
But never doubt I love.

That was Hamlet all right, I didn't need a signature to tell me that much. He couldn't write a love-poem without getting into astrology and metaphysics. And it wasn't all that bad a piece of verse—at least it was succinct. But the letter continued with his protestation and apology—another lover's convention—that he was so poor a poet and hadn't the art to count the number of his sighs and groans and make them scan, in decent verse. All that he could sincerely do was to express the truth: that in the whole world she was the one he loved best. And he ended with a lover's assurance:

As long as there is breath in this body, I am yours, my dearest love—yours forever. Adieu.

It has since passed through my mind, in the light of everything that had happened and was to follow, that the adieu was almost prophetic, coming before the ghost's repeated farewell and the separation that lay ahead. But Gertrude was impatient for him to conclude.

'And...? And...?'

'And, Your Majesty, it's signed—Hamlet!'

So he got there in the end, and was pleased to repeat that his dutiful daughter had shown him—so he said—not only this letter but more in the same vein, what Polonius referred to as Hamlet's 'solicitings', making his approaches sound almost improper, and every single approach had been duly declared. Ophelia was obviously an angel of obedience, though anybody familiar with the Polonius menage would know that he ran his household as Claudius ran his court, with spies and informers everywhere, and

Ophelia would have had little choice in the matter of transparency. Unable to read, she would have asked for an interpreter, and no one valuing employment under the chamber-pot ought to have failed to turn over something as significant as a royal love-letter, especially one from the Prince of Denmark. Very shortly the poor girl would now hear that so intimate a missive had been read out in public. Nothing private in Elsinore, not even in your love life, and especially not if you happen to be Ophelia, and your father's a big enough wig to be worried about protecting his reputation. And this is all that concerned him now.

Claudius on the other hand asked the obvious question.

'But what does Ophelia think? How does she feel about it, about Hamlet? How has she reacted to his letters, his pursuit of her?'

Polonius was clear about this. He had no interest in his daughter's point of view, if she had one. What she thought about it or didn't think, what she felt was irrelevant. He had only one question to put to Claudius.

'What do you think of me, Your Majesty?'

Claudius was clear about that.

'A faithful servant, and an honourable man. Of that I have no doubt.'

'And I wouldn't want you to doubt it, or to think otherwise. And that is why I took immediate action and gave her strict instructions. Of course I'd seen it coming, this little love-affair, let me tell you, long before she told me about it. And under no circumstances was I going to become a medium of communication between the two parties. What would you think of me, I asked myself, if I'd let myself be turned into a dead-letter-box for these messages, for the pair of them to carry on with their courting on the quiet? No—there's courting, and there's the court. Or if I'd winked at and played along, played dumb, if I'd been complacent about it, or even complicit? If I'd failed to appreciate the political implications of the affair? And it's not only letters. They've been seeing each other. Imagine. Absolutely not, I said, I spoke plainly to her on the subject. I admonished her, gave her a good scolding, not a beating. Look here, I said, this isn't just any man you're fooling around with, it's the Prince of Denmark we're talking about here, do you understand what that means? He's the heir to the throne, the king has said so, he's above your station, way beyond your reach, outside your destiny. Whatever your stars tell you, or your love-charts, listen to what I'm telling you now: forget it. The affair is at an end. And it's time to learn your place. Have you got that? And then I ordered her to keep herself under lock and key. From now on no meetings, no messages, no messengers, no love-tokens, trinkets, no gifts of any kind, no nothing. And she followed my advice—my orders—like the good girl she is, a daughter fit for her father, and a sister fit for her brother. And then—well, you know the rest. The black mood fell on him, he stopped eating, stopped sleeping, stopped behaving normally, became unstable and irrational, lost his wits, his taste for life, his direction, everything, and subsequently deteriorated into the state of complete madness into which we know he has fallen, so sadly for all of us. And now at last we know the cause.'

An enormous yes. A huge smile. Unburdened satisfaction. The chamber-pot had dumped, drained itself, and now awaited the round of applause for a job well done.

It didn't come.

'Hmn.'

Claudius was unconvinced. He looked at Gertrude.

'What do you think? Could it be this?'

Gertrude was no expert on the meanings or mainsprings of madness and didn't pretend to be. But she knew her son. Or thought she did.

'I don't know. But I think it's quite likely. In fact, yes, highly probable.'

The chamber-pot had a higher opinion of itself, and put it to His Majesty.

'Have I ever been proved wrong? Have you ever known such an occasion?'

'Not that I can think of.'

'And if I'm wrong in this case, you can chop my head off.'

Claudius smiled.

'No need for that. But all the same I'd like to be more certain. How can we try it further, put it to the test? Madness, mental illness, call it what you will, it's a disorder, a distemper, it's a disease, and it needs to be, like any ailment—you know—probed.'

'Exactly, Your Majesty. And I'm the man to probe it.'

'I'm sure you are. But how exactly—in what way?'

The chamber-pot brimmed again.

'There you have me. And I have the answer.'

'What is it?'

'You know how he paces the lobbies, walks up and down endlessly in this very one here, for hours at a time?'

Gertrude nodded.

'I know, I know. It's a sad sight.'

'Sad indeed, Your Majesty, but also our opportunity. And at the next chance we have, I'll loose my daughter to him. We'll arrange it so that His Majesty and myself will be hiding behind an arras—I mean, diplomatically screened, as it were, so that we can hear what goes on between the two of them, and draw our conclusions. And if I'm wrong—'

He pointed again to his head and shoulders and Claudius waved the gesture away with a grin.

'Then not capital punishment, Your Majesty, but political punishment. Execute me from my post as your policy adviser—and send me out into the fields. I'll be a farmer like old Adam, and till the thistles. I'll be a peasant and drive a cart. I'll be a drover and keep cows. I'll—'

'Ssh!'

Gertrude could never endure his verbosity, but this time she was urging everybody to keep quiet.

'Fingers on lips! Look, here he comes now. He doesn't see us, poor boy, he's deep in his book.'

The chamber-pot spun round.

'Away! Away with you, all of you! Pardon me, Your Majesties, you too, and you, Horatio, everyone, I beg you, off you go. I'll waylay him. It's a chance not to be missed. Leave him to me.'

Hamlet's Account to Me: Of How he Ran Rings Round the Chamber-Pot

Deep in my book, was I? There was a time I was deep in books, and nobody knows it better than you, Horatio, old friend. But my books and I had a parting of the ways some little time ago—you know that too—and there's nothing so useful as a book to lose your face in if you want people to think you're not aware of them, or don't know what they're up to. I knew all right, because they were so deep in each other they didn't hear me coming. I saw them before they saw me—I'll dramatize it for you in a moment—and I not only saw but I heard… their plot to probe me, the poor fools, to spy out my problem, to diagnose me, for God's sake, and for that I could almost have forgiven them.

Almost. They were concerned for me, after all, up to a point, though mainly concerned for themselves, and for each other. But one thing I could never forgive, and I never will forgive. I overheard that old piss-pot say that he'd loose his daughter to me. Loose! What a pathetic old pimp! He just couldn't help himself, could he? Loose! a choice turn of phrase, and one that gave him away. Loose! It's what the farmer does when he releases the cow to the bull—for a red-hot rod and a good old-fashioned fuck, the bastard! Planning to use his daughter as bait, to hook me. And did I know she wasn't a willing hooker? How do I know it now? How can anyone be sure of who's who in this execrable Elsinore? Excremental, I should say. The tongue follows the tainted brain, and I have only foul things to say, about discharge and droppings and putrefaction and… and oh! My sainted aunt-mother! Who's this who's just hove into my weather-eye on the port side of sanity?

'It's me, my lord.'

'And who are you?'

'The Lord Chamberlain, my lord. Don't you recognise me?'

'Recognise you? Of course I bloody recognise you! Do you think I'm mad or something? I know you as well as I know my own mother—I'm sorry, I mean my aunt. Yes, I got confused there, it's such a confusing set-up here in Elsinore, don't you think? How do you find it? Ah, but in your case there's no problem is there? No, no problemo, old Italian angler, no worries, no sweat, and of course I recognise you, how could I fail? You're a fishmonger.'

'A fishmonger? No, no, now you *are* confused, my lord.'

'Am I? No, I don't think so. Of course I suppose I could have said fleshmonger—but no, I'll stick with fishmonger.'

'Why fish rather than flesh, my lord?'

'There you have me. Because a diet of salt fish is conducive to fertility.'

'And what have I to do with fertility?'

'Nothing—directly. But indirectly—well, salt stirs up lust, you know, and furthers procreation.'

'None of which is any concern of mine, my lord.'

'On the contrary, master fishmonger, it concerns you most closely. Haven't you read Plutarch?'

'Plutarch?'

'Or heard it said that females without any copulation with males can conceive merely by the licking of salt.'

'Which seems unlikely, my lord.'

'Which gives fishmongers' females great advantages in the matter of procreation.'

'Their females?'

'Yes, their females. Their wives, for example. Or their female offspring. They're unusually prone to breed. All the more so should they happen to be simultaneously seductive and comely.'

'Still nothing to do with me, my lord.'

'Really? Then I beg your pardon once more. I thought you were a lecher and a pimp.'

'My lord!'

'I mean honest. A whoremaster's an honest man, isn't he?'

'Is he?'

'Of course. He sells female flesh and makes no bones about it.'

'Bones?'

'Flesh and bone. He doesn't dissemble, doesn't pretend he's anything other than what he is, a pander, a procurer. But you now, you—do you know what Solomon said about it?'

'About what?'

'He said that out of a thousand men he could find one good man, but out of a thousand women—'

'Alas?'

'Alas indeed. One good woman he simply could not find. And yet he flattered us men, don't you think? I mean the odds against finding a good honest man—more like ten thousand, wouldn't you say?'

'Ten thousand?'

'To one.'

'It's likely enough, my lord.'

'Closer to the mark, I'm glad you agree, because if the good old sun up there can breed maggots in a dead dog...'

'A dead dog? Now you've lost me, my—'

'No, not at all, quite the reverse, I've just found you, you see, found you out. You look worried. And now it's you who looks confused. But never mind, let me educate you. Have you ever seen a dead dog? Of course you have. I saw one once. It had been dead for days on end and its insides were open and hanging out, and alive with maggots, I mean crawling with them, thousands of them, that carcass, it was like a roaring metropolis, the veins like streets and the arteries of commerce, and the maggots like citizens riding and perambulating and going about their business, you could hear them, and my God, the din they made in that dog!'

'I don't follow what you're saying, my lord, I don't get your drift.'

'Don't you? A bad teacher, I'm sorry. Let me try again. Can we agree that a dead dog is a good piece of carrion flesh to be kissed?'

'Kissed? No!'

'I mean kissed by the sun, stupid! Now you're a poor pupil. A bad learner. We'll both have to do better. Let's start over. Back to basics. The sun is the source of life, yes? It has procreative power, but it's a power which produces foul and corrupt forms of life, yes?'

'In what sense, my lord?'

'In the sense that the corruption lies not in the sun itself but in the thing it breeds from.'

'What thing is that, my lord?'

'Anything. Take your serpent of old Egypt for example, which is bred of pure mud by the operation of your sun. Or take any dead carcass. Its stench is made stronger by the sun, but it comes out of its own corruption and rottenness. Agreed?'

'If you say so, my lord.'

'Not if my lord says so, but if the Lord says so. Let's get back to the dog. So the sun is a god, right? And a dead dog is carrion, right? And a whore is also carrion, right? I mean she exists only to be preyed on by scavengers—men. Still with me? So, the sun kisses the dog and breeds maggots from it by his hot kisses, right? And a god kisses a whore—why shouldn't he?—and breeds people. Well, people are maggots, aren't they? And let's face it, old fishmonger, this world we inhabit is so corrupt that it perverts even divine influence, the sun, even heaven itself—God, this is like drawing teeth! Do you have a daughter, by any chance?'

'I have, my lord.'

'Well then, there you have me! So, whatever you do, don't let her walk in the sun.'

'Why not, my lord?'

'You've been paying no attention, have you! I mean in public. Best keep her locked up, away from the son—that's the other son I'm talking about now, keep up, you know, a king's son, for example, anybody's son, really. Take me, to take another example. If I were to kiss your daughter—well now, what would that result in, do you think? What would it lead to? She might be a nice piece of meat. Or supposing I were to have intercourse with her standing up—what would that lead to? It might lead to dancing—and that's dangerous, and wicked. It could even lead to marriage, to a sudden wedding. What do you think? But one thing we can be quite sure of, it would result in the breeding of babies, and in even more meat for maggots. Don't get me wrong, I mean conception is a good thing, children are a blessing, and it's a blessing to possess understanding, and to have the power to produce, to procreate, to be fruitful, to multiply. An extremely ancient privilege that one, as old as Adam, because if you remember, Adam knew his wife, and she conceived. He may not have understood her exactly. I mean, what man really understands his wife and what she's capable of, like accepting bribes from serpents, for example. Even kings and queens do it. So he may not have understood her exactly, but still he knew her, and you see what happened.'

'What was that?'

'She conceived, you bonce-head! I've been wasting my breath, haven't I? Pearls before swine. Artificial pearls perhaps, but perfectly genuine swine. You're just too old to learn, aren't you? I'll give you one last chance. Are you ready? She didn't understand what he meant, didn't get his meaning until the deed was done, and by then it was too late, she was so innocent—ignorant—same thing—but still she conceived. And she bore a son. Know your bible, do you, old man? You'd better, because anybody can see you're nearer the end of your life than the beginning, and you'll soon be going to meet your maker, and then we'll see what's what, then we'll see who's who. Where was I? Ah yes, she bore a son, and his name was Cain. And lo and behold, she'd just given birth to the first murderer, the man who murdered his brother, and made fratricide a fashion, not generally, of course, but among certain sects and scions of society, kings for example—or men who would be kings. I'm tired of this. If you want to know, I'm tired of everything, of all of you. I'm certainly tired of teaching. Here endeth the lesson. Take a break. And if you don't want your daughter to conceive—look lively now.'

After that little performance I buried my head back in my book and forgot he was there. As part of the act. Left him to mutter away to himself.

'Still harping on my daughter, eh? But he didn't recognise me at first—he thought I was a fishmonger. Far gone, far gone, I fear. And now that I remember, I myself suffered for love in much the same way. I did, in my young days at any rate, the days of my folly. I'll have another stab at him. My lord?'

'Still here?'

'Yes indeed. What are you reading, my lord?'

'*Ord, ord, ord. Slova, slova, slova.*'

'My lord?'

'Words, words, words.'

'What's the matter?'

'Between who?'

'I mean the reading matter, the subject matter.'

'Ah, pretty slanderous stuff actually. Do you know, this satirical rogue of a writer—have you read Juvenal?—has the impertinence to say that old men have grey beards and wrinkled faces, that their eyes are constantly secreting slime—you know that gummy stuff you get from plum-trees when they're discharging their resin, really sticky. And if that's not libellous enough, he goes on to say that they don't have all that much sticky stuff that matters in their brains, a huge lack of grey matter, no intellect to speak of, together with terribly spindly shanks, the sort of hams that don't have much meat on them, no good eating, if you happen to be a cannibal, not enough zip, you know, no vim left in the old pins, a bit like yours in fact, suffering from the old age problem, I'm afraid, plenty juice in the eyes but none in the poor old stumps. Old, old, old. All of which is unquestionably true, and I for one don't deny it, but you must admit it's scarcely decent to put it down in a book. I mean, look how it applies to you, I'm sorry to bring that up again but you must agree you're the prime example—and by the way why are you walking backwards, like some old crab?'

He had no choice of course other than to retreat, when he saw the mad Hamlet, as he took me to be, bearing down on him, and demonstrating each and every aspect of his enfeebled old age with an accusing finger wagging at him, and pointing from the text to himself and back again, until I tired of it, and of him, and got back again to my book. By that time I'd led him out of the lobby and up into the fresh air, which he obviously thought bad for me, as doctors tell us. Mad people need to be locked up, and kept in the dark.

'Will you come inside, my lord? Will you walk out of the air?'
There was only one answer to that.
'Into my grave.'
And it did make him think—not too deeply.
'Well, the grave is certainly away from the fresh air.'
'A long way, old man.'
'Our long home?'
'A long way from home.'

Method in madness was his not altogether erroneous conclusion. Even reason in madness—he got that far with it. Insanity obviously had its own insights, perhaps even superior to our humdrum workaday wits, and I wasn't babbling inanely, at least not complete nonsense. But the mad act had paid off. He talked to himself as if I weren't there, as if I were stone deaf.

'I'll leave him now, and I'll contrive it so that he runs into my daughter, at the soonest opportunity.'

Will you, old engineer?

'As if it's entirely by accident.'

Oh, you practised plotter, you devious old wangler.

'Still in his own waxy world, poor prince.'

You'll find yourself on the sharp end of one of your own schemes—one of these days.

'My lord?'

'My old whoremonger?'

'He's back on that burden again. My lord, I will now take my leave of you.'

'You can't take anything from me that I will part with more willingly—except my life.'

Except my life, except my life, except my life.

'Then I'll go at once.'

He began to bow himself back inside. All the way.

'And so, blondie, it's goodbye.'

He used to call me blondie when I was little, pretending he was the court fool. I wasn't fooled then and I wasn't fooled now.

'Goodbye.'

Goodbye then. At last, goodbye. And don't hurry back. I'll see you with your hook and line, your obedient daughter. God, these tedious old fools!

I gave up my dance around the chamber-pot and went back to my book.

Hamlet's Account of How he Rattled Fork and Knife

No sooner had the chamber-pot taken its leave, crammed with new matter, than the two tools appeared, re-christened now in my book as the two testicles—pretty wobbly waltzers in anybody's book, you'd have to say, though they fitted together snugly enough in the king's purse. Prick and foreskin might be more to the point: two parts of the same member. I knew they'd need a different sort of handling from Polonius, who'd obviously directed them up to where I was having a quiet read. Apparently. I started by seeming surprised to see them—to hear them, I should say. I had my back to them and was still immersed in Juvenal. Who wouldn't be, in Elsinore? No lack of material here for an old satirist.

'My honoured lord!'

'My most dear lord!'

You were so spot on, Horatio—about the number of syllables. The derivative duo—parrots parodying one another. Catspaws, pawns and puppets—on a very short string. When they micturated their two urinal streams met in a chromatic descent. They probably farted together in their sleep.

'Good God almighty! I don't believe it! It's my old collegianers! Or should I say my fresh young friends? What the hell are you two doing here? Have the brothels gone out of business in dear old Witters? You'll find plenty of flesh here in Elsinore, Denmark's a drab these days, fit for the stews, and just up your street. Or streets. But never mind that—how are you both?'

'Oh, pretty average you know.'

'Plodding along, you know.'

'Keeping our spirits up.'

'Happy to be still on the earth.'

'Not under it.'

'If not over the moon.'

'Or high on Fortune's wheel.'

'Or the button on her cap.'

You'll notice I don't bother to say who was saying what, which speaker was which. Not that it mattered. Or matters. It didn't and doesn't. They spoke with one voice, as always. To suit the company and the note of old-time nostalgia, I immediately set about lowering the tone.

'So you're right up there, then?'

'Up where, my lord?'

'Up Lady Fortune.'

'Well, as we said—'

'Not exactly at her feet.'

'Not sucking her toes?'

'No—nor on the crown of her head.'

'What about her maidenhead?'

'My lord?'

'Her middle parts—you know.'

'Well, we're her privates in another sense.'

'What other sense is there?'

'Her ordinary citizens, you know?'

'Yes, I know. But do you know her genitals?'

'Well, on the quiet, you know.'

'Ah, back-door stuff?'

'Back-stairs.'

'Hole-in-the-wall?'

'Hole and corner.'

'The Janet Jakes?'

'In the closet.'

'In the ladies' room?'

'In the privy.'

'And in the pink?'

'If you put it that way.'

'I do. And so—in the cut?'
'The cutting edge.'
'Of Fortune?'
'All the way.'
'Down under.'
'Under the covers?'
'Under cover.'

'Ah, so! Undercover envoys! Secret agents! Moles! Spooks! Spies!'

'Oh no, my lord!'

'Oh, yes, my lord! But when I say spies, I mean—to spy out the secret parts of Fortune, that well-known whore. Hobnob with her and you'll end up acquainted with her private parts.'

'My lord!'

'My lord!'

'That's me. Still me. But I think we're done here with this chit-chat. Let's move on, shall we? What's new?

'New?'

'New?'

'New, yes, new. I mean—what's the news?'

Two blank masks. They hadn't a clue.

'Come on, what's going on in the world? Tell.'

'Nothing, nothing much, except that the world's grown honest.'

'Honest! Then it's the end of the world, I fear. Has the moon turned to blood, did you notice? Honest indeed. Welcome to Denmark is all I can say. She'll change your mind for you on that score. One more whore in the world—won't make that much difference of course to the whole world, I don't suppose. But if you've been whoring at the hands of Lady Fortune, can I ask you why she's sent you here—to prison?'

'Prison, my lord?'

'Prison, my lord!'

'Oh, yes, Denmark's a prison, didn't you know?'

'Then the world itself's a prison, you might as well say.'

'You might as well. We're trapped in time and space—that's an open prison, by the way. But it has plenty of cells and dungeons—look about you—and Denmark's one of the worst.'

'We don't think it's so bad.'

'Not too bad.'

'Is that so? Then it's not good to me and not bad to you, as there's nothing good or bad but thinking makes it so. To me Denmark's a prison.'

'Ah, well now, that's because it's too narrow for your mind, perhaps. And for your ambition.'

'That's got nothing to do with it. Listen, I could be confined in a nut-shell and count myself a king of infinite space—'

'Not king of Denmark then?'

'Were it not that I have bad dreams.'

'You see, that's your ambition showing through again.'

'How do you draw that conclusion?'

'Well, ambition is made of dreams, isn't it? And whatever the ambitious man achieves is a mere shadow of what he'd like to be.'

'Dreams, shadows—same thing.'

'Granted, my lord, but ambition—that's so up in the air it's even less than a shadow. A shadow's shadow.'

'In which case great kings and heroes are mere shadows, and your average beggar is the only real man.'

'You're losing us there, my lord.'

'Am I? Then think: our proud monarchs and our puffed-up celebrities are mere shadows, because they embody ambition, and ambition, as you've just said, is a shadow. Beggars therefore must be bodies, the exact opposite of shadows, being socially opposite to kings and conquerors, the paragons of our race. But what do bodies do? Come on, do you have an answer?'

'We're really lost now.'

'They cast shadows—stay awake! And therefore your monarch—shadowy ambition, if you like—is merely the shadow of your beggar, the beggar being the body—the substance, if you prefer.

And as for your outstretched heroes—have you ever observed a graveyard in the early morning, say at sunrise, or again at sunset?'

Two blank faces.

'Then you'll have noticed how those imposingly tall tombstones of great men are made to cast particularly long shadows, stealing across the grass when it's very late, or early.'

Open mouths, saucer eyes.

'And the same outstretched heroes, those champions dead in the dust. What are they but long shadows, elongated nothings? And the taller your tomb, the longer its shadow.'

'And so?'

'And so much for ambition, the subject you two raised—I didn't. Why are we even discussing it? I'm sure you've had enough of this tiresome talk. I have. Frankly it's the sort of quibbling that will go down well at court, much better, in fact. So that's where I'm headed for. Right now.'

'We'll go with you.'

'Right now.'

'Will you? Why? To pick up your souls on the way?'

'Our souls?'

'Yes, your souls. Did you leave your souls outside? Or back in Witters? Or are they in the king's pocket, perchance? Or up his arse?'

'My lord!'

'My lord!'

'My lord, good Lord, what you will. But why else would you come with me?'

'To keep you company.'

'Yes, we'll, we'll…'

'You'll watch out for me? Will you really? You won't lie in wait for me instead, will you?'

'What do you mean, my lord?'

'No matter. But I wouldn't want you to wait upon me either. Frankly speaking, my retinue—a pretty wretched one. I'm only a prince, after all, dreadfully attended—apart from the bad dreams, I mean. They are extremely zealous attendants, the ones that haunt me. But as we're old friends, can I ask you something?'

'Ask away, my lord.'

'Why are you here? Why did you come?'

'To see you, of course, to pay you a visit, no other reason.'

'After all this time? I'm honoured, and I don't know how to thank you. I don't believe I have enough on me at the moment—'

'My lord!'

'Good lord!'

'No, hardly a halfpenny, though mind you, even that would be overpayment, wouldn't it, considering that what you're giving me in exchange is worth sweet nothing. I mean it's pointless, if you're not even being honest with me about the reason for your sudden visit.'

White faces now. Not scared—but cornered, confused, caught out.

'You were sent for, weren't you? You didn't come of your own accord. You were summoned. Come on, own up, be direct and decent. Be honest with me.'

'What do you want us to say?'

'Say? Say anything you like, anything irrelevant, anything you care to come up with. Look, you don't even have to confess, I can see it in your eyes, in your faces, you can't disguise it, you clearly have some dregs of decency left in you, some sense of shame. So why don't you stop all this dodging and ducking the issue? Stop pissing about! Let's put an end to it now! I know very well that the good king and the good queen have sent for you.'

'And why would they do that, my lord?'

'That's for you to tell me. But let me beg you then—we were once friends together, we were young—won't you level with me at last? Tell me you weren't sent for. Or tell me you were.'

The two faces turned to look at one another. The two heads came together. The two breaths met. They practically kissed. The two tongues spoke as one.

'We were sent for.'

Finally.

'No need to say any more, then, not now. Later I'll tell you exactly why you were sent for, and my saying it first means you'll not be giving anything away, and your understanding with the king and queen, your little pact, or paid pact, or whatever it is, won't be broken. How's that? Agreed?'

'Agreed.'

'Agreed.'

Times two.

'Then, gentlemen, you are welcome to Elsinore. You've come to the right place, the place where everybody lies and schemes. You'll be at home here—as hirelings of the king, which is what you are.'

'It's not like that.'

'Not really.'

'Of course not, nothing's real, so let's shake hands on that. But there's one thing I should say, that I need to say—to confess, if you like.'

A confession! You should have seen how their faces lit up—with expectation, and hope. I could read money in their eyes, reward. They didn't believe their luck, didn't think it was going to be as easy as this, to work for a royal return, to come to Elsinore all prepped to hack into me and sweat for my secret, for their filthy lucre, the velvet pelf to ease their arses, only for me to hand it over to them on a silver platter like John the Baptist's head—and they didn't even have to dance before the king.

So what did I have to confess, then? A gathering blanket of boredom. A self-diagnosis—of my melancholia, my misanthropic world weariness. Suddenly there was nothing new under the sun, and the sun itself was as cold and barren as the moon, an out eye, a sort of socket in the sky. No dawns came up like thunder now, and the west never embered again, like a lingering love affair, not anymore. Lately I'd simply lost all my appetite for life, my old zest, my *joie de vivre*. I'd fallen into lethargy and dejection, nothing any longer seemed worthwhile, the entire earth an isthmus, a bank and shoal of time, washed by the two eternities of past and future, and nothing in the present left to satisfy. The heavens no longer declared the glory of God—I couldn't see what the Psalmist had seen—and his dazzling handiwork, the stars, what were they but a gathering of gases, poisonous, pestilential, meaningless? Oh, and the human race? That last culminating touch of God's cunning hand? Well, let's ask ourselves, I whispered to the four twitching ears—though I could see how their expressions were changing as they felt the royal reward slipping through their fingers. Still, let's ask the question.

'Ask it, my lord.'

'What is it, my lord?'

'The question, gentlemen, is this: what is a man? I pause for a reply.'

No reply. Not surprising. A difficult one.

'Not to worry. Let me answer it for you. A man. What a piece of work he is! Just think: able to reason, to imagine, to achieve the infinite, to reach beyond the stars, not only that but his very anatomy so expressive of his abilities, so beautifully designed, and able to move like an angel and understand like a god. Like a god! My God! This creature is the beauty of the world, the peak of creation, the paragon of all animals. And yet and yet. And yet.'

'And yet?'

'My lord?'

'And yet to me what is this quintessence of dust?'

'Dust, my lord? That's all? Just dust?'

'No, not just dust—the finest dust, the richest dust on earth. The graveyards are full of it, clad with it, larded with it, with us, it's us that you can hear and feel and taste in the wind, the wind that blows us all over the world, man, woman, you, me, all of us are part of that rich quintessence, we belong to it, it's our beginning and our end, that's all. So now you know what I think of it—nothing.

I think nothing of nothing. And that's why I take no delight in man. No, nor in woman neither, though I can see from your grins that you think a woman might just make me change my mind. No, not any more, that's over for me, it's in the past. Oh, but before you go, there's just one last thing I have to tell you. You'll want to know this. You'll need to know it.'

The money look came back into their eyes.

'Tell us, then, tell us what it is.'

'It's this. My uncle-father and my aunt-mother are deluded.'

'Mad?'

'Not in that sense, no, not them—they're criminally sane, in fact. No, by deluded I mean duped. They're deceived.'

'In what way?'

'Ornithologically.'

'How?'

'And meteorologically.'

'What?'

'And melancholically.'

'You've lost us again.'

'Then learn. I am mad, yes. But I'm mad as the wind, as the wind changes. Let's put it this way. Let's say I'm mad only in a certain direction—north-north-west. When the wind is southerly, I know a hawk from a handsaw.'

'I should hope so.'

'Hope you would, my lord.'

'Then hop away—and away with hope. For you know what they say?'

'What?'

'What is it that they say?'

'They say hope springs, hope springs…'

'Yes?'

'Yes, yes?'

Hope springs infernal.

The Players Arrive At Elsinore

Hot on the handles of fork and knife came the travelling players. Rosencrantz and Guildenstern had overtaken them on the road to Elsinore and Hamlet's spirits were lifted by the news of their arrival. Before I give my account of what followed, however, I wish to make a note of my own on Hamlet's cryptic comment to the duplicitous duo concerning the hawk and the handsaw. I make no apologies for this academic impediment to my report. I have already admitted to being an old pedant—old in approach, if not in years—who will have everything clear and accounted for, according to my remit. And Hamlet never construed his quibbles; it was part of his nature to make you puzzle them out for yourself, and fork and knife were not accomplished in the art of wordplay.

Let me remind you exactly what Hamlet said.

I am mad, but only north-north-west. When the wind blows southerly, I know a hawk from a handsaw.

His words, to the best of my recall.

It's not unusually abstruse but it suits my own nature to offer an explanation. A hawk, or hack, (note the pun) is the name given to a workman's tool, a heavy cutting tool of the mattock or pick-axe type, easily distinguishable from the much lighter and neat-cutting handsaw, so that no workman worth his salt would have any difficulty in telling between the two, even if blindfolded. A hernshaw is also the word for a heron, so there you have another piece of wordplay, and the ornithologist, like the artisan, would likewise have no difficulty in distinguishing between a heron and a hawk—I am tempted to say again, even if blindfolded, since any hunter or sportsman will assure you that he can tell a type of bird by ear alone, if it is passing close enough for its wing-flight sound to be detectable, in addition, of course, to its call.

Now to falconry. Heron-hawking, or hawking at herons, is one of our best-loved sports, especially among princes such as Hamlet. Any bird when roused, especially a bird heavy on the wing, such as the heron, normally flies with the wind. If the wind is in the southern quarter, the heron will fly northwards, away from the sun, and the eyes of the falconer, as they follow the flight of the heron and the pursuing hawk, will not be dazzled, and so will be capable of discerning which is which. The heron, incidentally, will generally try to elude pursuit by heading for the sun. I should add that a north wind, driving both birds south, or into the sun, will thus make it difficult to distinguish between them at a distance, despite the difference in size. In ancient Egypt, by the way, the hawk was the symbol of the north wind and the heron the symbol of the south. I know my Egyptology. What Hamlet knew—and hinted he knew—was that a treacherous wind had carried the pair of pretenders north from Wittenberg to Elsinore.

I should say that while most or all of these meanings would have been lost on fork and knife, they presumably understood Hamlet to be saying that he saw through them, that he could tell an innocent bird from a predator, the hunter from the hunted, that he knew them to be not the friends they pretended to be, but birds of prey, and that he was not so mad as not to recognise that they were rogues, and tools too, a murderer's tools, while also implying either that he was merely touched or tinged a little with madness, as the north-north-west wind has very little west in it, or that he was only mad when he wanted to be!

I now take off my scholastic cap. And as for fork and knife, with that last quip and quibble stinging their four eyes, they were swept aside when Polonius ushered in the actors, and Hamlet's old interests, an excitement so recently lost to him, were rekindled. Here was a big breath of fresh air blown into Elsinore, bringing with it an aesthetic stringency and surge of otherness into the prison world, and offering an exit from obligation and responsibility, from the pressure of duty. Here was a bracing alternative to the corruption and claustrophobia of the court. It was another world, an unreal world, you could say, because the players were in one sense no different from the people around Elsinore—they too were feigners, not real people, but their kind of feigning was different—it led to a finding out of what is really true on the stage of life, where most friendship is feigning, most loving mere folly, and I watched Hamlet dive into their world head-first with a great big splash. At first he vented his relief and expressed his elation by targeting the chamber-pot. He didn't give him his homely nickname but elevated him instead to scriptural status, though anyone conversant with the scriptures would have understood that the apparent dignity conferred was indeed a hollow compliment.

'Well, look here, everybody, see what the cat's brought in! It's old Jephthah, judge of Israel, don't you know—and what a treasure he had! What a treasure you had!'

The allusion was lost on the un-spiritually-minded Lord Chamberlain.

'What treasure was that, my lord?'

'What, you don't even know what a treasure you had? Perhaps you still have it. Here, let me quote it to you. This one's from an old song.'

> *One fair daughter, and no more,*
> *The which he lovéd passing well.*

Polonius smiled—knowingly, as he thought.

'Still on about my daughter. But we know why that is, why he's always harping on the same string.'

He spoke about Hamlet as if he weren't there, as if he couldn't hear or understand what was being said. And it was all meat and drink to him, all confirming his theory that the prince had lost his wits for love of his daughter.

'But I'm right, am I not, old Jephthah?'

'About what, my lord?'

'About the daughter.'

'What about the daughter? What daughter?'

'Old Jephthah's daughter, who else?'

'Well now, my lord, if you choose to call me Jephthah in your present infirmity, that is entirely your affair. But I do as it happens have a much-loved daughter—and that is entirely mine.'

'No it's not, that's not how the song goes on, you're misquoting, but well spoken nonetheless, old Jephthah, well said.'

'Thank you, my lord, but why Jephthah, may I ask?'

For a moment it looked as if Hamlet might break a lifetime's habit and explain the reference, that Jephthah, not entirely unlike Agamemnon, had vowed to God that if he were successful in war, he would sacrifice the first creature he met on his return home. Sadly, tragically, he encountered his daughter, who had come out so joyfully to welcome him back, and refusing to break the oath, he kept his word and slaughtered her. But before he did so, the poor wretched girl went out and bewailed her virginity. She was too young to die, and was to die unmarried and unknown to man, one of the pale primroses that, like the daffodils, come before the swallow dares and take the winds of March with beauty, and yet they too die unmarried before they see the sun in his strength, a malady to which young greensick girls are prone.

Ophelia was no greensick girl, and as to her dying a virgin, Hamlet had no foreknowledge of that, but did know of old Polonius's readiness to sacrifice his daughter, and not for God, to use her for his own ends, and those of the corrupt king. And that, as it happened, was the point at which the players came in, and Hamlet thanked God for the sudden abridgement of his tedious dealings with knife and fork and chamber-pot, and he spread his arms wide to welcome the good spirits of the theatre, as their covered cart trundled in bumpily through the castle gates and into the courtyard, an escape-world on wheels, clattering into the grim prison-world of Elsinore.

In they came, dancing and cartwheeling and somersaulting and walking on their hands, and with a brave little flourish of horn and recorder and drum, so much scaled down from Claudius and his cannoneers—no guns lugged from Wittenberg to pledge an afternoon's or evening's entertainment. No need. They were their own big guns, capable of turning a few wooden boards into a battlefield of blank verse, with actions and utterances that would lift you up and away out of Elsinore, liberate you from the present moment, and fill the air with sound and fury. Hamlet was ecstatic and gave them his own drums and trumpets, and full battery and orchestra.

'Welcome! Welcome, old friends! It's a mad world, my masters, but welcome to it! Just look at this—our lead player's gone bristly since Wittenberg. Have you come to beard me in Denmark, then? And you, young lad—or should I say young lady?—you've grown taller since I last saw you. Is that high heels or hormones, I wonder? And how about the voice? Is it broken yet? Speak a line.'

'My lord?'

'Ah! Say no more, you're safe for a few months more, I'd say, shrill enough to play Cleopatra, or any part that needs a ring and not a rod. I was afraid you might have been deflowered by now! Well then, my masters, my good friends, let's get straight to it, like French falconers, let fly at the first thing that comes to mind. What'll it be?'

The lead player spread his arms.

'Anything, my lord! What would you like?'

'Oh, something passionate, I think, something with plenty of fire and feeling.'

'Plenty of that in stock, my lord. Any one in particular?'

'Something old world? Yes, something old-fashioned, antique style, yes?'

The first player nodded, beamed, spread his arms even wider, fingers fluttering, beckoning expectantly. Hamlet laughed back at him and clapped his hands.

'I heard you deliver a speech once, and a cracking speech it was too, a really memorable one.'

'From what play, my lord?'

'That's the thing—it was never acted—except maybe once, now that I remember.'

The player's face fell.

'It doesn't sound too popular, my lord.'

'It wasn't. It was far from popular. I'd say it was the opposite. It was caviar to the general, you might say, wasted on the groundlings, no ribaldry for the rabble in that one. But there were some who saw it whose tastes echoed mine to the full, some of them superior even, who had a high opinion of it. Let me think now, it was about the Trojan War. And there was one particular speech—'

'Aeneas' Tale to Dido!'

'That was it! You've got it! God, I loved that speech! Can you still do it?'

'Well now, it's been a while... but you know what they say, an old actor never dies, he just dries up, and what I can't summon up, I'll make up!'

'That's the spirit! You're a terror for the boards! Right then, let's have it! Let's give it a whirl!'

By this time a small crowd had gathered round the wagon, mostly scullions, and some soldiers, but a few curious courtiers too, following Polonius, and also the now ubiquitous fork and knife. For most it was a spot of relief from the routine rather than a splash of culture. Everyone waited expectantly.

'Just a second, though.'

Hamlet was thoroughly into the spirit of the thing. He insisted that the extempore audience be given something of the background to the speech they were about to hear. I knew it, naturally, and was not put out when he appointed the task to me.

'Horatio, my friend, you're the man for this.'

In point of fact, if I am honest, I confess I felt rather pleased to be offered the opportunity to display my learning.

'Not too long though, Horatio. You know what old Jephthah always says.'

'Brevity is the soul of wit.'

Muttered with shrugs and some grumbly faces from among the courtiers. They knew all about Polonius's brevity, preached rather than practised. I took the point, and explained very quickly how, after the fall of Troy, according to Virgil, Aeneas had landed at Carthage, where Dido was queen. He told her all about his experiences, and she was so moved, she fell in love with him. The affair ended sadly for Dido when he left, but I assured the spectators this had no bearing on the speech, in which Aeneas is describing the scene in which Pyrrhus enters Troy, storms the palace, and slaughters old King Priam.

'It's a bloodcurdling business,' I said, 'but you need to remember that Pyrrhus is a son bent on vengeance. His father, Achilles, a great warrior, had been murdered, you see…'

A shout from the crowd, a soldier's, protesting.

'He worn't murdered! He was killed, worn't he? Killed in action he was. Death in action, death in the field, that don't count as murder!'

This nettled me a little, so I explained that the great warrior had been killed by Paris with an arrow to the Achilles' heel.

Don't go into it, Horatio! No footnotes!

I'd have rounded out the picture a little but contented myself with pointing out that Paris hadn't faced his opponent fairly, like a man, in open combat, but had done it from a distance.

'He did it the coward's way!' shouted Hamlet. 'With an arrow! And I'll wager it was tipped with poison!'

And now, I said, the son wanted his revenge for his father. I was aware of Hamlet looking at me intently at that point, and it came to me that he'd unconsciously chosen the speech for reasons only he and I knew of.

'Finish it, Horatio!'

I could see him working himself up. Two months had gone by since the ghost and he'd done nothing, taken no action, only an act. Now he wanted action. And yet the action was acting…

'Quickly, Horatio! Let him begin!'

I hurriedly described how Priam was killed, and how his widow, Hecuba the queen, was left blinded by tears, and in a truly terrible state, following her husband's gruesome death. Hamlet couldn't let that go.

'A lesson to all queens—how to grieve for their dead kings! And Dido killed herself! No Didos in Denmark! No Hecubas to hang round their murdered husbands' necks! And now, old friend, the stage is yours, the stage of Elsinore…!'

The player was scratching his head and stroking his beard.

'Have you forgotten it?'

'No, no, my lord, I'm ruminating. Where to begin…'

'Let me start you off. How about the line *The rugged Pyrrhus like the Hyrcanian beast*? No that's not it, that's not how it begins. It starts with Pyrrhus. Let's see, let's see. *The rugged Pyrrhus, he whose sable arms*... yes, that's it, that's the line.'

And Hamlet cleared his throat and began.

'The rugged Pyrrhus, he whose sable arms,
Black as his purpose, did the night resemble
When he lay couchéd in th'ominous horse,
Hath now this dread and black complexion smeared
With heraldy more dismal: head to foot
Now is he total gules, horridly tricked
With blood of fathers, mothers, daughters, sons,
Baked and impasted with the parching streets,
That led a tyrannous and a damnéd light
To their lord's murder. Roasted in wrath and fire,
And thus o'er-sizéd with coagulate gore,
With eyes like carbuncles, the hellish Pyrrhus
Old grandsire Priam seeks'…

'And so on.'

And Hamlet jumped up onto the players' wagon to hear the speech.

But the chamber-pot couldn't resist a gyration.

'Well delivered, my lord! A good command of verse there!'

And he gesticulated to the little gathering to give Hamlet a round of applause. Much loud clapping and cheering, and Hamlet stood up and bowed from the cart. When it had all died down the first player waited for silence, whipped his long costume-cloak dramatically across one shoulder, paused for effect, raised an arm to the sky, and declaimed.

> *'Anon he finds him*
> *Striking too short at Greeks, his antique sword,*
> *Rebellious to his arm, lies where it falls,*
> *Repugnant to command; unequal matched,*
> *Pyrrhus at Priam drives, in rage strikes wide,*
> *But with the whiff and wind of his fell sword*
> *Th'unnerved father falls: then senseless Ilium,*
> *Seeming to feel this blow, with flaming top*
> *Stoops to his base; and with a hideous crash*
> *Takes prisoner Pyrrhus' ear. For lo! his sword,*
> *Which was declining on the milky head*
> *Of revered Priam, seemed i'th'air to stick,*
> *So as a painted tyrant Pyrrhus stood,*
> *And like a neutral to his will and matter,*
> *Did nothing.*
> *But as we often see, against some storm,*
> *A silence in the heavens, the rack stand still,*
> *The bold winds speechless, and the orb below,*
> *As hush as death, anon the dreadful thunder*
> *Doth rend the region, so after Pyrrhus' pause,*
> *A rouséd vengeance sets him new awork,*
> *And never did the Cyclops' hammers fall*

On Mars's armour, forged for proof eterne,
With less remorse than Pyrrhus' bleeding sword
Now falls on Priam.
Out, out, thou strumpet Fortune! All you gods,
In general synod take away her power,
Break all the spokes and fellies from her wheel,
And bowl the round nave down the hill of heaven
As low as to the fiends.'

That was when Polonius yawned.

'Rather too long, perhaps?'

Hamlet rounded on him furiously.

'To the barber with it, then, along with your beard—also too long! Or to the surgeon—too long in the tooth, perhaps? Or to the headsman. He can decide which of you is best shortened by a head! Carry on, old friend, come to Hecuba, the mobled queen, remember? She was all muffled up, already in her weeds, not in a wedding dress! Oh, you black weed…! Weeds of Lethe, but not for Hecuba! There was a queen who knew how to mourn! When did you last see one like her? Another lesson—from Troy to Elsinore! Proceed!'

'But who, ah woe! had seen the mobled queen
Run barefoot up and down, threat'ning the flames
With bisson rheum, a clout upon that head
Where late the diadem stood, and for a robe,
About her lank and all o'er teeméd loins,
A blanket in the alarm of fear caught up—
Who this had seen, with tongue in venom steeped,
'Gainst Fortune's state would treason have pronounced;
But if the gods themselves did see her then,
When she saw Pyrrhus make malicious sport
In mincing with his sword her husband's limbs,
The instant burst of clamour that she made,

Unless things mortal move them not at all,
Would have made milch the burning eyes of heaven,
And passion in the gods.'

'Stop! Stop the performance!'

It was Polonius who had shouted, and some of the crowd were certainly pointing and looking at each other and murmuring. The actor had entertained them. He had delivered the lines in a sonorous voice and a magisterial manner—until he came to Hecuba. And that was where he'd started to lose control. He was overcome with emotion, the sheer tragic pathos of the scene the lines were describing. Some actors say yes, lose yourself in the part, be that other person, the one who isn't you. Others say no, stay in control, it's not real, it's a stunt, it's acting. But this old actor was no longer acting. He'd turned pale, there were tears in his eyes, and finally he broke down. Hamlet was staring at him from the cart. He looked frozen. Polonius made another appeal.

'My lord!'

Only the prince could declare the little performance at an end. He leapt down from the cart and strode over to the first player. He took him in his arms.

'Well done, old friend, I'll hear the rest of it another time, when you're recovered. Meanwhile, my Lord Chamberlain, please see to it that these players are well accommodated and well looked after, treated as my friends, do you hear?'

Mutterings of a different sort now from some of the crowd. You could plainly hear words like vagabonds and beggars and scum, and shouts about graven images and the lash. Hamlet glared at them.

'It's silk they deserve, not the lash. They've earned a place in a palace. They're the mirror of your time, the story of your age. And they sum you up, as nobody else can do. So beware: it would be better for you to have a bad epitaph after your death than a bad report from them while you're still here.'

Much pursing of the Polonius lips.

'My lord, I will treat them according to their rank.'

He saw a frowning Hamlet bearing down on him and added—
'Their merit.'

The correction didn't pacify the prince.

'Merit, did you say? By Jesus, man, better than that! Treat every man in accordance with what he deserves and which one among us will escape the lash? We'll all be whipped through the streets… like these poor fellows. Common players indeed.'

'My lord—'

'Enough! Treat them as you'd treat yourself. And if they do deserve less than you offer them, the more deserving you are—for your generosity. Take them inside.'

Looking as dignified as a Lord Chamberlain should look, Polonius signalled to the actors to follow him, and walked to the doors with great gravitas, followed by a line of capering and frolicking figures, making faces and funny noises and aping the great office bearer. Had they known his nickname, the mimicking would have taken a much smuttier turn.

'And,' shouted Hamlet to the scattering little assembly, 'we'll hear a play tomorrow!'

He ran up the line and stopped the first player.

'Listen, old friend, can you play *The Murder of Gonzago*? Can you put it on in time?'

'Absolutely.'

'Right. We'll have it tomorrow night. And could you learn off a short speech, say a dozen lines or more, which I'll write myself tonight, just something I have in mind, that can be inserted into the play? Could you do that for me?'

'Easily.'

'Excellent! Then follow that great man, so high above your station. And don't make too much fun of him, will you?—even though around here he does get called the chamber-pot!'

The player skipped off laughing and Hamlet turned and saw the pair.

'And on a slightly higher level than the chamber-pot—it's fork and knife. Still here, are we?'

'If we're still welcome, my lord.'

'Oh, more than welcome. Welcome to Elsinore. I told you before, it's the best place for you. Prison. It's your home from home. And now leave me—now!'

They trotted off.

'And you too, Horatio—no offence. I have things to see to. And things to think about.'

I asked myself what he would be thinking about. I knew one thing: that the arrival of the actors had had a destabilising effect—this is what actors do—bringing the unreal into the real—and before we knew it, Troy was more real than Denmark, and Elsinore had begun to totter, and to slip from under our feet. What exactly was happening? What was going to happen? I could only wait for Hamlet to tell me.

What Hamlet Thought About

He called me his other self, his spirit's mirror, his council's consistory. I, Horatio, at your service, reader, was never near to being the first two, and I'm not sure how far I qualified for the last. Still, I acted as his sounding board, though much of the time I felt more like an empty tunnel in which his thoughts echoed. Let me echo them over again.

He said that when he saw that actor overcome by an emotion that was a thousand years old, two thousand, three thousand, who knows where and how it originated, he felt humiliated and ashamed, and worthy to be shown up for a worthless wretch. And as for whipping, he said, he whipped himself to pieces, meting out the lashes in his mind. Here was this player, blinded by tears, his voice cracking, appearing completely deranged, his entire body matching his mentality, his imagination—it was no act—and for what? For a fiction. For a woman who, if she'd ever lived at all, had been dust for over thirty generations, and may have been nothing more than a writer's figment and an actor's dream. And yet he wept for her. For Hecuba! What's Hecuba to him or he to Hecuba that he should weep for her?

And that's when he asked himself…

What would he do, this actor, had he the call to action, the motive for emotion that I have? The cue to come before the audience shaking with rage and grief? My God, he'd drown the stage with tears, deafen the spectators with his declamations. The guilty would go mad and the innocent would be appalled, for fear of falling into the same pit and pitiful state of suffering and sin. Even those ignorant of the crime, or the atrocities behind the story, would be utterly stunned. Oh no, this actor wouldn't wow the crowd, he'd crush it, he'd waste them in their seats, or where they stood, even if they were groundlings.

And now look at me! How do I look, apart from being a dreamer and a sleeper, a sleeping-sickness sufferer, a corpse without a spirit left in it, without the backbone and the guts to fight my cause and put my purpose into action: to avenge a king who was robbed of his crown, of his queen, of his life, of everything? Instead of which I've done nothing, I do nothing. Why? Am I a coward? Who's preventing me? Nobody's standing in my way, nobody's giving me a going over, nobody's calling me a liar and forcing me to choke on the insult. Christ's bleeding wounds, what am I? I'm pigeon-livered and without a single glob of gall to bring him to his bitter end! I'm a craven, a chicken, a yellow-belly, a renegade rat, a pusillanimous poltroon—go on, pile on the self-reproaches you prattler, you non-doer—or I'd long since have tossed this murdering fucker's tripes to the air, to feed the vultures, the bloody, bawdy, lecherous bastard! A poisonous bastard! A treacherous trickster! A lecherous wretch! A vile, inhuman, cold-blooded cunt! Am I done…?

No, he hadn't done. All that and more, piling on the profanities, putting on the agony, putting on the style, acting it out to himself, his only audience apart from me, getting it out of his system.

Which he finally did. And begged my forgiveness for the self-display. I could forgive him if I chose, he said, but he couldn't forgive himself for his behaviour: a man impelled by hell and heaven together to avenge his own father, and who stood instead like a slut in the streets, like a working whore, unpacking her arsenal of words, cursing like a scullery drudge, a scullion, the lowest of the low! Enough, enough. No more.

And that's when he revealed his plan to me. It had come to him while watching the player break down during the Hecuba speech.

'That's when I remembered hearing that criminals and guilty sinners, sitting in a theatre, have been so stricken by the parallels between the play and their own misdeeds, that they've come out of the closet and confessed to their crimes. Murder will out, old friend, most miraculously.'

And so the plan was to have the players put on a play before the court that would reproduce as far as possible the circumstances of his father's murder.

'I'll watch him like a hawk. I'll probe the bandaged-up wound of that guilty conscience of his—there's got to be a drop of conscience somewhere in that sack of slime. If he just blinks or flinches—even one single flicker of the eye—then my course is clear. And I'll chop him down on the spot!'

And then that familiar look came over him.

'Of course, I have to be sure, you understand?'

'Sure of…?'

'Sure that he really is guilty. Of course.'

'Yes, of course, guilty. But… the ghost… your father's spirit?'

'May be the devil. Who knows? And a devil, as we know, has the power to assume any shape it pleases, and that pleases us, and deceives us, for its own evil ends, such as to damn me by leading me to commit murder. You know how I've been in such low spirits this past while. I've not been myself. I've been acting, of course I have, but there have been times when it hasn't been an act, it's been this… this miserable grief, this wretched melancholy. And the devil can use that against you, as you know. No, I need stronger grounds than I've got, grounds to move against him. I need to be surer than this—I mean to be surer about this ghost, and what it's said to me, if it even was a ghost that was speaking, and not something else… No, the play's the thing, the play's the thing—in which I'll catch the conscience of the king! Look at that—I even rhymed! Our old actor friend has done me good. I could well be on stage myself at this rate. Joking apart, I feel like an actor myself, in some great play. But not an actor putting on an act, more like our old friend there, playing the part for real. If that makes any sense…'

It made sense. Except that when Hamlet said he doubted the ghost, I saw a certain uncertainty in his eyes, an uncertainty I'd seen before. The eye, they say, is the index to the soul. And something in my friend's soul leaked into the eye and out into the open. I realised that when he said he doubted the ghost, the truth was that he doubted his own doubt.

PART THREE

Enter Osric with Information and a Flourish

There was a slippery sycophant in Elsinore called Osric, a courtier who'd sell himself to anyone if it came up his back or fitted his passing whim, and who'd blithely betray you just as whimsically to the next buyer. Curiously it wasn't a question of cash. He was well-heeled as it was, and a great purchaser of property and land, and yet, oddly enough, not greedy. Osric—it was this simple—simply liked to be liked, and liked especially to be liked by the gentlemen of the court as opposed to the ladies. With the fair sex he was equally charming—he couldn't help himself—but was not inclined to pursue them, preferring to seek the company and favours of his own sex, and if you happened to fall into that category he'd butter you up and bend over. Such was his nature.

Hamlet called him the water-fly—because he fluttered along the filmy skin of court life, mingling with the insects and the surface scum. And as he was a floater he could be found anywhere and everywhere about the court, bowing in, bowing out, but always bowing, his big plumed hat in hand, never on his head, waving it about, waving it in your face, saluting you, saluting the empty air, winnowing the gossip, chattering, flattering, obsequiously, pointlessly, effortlessly, endlessly.

As such, Osric was a useful fund of information on court news, who's in, who's out, that sort of tittle-tattle, which he'd divulge as easily as breathing, if you steered the talk to where you wanted it to go. Then he'd gabble happily, feeling himself the centre of attention and the beating heart of court affairs and tell you all that you needed to hear, always remembering that he'd then swan off with his plumes in the air or fanning his perfumed wake and leak to the next party anything he'd managed to glean from you in the passing. He'd then sell you out for a smile, and sell the purchaser for a flourish of feathers and a farthing's worth of clack. Osric epitomised the easy inconsequentiality and untrustworthiness of Elsinore, its smoke and mirrors illusoriness. He was its comic mask and its smiling face, imitating that of the original smiler, the corrupt and grinning king.

It was Osric who smilingly and wordily regaled me at my request with what went on at court following Hamlet's first meeting with Rosencrantz and Guildenstern. The pair were immediately summoned by Claudius to submit their report, and if what Osric had to say was an accurate account of what he'd heard, overheard, or gleaned from gossip, the fork and knife report was itself not altogether accurate. Primarily they failed to confess that Hamlet had seen through them from the start as hired spies, and they gave a distorted version of his reaction, claiming that he'd opened up to them freely—quite the friendly prince in fact. And they'd also said that Hamlet had stood aloof on the matter of his madness, failing to disclose that in fact he'd offered them an entirely unforced and candid explanation of his so-called insanity: it was not madness but melancholia. He'd lost his faith in God and man, in the meaning and value of existence. He'd lost his appetite for life, lost the will to live. And so: as spies they'd so far proved themselves pretty incompetent. Their subject had seen them coming, and their spy-master employer had been given a blandly misleading record of events, to say the least.

Claudius was not convinced in any case. On the contrary he was all the more persuaded that the recent mad behaviour had been a front, or largely an act, and he was becoming increasingly anxious and apprehensive, although he'd been relieved to hear that the arrival of the players had lifted his nephew's spirits—nephew, not son, was the relationship in the current uncertainty—and he was even happier to learn about the play shortly to be performed. Even so, he had no intention of leaving it at that, and had declared that he now proposed to pursue the Polonius plan. Ophelia would be placed in Hamlet's way, and he and Polonius would ensconce themselves in order to overhear the encounter, and determine whether Hamlet really had gone mad for love, or if the affliction—assuming it was real—had some other cause, which could be looked into and hopefully remedied. All with Hamlet's own health and welfare in mind. Of course.

Ophelia's was a dumb presence at this discussion. She was never asked for her opinion—(well now, how could she even have an opinion, asked Osric, she being a mere girl?)—or whether she was willing to participate in this little piece of deception. Girls obey their fathers, quite simply. And Polonius quite simply thrust a pointless prayer-book into her hands and told her to kneel and look pious—illiterate but virtuous. The word was that Hamlet was headed that way. The others were ushered from the scene. King and Lord Chamberlain hid themselves behind the arras and waited. And Ophelia waited as she'd been ordered. And her lips moved in prayer, as she had been ordered. Two in hiding, plotters, one out in the open, but still in secret as it were, part of the plot, and one unsuspecting as yet, still on his way. It was a shifty scenario that somehow summed up Elsinore.

Hamlet and the Sea of Troubles

To be or not to be: that is the question. Just for a moment it feels like Wittenberg all over again, when we were asked to debate a 'question', a subject for argument in one of our scholarly disputations, all very orderly and academic. And put this way, the question itself sounds simple enough, doesn't it? To be or not to be: six grave yet flighted monosyllables, whanging for an answer, yes or no. Not too difficult a decision on the face of it, you'd think—not a whole range of alternatives there: action or inaction, a movement this way or that, or no movement at all, nothing; to be, or not to be. And yet even as I ask the question,

I ask myself exactly what it means, what exactly I am asking and why I'm asking it, as I perch here on the rocky edge of Elsinore, staring out to sea…

The sea, the sea, infinitely stringent, utterly intransigent, eternally refreshing: cold, brutal, balmy, bewildering, bipolar. And troubled, like me. It's a projection, isn't it, a sea of troubles, heaving around the distracted globe of the head, a skull holding an entire ocean of interrogation, of endless questions, until eventually it will hold only emptiness. Or earth.

Let me look at it again. What is it that I see?

Blue water and the four points, each pointing to infinity, unfenced emptiness, unfenced existence—unfenced except for that single sweeping long hard line of the horizon, fencing you in. Or so it seems. Actually it's an illusion—the skyline's line doesn't really exist, it's a trick of distance, a deception of the eye, and knowing it doesn't exist, you begin to understand that it's not a confining line but an alluring one, beckoning you instead out of Elsinore, out of sight and sound of all of them, until suddenly you know you can cross that illusory line, lose yourself in the blue bliss of nothingness. But first you have to cross the sea of troubles, far out from the wishless swish of the water, close into shore, the waves that beat at Elsinore. And long before that you have to answer the question…

I keep on putting it to myself. To be: to be—what? The avenger? And step into the part cast for me by a ghost, yet another troubled and uncertain and unauthenticated thing? As troubled and troubling as the sea that roars so close to Elsinore. I can't get either of them out of my head—the sea, and that question that roars so loud. Should I accept the role of the killer, and murder my murderous uncle? Or say no—no I will not submit to the two syllables, I will not obey my father, I will leave him unavenged, leave the murderer free to fuck my mother in my father's bed, the royal bed of Denmark. Can it really be that? Can it be not to be?

Can it be the three syllables? What sort of a son would I be then? I think about it and I think no, surely to God, no!

And yet. If I were to take this dagger and take my revenge right now, slit his throat, spill his murderous guts into the sewers, wouldn't it be an act of suicide? How could I explain my action in committing murder? How else would it look, other than the act of a disappointed heir, an uncle-murderer and a regicide, who'd be tried accordingly, and only one possible witness that could be called to testify on my behalf—and with what likelihood and to what effect? Has a ghost ever been known to appear in court, to stand up and swear? And what would my case consist of otherwise? A scary story, a yarn, riveting enough for a winter's tale around the fire, but no more substantial than smoke, or the fumes of Rhenish that begot it no doubt. So that my act of revenge would result in an act against myself. By committing murder I'd be committing suicide. And I ask myself: is suicide what I'm really ultimately contemplating? To be would mean not to be, and a simpler way forward into non-existence would be to take arms not against the slings and arrows flung by fate, but against myself, against my own inner sea of troubles—and by opposing, end them.

So it's back we go again, back to the infinite emptiness I see staring back at me from this rocky ledge—a man pondering the sea and thinking how easy it would be to slip into it and pull a wave like a bedcover over his beating head and go to sleep, just sleep, nothing more, sleep that knits up the ravelled sleeve of care, the kind of sleep that slides into your soul and ends the heartache, the shocks and blows of time, and all the ills suffered by the flesh—yes, by God, yes, that's an ending deeply to be desired, the longed-for sleep of death. Sleep, sleep, sleep...

But what sort of a sleep is it, the sleep of death? Suppose... just suppose that once you've shuffled off all the bustle and bitterness of your days, you suffer the downside of sleep, the sleep that's shaken by dreams, the fitful fevers and foul whisperings, the tortures of the mind and rooted sorrows that rack you nightly when tainted brains are laid on listening pillows, and the very pillows are infected, and there's no dawn to end your suffering, because this is death, and death has no dawn. Imagine then if this is what you've lived for. You've borne the whips and scorns of time and the age, you've endured oppression, the arrogance of dogs in office, who kick you in the teeth and foot you from their way as if you were the unworthy one, the ugly cur, and you're spurned not only by them but even by those you love, devotion despised and rejected. Why would you go on taking the punishment like a beaten donkey, grunting and sweating beneath his burdens and waiting for the last blow, death, to unload him—why would you bear it a moment longer when you can obtain your own release and peace by the single thrust of a naked dagger? Go on, then, thrust, thrust, thrust…!

But you don't. Why? Because you don't know what's to come, you don't know what happens after death, it's as simple as that, it's the child's fear of the dark that stays your hand, the dread of the undiscovered country, that's what confounds you, breaks down your resolve, because it's a country without a border, or it's a border that can't be crossed, not by any returning traveller, not ever… except by a ghost? And a ghost is not one of us, not any more, it's neither man nor woman, and may even be a devil, who knows, and so it's better the devil you know, for we'd rather endure what we know than the thing we know nothing of.

How to oppose, then? To do away with our troubles to do away with ourselves? Should we passively submit or actively resist? And if you do resist… slings and arrows you can evade or deflect. Or you can take them and still survive. But in an ill-matched combat with a formless foe, or an overwhelming enemy, you have no chance, and no option but to accept the heart-ache, the tiredness of living before the fear of dying, the dread of something after death. Face it, face the truth, we know nothing of the terrors of the afterlife, if they exist at all, unless we go back to believing in ghosts, something that now begins to fade like a childhood dream, and I ask myself now if it ever really happened…and there's no answer to that, but another answer comes back to an unasked question… no, no, no.

No, it's not death but life that tries us. And thinking about all of this, and endlessly dissecting it, makes us thought-sick, and a prey to anxiety and irresolution, we lose our nerve, and the great things we could have done suddenly come to nothing, like ships lost at sea, or like great rivers that roll all that way only to lose themselves in sandy wastes, and at the end of their long courses never even reach the sea…

The sea and its treacherous and capricious currents—we're back again to it, the sea, as here I sit, still staring out, still being stared out by it, still doing nothing, still lost to all action except the action of facing the question. And the real question is: is life in the end worth living? Is it preferable to have it or not? It's the only serious question of philosophy. And it's the question to which I must finally reply. I have to make a decision, I have to give an answer. It's a delicate balance: the desire for death and the fear of death, the pains of death and the pains of life. But if it were a formal debate, its conclusion would be clear: that although the life we humans live prompts a longing for death, we'd rather endure the life we have than face the alternative, which is the fear of the after-life, the fear of the unknown. What I am debating here is not merely my own personal predicament, but the pros and cons of human existence. And yet if I overhear myself correctly, I believe I hear myself saying that having contemplated death, and even suicide, I come down finally on the side of life—in spite of everything, in spite of the daily burdens, the calamity, the contempt, the merit unrecognised, the love scorned, and in spite of the sad fact that I continue to sustain life through continuing inaction, even if in the end it is not worth sustaining. A wise man looking down on such an abject panorama from a high place might well be tempted to self-destruction, as I have been. But so far I have resisted the temptation. Why? Possibly only because, quite simply, suicide would have been a decision. And the only real decision I made in the end was to leave my sea-girt settle, leave the sea to its troubles, come back over the parapets, and put on my peripatetic act again, once more strolling idly through the lobbies of Elsinore, to keep the king on edge. And that was easy. That was no decision at all.

Ophelia's Confession — and Country Matters

Stand there, Ophelia. Sit there, Ophelia. Be still, Ophelia, be quiet. Pick up your needle, Ophelia, work up a tapestry, but not a tapestry of longing, or lust for life, or a thrust of the loins, leave your loins out of it, my girl—no arrows of desire, if you please, not in your little tapestry, leave the arrows to those who can bring on the bows of gold. As for you, easy live and quiet die. You may dance, of course, but to your teacher's lute and lesson, not to a man, or with a man, or for a man—not like Salome, whose dancing cost a man his head, and could cost you your maidenhead. And now—for now you can kneel, Ophelia, kneel and look modest, look solitary, look lonely…

Look lonely. How hard was that? That was the easy part, it was the simplest thing they ordered me to do, it needed no rehearsal, no book, even if I could have read it, unlike the prayer-book they put into my illiterate fingers, so that my loneliness could be stained with a touch of devotion, so they said. A little staining was all I ever wanted, though not with devotion. He could have stained my lips…

And move your lips, Ophelia, move your lips in prayer, or as if in prayer, your lips, that's it, go on, your lips, your lips. No, not your hips, you silly girl, your lips, your lips.

My lips. Lips that I'd longed for him to kiss, to stain with his, and colour my innocence, my ignorance. Maybe he had longings too, that hurt like mine. He said he did, but he never got that far. His real longings seemed to pass me by, bound away, elsewhere, like ships scenting the skylines. Letters and love-tokens were as far as he got, and as far as I ever got on the closed road to knowing a man. Now I was alone—or so he may have thought, for a moment, perhaps, before he remembered the eavesdropping scheme—but still he couldn't kiss my lips, because the breath between them belonged to God. I was at my orisons, and he couldn't soil my spirituality, he couldn't sully my flesh. He hated the sullied flesh. Or maybe he simply hated the flesh. Perhaps they should have arranged for us to meet not here, in these unquiet interiors, but up on the parapets, or outwith Elsinore altogether. How would the graveyard have suited, I wonder? Then I could have laid myself down on one of those cool mossy marble table-tops, hands clasped chastely, piously, across my bosom, and waited for his kiss on my marble lips. He once told me he was at home among tombs, a ruminator of the dead, digesting them like a cow with his lonely, soulful, bland and sometimes blank eyes. Oh yes, fine decent folk, the dead, he'd say, implying... and who needs the living? Who'd want them? That's when I heard him coming.

'Ah, the fair Ophelia.'

The fair Ophelia? Yes, that was me, accustomed as ever to being addressed or referred to as if I wasn't really there, the invisible bitch of Elsinore, the distaff, the spinner and the knitter that never saw the sun, never lay down in it, or for it, the thing in a petticoat, the fair Ophelia. And why all of a sudden the affected language? Followed by the removal of my name—now it was 'nymph', 'greetings, nymph', or some such empty appellation, along with an irrelevant reference to his sins. I wasn't thinking about his sins. I wasn't even thinking about my own. How could I? I don't have any. I wish to God I did.

So what to say? What could I say? Long time no see? That would have suited me. But it wouldn't have suited him. His mood needed something to equal the affectation of the fair nymph at her orisons. Try this then: how does your honour for this many a day? Now there's a statement! And I gave it to him. Oh yes, we both know that my father came between us, but we both know too that you did nothing about it. You could have thrown me across your charger and exited Elsinore with your fair prize, her hair flying in the wind. You could have hired a ship…

'So how are you, then? My lord?'

'I humbly thank you, well, well, well.'

I got the message. He was addressing me as if I were a complete stranger. Humbly. Thank you. Well, well. So I reached between my breasts and brought out the evidence. Some of it. His eyes flickered. He'd never reached in there.

'What's this?'

'It's your bits and bobs, your love-tokens, remember? Your little keepsakes. Only I can't keep them any more, not for my own sake at least. I've wanted to give them back to you for some time now, as it's some time since it felt like they meant anything to you.'

'To me? How could they? I never even gave you these, never.'

I was no stranger to his word-games, though once they'd been love-larks. Was he saying that he was now a changed man from the one who'd given me these little gifts? Or was I the one who had changed, supposedly? Was I to blame? I wasn't about to accept the blame—it was unfair and untrue, and I reminded him of his love-letters, and of all the tender talk between us, and I insisted I was in no mind to hold on to gifts when the giver had gone so cold. I let him have it. And to give an extra edge to my exchange, I dipped my hand again into the white valley and brought out the rest, the actual jewels. They'd been warmed between the drifts—I wasn't going to spare him the shiver of excitement. And it worked. He went off again into his word-games.

'So—innocent are we, then? A good old vestal virgin?'

'What do you mean?'

'I mean that your charms can have no connection with your chastity, beauty and chastity being incompatible.'

'And why should they be so?'

'Because beauty breeds temptation, and temptation dishonour—you know how the proverb goes. A woman may be as ugly as sin but is therefore all the safer from sin thereby.'

'And how safe does that make me, would you say?'

'Oh, safe as houses. After all, we're not about to have intercourse, are we? Or are we in doubt about that? You know what they say:

If you wish to sin, stick it in.
If in doubt, pull it out.

By the way, have you heard the one about the young sex-seeker? Just before he fucked her he asked the girl what she was called, and when she told him it was Mary, he packed away his doings, codpiece and all, and went off instead to found a convent dedicated to the Virgin.

'Ah, so what's in a name?'

'Yes indeed. And what's in your name, do you know?'

'I've no idea.'

'Then let me tell you. It's from the Greek. It means 'helper'. Are you my little helper? Or are you someone else's?'

'I don't know what you're talking about.'

'What I was trying to tell you a moment ago is that your looks will corrupt your chastity soon enough. This could have been unthinkable but now it's all too true. I loved you once.'

'So you made me believe.'

'You shouldn't have let yourself be taken in. It's still there, you know. He's still there.'

'Who is? What is?'

'The old offending Adam. The savour of sin. You can't get rid of it. I never loved you. Never.'

'Then I misconstrued you it seems.'

'No you didn't. I mis-con-screwed *you*, little miss, and you missed your chance with me.'

'The more fool me for believing you.'

That's when he lost it.

'Believe? Belief? Fuck your beliefs! And fuck you! Why don't you fuck off? Get yourself nunnified. Get into a convent—or into a brothel.'

'Same thing?'

'Same thing—they don't breed there, breeding is out. There's the nunnery where the wiles of women are renounced, and there's the other kind where they flourish.'

'And which do you propose for me then?'

'Ah, what would you like me to say, I wonder? Ideally for you the sanctuary from marriage and from the world's contamination? Not the sort of nunnery where two pairs of slippers lie at the bedside and four bare legs are in action, eh?'

'So you like to picture it, do you? All in your head?'

'No, I'd like *you* to get the picture. The nun is the bride of Christ and the whore is the bride of all who come to her, but not to breed. You can either suck up to sister Josephine, lick her tits, or give your madam a good going over after you've done with your customers, it's all the same to me, but why lie on your back and breed more sinners? Why was I bred, for example? Why did my mother spread her legs and shove me out into the world? For what? I'm a proud bastard. I'm ambitious. And I'm bent on revenge. Revenge! Do you hear? Do you hear? I know you're listening. You bastard! And I'm not the only one. We're all at it, we're all after you, all hot on your trail, you'd better believe it… Where's your father?'

It was the test question. He was putting me on trial and I'd no option but to fail the test, and be found guilty. We both knew where my father was but I couldn't tell him, not out in the open. I had to lie. And I did. I told him where my father was. Where else would he be?

'At home.'

'Whore! You whore! That's what you are! That's what you all are, whores, every last one of you! Not worth a tart's fart. And you make cuckolds out of all of us, every one! Did Eve paint her face in Eden do you think? You painted fucking prostitutes! You hip-swingers, you sweet talkers! You jigging Jezebels! You ambling bits of arse! You're no better than those brawny big-breasted farm girls who take on the bull and count the horn a pleasure. Marry you? Let me tell you now—there will be no more marriages. We've had one that's been more than enough. As for those that are married already—they can all live, all except one. Can you guess which one? It doesn't matter. Just get to your convent—or to your cunt-house. Doesn't matter either way. Impregnation's off the agenda. Keep a tight fanny. And all arrows in their quivers, got it? Enough. I'm fucking off…!

Oh dear. But never mind, dear. Dance, Ophelia. Dance to your daddy, dance to the Prince of Denmark. Dance to the expectancy and rose of the fair state, the glass of fashion and the mould of all good taste—his crudities apart—the unmatched form and feature of blown youth, blasted with madness! Dance? Yes, dance to sweet bells jangled, jarring, out of tune and harsh, like bells at Polish funerals, they say, refusing to make love, I sucked the honey of his music vows but he never sucked my tits…

'To hell with tits!'

It wasn't the grinning diplomat that crept out now from behind the arras with my father, putting words into my head that I'd never have used, though I'd overheard my brother often enough, smirking with the gallant lads about the women they'd entertained. The king who came out was not the one who'd gone in. King Claudius was now a king of concerns, and they weren't about his nephew's mental health. And needless to say I didn't exist to hear them, though I did—clearly. When you are a non-person you hear everything clearly, simply because you aren't there.

'Fanny? His mind's far from fanny, that's clear enough. Woman trouble? Unrequited love? Lust? No, that's not it. There's something else. There's something in his soul, something brooding in his blood. I don't know what it is, but it's something dangerous, and I don't like it. And to forestall it, I've decided. I want him out of the way. I have a mission for him. I'm sending him out of the country. I'm packing him off to England, to collect our tribute, our peace-money. It's long overdue. And he's the prince, our ambassador. Who knows, maybe the voyage will do him good, the sea-air, a change of scene, new sights and sounds, they might help him, help to expel whatever it is that's festering inside him and bring out this... this unsafe, this dangerous behaviour. What do you think?'

The question—if it was a question—was addressed to my father. Neither of them asked me what I might think. The Lord Chamberlain's daughter doesn't think. Ophelia doesn't think. It's not what she's for. What is she for, then? What am I for? Nothing. Nothing for now but to overhear the next piece of the plot, with ears that are deaf shells. The play would go ahead. And after the play my father would hide himself again, one more arras, this time in the queen's bedroom, where the prince would be summoned to speak to his mother. One last try. Perhaps she could tease out of him whatever it was that had split him apart from his old self. And perhaps, one of these uneasy afternoons or anxious Elsinore evenings, my father would hide himself once too often...

Before the Play

He couldn't help himself, of course—the lead player had to be given a Hamlet lesson in acting, during final rehearsals, paying particular attention to the performance of the speech which he'd penned himself for insertion into the Gonzago play. Don't murder it, whatever you do, or I might as well bring in the town-crier to give it all he's got—straight from the belly. And don't saw the air with your arms like that—you're not a windmill, and there aren't any groundlings here to play up to, so you needn't tear the speech to tatters. And if you're bringing on the clowns, keep them under control, none of their ad-libbing. One last thing—no dumb-shows. They're for idiots, and I don't want them in this particular piece, it would be out of place. Are we understood?

The old actor swallowed the lecture as if he'd been a novice, nodding and grinning, and looked to me ready to go on and strut his stuff as he always did. He didn't know what I knew, that the speech he was to interpolate was crucial to more than the play itself. It was no mere slice of blank verse to please a prince's whim, it was the bait in the mouse-trap to be set that night for the catching of a piece of vermin: King Rat. Hence Hamlet's obsessive attention to detail. I also knew that Hamlet was not only keyed up to a high pitch of excitement, but that although he did not necessarily understand this himself, the play was not unlike the antic disposition—itself a sort of performance—a device which presented him with a specious control of the situation, and of his own intractable problem. Not that I fully understood it myself at the time, but I believe I was coming closer to realising that both feigned madness and play-acting offered him an escape from his dilemma by allowing him to pretend to himself that he was coping with it. Right now he was at the top of his form, both on edge and in high spirits, almost to the point of hysteria, certainly hugely elated, because at last he was acting, not acting. This was action and not an act. Or so he thought.

All was bustle and bells. Fork and knife and chamber-pot were fussing about. The word was that the whole court would watch the performance, including king and queen. Gertrude was reportedly relieved and delighted that her son was acting more like his old self again. She was not a great one for the theatre but on this occasion she was eager to attend and was making ready. So was Claudius, though from what Ophelia had just told me, he was likely to form an extremely wary member of the audience. There was also to be music as a prelude to the evening's entertainment. Just before it all began Hamlet called me over—and rather took me aback, I have to say, with something of a speech. It wasn't prepared, I could hear it coming from the heart. He'd never spoken to me quite like this before.

Apparently I was the best person he'd ever encountered in his whole life, the truest friend and the most decent man: good, honest, upright, impartial, blameless—he ran out of adjectives and I demurred, naturally, but he swept my protests aside, he was in deadly earnest. So I let him continue.

'You know how this corrupt world works, you know as well as I do—by flattery. Arse-kissing and arse-licking, just look at all of them bending over. But why should I flatter you, my friend, when we both know you haven't a penny to your name? You're a poor scholar. Let's be blunt, you haven't a pot to piss in. That's why I love you. You're cool, you're practical, you're ordinary, in the best sense of the word, you're all the things I wish I were, or could be, and can't be. And you don't belong here among these honey-tongued hypocrites, these fucking flunkeys...'

He wasn't getting into his stride—he'd lost his stride, he'd crossed the line, and I tried to halt him but couldn't.

'No, Horatio, listen, I want you to listen. I've had dealings with many people in my time, but from the day I got some sense into my head, since I knew what was what and who was who—you know what I'm saying?—I knew that you were the only one, that you were my soul-mate, my one and only, how else can I put it? You were the man for me. Why? Because I've watched you, you've taken all the shit, all that life could possibly throw at you, good and bad, the blows and benefits alike, and you've taken them all on the chin. You endure everything and you're hurt by nothing. Again, why? Because you're yourself, you're your own man, you're no mere pipe for fate's finger to sound you out, to pull any note it pleases out of you. How else to express it, my friend? You're not passion's slave, you're not the victim of your own temperament, not like some of us, not like me. And that's why I wear you right here, here in my heart's core, in my heart of hearts...'

I thought for a moment he was going to kiss me. Maybe he saw my little flutter of panic. I wasn't certain what the kiss, if it had been made, would have signified, or consisted of, how exactly it would have been expressed. I'm not that sort of man. Had there been a woman… But this is outside the scope of my remit. At any rate it was at that point that my old friend took pity on me, perhaps, and put me at my ease.

'I'm going on too much about this, I know I am, too much information. Forgive me, friend. Let's get back to business.'

I was glad to. And the business was the play. One scene of it in particular came close to acting out the very circumstances of the old king's murder. The agreement was that at that point in the action I'd pay close attention to Claudius and his reaction, if any. If the specially prepared speech didn't work the trick of exposing the king's guilt, then we could conclude perhaps that the apparition had indeed been diabolical, and the whole story of the murder some species of hellish fiction.

'Watch him like a hawk, Horatio. And my own eyes will be riveted to his fat face. If he flinches for a second, just one second, he's guilty. But let's watch the performance… and watch the king at the same time. Afterwards we'll compare notes. Here they come—they're coming now to the play. I hear the music. Time for me to put on my mad act. Get yourself a place. Close to the king…'

The Mouse-Trap

Darkness and candlelight, drums and trumpets, and instead of cannons—music a Danish march, stately, ceremonious, to which the whole court entered, expectant, eager for the unaccustomed entertainment. Claudius opened on a bold, breezy note.

'Well now, Hamlet, and how are you faring this evening?'

The prince went straight for the wordplay.

'Faring. Ah, how am I faring? As well as any chameleon, if you know what I mean.'

Claudius didn't. How could he?

'You'll have to explain that one to me, I fear.'

'With pleasure, Your Majesty. The chameleon lives on air, or so they say, and the Elsinore air is extremely appetising, don't you find?'

'How is that?'

'How? Because it's crammed—with promises. And so I eat the air, promise-crammed, and yet I'm still not satisfied. Want to know why?'

'I know you'll tell me.'

'Because that's all they are, these promises, empty air.'

And I'm still only the heir—he could have added, but kept the pun implied, and if Claudius understood the implication he didn't give it away. Hamlet turned his attention to Polonius.

'Ah, my Lord Chamberlain! You were once on stage yourself, weren't you?'

'My lord?'

'At the university, I mean. I think that's what you once said, when you were a student—about two hundred years ago, was it?—you took the boards, did you not now?'

'An amateur, my lord, as a mere amateur. And yet, now that I remember, I was accounted a good actor.'

'Well now, why doesn't that surprise me? And what did you enact?'

'Julius Caesar, my lord. I was killed in the Capitol. Brutus killed me.'

'*Et tu Bruté*? Oh, what a brutal deed was that—to kill such a capital ass! You were in the wrong place at the wrong time. Still, no Capitol hereabouts, eh? This is Elsinore. You should be safe.'

A ripple of laughter from the courtiers. And the queen was enjoying herself, greatly encouraged by her son's sudden merry mood.

'Come over here, dear boy, sit with me.'

Hamlet gave her a brief bow and turned instead to Ophelia.

'You must excuse me, Your Majesty, here's metal more attractive! She's magnetic, don't you know? I'm drawn to her!'

He kneeled down in front of Ophelia and spoke in a loud exaggerated whisper so that everyone could hear.

'Well, lady, shall I lie in your lap?'

Ophelia shook her head.

'I don't think so.'

The entire audience was watching, listening.

'What's the matter? I could lie on you, in you, with you. Or I could just lay my head in your lap, if that's all right?'

'Then how would you see the show?'

'Ah, but you could show me a better show, with my head in your lap. I'm sure you could, that is if you're not ashamed to give me a show. But that's not what I meant.'

'What did you mean?'

'What do you think I meant? Do you think I meant cunt-rie matters?'

'I think nothing.'

'Nothing. Now that's a very pretty thought—nothing—a perfect one to put between a lady's legs.'

'How so?'

'Because it's nothing. And nothing's a zero isn't it? Or it's just a hole. Or there again, if it's a perfect circle—let's see now, what's a perfect circle? Oh, it's infinity, isn't it? It's truth. So truth lies between your legs. And so do I!'

'In your dreams.'

'In my wet dreams.'

'So you're having a good time, then?'

'You can see I am. I can do you songs and jigs too, if you like, and jokes, I do jokes. And why not indeed? Why should a man not have a good time? After all, just look at my mother over there, she's having a whale of a time, don't you see? And my father only dead these two hours.'

'It's a bit longer than that—it's twice two months. Can you count too?'

'I think I can. Twice two—that's four months! So long? Good God, then it's time I got out of these mourning clothes. I should give them to the devil and join the rest of you. I mean, if wearing black means so little… Still, fancy you remembering my father. No-one else around here seems to. But if you do, then there's some hope a great man's memory might last as long as half a year. Dead four months and not forgotten yet. Yes, there's hope for us all—well, for some of us, I hope, not all. But hush-a-bye! I must sing dumb—here come the players!'

I was sitting right next to Ophelia, opposite the king and queen, and I watched Hamlet's face turn black as thunder as the players came on. It was clear they were about to preface the action with a dumb-show. The bare bones of the plot would be mimed, showing what was about to happen on stage. It wasn't only that Hamlet had forbidden the question of a dumb-show. This was no mere matter of aesthetics. Claudius would be given more than an inkling of what was to come, and would have time to steady his nerves. The spring would be removed from the trap and the bait would have lost its flavour. But as he caught my eye, I pointed away from the stage to something I'd just noticed. The king and queen were so far paying no attention to the players. Polonius had approached them and they were deep in whispered conversation. Hamlet had looked ready to commit murder but he let the mime go ahead.

On came a king and queen, obviously in love, making all the relevant tender gestures. He then lay down on a bank of stage flowers, representative of an orchard, or a garden, and she left him there to enjoy his sleep. It was cut short—or rather it was lengthened, into the eternal sleep. A furtive-looking fellow came on, removed the sleeper's crown, kissed it, poured poison in the ear, and stole away as the murdered man writhed in his last agony…

I glanced at Hamlet. He had one eye on the real king and queen. They still had their heads together with Polonius. Obviously in attending the play they were merely humouring the prince and were awaiting the actual performance.

The player queen came back to wake her husband, found him dead, and went through the motions of tearing her hair and rending her clothes. But the poisoner came back on and condoled her as the dead body was carried off. The condolences then turned to caresses, and to gifts. It didn't take him too long to break her down. She embraced him and he put on the dead man's crown. It was over.

Almost. One of the players then stepped forward and Hamlet shot me another furious look. A presenter! As if the dumb-show hadn't been enough, the speaker was now about to explain the precise meaning of the dumb-show, and Claudius and Gertrude were now all eyes and ears…

But no. The speech turned out to be a short inconsequential jingle.

For us and for our tragedy.
Here's stooping to your clemency,
We beg your hearing patiently.

Ophelia smiled.
'So brief.'
'As woman's love.'

Hamlet never missed a trick. He was unsmiling but he was relieved. The play was saved—and went ahead, with everyone now watching.

Enter on the dais two Players, a King and a Queen

Player King. *Full thirty times hath Phoebus' cart gone round,*
Neptune's salt wash, and Tellus' orbéd ground,
And thirty dozen moons with borrowed sheen
About the world have times twelve thirties been,
Since love our hearts and Hymen did our hands
Unite commutual in most sacred hands.
Player Queen. *So many journeys may the sun and moon*
Make us again count o'er ere love be done!
But woe is me, you are so sick of late,
So far from cheer, and from your former state,
That I distrust you. Yet though I distrust,
Discomfort you, my lord, it nothing must,
For women fear too much, even as they love,
And women's fear and love hold quantity,
In neither aught, or in extremity.
Now what my love is proof hath made you know,
And as my love is sized, my fear is so.
Where love is great, the littlest doubts are fear,
Where little fears grow great, great love grows there.
Player King. *Faith, I must leave thee, love and*
    shortly too.
My operant powers their functions leave to do,
And thou shalt live in this fair world behind,
Honoured, beloved, and haply one as kind
For husband shalt thou—
Player Queen. *O confound the rest!*
Such love must needs be treason in my breast,
In second husband let me be accurst,

None wed the second, but who killed the first.

At that point Hamlet stood up and shouted: 'That's wormwood, wormwood!'

> Player Queen. *The instances that second marriage move*
> *Are base respects of thrift, but none of love.*
> *A second time I kill my husband dead,*
> *When second husband kisses me in bed,*
> Player King. *I do believe you think what now you speak*
> *But what we do determine, oft we break.*
> *Purpose is but the slave to memory,*
> *Of violent birth but poor validity,*
> *Which now like fruit unripe sticks on the tree,*
> *But fall unshaken when they mellow be.*
> *Most necessary 'tis that we forget*
> *To pay ourselves what to ourselves is debt,*
> *What to ourselves in passion we propose,*
> *The passion ending, doth the purpose lose,*
> *The violence of either grief or joy*
> *Their own enactures with themselves destroy,*
> *Where joy most revels, grief doth most lament,*
> *Grief joys, joy grieves, on slender accident.*
> *This world is not for aye, nor 'tis not strange*
> *That even our loves should with our fortunes change:*
> *For 'tis a question left us yet to prove,*
> *Whether love lead fortune, or else fortune love.*
> *The great man down, you mark his favourite flies,*
> *The poor advanced makes friends of enemies,*
> *And hitherto doth love on fortune tend,*
> *For who not needs shall never lack a friend,*
> *And who in want a hollow friend doth try,*
> *Directly seasons him his enemy.*
> *But orderly to end where I begun,*

Our wills and fates do so contrary run,
That our devices still are overthrown,
Our thoughts are ours, their ends none of our own—
So think thou wilt no second husband wed,
But die thy thoughts when thy first lord is dead.
Player Queen. *Nor earth to me give food nor heaven light,*
Sport and repose lock from me day and night,
To desperation turn my trust and hope,
And anchor's cheer in prison be my scope,
Each opposite that blanks the face of joy
Meet what I would have well and it destroy,
Both here and hence pursue me lasting strife,
If once a widow, ever I be wife!
Player King. *'Tis deeply sworn. Sweet leave me here awhile,*
My spirits grow dull, and fain I would beguile
The tedious day with sleep.   [he sleeps]
Player Queen. *Sleep rock thy brain,*
And never come mischance between us twain!   [exit]

At this point in the action Hamlet called across to the queen.

'Well, madam, how do you like the play? Does it suit you?'

If she sensed an insult after the talk of second husbands, Gertrude swallowed it.

'The lady is overdoing it, I think.'

'No, that's the wormwood working on her, mother.'

'Wormwood?'

'She must have picked some from the garden—when she left her husband sleeping there. You know what they say—chew on the old wormwood and it will purge your digestive tract of worms.'

'What on earth are you saying? What has that got to do with the play, or with her?'

'Guilt, mother, gnawing guilt, it has to be brought out, got out of the system, expelled.'

'And why should she feel guilty?'

'Wait and see.'

Claudius came in on her side.

'Do you know the plot? It doesn't contain any offensive material, I take it?'

Hamlet gave one of his mad laughs.

'Offensive? Well, there's one offence…but no, no offence, not really, not unless you find poison offensive, I mean it's only a play, after all, they're not committing real crimes, they're only playing at it, playing with poison—poison in jest!'

Claudius was keeping a straight face.

'I didn't catch the title of the play.'

'Oh, didn't you? It's called The Mouse-Trap, at least that's what I call it, because it's about trapping a rat. Its real name is—let me see—ah yes, *The Murder of Gonzago*. It's the story of a murder done in Vienna. Gonzago is the duke's name—well, he was a king, really, and he had such a lovely queen, Baptista she was called. But you know what these Italians were like—some of the women were worse than the men, devilish pieces of work, but we needn't let that concern us, not here in Elsinore, we're all innocent here, are we not? We're all the king's horses here, and no saddle-sores to trouble us, we're all in such fine fettle, like they say in the proverb, our withers are unwrung… Oh, look, here comes Lucianus!'

All this time the players had been hovering, waiting for the best moment to resume the action. King and courtiers could talk their way through an entire play if they felt like it, irrespective of what audience or actors thought of the interruption, but in spite of the dreaded dumb-show, these players knew how important their performance was to Hamlet, and they'd paused the action just before the climax. Now the climax had come, and the lead actor had come on in a black doublet, dressed just like Hamlet, and holding a vial. He strutted mincingly, melodramatically, towards the sleeping king, making threatening gestures and grimacing wickedly. Hamlet stood up and pointed at him.

'Yes, this is him, it's Lucianus, Lucianus! Take a good look at him, everybody, and watch him closely, see what he does! He's the king's nephew. And he's the avenger, yes? But avenger of what? Of the first murder, the brother's murder, So he's both brother and nephew, killer and avenger. And what do you think he's just about to do...? What do you think, Ophelia?'

'Why don't you tell us?'

Everybody was starting to get edgy. They could sense something critical. The air was charged. Only Ophelia, strangely, seemed to be able to bandy words with him, to appear conversable.

'You might as well tell us—you're as good as a chorus.'

Hamlet leered back at her.

'Oh, I can do better than that! I could be a puppet-show reporter—if you could swing your two puppets for me.'

She answered him with a smile and a whisper.

'You mean my breasts, I take it?'

He didn't like the directness.

'Oh yes, let me trifle with your tits!'

She refused to be shocked.

'Oh my, you're keen aren't you? I can feel it.'

'Careful what you say! If I'm as keen as you say, it could cost you a groaning to blunt my appetite and take off my edge.'

'A groaning, really? How about a moaning? On my side of the bed only. Girls groan when the lads are having their wicked way, or when we're paying for their fun nine months later. We moan when we're the ones having the fun. How about it—can you make me moan?'

He'd asked for it and he got it.

'You tart! You'd moan all night long before you brought me down!'

Still she was not to be intimidated.

'Wittier still, so you think. But even less the gentleman. Better and worse.'

'Oh, better and worse, eh? Now you're the witty one. You remember the marriage-vows, do you, little virgin? For better or for worse. You take a man to be your husband—or maybe you mis-take him, or you take another man to your bed—and goodbye to your first husband, let him rot in hell! Anyway, to hell with all this! Let's get going, Lucianus! Leave off with your stupid faces! You didn't listen to a fucking word of what I said, did you? Get on with it, man, this is your cue! The croaking raven bellows for revenge...!'

The actor ceased his antics and began. The whole court stirred in their seats. You could hear it intensely, the sudden intake of breath. The king's nephew was about to kill him...

Thoughts black, hands apt, drugs fit, and time agreeing,
Confederate season, else no creature seeing,
Thou mixture rank, of midnight weeds collected,
With Hecate's ban thrice blasted, thrice infected,
Thy natural magic and dire property
On wholesome life usurp immediately.

In went the deadly drug—and all eyes turned to look at Claudius, who was being murdered on stage. Hamlet was standing up, shouting at the top of his voice.

'He's poisoning him in the garden for his crown! Gonzago is the victim's name! The murderer doesn't need a confederate, as you can see—the occasion itself is the only ally he needs, there's no-one else to see him, people could think what they like, they might even assume he'd been bitten by a snake...'

Claudius had turned pure white, his face a mask of fear. He knew now that Hamlet knew. He tried to rise and fell back into his seat.

'It's a well-known story, and written in very choice Italian, highly readable, if you're into Italian. You'll see in a moment how the murderer not only gets away with it, but gets the love of Gonzago's gorgeous wife—the queen!'

Claudius had managed to totter to his feet. Ophelia rose too.

'The king—what's wrong with him? He needs help.'

Gertrude rose, reaching out to her trembling husband, terrified, uncomprehending. The entire gathering was on its feet. Hamlet was wild with excitement.

'What, frightened by false fire, are we? It's only a play, for God's sake! It didn't really happen, did it? Did it?'

Polonius hurried over to the dais and faced the baffled actors.

'Enough! Stop the play!'

Claudius clapped his hand to his face, a stricken figure in the flickering darkness. Some of the candles had gone out. He screamed.

'Light! Give me some light!' Hamlet raced to the nearest guard, snatched his torch, and ran across to the petrified king. He thrust the flaming brand into his face.

'Your light—Your Majesty!'

Claudius swept the torch aside—it went flaring among the spectators—and rushed from the hall, stumbling and staggering, his arms flailing everyone aside.

'Away! Away!'

Polonius shouted for lights. The audience didn't wait for them. Everyone followed in the wake of the fleeing king, streaming from the hall in complete confusion. The actors ran too. They thought they were in trouble. Hamlet and I were the only ones left. His head was in the clouds. He closed his eyes and raised his hands to the roof. He was elated, throbbing with triumph, ablaze with his achievement.

'Music! Let's have music! Tell the players to bring in the recorders!'

He danced around the hall and burst into a ballad.

Why, let the stricken deer go weep,
The hart ungalléd play.

'What do you think, Horatio?'

'About what?'

'Can the queen go weep—from the heart? And her horned husband escape my hunter's arrow? Or shall I try minstrelsy instead?'

'I think you should try whistling—if that's the best you can do as a singer!'

'Oh, you mean dog, Horatio! How about an actor, then? What did you think of the speech?'

'A bit overdone, since you ask! But he didn't finish it, did he?'

'He didn't have to, it worked so well. Even at the worst I could get myself a share in a theatre, don't you think?'

'Half a share.'

'Oh, no, come on, old friend, this is worth a forest of feathers and a pair of rosettes for my fancy shoes, and I'll tread the boards with the best of them. It's a partnership in a pack of players for me. And I'll go to the dogs and be famous in the world! Meanwhile the king is dead—who was a god while he lived. And now long live the king! But not for too long, eh? The peacock has lost his strut at last.'

'He's lost something of it—he flew off fast enough.'

'God, Horatio, you're a famous friend—and I'll take the ghost's word for a thousand pounds! You saw it, didn't you?'

'I saw it.'

'At the moment of the poisoning?'

'It was unmistakable.'

'Unmistakable. You couldn't fail to see it.'

'Everyone saw it.'

Everyone had seen it. But not everyone knew exactly what they'd seen. Apart from Hamlet and myself, the only other member of the audience with the inside knowledge of what he'd witnessed was the guilty king—and he'd been allowed to escape, and I found myself asking myself at that point: why? I was also asking myself: why hadn't Hamlet made the murderer the king's brother? Why had he stopped short of pressing the resemblance as far as it could go? By making Lucianus the nephew instead of the brother, he'd set up a rehearsal for a strike against his uncle, and it wasn't only guilt and confusion that made Claudius run for it—he was terrified for his life, convinced that Hamlet was about to murder him in public. And at the crucial moment, what would have been the moment of total retribution and triumph, he'd let him go. The revenger had not only failed to complete the task, he wasn't even thinking about the task, he wasn't in the revenger's world at all, the real world, he was caught up instead in the fabulous atmosphere of the theatre and its thespians, the moonshine of deception and pretence. But could I say as much to him? Should I mar his moment of success that in more than one sense was not only no success at all but its opposite, failure? Failure—and danger to himself, because of what was now bound to follow: consequences. They would be inevitable, once Claudius had pulled himself together.

Even as I was listening, and pondering what best to say, how to advise—along came the first two of the consequences: the fated fork and knife.

'Can we have a word, my lord?'

'Only one word? You can have an uncut chronicle if you like.'

'Just one word, that's all. The king.'

'Oh yes indeed, the king! What about him?'

'Is withdrawn to his rooms.'

'Very wise, wouldn't you say?'

'And is dreadfully upset... disturbed.'

'With drink?'

'With anger. He's beside himself. Out of sorts.'

'Then shouldn't he see a doctor? The doctor could give him a purgative perhaps, get it out of his system, whatever's in there.'

'That's not really what he—'

'Or I could offer him one myself.'

'Offer him what?'

'A purgative. Or a little blood-letting, maybe? Being bled can work wonders, you know.'

'My lord—'

'On the other hand, if I were to put him to his purgation, it might make him worse, who knows? After all purgation, true purgation, can involve confession, and eliciting a confession isn't always too easy. It should be made freely, if the confessor is anxious to avoid purgatory. Do you think he is?'

'We think you're not making much sense—forgive us, my lord—you're rambling, you know, you're rather wild.'

'Wild! God forbid. Very well. I'm tame. Carry on.'

'Thank you, my lord. The queen has sent us to you.'

'You're very welcome. I'm glad to see you. And how are you both?'

'No, my lord, you know very well you're playing with us, making fools of your friends. If you won't give us a rational answer, a sound answer, a sane answer, then we'll end it there, we'll say goodbye.'

'But I can't.'

'Can't what, my lord?'

'Can't make you a sane answer. I'm mentally ill, you see, my mind's diseased. But tell you what, let me try anyway. My mother, you were saying?'

'Is quite bewildered. And alarmed. You've put her into a state of complete shock.'

'Really? What kind of a son am I, I wonder now, to shock a mother in this way? Anything else?'

'Yes, she'd like to speak to you in her private room, before you go to bed.'

'Ah, bed. Shall I ever go to bed? There are so many other matters to put to bed. But I'll do as she asks. I'll obey my mother were she ten times my mother. At the last count she was, let's see, only twice my mother, was it? Still a long way to go. Anything else? Or is that it?'

'My lord—you were once a friend.'

'And still am. And can pick and choose. If you two are still friends, not thieves.'

'It's because we're friends that we'd like to try to keep you at liberty, keep them from locking you up. We might as well stop beating about the bush; they see you as a menace, so it would help if you could let us understand the nature of your illness, the cause.'

'The cause? Oh, that's an easy one. I'm a frustrated heir, as you well know. Everybody knows that. I want to get on, make my way in this world, flex my muscles, fulfil my ambition. We spoke about ambition before, didn't we?'

'We did. And if we didn't say so at the time, let us remind you now—His Majesty has already appointed you to be the next king.'

'Yes, yes, that's true—and optimistic. But you know what they say about that.'

'What do they say?'

'Oh, come on, you know the old proverb. While the grass grows the silly horse starves. Which reminds me of a true story. Do you know it? Let me tell you. There was a peasant who'd been condemned to death by his king, and he begged for a reprieve, and the king said yes, very well, he could have his reprieve—he'd give him one minute. But the peasant said no—he wanted a year. The king was tickled. 'A year! Why should I give you a year?' 'I'll tell you why,' said the peasant. 'Give me a year—and in that year I'll teach your horse to talk.' The king agreed. The peasant's friends, however, were understandably baffled, and so he explained his thinking to them. 'Look, I have a whole year now that I didn't have before. And a lot can happen in a year. The king could *die*. The *horse* could die. *I* could die. And who knows—maybe the horse *will* talk!' What do you think, friends? A marvellous example of optimism, eh? And pragmatism. But while I'm waiting for His Majesty to die—well, I could well die myself. Of boredom... Ah, no! Hang on! Boredom begone! Here come the recorders. Ready to face the music?'

The players came running in and presented the instruments. Hamlet took one and turned round with it to the hovering pair.

'Step aside, please. Why are you hounding me like this? Do you want to drive me into the net? See me caught up in your snare? All trussed up and ready for the beheading and the disembowelling? A tasty dish to set before the king, what?'

'Oh, my lord!'

'Oh, my lord—what?'

'We do have a duty—to the king and queen, and if that makes us too bold, well it's our love for you that's to blame. True friends don't worry too much about manners, do they?'

'I don't know about that, but I'll tell you what, let's hear you play a little on this pipe. Here, take one each.'

'We can't, my lord.'

'Please.'

'Trust us, we can't.'

'I don't trust you. So I must beg you.'

'We have neither the training nor the talent. We simply don't have the touch.'

'It's as easy as lying. Look, see these little wind-holes? We call these the stops. Apply your fingers and thumbs, as I'm doing now, see, breathe into it, and listen—lovely music will come out of it. Go on, do it!'

'But we couldn't produce good music—it would just be noise, nothing more, no harmony, nothing, we just don't have the skill.'

Hamlet snatched the instruments from them and threw them away. The players hurried to pick them up.

'So you don't have the skill. My God, you think little of me! True friends did you say? Do you think I'm a complete idiot? You want to play on me, you want to know all my stops, you want to make me sing, you want to suck the soul out of me, you want to pluck out the heart of my mystery, you want to sound me out from top to bottom, from the lowest notes to the highest, range right through me—and there's so much music to be got out of this little pipe, and yet you can't make it speak? Not one fucking note? You cunts! Do you think I'm easier to be played on than a fucking pipe? And you won't know what the frets are either, will you? Well, I've got news for you, you can fret me well enough, make me angry enough to want to kill you, to wring your treacherous necks, you snakes, but you can fret me all day, fret to your false fingers' content—and still you'll never learn to play on me. I'm too deep for you, you see. The music of the night—it's lost its power.'

'My lord!'

Now it was the turn of the chamber-pot, rolling in, looking dizzy.

'And God bless you too, old trout! Have you come to be tickled? And landed?'

'My lord, the queen is waiting! She wishes to speak to you—at once!'

Hamlet took him gently by the arm. Polonius tensed nervously but allowed himself to be walked over to one of the high windows.

'Do you see that cloud up there—the one that looks almost like a camel?'

'Good Lord, it's true—yes, it's like a camel.'

'Actually it's more like a weasel, don't you think?'

'It's backed like a weasel.'

'Or like a whale?'

'Very like a whale.'

'Right you are, then. We've done musicology. That was zoology. And here endeth the second lesson. So now I'll go up and have a word with my mother, then. I can't play the fool here any longer. I've had all of you up to here. You've wound me up, bent me like a bow. Up to breaking point.'

'And so your mother, my lord?'

'And so I'll come to my mother, by and by.'

'I'll say so.'

'By and by is easily said. Now leave me alone.'

A Short Note on Hot Blood

The fork and knife and chamber-pot were dismissed. I stayed—and he spoke briefly to me before proceeding to his mother's closet. Still I waited for some sign of action from him, even a verbal sign. I am not a bloodthirsty man—my preference is for peace—and I could have wished that the entire affair might have been unravelled in some court of justice, one in which even kings are not above the law. At the same time I could sense the whole thing gradually eating into my friend and eating away at him inwardly. I did not foresee the outcome—no-one could have done so—but I began to fear that whatever outcome lay ahead would be bloody. It had to be. And it was for his sake that I wished it would not be dragged out to an even worse conclusion. But one man stood in the way of that preferred end: Hamlet himself. Not one word of what he spoke to me on this occasion bore any relation to his uncle—or to the revenge task. He spoke instead of the witching time of night, of yawning churchyards, and hell spouting out contagion and hot blood into the world. Not into the real world, that was for sure. He wasn't living in the real world, he was still inhabiting the actor's part of the revenger—*Now I could drink hot blood!*—enjoying the imagery, not the action. It was the stuff of fantasy. And as always, conditional. Now *could* I drink hot blood… He could, I thought, if he were the revenger. But he wasn't—he was dressing himself up in the role, and I thought it sad but true. Even as he prepared to go and meet his mother, he imagined he was Nero—and immediately rejected the very image of himself he imagined he was inclined to act out, rather than afraid that he actually would.

'Nero had his mother murdered,' I said. 'Tread lightly in her closet—and skip that bloody scene, whatever you do.'

Suddenly he was calm again.

'Don't worry, my friend. I will be cruel only to be kind. I'll speak daggers to her, of course—she deserves it—but her life is safe, if not her soul. Let's face it, she's earned her disgrace, supped up her own shame—she's gorged on it. I'm sorry. Harsh words await her. But I'll never ratify them by actions. Her fate is sealed—but not by me. The deed won't come from me, it won't be by my hand, I promise you, but from whatever hand, that remains to be seen.'

Osric Overhears What God Did Not

Claudius was frantic with fear and worry. Osric didn't know the half of it, of course, and simply assumed that the king was afraid for his life—which he was. But he was also guilt-ridden and conscience-stricken, as Osric later discovered when he hid himself in the king's private chapel and heard everything: a confession.

Before that, Claudius had a sudden change of mind. The original plan had been to get Hamlet out of the country by appointing him as the princely emissary to England, to collect the overdue tribute money. Now, however, Rosencrantz and Guildenstern were to accompany him—as guards for his own good. But they were to be more than mere guards. Another murder was hatching in the peacock's plumes, fluttering in agitation. As Hamlet had said earlier, the strut had gone out of him. Now he was panicking.

Polonius came hurrying by to report that the prince was on his way to his mother's closet, and that he'd get there first and lurk behind the arras—where else?—in an advantageous position; that was the plan at least, to overhear what was said.

'After all, Your Majesty, she may be the queen, but she's also his mother, and motherhood makes women partial. She may knead the facts a little, with a woman's hand, a mother's touch, and report in his favour. She may underestimate the danger he presents. And he is dangerous, of that there is now no question. In his present mood, who knows, he could even kill. It could be you. Or me. What do you think?'

'I think you're right.'

'Am I ever wrong? I've told you before.'

'I know. Go quickly—and keep me informed.'

'I'll call upon you before I go to bed, and tell you what I know.'

Polonius didn't know that he was going to bed early that night. But he went off and left the king to fall to his knees in front of the little altar, with Jesus looking down on him from the cross, Jesus who forgives, if the one who prays to him is worth forgiveness…

O, sweet Jesus! Oh, God, my crime is rank and rotten, I know! It stinks to high heaven! It stinks out all the earth! It's the first and worst of all murders! It's got God's curse on it, the curse of Cain, the brother-murderer! I'm trying. Christ, I'm trying—to pray, but it's my guilty conscience that keeps getting in the way. It defeats my intention. I'm paralysed. I kneel here and I'm bound for nowhere, except for hell. I clasp my hands in appeal—and all I see is the hand with which I did the murder. I have fat little hands, red hands. Supposing this one here were thicker than itself with a brother's blood—isn't there rain enough in the sweet heavens to wash it white as snow?

Isn't that what scripture tells us? *Though your sins be as scarlet, they shall be as white as snow, though they be as crimson, yet shall they be as wool.* Isn't that the line? But what's the use of all that rain and snow, if a man fails to confront his crime? I'm down on my knees. I'm begging for mercy. Can I look up to heaven and look God in the face? Surely I can. My crime is in the past—now I can look to the future.

But how can I pray for forgiveness when I still retain the things for which I did the murder—my crown, my queen, and my ambition? Can a man be pardoned and still hold on to his ill-gotten gains, the profits of his crime? That's how it works in the world out there, in that sea of iniquity and all its corrupted currents and sharp practices, all those gilded fists bearing bribes. There you can bend the law and buy it out, but it's not like that in heaven—God's courts are clean, and the angels sweep corruption from the gates and down to hell, and there's no amount of shuffling of the feet or of the cards, no evasions or excuses that will get you off—no, there your crime is exposed and your sin stripped bare to the very bone, and there we're compelled to submit every ounce and iota of evidence against ourselves and await the judgement.

So: *quid restat?* What remains? What's left but to try for what repentance can achieve? What can't it after all, when repentance is what is called for? But what can it achieve when a man can't truly repent, not from the heart? Repent? No, there's no repentance in my heart, not for real, not deep inside, where my heart's as black as death, I know it is, and so is my soul, it's trapped, it's a bird stuck in the snare, and the more it struggles, the more enmeshed it is. Oh, God's good angels, help me as I bend the knee to you, and try to make this heart of steel as soft as sinews of the new-born babe. And if you hear this prayer—perhaps, perhaps… all may yet be well…'

Even Osric was appalled, and afraid—and almost regretted his own action in earwigging on the king himself. He didn't know what to do at first. But every man has his price, especially Osric, and eventually an arrangement was reached. As you will hear. And at the time, Osric knew very well that even as Claudius was doing his futile best to repent one murder, he was already planning another. He'd killed the father. Now he was working up to killing the son. Rosencrantz and Guildenstern were going to be more than guards—they were the unwitting ushers to an execution. Or maybe they knew, or half-knew… The Claudius prayer for forgiveness was a false alarm. God, if he heard it, was not fooled. And Claudius didn't even fool himself. Words without thoughts, as he well knew, never even reach God's ears.

Hamlet's Last Chance

I was on my way to my mother's closet when I saw that prick Osric flitting about by the king's chapel. What was he up to?— the usual bowing and scraping and bending over, I supposed, flirting with king and court, feathers for the peacock, or for his own ease, as he liked to say as he fanned himself, fanned the ignorant air, fannying about, into everything except an actual fanny. Fair enough, I thought, let him be about his business. But why the chapel? What was he up to now? I hung on, and approached… no sign of him now, and I was about to pass on to the queen's bedchamber when I stopped. I could hear somebody speaking softly. I came up on the quiet. The door to the chapel was ajar…

Christ Almighty—it was him! He was kneeling. He was praying. In a whisper. He had his back to me. His hands were clasped. And he was bent over bowed, naked to the blade, defenceless to the thrust. One thrust. I unsheathed my dagger. This was it. This was the moment I'd been waiting for so long. Now I could do it. He was alone and unguarded and didn't even know I was there. Unsuspecting. Unaware. And no witnesses. Yes, now I could do it. At last. I could. Now that he was praying. And I would. Could. Would, would… and yet I couldn't, couldn't. I couldn't.

How could I? If I'd killed him where he knelt, I'd have sent his guilty, filthy, newly scrubbed and purged soul straight to heaven. Prayer, confession, contrition, repentance, absolution, God's pardon—the whole spiritual package. And he'd spend eternity in heaven with the angels, while my father's spirit roasted in purgatory…

And so—revenge? Would that be revenge, to give him his ticket to heaven, newly minted and free of charge? God, no! That wouldn't be revenge, it would be doing him the ultimate service, which he could have virtually hired me to perform for him. You could even put it the other way, that I'd done the hiring myself, that I'd chartered him to murder my father, and now I was handing him his wages, and at the highest possible rate: forgiveness, salvation, eternal life. Fuck, no! He took my father furtively, grossly, full of bread, in the blossom of his sins—no fasting, no prayer, no spiritual preparation, nothing to speed him safe on his way, to help him to heaven, instead of which an account unaudited, unsettled, and in no fit state to be presented to his maker, but heavily in debt, and food for the flames.

And I asked myself again—what sort of revenge would that be, to take him at the moment of his purgation, all fit and furnished for the next world, seasoned for salvation, a dish for the gods? God, no! Still no, no, no! Sheathe your sword and wait—wait for some awesome opportunity, one that will ensure his damnation. Wait till you can catch him drunk asleep, snoring his fat, befuddled boozy head off, or in the throes of some other deadly sin—if not gluttony, then anger, when he's in a rage, when he's gambling or swearing or in some stupor, any act that has no flavour of forgiveness in it—or, even better, better still—when he's in the incestuous pleasure of his bed, when he's fucking my mother, that's the best time to get him, right between her legs, off balance, and then, that's when I'll trip the bastard and send him head over heels out of bed and into space, and his feet will kick at heaven as he heads for hell, where his black damned soul will rot forever… yes, yes, yes!

Very well then. My mother is waiting. This prayer of yours has kept you alive—for the moment. But it's a postponement, a palliative, nothing more. Your end is nigh, as they say. Your state is terminal. Finish your prayer. And I'll be back to finish you—when the time is right.

A Note on The Above

This is the essence of Hamlet's reasoning, as he expressed it to me. I have thought about it over and over. On the one hand I could hardly have wished for my friend to kill a defenceless man in the act of praying. Nor could I hear his argument without a shudder: that it was not enough for him to kill his enemy's mortal body—he wanted his immortal soul to suffer in hell, not only death but also damnation, eternal torment. What kind of revenge would it be to kill an enemy when he would soar straight to heaven, instead of waiting till he was fit for the downward descent, his pious armour off? No—strangle the bastard with all his sins about him. Stab him so hard that his bloody crimes spurt out all over him, and redden him for hell! And everyone would have applauded, including me, who might have forgiven even my best friend such ruthless cruelty.

On the other hand, I continue to ask myself: was this really what Hamlet was thinking at the time? Was it a genuine argument? Or was it merely an excuse for more delay? In my heart of hearts I have concluded that this is what it was, a mental means of not only excusing his delay, but of prolonging it. I have already noted that Hamlet was never going to kill Claudius, or that at least he was never going to arrive at that decision. In respect of the above episode, however, there remains a grim irony of which Hamlet was unaware. It was only later, after the conclusion of all of these terrible events, that Osric, under questioning, revealed the last words of the king's prayer, his desperate admission that the prayer was ineffective because he was not truly contrite. His plea was false, and if Hamlet had killed him at that moment he would have sent his spirit straight to hell. And things would have taken a different turn from then on. Whether I would have wanted it that way is in the end an entirely different matter.

In Gertrude's Bedchamber

Horatio has asked me to let him have an account of what took place in my closet on the night the Lord Chamberlain was killed. Increasingly he senses that my son's version of events requires to be sifted through another head than his. And increasingly I have come to confide in Horatio as a good man in Elsinore, a man to be trusted. That, I may say, is an inevitable afterthought. At the time I wasn't even thinking, I was so distraught by what had happened, and by the terrible things he'd called me, and accused me of. I couldn't go to my husband, not after the things that had been said. My nerves were in shreds and my heart in tatters. I fell into Horatio's arms and poured it all out.

This is what happened. I had sent for my son and I heard him coming. He was calling my name loudly as he approached, echoing it through the corridors. The Lord Chamberlain was with me and whispered that he'd silence himself behind the arras. He ensconced himself just in time—he was safely hidden. Or was he? The curtain flickered. It caught Hamlet's eye just as he came in but I swept up to him at once and spoke to him sternly.

'Hamlet, you have greatly offended your father.'

'No, mother, you have greatly offended my father.'

'How is that? I've done nothing. What are you saying now?'

'That man's not my father. You've forgotten who my father is.'

'I think rather that you have forgotten me. Do you even remember who I am?'

'All too well. You are the queen, your husband's brother's wife, my father's wedded widow, my uncle's forbidden bride, his incestuous bed-mate—and as I can't change it, much as I'd like to, you are my mother.'

There was no talking to him in that mood.

'Very well, if you won't speak to me with respect. I'll bring along those who'll speak to you, and you'll stand there and listen.'

I brushed past him and made for the door, but he seized me by the arm and hauled me roughly back into the room.

'You're going nowhere—you're going to see inside yourself at last, instead.'

His eyes were flashing. I thought for a moment he was going to murder me. It wasn't my son, it was a madman standing in his place, on the loose in my room. His hand was on his dagger. I screamed. That was when the cry came from behind the arras, Polonius shouting instinctively for help, giving himself away. It all happened in a matter of seconds.

'What's that—a rat? Dead for a ducat, dead!'

He whipped out his sword and lunged at the arras, stabbing hard at the sudden movement in the curtain. It bulged out, the body behind it impaled. It would have fallen, but Hamlet stood there for what felt like forever, supporting what was now a corpse, still hidden on the other side, still held there upright but dead. He'd run him right through. There was no time even for a groan.

'Oh, God! Hamlet, what have you done?'

'I don't know! Is it the king?'

He withdrew the blade, dragged at the curtain, and the arras collapsed, revealing the dead body of Polonius, eyes wide open, staring into eternity.

'Oh, my God, my God! Do you see what you've done? That was a savage act—a bloody deed! A brutal crime!'

'Brutal? Bloody? Yes, mother, almost as bad as kill a king and marry with his brother!'

'As kill a king!'

'You heard me! Yes, lady, that's what I said!'

And that's when I knew he really had lost his mind. He was accusing me of murder, the murder of my first husband, whose death, as we all know, was a terrible thing but it wasn't murder. Clearly my son was deranged. He kneeled down at the body, closed its eyes tenderly, then hissed into the unhearing ear.

'You fool! You stupid interfering pathetic old fool! You couldn't keep out of it, could you? You just had to stick your nosy beak in once too often, didn't you? And you got it bitten. What a pity. I thought it was him. And now it's you—gone on to meet my father. Tell him I stuck the wrong one. The bigger one is still to come. King Rat will soon be on his way…

I was standing there shaking uncontrollably, the body still on its back, and I was thinking of what would now follow, the outcry. He grabbed me again even more roughly and forced me into a chair.

'Stop wringing your hands, woman! I'll wring your heart for you instead, if you've got anything heart-shaped left in there, behind those brassy breasts! Still getting them sucked, are you? King Rat still likes to nibble a nipple, does he? Still fancies gnawing on a tit?'

I'd never been spoken to like that. I tried to stand up.

'Sweet Jesus, what have I done that gives you the right to throw bilge over me as if we were in a brothel? Can you tell me what it is you think I've done?'

'Done? Done?'

He shoved me back down into the chair.

'What you've done would turn virgo intacta into a tart! You blister the innocent rose between a sweet girl's legs! You change a church into a den of thieves, a marriage-oath into a gambler's curse, a bridal-bed into a hearse—the wedding-hearse! Christ, you make the angels weep! You turn the moon to blood and make the stars above us sick...'

'I still don't... I don't understand what you mean!'

'You don't? Then look!'

He propelled me to the bed, took my head in his two hands, held me hard, and forced me to look at the portraits on the wall, above the bed's head.

'There you are! Two brothers, two husbands. The question is, who looks down on who? Which is your side of the bed? Does my father watch his murdering brother fucking his wife? Or is that the fat king's privilege? Maybe you'd like to come in the middle, to do it between the two husbands? Just look at the one on the left. What do you see? A man? No, not a man—a god! It's the sun-god, golden-haired, a brow like Jupiter's, eh? An eye like Mars to threaten and command his forces in the field and take the field by force! A stance like Mercury just landed, the graceful messenger of all the other gods—God, what a man was there! What a man he was! What a father to your son, what a husband for your bed! What a husband you had! Once. And what came next? A toad, a squatting thing, a thing of slime, a mildewed ear of corn, blasting and withering the rest of the field with his poison. Poison! God in heaven, have you eyes? Can you still see, or have you gone blind that you could have fed on this fine mountain of a man only to get down on your knees second time round and grub about on a barren moor like a sheep waiting to be shagged, to be fucked by a goat! And for what? For love? What kind of love? You can't even call it love, not at your age, when the libido's lost to the lowest form of lust. Is that what's left to you? Is that all there is? Do you turn your arse to him in this very bed? Why don't you show me?'

He threw me onto the bed, turned me over, forced me into the position and came up hard against me. I truly believed he was about to rape me, but he turned me over again on my back and straddled me, bringing his lips close to mine for a moment, as if to kiss me, before whispering in my ear.

'You're turning your arse on Aphrodite, don't you see, if you do it that way with him? Even a mad woman would find some last drop of discrimination left at the bottom of her gutter mind to make you see you'd picked this man in a game of blind man's buff—no eyes, no ears, no sense of smell to tell you were making a bad choice, the wrong choice. I mean, fucking hell, what are you? You're a stately old ship, mother of mine, you're a creaking vessel, you've let the youthful mutineers take you over, telling your old bones they can buck in bed and not break, when you're abusing yourself like this in your maturity, pretending frost is fire, and doubtless mixing up the holes... Do you gobble his cock, you old whore? Do you sweat like swine between the sheets? Do you grease each other well? Are you stewed in your own stinking love-dew? Is the bed a brothel? Do you like to pretend he's a client and you're his piece of cunt? Do you talk about it while you're doing it? Filthy talk for a filthy sty? Does he whisper smutty nothings into your slack fanny? Does he kiss the lips, outer and inner? Does he stick his tongue down your tonsils? Does he get his thing in up to the hilt till you retch on his testicles? Do you know you're fucking a murderer, the vicious vice, the royal buffoon, the clown king, the cut-purse of the empire, the one that crept up to the shelf and pocketed the crown, a petty poltroon, a wretched specimen, a king of shreds and patches...'

He stopped, suddenly, in mid-sentence, as if stunned. I thought the fit was about to kill him, that he was on the point of dropping dead. I'd been trying to keep my hands clasped over my ears, to keep myself from hearing the terrible talk, the string of obscenities. Even though I knew it was his madness speaking through him, still I couldn't bear to listen to the things he was calling me, they made me feel so filthy, they were like daggers to the heart, and all the time he kept pulling my hands away from my head and forcing me to hear—until he let go of me and froze like that, staring across the empty room.

'Father.'

I followed his stare, saw empty air, and knew now for sure that he'd gone over the edge into full-blown lunacy.

'So you've come again. I know. I knew. I know why. My revenge is blunted. I lost the spur. I let time go by. I let myself be imprisoned by events, by circumstance. I did nothing. I failed you, father. I'm not worthy to be your son.'

I put my arms around him and held him as tight as I could.

'Oh, my poor son, my poor, poor son. There's nothing there, my love, nothing but vacancy. There's only ourselves.'

'No, don't you see? We're together again, mother—you, me, father, just like we always were, before.'

'I know, I know. You've missed him so much, haven't you? And now you've willed him here—in your mind.'

'He's here. He's in the room. And he's telling me not to forget, to find the edge again. And I've to look after you, mother. You see? He still loves you. In spite of everything. Can't you see it? Can't you see how sad he looks, how distressed he is for you? He loves you so much. Look. see.'

'I see. But I see nothing. There's nobody there.'

'Nothing? Nobody? Nobody at all?'

'Nothing at all. I only see what's there. An empty room. Except for us. But I see what's in your mind, I do.'

'But didn't you hear him? Didn't you hear what he said about you? How affectionate he was? Didn't you hear anything?'

'Only ourselves.'

'But look! Look now, before it's too late! He's going—he's still in his dressing-gown but he's going, he's stealing away… through the door… look, look there! He's gone! Gone. We'll never see him again.'

'Oh, my poor dear boy, what can I say to you? This is the invention of a disordered mind. This is not you, this is madness.'

He smiled. I still had my arms around him. He was still straddling me but lifted me up into a sitting position and stroked my cheek and kissed me.

'No, mother, I'm calm. Look at me. Listen to me and hear how calm I am. This is not madness. I can repeat everything that has happened. I remember it clearly. Don't deceive yourself into thinking it's my madness speaking, when what I'm speaking is the truth. I know you'd want to apply my madness as a salve to your guilty conscience. You're saying that it's not that you're guilty but that I'm mad. But that sort of salve really would be only superficial, it wouldn't heal you—outwardly perhaps, but deep inside the infection would still be there.'

'Infection?'

'Moral infection. Sickness of the spirit. Confess it. Repent what's past, avoid whatever lies ahead, and never spread the compost on the weeds, which will only make them worse, and this lovely little garden of yours, mother—I mean your body—will go to seed. We don't want that to happen, do we? You can't use the ointment on your soul either. There's only one ointment you can apply there—extreme unction. Mother, you need absolution.'

Something broke in me.

'Oh, Hamlet, my son—my heart's cleft, you've cut it in two.'

'Have I? Then throw away the rotten half. And live a purer life with half a heart, with the good half. There's good in you yet. And you're still a beautiful woman.'

'What is it that you want me to do?'

'Easy. Say goodnight. But don't go to my uncle's bed. Assume that much goodness in yourself, even if you don't feel it, or have it. Habit is a deadening and corrupting thing, as you must know, but you can try to use it for the good.'

'What do you mean?'

'It's simple. Refrain from sex with him tonight, and that will make the next abstinence a little easier, the next still.'

'You should have been a priest, my son.'

'This is logic, not religion. By habitual determination you can almost change your character, re-mould the stamp of nature, your inborn disposition. Forgive the philosophy lecture. As for the Lord Chamber-Pot here—'

'Oh, God!'

'I regret his death, but it seems that God has put the lash into my hand, and I must wield it where it's due. He had it coming to him. But don't worry, I'll dispose of him, and I'll justify his death. If not, I'll have to answer for my crime. Killing a man is a crime. Still, he wasn't a king, was he? And sometimes you have to be cruel to be kind. Did I say that before? In any case, goodnight.'

He made to go but turned back and looked long and hard at me, not speaking.

'What is it? What else? What more can I do?'

'I've told you what not to do. Don't let that bloated toad tempt you to bed. You know how it will be. He'll start pinching your cheek and giving you little love-bites, marking his territory like a dog pissing on you, yes, marking you out as his little whore, you know how it goes. Then it will be the filthy stinking kisses next, and the fat fingers paddling in your neck, and so on down to your nipples, to make them hard, and your heart soft and your privates moist, so that by the time he's on you, in you, he'll be asking his questions, ferreting away, trying to unravel you, to discover my secret, to weasel out the truth: am I really mad, or only crafty mad? And you know the answer. Look at me now. Am I mad? You'd be mad to say so. I'm as sane as you are. Only—don't tell him that, don't betray me, don't give me away.'

I told him I'd take his part, I'd be on his side though the next evening should fall so hard, it wouldn't matter, I'd build myself over again for him, I'd be a bridge over his troubled waters…

And that's when he came on me, all over me, fondling my breasts and kissing me like a lover, his tongue between my teeth. I didn't know what to do but he stopped as soon as he started, his mind elsewhere.

'Mother, they're sending me away. I'm being sent to England, remember?'

'Oh, God, I'd forgotten, but I do remember. It's decided.'

'It's decided. And there are sealed letters. And there are two companions.'

'Rosencrantz.'

'And Guildenstern. My two good friends, my old fellow students.'

'Don't trust them.'

'I'll trust them—as far as I can throw them. As far as I can throw two fanged adders out of my way. They're in charge. As guards. They're carrying the mandate. And they're carrying me too, all the way, sweeping me to God knows what. But don't worry, I know them, fork and knife, tits and testicles, they're diggers, they're miners, they're sappers, underground workers. But do you know what? I'll delve just one yard below their mines—and blow them at the moon! They're dead men. Not by me. They'll be brought down by their own devices, just you wait and see. Oh, I love it, mother, when two powers meet in one straight line, and the outcome will be an explosive one—for one of them at least.'

He reached down and pulled at Polonius by the neck.

'This gentleman was a plotter, and I have to take over from him. Dead as he is, he has the power now to send me packing. The dead hand, mother, the strength of the dead hand. Don't under-estimate it. I expect I'll be out of here tonight. Never mind, I'll lug him into the next room meanwhile, get him from under your feet. And yet—'

He paused for a moment, studying the corpse.

'It's weird, isn't it?'

'What is?'

'He's so still now—and yet he never could stay still.'

'He's dead.'

'I know. But he's so—so quiet, and so secretive now, so serious and subdued. Is that what death is? Is that what it does? And in life he never could stop his yapping, the silly old dog, he could never hold his tongue, just never knew when to shut up, the poor old fool. And now he's so... so grave. Yes, he's ready for it now, the grave. The grave's the place for him. So let's get him under way—for the long journey. Goodnight, mother. It's goodnight from me. And I'll say goodnight from him. Goodnight. Goodnight'

A Few Notes on The Above

First I should say that the above account is not given in Gertrude's precise words. I have dramatized them, as it were, to render them readable, and bring the force of them before you, but the gist is faithful to what she said. Second, it is clear to me from what she said, that she was entirely innocent of the original crime; she never was an accomplice, not in the remotest sense. Third, I should say that she never knew what I knew. I never revealed to her anything concerning the ghost, or what Hamlet had told me about the circumstances of the old king's death. At this point she still knew nothing. And fourth, she failed to see the ghost of her dead husband because the husband's ghost chose not to be seen by her, but to spare her. That is my interpretation of what took place, though later Hamlet was to speculate to me that she saw nothing of her husband because she was no longer worthy of seeing him. Vice was incapable of looking virtue in the face. And that was a harsh judgement.

One other thing. I was struck by something in her account—Hamlet's question at the moment he killed Polonius: 'Is it the king?' How could he have thought it was the king? He had just left the king, kneeling in prayer in his private chapel, when he had had the chance to kill him. Hard upon that he was in his mother's closet. The king could not possibly have been behind the arras at that point. I conclude that he acted without thinking, on the spur of the moment, and that had he had the opportunity to think, to pause for thought, he never would have acted. Thought and action in Hamlet were irreconcilable enemies.

PART FOUR

Hamlet on the Loose

The killing of Polonius was a turning point. From then on king and prince were openly at odds, and Claudius dropped all pretence of referring to Hamlet as his beloved son, or even as his son. He was now a murderer, and as such he was the offspring of his mother's womb, with a little help from the loins of his warlike real father. He'd committed a shocking crime. It had to be confronted.

'Gertrude, where is your son? What bloody state of mind was he in when he left you?'

The queen did her best to excuse him.

'Mad! Mad as the sea and wind! It was a storm, a brainstorm. He heard something stirring behind the arras and struck out without thinking. It was an instinctive reaction, a spur of the moment thing, unpremeditated. He didn't mean to—he wasn't in control, he wasn't in his right mind, and he might have thought his life was in danger, that he was under attack… and suddenly there it was, the poor old man was dead, killed instantly.'

'As I would have been! Had I been there! Do you realise that?'

'I realise he's a danger to himself.'

'To himself! He's a danger to all of us, including you. Who will be next? And how can I explain all this away? They'll say I should have taken a tougher line with him! Should have kept him on a leash at least, or chained up, like the mad young dog he is. But I held back, I was indulgent, I was tolerant, because he's your son. And now your mother's love is mincing this matter, making it seem light to him. But it's not. And not to me either. I let him run out of control to the jeopardy of all of us. My God! And where exactly is he now? What is he doing?'

'He's…he's with the body, somewhere, I don't know. He's full of remorse. He hates himself for what he's done, in spite of the extenuating circumstances.'

'Circumstances?'

'The arras, everything. He wasn't responsible for his own actions. Even so, he's distraught.'

So Gertrude lied. Hamlet was not distraught, he was far from distressed, quite the opposite, he was buoyed up, and unrepentant, and yet the queen did all she could to disguise this. It was the first indication to me of a gradual parting of the ways between king and queen. It was from that moment on that I suspect she ceased to share the Claudius bed. Hamlet had got through to her. She was now, if not a broken woman, an increasingly fragile one. Claudius on the other hand was the inveterate survivor. Rosencrantz and Guildenstern were ordered to accost Hamlet and fish out of him if they could what he'd done with the body of the Lord Chamberlain. And the fretful king, unconcerned by the human loss of his right-hand man, agonised instead over his own image and reputation. The plan now was to call a council meeting and discuss what could be done to protect his name. The murdered Polonius and the missing corpse were not his immediate concerns. These were passed on to Rosencrantz and Guildenstern, who tracked down the prince and proceeded to question him.

'My lord.'

'That's me.'

'My lord, can you tell us where we can find the dead body?'

'Dead body. Of what? Of the body politic? That's been dead for months.'

'We mean the dead body of the Lord Chamberlain. What have you done with it?'

'I've given it to its next of kin.'

'Do you mean Ophelia?'

'No. I've compounded it with dust. That's its next of kin. It's next of kin to all of us.'

'Yes, but where? We need to take it to the chapel. It's customary, you know.'

'I know. But if I tell you where the body is, I'd be giving myself away—to a mere sponge.'

'A sponge, my lord?'

'Well, two sponges.'

'Sponges. And how so?'

'Because, pair of sponges, you soak up everything you can get, from the king. But you know what? He'll squeeze you dry and throw you away—once you've served your purpose.'

'My lord, enough of this. You must tell us where the body is—and then go with us to the king.'

'Must!? Tell you? Go with you? On what compulsion?'

'Because. Because the body—'

'Is with the king. But the king is not with the body. Know what I mean? Of course you don't. You don't know anything, do you? Listen. Learn. Two bodies—and two kings. And one king yet to be a body. Which king is that, do you think? Could the king's days be numbered? Could it be the king of nothing? Will you bring me to this king of nothing? Or shall we have a game of hide-and-seek instead? Let's see, who's the fox? Is it the king? Is it me? Or is it old Polonius? If so, where's he hiding, the old mole? We're coming to get you! But no—first, I'm it! First you've got to find me! Give me till the count of ten. One, two, three…'

The Council Meeting: Claudius in the Chair, Osric Taking the Minutes

'My lords. I'm doing all I can to locate him and to bring him before us—he's on the loose—and to get from him if we can the whereabouts of the body, which it seems he's hidden somewhere in the building. I hope to God it's not the privy. I know some of you may feel I should have let him feel the full force of the law long before now. The problem is—as always—the proletariat, let's be blunt, the ignorant masses—you know how the commoners dote on him, God knows why, and we don't want to rock the boat with all that mutinous crew in it, they'll take his part and give us trouble, they'll blame us, not him. Meanwhile, by sending him away on official business—it will seem a matter of policy rather than panic. Do you agree?'

At this point the meeting was interrupted. Fork and knife brought in the prince, guarded by heavily armed soldiers, and he was duly interrogated before the court, His Majesty putting the questions.

'Now, Hamlet, where is Polonius?'

'At supper.'

'At supper. Really. Where?'

'Not where he eats, but where he is eaten.'

'Meaning?'

'Meaning the worms are already at him, tucking in. Not a royal feast—not yet. But a high-level one.'

'Highly distasteful, Hamlet! Show some respect!'

'But the worms *are* showing him respect. These aren't your average worms, you know, they're political worms, and an entire assembly of them too, paying special attention to him. They're crafty little bastards, of course, but each worm is like an emperor. Oh yes, let me assure you, he's well attended.

'This is nonsense, Hamlet—mad talk.'

'You think so? No, think again. We fatten up cows, and other creatures, so as to get a good eating, and fatten up ourselves. And we fatten up ourselves for what? For maggots. For worms to get even fatter on. They'll chew on anybody, on all of us. Take your fat king and your lean beggar, for example—no difference, really, different dishes, same meal.'

'You're far gone, Hamlet. Far gone.'

'I can go further than that. Listen. A dead king is eaten by a worm, right? A man catches a fish with that worm, and eats the fish that has just fed on the worm, right?'

'And what is that supposed to mean?'

Nothing much. Except to demonstrate how a king can go on a right royal journey—through the guts of a beggar.'

'Stop right there!'

'And so on, all the way through the beggar's bowels.'

'Enough!'

'And out at his arse. So: a beggar shits a king—and the king turns out to be nothing more than a turd. What do you make of that? Neat, eh? And quite revolutionary. A free lesson from death the leveller.'

'For the last time, where is Polonius?'

'For the last time—or what?'

'You'll find out or what! Where is he?'

'In heaven. Maybe. Send somebody to see—though, you're much more likely to find him in the other place, the hot place, in which case you'll find him there yourself soon enough. But tell you what—I'll give you a month, and if you've still not found him, you'll smell him…just as you go up the stairs out there, into the lobby. He always loved a lobby, didn't he? Or an arras? He was a great arraser. And a lobbyer.'

Claudius gave the order to two of the soldiers.

'Go quickly—go and look.'

Hamlet called after them.

'No hurry—he'll stay till you come.'

Claudius cleared his throat and spoke formally, raising the tone.

'Hamlet, I have to be open and direct with you in front of this court. You have committed a heinous offence, and I am deeply grieved for my Lord Chamberlain. I am also greatly concerned for you, my—my nephew, and for your own health and safety. So here it is: I am sending you off at once, out of the country. You'd best prepare yourself. The vessel is ready in a port nearby, the wind's in the sail, the crew's aboard, your attendants await you, everything's in order—and it's hell bent for England.'

'For England.'

'That's right.'

'Good.'

'You think so? That's good, then. It's for your own good, you know, if only you knew my good intentions for you.'

'Oh, I do. I know your intentions. I see them clearly.'

'How is that?'

'I see a cherub that sees them.'

'A cherub?'

'Oh, yes. One with powerful eyesight. But they're all gifted in that respect, you know.'

'No. I don't know.'

'Why are kings so ignorant these days? A cherub has abnormal eyes. It can see supernaturally far—right across the universe. And it's also an angel of insight, did you know that? What a cherub doesn't know isn't worth knowing.'

'Really. Well, I'm sure you know.'

'I know. And now I know that I've received orders—to sail for old England. So heave away, then. Goodbye, dearest mother.'

'Your loving uncle, Hamlet.'

'Not my father?'

'And your father, if you like.'

'I don't like. Let's call you mother. After all, father and mother is man and wife, and man and wife is one flesh, they say. And so, let's make it my mother's flesh, shall we? My mother.'

He turned to his guards.

'Let's go then, soldiers—for England.'

Claudius nodded. But before going out, Hamlet walked slowly round the seated circle of counsellors, the king's henchmen, the coins he kept in his pocket. He gave each one of them a long slow stare, before which they shrank visibly, some of them obviously terrified of an attack. It was as if Hamlet was saying: I know what I'm leaving behind me, I know you for what you are—a circle of sycophants, a ring of toads. Then he turned and walked out swiftly, under heavy guard. The king turned to Rosencrantz and Guildenstern.

'Follow them closely, don't let him out of your sight, stay on his heels, get him across the plain, and embark as fast as you can, no delay, take the tide. I want him out of the country this very night. Away! Everything's signed and sealed, as you know, all's taken care of. Quickly, I urge you, I order you! And you, my lords, you may go about your business. The meeting is concluded.'

Everyone left. And the king was left alone—except for Osric, who did not commit the king's last thoughts officially to paper, obviously, but who was now privy to them.

'For England, then, Your Majesty?'

'For England. And England, if you value my love, and its importance to you, and if you bear in mind the power I hold over you, and the consequences of non-compliance—do not disregard my solemn orders, in these letters that you are about to receive, calling for the immediate death of Hamlet. Do it, England, do it! For now he's like a fever raging in my blood. He's killing me—and you're the cure. My fate rests on this, on you. You're my only hope.'

Hamlet Meets the Fortinbras Army

I was on the road to port, under guard, when I saw troops on the march, along the shore, headed inland. A single soldier crossed our path, on horseback, a captain. He was with the army but clearly had another charge. Fork and knife urged my guards not to let me accost him, but I insisted on dismounting and speaking to him.

'Captain, may I ask you: whose troops are these?'

'Certainly, sir, we're a Norwegian force.'

'But what are you doing here, in Denmark? What's your objective?'

'To attack some part of Poland. We have your king's permission for safe passage through your country.'

'Who's the commander?'

'Fortinbras, sir, nephew to old Norway.'

'And the mission—you make it sound random—is not to attack all of Poland? Is it the mainland? Or just some frontier?'

'Ah, there you have it, sir. To tell you the truth it's a waste of time—and lives. We're targeting a tiny patch of territory. It's worthless, got nothing going for it, nothing. Me now? I wouldn't farm it for five ducats. Not for anything you paid me. And if it were sold, it wouldn't fetch a penny more, either for us or for the Polacks. As land goes, it's worth bugger-all.'

'Well then, surely the Poles will never defend it.'

'Oh yes, sir, it's already garrisoned. And when we get there, there's going to be one hell of a scrap, let me tell you. And all for nothing.'

'So all those lives, including yours, quite possibly, to be sacrificed—for what? For a straw, and without as much as a murmur from anyone. Dear God, this is the corruption of the times, isn't it, when we can't even give a good reason for a man's death? What is it, then? Is it insolence, swollen pride, too much wealth? Do we need war because we're bored with peace? Whatever it is, it's all covered up, hidden away, like a cancer. You can't see it, but it's eating you alive.'

'Well now, sir—'

'I know, captain, it's not your job to go into any of that, is it?'

'You're right, sir, I have other duties to attend to.'

'Good luck with these, then. And thank you, captain.'

'God speed, sir.'

'And you.'

'And now we must press on, my lord—to port!'

Fork and knife, still mounted, still champing at the bit. Even their horses were restive, reprimanding me for my delay.

'Why don't you two press on? Go on ahead of me. Or better still, why don't you eat each other?'

'My lord!'

'Yes, I hear you for fuck's sake. Go on ahead, just a little. I'm thinking.'

What I was thinking was how everything and everybody sang out against me, and from every angle—common players, common soldiers, all exposing my dereliction of duty, all branding me a failure. What kind of man am I, I asked myself? I eat, I sleep, I let time go slipping underneath my feet, and I do nothing. I'm rotting. It's an animal existence. I might as well get down on all fours and eat grass. My mind's gone mouldy. Is this what I was meant for? To neglect my better self, my rationality, and wallow in oblivion, like a beast that has no understanding, no sense of time or purpose? Is it cowardice—this endless dissection of the consequences? Thinking too much about the whole thing? Thinking instead of acting, is that what it's all about? Whatever it is, I can't understand it, I have motive, means and opportunity, at least I've had means and ample opportunity—the motive never goes away, knowing I should do it, and knowing I have the justification to do it, and still haven't done it! Why?

And now see what's happened. Along comes this great army, commanded by a young prince, a paragon of action, full of ambition, full of charge, taking the field like a god, and scorning the consequences, showing complete contempt for death, exposing himself to the unknown, to all the dangers of war—and for what? For an egg shell. For fuck-all. Now there's a man for you! All right, you may say, the land he's fighting for is nothing, it's a trifle, and fighting for trifles isn't a matter of greatness, it's sheer belligerence, it's uncalled for aggression. But if you fight even for a trifle when honour's at the stake, when it's a matter of principle, then the trifle is no trifle, it's what you have to fight for, no matter what the cost, even if it's your life. That's what this man is doing now, and all his soldiers follow him, without a question in their heads—for honour's sake. And look at me—my father murdered, my mother corrupted, defiled. I've suffered in my mind, I've lost my reason, lost my way, I hardly know myself, I've let a criminal get away, unpunished, while to my eternal shame I see twenty thousand men going blithely to their graves, like beds, and again for what? For a political whim, for a trick of fame and fate, fighting for a piece of land which is so small, the two opposing armies can't even do battle on it—there isn't the fucking room, for fuck's sake, and when it's over there won't even be land enough to dig the graves for the casualties—they'll have to find some other graveyard in which to bury the dead. God in heaven, what a quirk of fate! I was meant to meet this army! If only I could have met its leader! But he's given me the blood and balls I need. From now on I have only murder on my mind. At last I'm committed. I'm red-hot. My thoughts have turned to blood. King Claudius, is it? Well, uncle, what's it to be, extreme action or extreme unction? Whichever it is, I have to tell you, you're a dead king…

Ophelia's Insanity

Weeks passed. Hamlet was gone from court, bound for England. Polonius was under the ground, his eavesdropping ears deaf to the whisperings of worms, as Hamlet had said before he left, commenting on the incongruous reversal of fortunes: the Lord Chamberlain had fed on the worms of jaw-jaw, picking up from tittle-tattle. Now the worms were picking up from him, coming in at the ears, no invitation needed. Worms had become an increasing feature of Hamlet's conversation, I have to say, but he was taken away under guard before the hurried and clandestine burial, at which Ophelia was the only mourner—the only true mourner, her brother still being in France, and so far unaware even that his father was dead.

My most terrible memory of her is when they locked her into an iron farthingale, which was the first stage of the elaborate grieving procedure for her father. The farthingale was no more than a hooped petticoat of sorts, but in reality it was a kind of cage, like the iron bodice which they clamped to her bosom, almost as a form of medical restraint, as if she were already losing her mind. Then she held up both arms for her women, dutifully, as they decked her in black, black-veiled for the mourning, and her eyes glittered like fish-eyes behind the veil, like eyes that don't see, eyes that can't cry. Thus arrayed, she stepped out of her closet, walking awkwardly, disjointedly, like a clockwork doll, a doll without a heart, her hair piled high on her head like a tombstone, impeccably braided, brutally carved, from which the pinned black net fell down like a waterfall, silencing her grief. She was dressed not for obsequies but for madness.

It was after her father's funeral that Ophelia began to deteriorate, and her mind to give way. She roamed the corridors of Elsinore as Hamlet had done when performing his antics—it was almost as if she were following in his footsteps, only in her case it was for real. With the prince gone, her brother in Paris, and her father dead, the motherless girl was now totally alone, and her peregrinations through the castle rooms and corridors were no act. She appeared barefooted and half-clad, nightgowned in her madness, frail and exposed among heavy-booted soldiers. She kicked out angrily at wisps on the straw-strewn floors, squealing and beating at her head. Her hair hung loose and unkempt about her shoulders. Sometimes she held her breasts, one in each hand, lovingly, under the thin fabric, offering them to the empty air, as it were, and bursting into tears when the offer was ignored.

At other times she appeared on the castle battlements, not now barefooted, but in her dead father's boots, which were of course much too big for her, but which she had adopted, along with his greatcoat, also dwarfing her, drowning her, but in which she paced up and down for an hour at a time, marching from rampart to rampart, wall to wall, like an animal in a cage, and hitting out violently at anyone who came close or tried to help her. Not that she seemed to see them. Her eyes stared but never focussed, her face was far away, scanning the sea horizons. What she said when she spoke had no meaning. She rambled and stammered; her words were wandering and wild. She refused food, lashed out at anyone who brought it to her, overturned plates, threw them from her, smashed them to the floor. She ran from doctors, turning her back on them and retreating to the four corners, blotting her face and whole frame against walls, as if wanting to be soaked up, willing herself to dissolve and disappear. It was the saddest spectacle I have ever seen.

And during all this time the queen, when approached by servants and courtiers, refused to speak with her, or even to see her or come near her. Why, I wondered? Ordinarily, a sympathetic woman, tender and affectionate, Gertrude was obviously afraid of her in some sense. She seemed to feel guilty. It was as if Ophelia's sickness concurred with something in her own sick soul, something resulting from the scene in the closet, not so much the killing of Polonius, bad as that was, but the things Hamlet had said to her, forcing open her shuttered soul, shattering the happy gates of her oblivion, the moral coma in which she had been content to live. She was a woman who only ever wanted to be happy, and to see everyone happy around her. First Hamlet, and now Ophelia, had made that impossible. Happiness belonged to the past, and she was afraid of the future. She would never go the way of Ophelia—the stuff of madness wasn't in her—but I could see the once happy queen fading into a lonely lady who had lately lost her bright bearings and now had nowhere to go.

It was when I was urging Gertrude to do something to remedy the situation, that Ophelia suddenly burst into the room. She was carrying a lute.

'And where is our lovely queen?'

'Here I am, Ophelia.'

'Are you? Are you sure? I thought you were some stranger. How long have you been about this court?'

Too long, it seems. They say that life is short. But sometimes it seems long, too long…

Gertrude never said that, of course, but the look she gave Ophelia somehow implied the answer for which I have supplied the words, and Ophelia seemed to understand it.

'Never mind, sweet queen. If you travel far enough—in your mind, you know, far enough from Elsinore—you'll find your true-love again.'

'My true love?'

'If only you can tell him from the other.'

'My poor, dear girl. I don't understand you.'

'Don't you? Then let me sing it to you.'

She stared at the lute but made no attempt to play it. She sang sweetly enough, unaccompanied.

How should I your true-love know
From another one?
By his cockle hat and staff,
And his sandal shoon.

Gertrude reached out to her tenderly, meaning to stroke her tangled hair. Ophelia stepped back and put a finger to her lips.

'No, no, Your Majesty! Just listen!'

'But what is it, my love? What is it that you want us to hear?'

'He's not here, is he? In the Holy Land, perhaps? Or not far from Finisterre? Compostella? Walsingham? What do you think?'

She turned away from the queen. She was singing to herself.

He is dead and gone, lady,
He is dead and gone,
At his head a grass-green turf,
At his heels a stone.

Gertrude had tears in her eyes.
'How can we help you, my poor love?'
'By listening—to the floods and streams.'
'What floods, my love? What streams?'
'Our passions. The shallow ones—they murmur. But the deep are dumb. You need to listen very hard. Listen.'

True love is a durable fire,
In the mind ever burning,
Never sick, never old, never dead,
From itself never turning.

'But Ophelia—'
'Quiet there! If you don't listen, you won't hear.'
At that point Claudius came in. He made to approach the queen but Ophelia stepped in his way and held up her hand. The king stopped and she nodded and shrank to the floor, caressing it with one hand, and smiling quietly.

White his shroud as the mountain snow,
Larded all with sweet flowers,
Which bewept to the grave did not go,
With true-love showers.

Claudius had no notion of what to do or say.
'How are you, dear girl? How are you feeling today?'

'Oh, thank you, Your Majesty, very well, Your Majesty. But we must be careful of each other, you know. We must be kind. Fate is so sudden, isn't it? And can be so cruel. Look what happened to the baker's daughter, when Jesus wanted some bread. She wasn't kind. So may the Lord look after you. God, we know what we are, but we don't know what we may be, what may become of us. We are all so fragile. And there are so many unforeseens.'

The uncomfortable king nodded sympathetically and Ophelia burst out laughing. She stood up suddenly, picked up her lute, and attacked it with jarring chords and a harsh racket of sounds before throwing it away and dancing round the room, holding her breasts again, offering them again to the air, and singing lasciviously, leering and nodding and winking at everyone.

Tomorrow is Saint Valentine's Day,
All in the morning betime,
And I a maid at your window
To be your Valentine.

Then up he rose and donned his clothes,
And dupped the chamber door,
Let in the maid that out a maid
Never departed more.

Claudius never looked so helpless.

'Still distraught—on account of her father.'

Ophelia rounded on him, swept up close to his face.

'Oh, you think so, do you? You don't think it's him I'm thinking of, by any chance? It's got nothing to do with my father. He always said he was an old fool. He said he was a fishmonger. And I was never a maid at his window. If I had been, I'd have got him up all right, his little cock-robin, and standing too. I'd have made him stiff.'

'Oh, Ophelia!'

'I know, sweet queen, but there was no need.'

Gertrude made a gentle attempt to go along with her.

'Of course, my love, no need.'

'No need, that's what I said, no need for the door-knob. He could have had *me*! I'd have opened my chamber door for him—wide open!'

'Oh God, poor girl!'

'Why do you keep saying that? It's not what you should say. You know what you should say? What they all say, you know how it goes. The maid went in, he went into the maid, and when she went out again, she went out unmade. How do you like that—neat, don't you think? Only it never happened. I wanted it to happen. It never did. It never could. Sweet nothings between my legs. He never would act on it. Country matters—his head was full of them. But he never came into *my* cuntrie.'

The king's eyes were now beginning to dart about in his head, in that shifty way he had when he didn't feel in control. He made a signal to the two guards at the door. Ophelia saw it and giggled.

'Aha, so you would, would you?'

Before they could move she ran over to them holding out her breasts, enticing, appealing, mockingly theatrical.

'I'll give them another. I can sing like a siren, you know. And that will conclude my concert.'

Her hands slid slowly down her belly, fondling, fumbling, groping at the groin. She grinned at the guards, threw back her head, shook her hair into a tangle, laughed and sang.

By Jesus and by Charity,
Alack and fie for shame!
Young men will do it, if they come to it,
By Cock they are to blame.

'But bonny sweet robin's to blame if he rises to the occasion and fails to finish. And when pistol's cock is up, flashing fire must follow. It's a consummation devoutly to be wished. Who said that?'

'Guards!'

The two soldiers came on either side of her but she slipped away easily between them and curtseyed to the king.

'If you will be so kind as to let me finish. And then I promise you, I will be so amenable. And so open. Open little Ophelia. Always open and never filled. Unfulfilled Ophelia. Listen.'

Quoth she, before you tumbled me,
You promised me to wed.
And so I'd have done, by yonder sun,
If thou hadst not come to my bed.

She ran back up to the guards and grabbed each of them by the groin, one in each hand, and held them there. They were holding their pikes.

'You're well weaponed, lads, but you can't use them—not enough hands, eh?'

The guards looked imploringly at the king. Gertrude came up and whispered something in his ear. Ophelia released them and spread her arms wide.

'Would you care to tumble me, lads? Three to a bed? And a husband each side of me? All three ready to do the deed—and six galloping legs to get us there!'

Claudius motioned to the soldiers and they retreated to the door. All the Ophelia passion suddenly seemed spent.

'It's a lonely bed to lie on, friends. I hope everything will work out well. We must be patient. But I can't hold back the tears, you see, when I remember how they put him to bed, when I think how they laid him in the cold ground. My brother will hear of it, be advised, be prepared. Meanwhile I thank you for your time, and for your good advice. I know it was all well meant, and straight from the heart. But come away now, let's be off, where's my coach? Bring on my coach. Ah, here it comes! Good night, then, good night, ladies, good night, sweet ladies, good night, good night.'

Claudius signalled to the attendants who had come in with her, and they followed at her bare heels. Gertrude looked at her second husband as if from a great distance.

'It's all understandable, my dear. It's the poison of her deep grief.'

Poison. It was the first time I'd heard him use the actual word and it struck me as grimly fitting. It seemed to suit him—poison and death and deep grief. Oddly enough it threw him off his usual diplomatic stride and launched him into a lament, almost a Jeremiad, on the state of Denmark, now under general attack, not from foreign powers but from internal enemies: Polonius murdered by the prince; the prince, Hamlet—*your* son—turned violent and unhinged, and removed from the scene; the people muddied in their thoughts, whispering among themselves about the shadowy circumstances surrounding the murder and the secrecy and haste in which the funeral had been wrapped up, a funeral held without due ceremony—a decision which reflected badly on the sovereign; Ophelia gone mad; and her brother, already informed—or misinformed—secretly arrived from France, no-one knew exactly where in Denmark, eaten up by suspicions and doubt, and keeping himself inscrutable and aloof—though not from the many Claudius-hating rumour-mongers.

'All eager to infect his ear with their poisonous whispers.'

It was the second reference to poison, this time with the ironical image of the ear. How much longer, I wondered, until Claudius gave himself away under the inwardly gnawing effects of guilt? Was it a kind of blind admission, an indirect unconscious confession? He'd already confessed to God, but God's ear was not susceptible to the poison of pretended repentance. Even now, Claudius admitted, he felt like he was facing a military murdering-piece, scattering its hot shot at random, and killing him over and over. He was suffering superfluous death.

This last comment was almost prophetic. There was a sudden thundering of boots from the other rooms and the sound of doors being smashed open and battered down, the boots coming closer, sounding louder and more murderous. Claudius yelled at the guards.

'Where are my Switzers? Have them defend the door!'

An attendant came running in.

'It's too late, Your Majesty!'

'What's too late?'

'They're here, Your Majesty! They're here!'

'Who is? Speak, man!'

'The rebels, Your Majesty! They've stormed the castle! We're taken! The guards are overpowered! Save yourself, if you can!'

'Save myself? I am the King of Denmark! Who's the leader of these so-called rebels?'

'Laertes, my lord—the rabble are calling him king!'

'King! This is treason! Arrest them!'

Even as Claudius issued his order, the doors were broken down and the murderous mob burst in, headed by Laertes, with drawn sword.

'Where is he? Where is this king?'

The mob massed at his back, shrieking and swearing and bellowing threats. Testicles would be sliced off, and ears and noses. And only then heads…

'Kill the royal fucker! Slit his fat neck! Let's do it—now!'

Claudius, so feeble when faced with Ophelia, here showed remarkable composure and restraint.

'Laertes, can we talk—without this mob? Talk sensibly? How can I answer you like this?'

Laertes turned to his followers. They grumbled and swore but agreed to wait outside.

'I'll call you if you're needed. Give me some time with him. And guard the door. Nobody leaves without my permission.'

The broken door was closed on the muttering mob.

'And now, you vile bastard, give me my father!'

'Calmly, Laertes.'

'Calmly? Calm's a bastard! This sword's a true son!'

He advanced on Claudius. Gertrude threw herself between them and physically tackled Laertes. In spite of everything her instinct was still to cling to the king. The king was, as always, the diplomat.

'Let him go, Gertrude. And let me ask you, Laertes, what is the nature of your grievance?'

'Where is my father?'

'Dead.'

'Dead,' repeated Gertrude, 'but not by my husband's hand.'

'Then by whose? Tell me straight out, and none of your trickery, your diplomatic talk. Don't think I don't know you. And don't tell me about loyalty either, or obedience. To hell with that! My loyalty is to my father. Nothing else matters. I don't care what happens to me in this life, or in the next. I'm going to be revenged for my father, to the death—mine, or his murderer's, or both. My mind's made up.'

Claudius nodded, raised both palms.

'Then don't change it. I wouldn't want you to. But are you so blindly bent on revenge, justified as it may be, that you'll make no distinction between your friends and your enemies? And you have enemies, Laertes. Your father was dear to me. I grieve for him, deeply. I'm innocent of his death and I'll join with you in your revenge. Together we'll make the guilty party pay... wait! What's going on out there? They've agreed to let us talk.'

There was a sudden noise from the other side of the door, and shouting.

'Let her pass!'

'Let her go through!'

The doors were flung open—and in came Ophelia, obviously insane, barefooted and wearing only a flimsy shift. Laertes needed no doctor to offer a diagnosis. She didn't have to say a word. He looked at his sister, and broke down on the spot.

'Oh, my lovely sister! Oh, my dear girl! Oh, rose of May! When did this happen? When did she lose her mind? Who stole it from her? She's followed our father to the grave. She's buried with him. She might as well be. I can see she's gone.'

'She's gone.'

Ophelia caught at his last words, and echoed them.

'Yes, she's gone. She's the gone girl of Elsinore. She's gone after him. He's gone before. He's gone down, he's fallen low, so low. The wheel goes down, you know, it does for all of us. Listen!'

They bore him barefaced on the bier,
And in his grave rained many a tear.

'Do you hear that? Do you hear it? It's an old one, old and plain. The spinsters and the knitters in the sun, and all those innocent virgins, who weave their threads with bones—they used to sing that one. Do you know it?'

Gertrude shook her head.

'She's rambling, dear boy. She's been like this for some time—since your father died. She's beyond the reach of sense. She's, she's—'

'Gone.'

It was Ophelia who finished Gertrude's sentence, and repeated it.

'Gone. Yes, I'm gone. But look, I'm still bearing gifts.'

She reached into her nightgown and brought out a bunch of blossoms. The handful, it turned out, had been carefully selected, it was no random gathering, some secret sense had directed her, and she proceeded to distribute these to everyone in the room with an astonishing accuracy of symbolism which even some of the recipients would not have understood, and completely belying her disordered mind. She came first to her brother.

'Pansies, perhaps, no, wait—there's rosemary for you. I'd have given it to you at my wedding, but now it's a funeral. But still it's the same—it's for remembrance. We must remember them in their beds. We must always remember them there, whichever they may be, and whoever they may be. His is clay-cold, but do remember him, warmly. Does my lover remember me, do you think…? Well, no need to answer for him. Let's wait and see.'

Claudius was the next nervous recipient.

'There's fennel for you—and columbines. They say the serpent fed on fennel—his favourite food. So they say.'

Claudius kept a straight face, whether or not he knew that fennel was symbolic of flattery and deceit. Ophelia surely did, I thought so from her reference, scarcely veiled, to the dissembling serpent, and I have often wondered how much she knew, or suspected, though she can scarcely have known the real identity of the serpent that stung old King Hamlet in his orchard. Or did she see things in her madness that would have been impervious to reason?

'And be careful with the columbines. It's not their scent, it's their shape that gives you away. So you must be wary of them in wedlock—horns, you know? Be faithful if you can. Are *you* faithful? *Are* you…?'

She had turned now to the queen.

'Well, if you can't be faithful, at least you can be repentant—so here's some rue for you. It's for contrition. You can call it herb of grace on Sundays. Oh, is it a Sunday today? It doesn't matter. Be contrite if you can.'

Gertrude, unlike Claudius, was unable to wear a face mask. The tears sprang to her eyes. Ophelia wiped them away, stroked the queen's cheek gently, brushed the falling drops.

'That's all right, dear queen. Rue's for sorrow too, sorrowful remembrance. Do you have sad memories? Any? None? I have so many, I must keep some rue for myself, if you don't mind, but you need to wear yours differently, not like mine. I've nothing to repent of, you see, nothing really, nothing that I can remember.'

She swung round again to her brother.

'Did I give you pansies? For love-thoughts? *Penseés, penseés*... oh, but I have my own thoughts, so I'll keep some pansies too, all for myself, to remind myself of my troubles. Ah, now here's a daisy, the dissembling daisy—but there's only one, and it can't be shared. I heard of wenches who wore them in their bosoms, to warn themselves against all those promises that amorous bachelors make—before they disappear. As they do. Men were deceivers ever, eh? So I'll drop this daisy between my two breasts. Look—he'll never find it there. But I'll remember it, and it will remind me of the springtime, and the green cornfields, and the acres of the rye, and lie... lie...lying.'

She had given away all her flowers and her hands were empty. She fell quiet, and in the silence nobody moved or spoke. Then she caught my eye and came over to where I was standing apart, close to the cold chimney. She bent down to the hearth and picked out some half-burnt twigs from among the ashes.

'Dear Horatio, I'd have liked to give you some violets, for your faithfulness, but they've gone, they all withered, every single one, when my father died. They say he made a good end. Take these instead. They'll never dwindle.'

I took the burnt twigs from her as if I were accepting a bouquet of the choicest blooms, and she smiled.

'You see, Horatio? They'll never wither. You're too good to let that happen. And now I must leave you.'

She turned from me, turned her back on all of us, as if she had forgotten we were ever there, and walked out slowly, singing her last song.

And will he not come again?
And will he not come again?
No, no, he is dead,
Go to thy death-bed,
He never will come again.

His beard was white as snow,
All flaxen was his poll,
He is gone, he is gone,
And we cast away moan,
God have mercy on his soul.

'And to all Christian souls may God grant mercy, for we are all frail.'

She turned again to face us for one last time, though without seeing us.

'But see that you think none more frail than yourself. And so God be with you.'

As she left, one of the troopers reached out and placed his cape touchingly, tenderly, over her shoulders, cloaking her nakedness, her vulnerability. Laertes stood and sobbed, shaking uncontrollably, his head in his hands. Claudius placed a hand on his shoulder.

'Laertes, I share your grief. This is what I want you to do. Choose anyone you like, however many, and let them judge me on the matter of your father's death. If I am found to be in any degree guilty, or even involved in this, take my crown, take my kingdom, take my life. Otherwise my pledge is to see to it that you are given satisfaction.'

Laertes remained aloof.

'Very well. But here's a lot of explaining to be done: how exactly he died, the hushed-up funeral, the hurried burial, the absence of ceremony—Christ Almighty, there were rumours reached me that when they came to close the coffin at the graveside, even the very coffin nails couldn't be found. What in God's name was going on?'

'It's true, Laertes. They were itemised by the undertakers as missing. All a mystery, I assure you.'

'And all crying out to be questioned. I deserve answers—and I demand them.'

'And you shall have them. And the axe will fall on the guilty party, no matter whose neck is for the chop, even if it's mine. You have my word.'

They went out together, the queen separately. I was left holding the twigs which Ophelia had given me—violets of the mind, which in my own mind would never wither. It struck me that she had left the room without attendants. Claudius had given no order, and her brother had been wholly taken up with his demand for answers, and the king's promise of immediate explanation, and requital. I was about to follow Ophelia myself, but was distracted by the unexpected arrival of a gentleman of the court, with attendants. He was eager to speak to me. In that single second Ophelia was gone—not forgotten, but momentarily overlooked, and, as it turned out, badly, sadly, neglected.

A Sea-Breeze

The gentleman of the court was dubious.

'They're a rough-looking lot, sir, seafaring types—and they stink something awful.'

'And you say they want to speak with me?'

'Urgently, they say. They have letters for you, apparently. I said I'd see that they were delivered to you but they insisted on seeing you in person. Shall I let them through?'

'Bring them in.'

'Very well, sir. Hold your nose.'

There was a handful of them, and more than a whiffy fistful of sea-air. But they were courteous enough.

'God bless you, sir.'

'And you. What can I do for you?'

'We have letters for you, sir, if your name is Horatio?'

'It is. And what is the name of the writer?'

'Writer, sir?'

'Of the letters. From whom have you brought them?'

'Ah, yes, they're from the ambassador.'

'Ambassador? I don't—what ambassador?'

'The Danish ambassador, of course, sir—him that was bound to England.'

'You mean the prince?'

The sailors exchanged smiles, and their spokesman nodded.

'That's him, sir.'

He handed me a small package.

'He gave these—this—to you personally?'

'Oh, yes, sir, that's to say he handed us the letters. We wrapped them up.'

The wrapping was a tarry rag, tied with twine. The package too carried quite a whiff.

'Do you know where he is now?'

'We most certainly do, sir.'

'Can you bring me to him?'

'We most certainly can, sir.'

'Then let's do it. First a little refreshment, perhaps?'

'That would be very kind, sir.'

'Not at all. It will give me time to examine the package, and then we'll be on our way, as fast as we can. Is it far? Where is he exactly?'

More shared smiles, knowing but not shifty.

'We're not at liberty to say, sir.'

'Of course not. Then I'm in your hands.'

A Letter From Hamlet

Horatio, when you have read this over, let the bearers have access to the king. They have letters for him too—something to boggle his brains. We'd only been two days at sea when a heavily-gunned pirate vessel pursued us with hostile intent. We couldn't shake them off, and so we opted for a fight, in which we held our own, and they were unable to overcome us. That's when I made my decision. During the grapple, when the two ships were locked fast together, I managed to board them. At that moment they swung clear of us and so I became their only prisoner—or fellow mariner. They are sea-rats, ruffians, but also opportunists, as these free-booters are. They treated me well when they knew who I was and what I could do for them. They are bringing me home—I will not say to which port exactly, or add subsequent details, in case this falls into the wrong hands, but they will bring you to me, trust them. Let the king have the letters and join me as soon as possible, not sparing the horses. I have things to tell you that will strike you dumb, and even then it will not be easy to convey the essence of the issue in mere words. You won't believe the villainy. Rosencrantz and Guildenstern are on course for England, and there's a strong wind at their backs. Of that pair I have much to report. I can hardly wait to tell you.

Your friend,
Hamlet.

The Poison Plot

In spite of his aggressive assault on Elsinore and his direct defiance of the king, in the event Laertes waived his right to call Claudius to a public account, and contented himself with a private conference—just the two of them with their heads together. Or so he thought. Claudius never left anything to chance, and had appointed a well-weaponed Osric to be concealed within the ear of their talk, so that if Laertes, who had already acted dangerously, had suddenly turned ugly and taken advantage of the secrecy to revenge himself, Osric would have sprung a surprise of his own and come to the king's defence. Ironically, Osric's effeminacy was entirely misleading in one key matter: he was no dunce with the sword and had played many a bout to the detriment of his opponents. The following account of what was said between Claudius and Laertes is essentially, therefore, Osric's, obtained under questioning after these events were over, and those involved no longer able to speak for themselves.

At the start Claudius insisted on his innocence, making the point that the man who killed Laertes' father had also acted against him, and with intent to kill. That was a lie of sorts. Hamlet had certainly harboured murderous intentions—in his mind, but he had never acted on them as Claudius implied. Not knowing the truth of this, Laertes asked the next obvious question.

'Why didn't you take steps to stop him, considering that it was clearly in your own interest to do so?'

'Ah, there you have me,' sighed Claudius. 'I ought to have done, of course, and would have done, but for two special reasons.'

'Which were?'

'Which were—and still are. One is that the queen, his mother, dotes on him, and as I am absolutely devoted to her, I want to avoid upsetting her, it's as simple as that. Sad, I know, but true.'

'And the second?'

'And the second reason is an even stronger one. He's the darling of the masses—they dote on him. They think he's one of them. He has this way with common folk, as you know, he can talk to them on their level, and they like that, and think he can do no wrong, so if I'd proceeded against him as I should have done, it would have stirred them up, caused unrest. You know the rabble—always agitating, always against authority, and things have not been good in this respect, not recently. Letting him go unchecked, it was to a large extent a political decision.'

Laertes was not exactly impressed. Osric said that as he stood listening, he kept his hand on the hilt of his sword, ready for intervention. It did not prove necessary. Instead of reacting, Laertes sank back instead into apathy and self-pity.

'So. I've lost my father. And now it seems I've lost my sister too, as she's lost her mind. And she was... she was such a sweetheart, such a lovely girl.'

'She was. And your father was a loyal servant and a great friend. But your time will come, Laertes, don't lose a moment's sleep over it, you'll have your revenge. I'll see to it.'

The conversation was suddenly interrupted. A messenger arrived with letters for both king and queen. They were from Hamlet. Claudius must have been badly shaken. His plans for Hamlet had mis-fired. But he gave nothing away, and unsealed the letter addressed to himself, reading it aloud, so as to bring Laertes all the more into his confidence. He was about to be drawn into the world of plotting and poison.

The Hamlet letter still survives.

High and mighty, you shall know I am set naked on your kingdom. Tomorrow I shall be begging leave to look into your royal eyes, when I shall also, with your kind permission, report to you on the occasion of my sudden and strange return.

Claudius was puzzled and apprehensive.

'What does it mean? He was bound for England. Rosencrantz and Guildenstern were his attendants. He was under guard. And on board ship. And yet he's returned. Have all the others come back too? What's happened to the ship? Was the voyage aborted? Or is it some kind of trick?'

Laertes glanced at the letter.

'I've seen some of the letters he wrote to my sister. But I'm not sure. Do you recognise the style?'

'It's Hamlet's hand all right. But what does he mean by 'naked'?'

'Fuck knows! And fuck cares!'

Laertes stood up, kicked his chair aside, and paced up and down the room. Osric slowly began to unsheathe his sword.

'Just let him come! I'm sick in my guts until I can look into his eyes and pay him back for what he did.'

'I'm with you there.'

Claudius righted the chair and persuaded Laertes to sit down again. Osric slid the sword back into its scabbard.

'But how best to get your revenge? There are ways and means. It has to be worked out so as not to look suspicious. And right now I'm thinking of a plan of attack.'

'That's fine by me. So long as I'm the attacker.'

'It's exactly what I have in mind. And it will play out so that not only will he perish, but even his own mother won't suspect foul play, and will think his death accidental.'

'I'm beginning to like the sound of it. What's the plan?'

The plan was pure Claudius, right down to the last drop of poison. Word had come back from France that during his time there, Laertes had won a golden reputation for himself as a swordsman. This had nettled Hamlet, who was no mean swordsman himself and prided himself on his proficiency, and he had been envious enough at the time to ask that Laertes be brought back to Denmark purely for the purpose of playing a few friendly bouts.

'And now here you are, Laertes. He has his wish.'

'But why did it matter to him so much?'

'Vanity, Laertes. Vanity, vanity. Don't underestimate it, even in intelligent men who ought to be above the influence of envy.'

'And so—what does this lead to?'

It led to the fencing plot. If the letter was genuine, if it wasn't some trick, and Hamlet did return from the aborted voyage, he would hear nothing else but exaggerated reports of Laertes' expertise with the rapier.

'I'll make sure it's the number one story at court. Laertes, you'll be on everyone's lips, you and your rapier.'

And if out of envy, Hamlet were to rise to the bait, then a challenge would be arranged, one with an appropriate wager.

'He's honest and trusting by nature, Laertes. At least he used to be. And with luck that's where we'll get him.'

'I still don't understand.'

'He'll not examine the foils, don't you see?'

'What of it?'

'Before the match. He'll just assume that they'll be blunted, especially as it's a friendly set of bouts. Do you see what I mean?'

'Not exactly.'

'Laertes, you don't see it because it's so simple. Of course the foils will be blunted… all except one. That one will be lethal. And that's the one you'll choose when they're presented.'

'But what if he sees it, or chooses it first, by chance?'

'He won't. He won't even look, believe me. But don't worry, I don't leave things like that to chance. I'll have a special presenter—I have one in mind—in charge of the foils, so that with a little shuffling you'll have a deadly weapon in your hand and you can hit him seriously and make it look like it happened by an unfortunate accident, in a friendly exchange. Unfortunate but fatal. All because a stray sharp got into the pack. How do you like it?'

'I like it. And to make doubly sure, I have another idea. When I was in Paris I bought a potion from one of those quack doctors, a street-seller on the banks of the Seine, a charlatan, you know the type I mean.'

'I know. What sort of potion exactly?'

'A poison.'

'A poison. Ah! But how powerful?'

'Deadly. Dip a knife in it, and whoever it draws blood from, the merest nick, he's done for. This quack told me that certain medicines made from herbs culled by moonlight can save a man from death, such is their power—but not from this particular venom. This is mortal.'

'And so?'

'And so I'll touch the point of my foil with this contagious stuff—I can do that easily enough on the quiet—and I won't even need to give him a deep wound. One scratch and he's a dead man.'

Poison. Claudius warmed to the very thought of it. Poison was his thing—invisible, untraceable, effective, unfailing.

'Excellent! Excellent, Laertes, and we'll have the fatal foil anointed before they're brought in. My presenter—Osric, by the way—will see to that. But let's think a little more along these lines, even further. Supposing, just supposing something went wrong, and that our scheme was somehow spoiled, we should have a back-up plan, a fail-safe. Let's see, let's see… we'll lay bets on your respective skills, and prospects…Yes, I've got it! I can add one to your double, and make treble sure. You'll both be hot and sweating, and thirsty too—don't hold back, press him as hard and fast as you can to that end, so that he calls out for a drink. And I'll have one waiting for him—a poisoned chalice, so that if by any chance he escapes your deadly thrust, the drink will see to it, and finish him off. What do you think?'

'I think we have a plan!'

Ophelia's Muddy Melodious Death — And Dreams

There was a woodland stream on the landward side of Elsinore, just beyond old King Hamlet's orchard. It flowed very quietly among the trees, still waters, not deep. But deep enough. That's where she was found, half-floating but drowned, close to a willow-tree, the whitish undersides of its leaves mirrored in the glassy stillness of the water. There was a sad symbolism there, the willow being considered an emblem of regret and wretchedness, particularly pertaining to the sorrows of forsaken love, and from that sad tree those who have lost their loves sometimes make mourning garlands, which they wear, or hang up like mournful trophies.

She'd gathered garlands of flowers for herself before coming there: crow-flowers, daisies, and even nettles, noxious generators of pain and poison, to the delicate, slender and tender-handed, as she was. And those long phallic purples—orchids with the roots resembling testicles, which lent them a coarser name on the rough tongues of peasants. In their vulgar parlance they were known as pricks, crimson cocks, knobs with balls, and so on, whereas our chaste maids and unplumbed virgins, untouched by country grossness, chose not to go there, referring to them instead as dead men's fingers—macabre but modest, sexuality succumbing to death. That's where Ophelia chose to end it all, if choose she did. Could it have been a cry for help? Or did a branch give way? Or maybe she tumbled, hung with her trophies, her armfuls of wild-flowers, and fell in the weeping water. But it was her failure to struggle against her fate which later led to the verdict of 'doubtful', determining her death.

You will ask me—you cannot do anything other than ask me—how do I know all this? And if it was not for me to know, in particular, how did anyone know it? With all this pathetic and pathological exactitude surrounding her death, not to mention the floral element and herbal evidence, the attention to detail—where did it come from? how was it recorded? And the next obvious question: why did the recorder remain passive? Why did no one help her? Why did no one try to prevent her death? Why, quite simply, did nobody pull her out?

A shepherd's boy, it seems, was the only eyewitness, so they said, too terrified to intervene, or afterwards to say too much about the lewd lyrics she sang concerning cock-robins and cock-a-doodle-doos, and how she stroked the long purples and moaned of country matters and sweet nothings—the details had to be coaxed out of him—before the waters gathered round to cover her and put her to her bed. But she didn't drown at once, her dress spread wide for a while, filled with ripples, and floated her along slowly downstream, like a Naiad or a water-nymph, clinging to her natural element. Only it wasn't natural, and it wasn't long until her garments, heavy with their drink, pulled the poor wretch from her melodious lament to muddy death. She sank to her watery end, showing, it seemed, a complete unawareness of her physical surroundings, a situation with which the crazed mind is only too consistent and in which may be heard a voice from those deepest levels of the emotional being which sanity keeps secret. Elsinore's gone girl had gone before. The lost girl was now lost for always. Nothing could bring her back from the grave. It would be from water to earth. She was now the property of the gravedigger.

But she was not given over entirely into the hands of the gravedigger, she came into my hands too, or rather into my head. Soon after her death, she invaded my sleep, and still does. In my life, I must confess, I have not been much disturbed by dreams. Hamlet always maintained it was because I lacked imagination. It was not meant unkindly—he often said he'd much prefer a clear clean head like mine, free from consciousness, from too much rumination, and it's true, I'm too much of a pedant for the poetry of sleep, and the monsters of the deep unconscious mind. But every other night for a long time now I have seen her drowning, gathering flowers, I've heard her singing, speaking her thoughts, or expressing them through her eyes, her eyes that were so expressive. This, I admit, is outwith my remit, but as I draw closer to the conclusion of my narrative, I want to say something about these dreams.

Once I saw her rising from her grave and moving slowly upstage as it were, upstage to oblivion, as if in a play, as if we were actors, as Hamlet and I ran down excitedly past her on either side, to launch into the enthralling account of his sea-voyage. It was stirring stuff, and yet in that inspiring account Ophelia was quite forgotten. And the truth is that by that time, as indeed thereafter, Hamlet really had forgotten her. Not one mention, not a reference, not a single question. It was a muteness that struck me hard at the time and even astonished me, as you will surely understand. He'd been far from Elsinore, far off on the sea, he'd had adventures, encounters, and had returned.

Very well. But let me ask you, had it been you, what would your first thoughts have been on your return? Or if not your first, how soon until you'd asked: how was she, the girl you'd loved, supposedly, the girl whose father you had killed? She'd lost her mind and he never even knew. And I didn't tell him, I waited, waited for him to ask. And waited… Nothing. Silence. Ophelia was emotional history. For him she not only no longer existed, she need never have existed. And had it not been for that sojourn in the graveyard, the funeral procession, and the sudden shock of her burial—who knows? Up until then it was Hamlet who was the property of the gravedigger, so seduced was he by his songs. *In youth when I did love, did love…* It was a song filled with sentiments appropriate to age, but the awful irony was that the rough-tongued singer was standing in the grave of youth. And of lost love.

Over and over I dreamed of her drifting, drowned, downstream, garlanded with that sad willow, and with all the other blossoms—buttercups and daisies and dusty nettles, and ragged robins and those long purples, which she'd selected for her wreaths, dressing herself for death. And all the weeds and worts which she'd gathered in her madness and distributed to the court—she reappeared with them, walking amidst the whirl of dreams that infested my head, bending over me and murmuring into my pillow, whispering her herbal secrets: rosemary for remembrance, to strengthen the memory of the dead, but also for a memento between lovers, lest either of them forget; and pansies too for thoughts of the dead, love-in-idleness, heartsease for young girls; rue for the Queen again and fennel for the King, fennel for flatterers and columbines. But in one of the dreams she snatched back the rue she'd given to Gertrude, saying that Her Majesty had a dead and unmourned lover, and thrust the herb instead on the King, insisting he mourn for his soul, and telling him that the rue of regret included not only sorrow but repentance, and that goat's-rue had the property of abating carnal lust. As for the violets that had withered since her father died, they too seemed to be recalling a lost love, echoed by her song, which flowed through my restless head.

> *How should I your true love know*
> *From another one?*

I thought the song expressed her longing for the absent Hamlet, but in the dream she took me by the shoulders, turned me round and pointed me again to the Queen, saying that she was the one who had failed to distinguish her true love from another one, and had left off lamenting him with the true-love showers she should have wept… *like Niobe.* I heard Hamlet's voice coming in, but there was no Hamlet, and now she was singing the song of a woman who was searching for her departed lover and despaired of his return, until she switched suddenly to the funeral elegy again. *He is dead and gone, lady,* as if to give the lovers' separation the anguish of finality together with some strain of accusation—of failure and unfaithfulness in love.

Fleeting confusion? Yes, the stuff of dreams. I make no attempt to put these chaotic scenes in any sort of order. They are at best impressions, episodes extracted from the whirlwind from which I surfaced with beating brains and thumping heart, and my head still thick with her dream-talk and with sleep; and unless she were to return from the dead and speak clearly, these befuddled phrases of mine which I have committed to paper must stand out as her last words, spoken from beyond the grave and heard only in my head. Even now I can't shake her from my sleep.

Or erase the images—which of late have become even more outlandish and surreal. I saw her in that terrible iron farthingale again, this time like a love-bird in a cage, holding up her arms like wings, which turned suddenly, quickly into the wings of angels, as if she might float free of her confinement, like a spirit. But she remained trapped—the flapping wings became those of a bird of prey, and it was as a screaming eagle that she tore the cage to tatters, and with talons extended escaped, and came swooping back down on all of us.

At other times it was the booted Ophelia, booted and great-coated and guarding the ramparts, marching up and down wordlessly, as if obsessed, her hair floating wide, her flashing eyes, staring across the battlements, out to sea, scanning the skylines for his return…

And once, when she was dispensing the herbs and flowers all over again in her last mad appearance to the court, Hamlet suddenly showed up. There he was, back from the sea, and he was holding out a hand to her, expecting to be allotted his chosen bloom. But she smiled at him coquettishly.

'Ah yes, you too, sweet prince, take these, these are for you.'

And she reached down into her nightgown, deep between her breasts, winking all the while, and brought out… a fistful of six-inch nails.

Everybody gasped. They were the missing coffin-nails, the disappearance of which had been itemised by the undertakers, prior to her father's internment.

'You see, my prince? I've left the best for you. I've kept them specially. They're the finest funeral flowers, you know, they'll never wither, not like love. But I can give you a withering, my love, now that I'm free. You were always the man for speeches, weren't you? Would you care for a withering speech, my dearest? It doesn't much matter what you care for, you're going to get it anyway. Listen, here it comes.'

Doubt thou the stars are fire,
Doubt that the sun doth move,
Doubt truth to be a liar—
But never doubt I love.

'Recognise the words? You see, I can read now. At one time lips were all I could read—the whispering lips of my ladies of the court.

Now I can read minds. And letters. And verses. They're not particularly eloquent as verses go, quite conventional wouldn't you say, coming from such a profound lover? And rather disappointing actually. But they're your words all right—and not just because you've signed your name at the end of the letter. No, it's not that—there's another signature there, apart from your name. The poem—it has your name written all over it, don't you see, don't you get it? In every single line of it, listen, what do you hear? *Doubt, doubt, doubt, doubt.* So you were telling me not to doubt you. But you know how it is—the more you tell someone not to doubt, the more you sow doubt in that person's mind. And in your own mind. That's where the doubt exists, and it's your own doubt which makes you keep on repeating the word. Let's face it, doubt is your middle name, sweet prince, it's the Hamlet characteristic. You were a doubtful lover, you were always acting out the part of the lover, weren't you, never really and truly in love, and your doubtful poem has enough double meanings to be ultimately enigmatic, don't you agree…?

In all this time—such was the dream-stuff—Ophelia's lips were not moving and she was not speaking, and yet I could hear the sound of her thoughts, paralysed and listening to her, the girl he might have married and didn't.

'And why, sweet prince, why, why? Not because I returned your letters and shut my door on you? No, you know perfectly well how it was with me, and it suited you very well. You weren't afraid that I'd prove false to you. You had a far greater fear than that, didn't you? You were terrified that I really would value your love, and would even return it. That's what really spooked you. That I'd be a breeder of sinners, because that's what love and marriage lead to, the propagation of our kind, human corruption. Why breed more mouldering meat for maggots? When I could go out instead and bewail my virginity, to do precisely as my brother ordered, not to yield my chaste treasure to you. But little did dear brother realise, little did he know, he was judging you according to his own unchaste behaviour. You had no interest in my chaste treasure, and you left it with me, unopened, unrifled. And that was your tragedy. And mine. I'll be buried in my maiden purity with my constant and forsaken love all unfulfilled, while you, my friend, you'll dwell on and on. On what? On the quintessence of dust, the reason unused, the mutiny in the matron's bones, farewell, dear mother, the nasty sty, the prison, the mildewed ear, the ulcer, the maggoty marriage, which you shun like the plague of procreation, denying your own nature, rejecting the part that life prepared for you, just as you failed to fulfil what nature demanded of you in respect of revenge. Oh, I know all about that now. I'll be with your father soon, in eternity. If you have nature in you, don't endure it, don't bear it—remember? Ah, but you did bear it, and nature *was* resisted, and vows unfulfilled. Both in love and in revenge, you were in denial, let's face it, you were a loser in love and a loser in war. But tell you what, you keep the coffin-nails, I'll go gather more flowers…'

At times it was Ophelia speaking, or somehow sounding out her thoughts. And at other times she was ventriloquising her words, so that they seemed to be spoken by myself, or Claudius, or Gertrude, or the Ghost. But at the end of the last dream, I woke up with that last thought of hers in my head—Hamlet was forever associated with coffin-nails, and with dust, and Ophelia with violets. God rest her fragrant soul.

PART FIVE

Grave Matters

The sailors took me to Hamlet's secret location, and from there, travelling over land, we made our way to Elsinore, approaching circumspectly by the graveyard, where few folk above ground would be alert to our arrival, and those down below were past caring. An ideal, incurious audience, the dead, Hamlet half-jested to me—'unlikely to blab'. He was wearing seaman's clothes as a rough disguise. But as we approached, we were met not with silence but with loud coarse voices raised in debate: two grave-diggers, a sexton and his mate, were arguing about the expected occupant of the grave they were preparing. The incoming tenant was a woman, apparently, who appeared to have done away with herself. The sexton was questioning the correctness of a Christian burial.

'Look at it this way, she tried to get to heaven early—she didn't leave it to God to decide. Now that's murder, it's self-murder, and that's not heaven, it's hell.'

The assistant digger shook his head, and we settled ourselves behind a tombstone to hear the argument.

'That's as may be, but the coronator's held a bequest—'

'You mean an inquest, you ignoramus—and he's called the crowner.'

'We're in for a treat,' Hamlet whispered. 'Let's hear them out.'

'Well, whatever he calls himself, he says it's to be a Christian burial, so let's get her plot dug straightaway, and let's dig it straight, not one of them skew-whiff pits.'

'Hang on, not so fast there! If she drowned herself in her own defence—'

'She did. It's been decided on. But now you're the one's got it wrong. How in God's name could she kill herself in self-defence? You mean self-*off*ence. She committed an offence.'

'What offence was that?'

'Heaven help us, *se offendendo*—don't you know any Latin? After all them funerals? It was an offence against her own body. And the body's a temple. And that's a crime, don't you know that neither?'

'I know this much, that if water comes your way and drowns you while you're minding your own business, you're not guilty, but if you go to the water of your own free will, then you're guilty of your own death. Argo—no holy burial for you!'

'And now it's you showing off your ignorance. It's your bad Latin again. It's never *argo*, it's *ergo*.'

'Ergo or argo, if she hadn't been a grandam—'

'You mean *grande dame*, a gentlewoman. You don't know no French neither.'

'If she hadn't been a nob, she'd have been slung into the ground outside these here walls—unconstituted ground.

'Unconsecrated. You've got no more brains than that spade.'

'Talking of which, hand me that same spade, goodman delver.'

The sexton jumped down into the open grave.

'I'll finish it off for her. But she finished herself off, that's for sure, and more's the pity that the gentry should have the right to drown themselves or hang themselves more than their unwashed fellow Christians. See this spade? When the world was first made, when the Lord God created it, this spade would have made me one of the gentry.'

'You—a gentleman! How so?'

'Cos any man using a spade in them days was a gentleman— gardeners, ditch-diggers, grave-makers, they all did what Adam did.'

'You mean they ate apples?'

'Apples nothing, you bumpkin! That's another story. I mean they followed in his gentleman's footsteps.'

'So Adam was a gentleman?'

'Course he was. He was the first ever to bear arms.'

'Never. He never had no arms. He never did.'

'Course he did, you clown. Are you a complete heathen? What does scripture say? The scripture says Adam digged. Eve span and Adam digged.'

'So?'

'So, you dimwit, how could he dig if he didn't have arms? But let's carry on with your schooling. Here's a question for you, and if you can't answer this one, then you'd best go confess yourself and be hanged.'

'Right you are. I'm ready for it.'

'Listen then. Who builds stronger than either the mason, the shipwright, or the carpenter?'

'Easy! The gallows-maker. The frame he makes outlives a thousand tenants.'

'Ha! A good answer at last—and a witty one. The gallows does pretty well. But ask yourself this: how does it do well? It does well to them that does ill—evil-doers. Now you're speaking ill—not of the dead but of the church, because, you blockhead, you're saying that the gallows builds stronger than the church. Argo—ergo, you see, I've learned it—ergo the gallows may do well to you. Better try again.'

'Right. What was the question again?'

'Who builds stronger—'

'Ah yes, who builds stronger than a mason, a shipwright or a carpenter?'

'That's the question. And can you answer it before one of us dies and ends up in that there hole?'

'I've got it!'

'Go on, then.'

'Hell! I had it! It was in my noodle. Now it's gone again.'

'Well, cudgel your useless crown no more about it. No use flogging a sluggard ass.'

'It's a dead horse.'

'A horse isn't an ass, but you are, and an arse into the bargain. And next time this question is put to you, say 'a grave-maker'. The houses the grave-digger makes last till doomsday.'

'Ah.'

'Ah, yes. And now after schooling you, I've got a big thirst on me. So get yourself off to Yohan and fetch me a flagon of good strong ale. Time you bring that back here I'll have the doomsday house all dug out.'

The newly schooled yokel wandered off. I was about to suggest we move on, but Hamlet made a couple of gestures, fingers to his lips, and hand cupped to the ear. He wanted to watch the sexton at his work, and otherwise seemed content to stay. Somehow he seemed relaxed and at home in the quiet but grisly surroundings. He was in no hurry. The sexton dug deeper, his head now barely level with the ground around the hole. He sang as he worked, scooping out spadefuls of soil and tossing them onto the growing pile.

In youth when I did love, did love,
I thought it really sweet
To pass the time till wedding-bells
By putting up me feet.

It was nonsense, but the tune was catchy and he grunted happily as he shovelled and sang. Hamlet had been smiling during the debate and the schooling lesson, but he frowned slightly now and looked serious. He was clearly struck by the incongruity—the grim work, the jolly song, and someone's sad end.

'Do you hear that, Horatio? Does this old bugger have so little feeling of his business that he serenades himself—while digging someone's grave? A human being is about to be put into that hole. It's so—out of place.'

'He's grown used to it, that's all. He's done it so long he's become indifferent, hardened. It's a job. And he'll need hard hands for it. Idler hands like ours—no offence—can afford to be more fastidious, I suppose.'

'Yes, can't be too sensitive in his line of work. Listen, he's off again—next verse coming up.'

My lusts they do me leave,
My fancies all are fled,
And tracts of time begin to weave
Grey hairs upon my head.

'More of the same,' I said. 'Shall we leave him to it?'

'No, Horatio, let's not be discourteous. A singer needs an audience. This one deserves it.'

For age with his stealing steps
Has clawed me into his clutch,
And lusty life away she leaps
As if I'd never been such.

'Hup! Ho!'

A skull suddenly came flying up out of the pit and rolled right up to where we were crouched. Hamlet grasped my shoulder, stared, and pointed.

'That skull had a tongue in it and could sing once—just as lustily as this old lout. Maybe louder. Maybe better.'

'Who knows?'

'And just see how he treats it—chucking it out of its resting place and hurling it about as if it were Cain's jaw-bone.'

'Why Cain in particular?'

'The prime killer, Horatio, the brother-murderer. Or it could be the brain-box of some crafty politician, don't you think?'

'Could be.'

'Some subtle schemer, who'd cheat God if he could. And now this lubber lords it over him.'

'Quite a thought.'

'Food for thought, Horatio, food for worms too. Or some popinjay courtier perhaps, some fop like our Osric, just imagine, with his 'O good morning, my dear one! How *are* you, my lord—if it's not a rude question? And how goes that champion charger of yours? Such a fine horse! How I wish it were mine!"

'You sound just like Osric—a good mimic!'

'Or it could have been my lord's lovely lady. Where have all her looks gone to now?—all atomised and faded, flown to nothing.'

'Well it could be anybody.'

'Exactly, Horatio. Somebody who was once somebody could now be anybody—any body. And now my lovely lord is married again, to my lady Worm. Ah, but he's missing his chinwag, no jaw-jaw, no jawbone to chatter with, and getting knocked about the bonce instead with a sexton's spade. The old oaf ought to be more careful with his customers. That skull could be a drinking-bowl if he doesn't break it.'

'Hup, ho!'

'Look, Horatio, there's a fistful of bones thrown up—just like little logs. You could have a game with them, ninepins maybe. Whose were they, do you think?'

'I've no idea.'

'God help them, did they cost so little to bring up—when they were alive and growing, I mean—that we can afford to caper with them now, like kids' skittles? Doesn't it make your own bones ache, just thinking about it?'

'It would—if you thought too much about it.'

'And off he goes again.'

A pick-axe and a spade, a spade,
Also a shrouding-sheet,
And a house of clay to be made
For the next guest so neat.

'Hup, ho!'

'Another skull, Horatio! Let's see now, let's say it's a lawyer's. Now where did his legalities get him, and his expertise? Where are all his hair-splitting quibbles and quiddities? Where are his properties and deeds? What's happened to all his tricksy talk? Why has he gone so quiet? Why's he letting this unlettered oaf away with it? An uncultured sod knocking him about his noodle with a dirty old shovel, and he's not taking out an action against him—no charge of assault and battery? Well, it's hard to credit, isn't it? This chap in his time could have bought up so much land. Just think of all the documents and deeds and debts, the witnesses and warrants and signatories, the acknowledgements, the indentures, the securities, the inheritances—and the fines! Think of the fines and the finishes, the *finis*, ending up here with his fine mind full of fine dirt, and his grey matter crawling with grey slugs, not to mention all the conveyancing, only to get himself conveyed into this grave. And all the boxes in that office of his, the deed-boxes, turned into a dead-box that would scarcely hold all the paperwork—I mean, the skull's a dead-box, isn't it? A dead brain-box? And as for him, as for master lawyer here, what does he actually inherit in the end? How much land did he really need? How much land does any man need? Six feet does the trick, don't you think? This chap for example—does he need a foot more?'

'Not a foot more.'

'Agreed. And what about all that parchment? Parchment's made of sheep-skins, isn't it?'

'And of calves-skins too.'

'Sheep and calves, that's us. Our own skins are parchment. Aren't they, of a sort? And even our skulls are not much stronger. Not by the look of things.'

'Not from where we're sitting.'

'And from where we're sitting, this rough grave-maker is the king of the dead, the lord of all the land hereabouts. And the fine dappered lord who while he lived wouldn't let the wind blow on him—here he's shovelled aside and hurled on a dung-hill, and his proud lady, who wouldn't let anyone get a sniff of her until she'd gone out perfumed with amber—she has to content herself with the earth as a bedcover, and worms and maggots for maids, and for toads and adders to eat out her eyes. And this character here won't have it any other way. Well now, I'm going to speak to him.'

We stood up and came to the edge of the grave, looking down at the sexton. He wiped the sweat from his forehead with a bare begrimed arm, and paid us no more attention than if we'd been corpses. Hamlet footed a scattering of soil into the grave to attract his attention.

'Whose grave is this, master digger?'

'Mine, sir.'

An unexpected answer. A clever clogs, as we'd already overheard. Hamlet winked at me, indicating he'd be happy to spar with him.

'It must be yours, as you're in it.'

'And you're not, are you? So it's all the more mine.'

'Except that it's for the dead, not for the quick, and as you look quick enough to me, you're not giving me the right answer, are you? What man are you digging it for?'

'For no man.'

'I see. For what woman, then?'

'For no woman either.'

'Really? Who or what is to be buried in it, then?'

'Ah, well now, someone who *was* a woman, but now she's no longer a woman.'

'And why is that?'

'Why? Because, would you believe it?—she's dead. So now she's neither man nor woman. She's nothing.'

'What a pedantic little bastard it is!'

I was taken aback. Hamlet seemed nettled. He's always been easy with his social inferiors, taking a pride in his lack of pride. It was one of his most endearing aspects. Now I sensed a change. I couldn't understand exactly what it meant. But the Hamlet who had come back from the sea was not quite the same man. Somehow there had been a sea-change. But he regained his composure.

'How long have you been a grave-digger?'

'Oh, that's an easy one, sir. I can tell you to the very day. I started digging on the same day our last king overcame Fortinbras.'

'Oh, yes? And how long ago is that?'

'You don't know that? Any fool can tell that. It was the very day that young Hamlet was born—the prince, you know, the one that went mad, and was sent away to England.'

'Ah, yes, of course, I'm with you now. But why England, can I ask? Why was he sent there?'

'Why? Because he went mad.'

'That's no reason.'

'It's the best reason there is. He'll get better there. And if he don't, it's no great matter, not over there.'

'Why?'

'Because the madness won't be seen in him there. He won't stand out.'

'Why not?'

'Why not? My God, you can't be as stupid as you look, can you? It's not possible. Because, you see, over there, the men are as mad as he. They're all mad there. Haven't you heard of mad dogs and Englishmen?'

'Right you are. You know a lot, it seems. Do you happen to know how he came to be mad?'

'Ah, very strangely, they say.'

'How strangely?'

'By losing his reason. What can be stranger than that? He became a stranger to himself. He just went out of his mind.'

'On what ground?'

'Ground? What ground? Right here, stupid. Here in Denmark. I've been sexton here, man, and boy, oh, let's see now—thirty years.'

'Thirty years. Speaking of years, let me ask you something. How long will a man lie in the earth before he rots?'

'O, Jesus, that depends.'

'On what?'

'On what condition he's in when we put him in. These days, I have to tell you, we've got some as are rotten before they die, long before they're even corpses—rotten with the pox, you see. Some are so rotten they don't hold together enough even to withstand the burial process, the laying-in, sir, cos they're falling to bits as it is, with syphilis.'

'All right, but leaving that aside for the moment, how long will a body hold together—in general, I mean?'

'Generally eight years, maximum, maybe nine. A tanner will last you nine years.'

'Why a tanner?'

'Think about it! Do I have to school you too? He's been tanning hides all his life. And his own hide is so tanned with his trade that it'll keep out the water for quite a while, the moisture in the soil, you know, and there's nothing worse than water to rot your corpse. No sir, water's the worst bugger in the world to get into your dead body and waste it away, oh yes, a real decomposer is your water… Oh, well now, would you believe it?'

He bent deep down and rummaged briefly before coming out with his find.

'Here's a skull now. This skull, I can tell you, has lain in the earth here twenty-three years.'

'Twenty-three. That's very precise. How can you be so sure—as it's just another skull?'

'Because it's not just any old skull—it's got a cap on it.'

'A cap? What sort of cap? What do you mean? Whose was it?'

'A whore's son if ever there was one! A mad chap! A daft bugger, so he was! As daft as a brush! Here, let me show you.'

He brought up the skull and placed it squarely on the edge of the grave.

'There you go. Who do you think that was?'
'I've no earthly idea.'
'Let me make it easier for you.'

He reached down again into the pit and picked up a jester's cap. The bells were choked with earth but still jingled faintly. He placed the cap on the skull and fitted it firmly.

'There's your man.'

Hamlet gasped.

'Ah, you've got him now, have you, near enough? Bugger him for the mad wag that he was! He poured a flagon of Rhenish on my head once. Not got him yet? No? Well, let me tell you. This same skull was, sir, Yorick's skull—the old king's jester.'

'This?'

'This is he.'

'Let me see.'

He took the skull in his hands and took off the cap.

'Yorick! Poor old Yorick! I knew him, Horatio—an inveterate jester, but not just a joker, he had imagination, he could make you think as well as laugh. He died when… my God, I must have been about seven, I reckon, from what this digger-up of bones is telling me. He used to give me piggy-backs, and he'd get down on all fours and romp around the castle with me riding him and lashing him with a pretend whip. He was such a clever clown. And now—O sweet Jesus, how fucking horrible is that, how he looks now! Is that how we all look? Is this really what happens to us? Dear Christ, it makes you want to vomit!

'Look, look Horatio! I used to kiss this chap, I loved him so much! See, this is where the lips must have hung. I kissed them God knows how many times. He was like a second father to me. And now just look at you, old son! All those jokes and jigs and songs of yours, all those flashes of wit that used to get the whole table roaring with laughter. You'd have them rolling beneath the benches. And now there's nobody left to laugh at you, now you can't even mock your own grinning, you're so down-in-the-mouth, so to speak, lacking the lower jaw, old chap. But if you can still manage a word or two from your old repertoire, why don't you get yourself along to my lady's chamber? And tell her, no matter how well she paints her face, even if she paints an inch thick, in the end she'll look just like you, and nobody could tell the difference, filly or fool, same thing in the grave, with the flesh all gone, and down to this, the last faceless fact, the anonymous cold bone. You liked to make them laugh. Well, make her laugh at that… Horatio, tell me something.'

'What's that?'

'Do you think Alexander the Great looked just like this—when he was in the earth?'

'Much the same.'

'And smelled the same?'

'The same way. Why not?'

'They say that apart from all his conquests, and his personal beauty and all that, he had a very fine skin-colouring, quite exquisite apparently, and a sweet smell. His entire body had this delightful aroma, so I've read, and his apparel too, everything he wore took on his fragrance, and he lay naked for many days, they say, before they buried him, and still smelled as clean and fresh as he'd been when he was alive.'

'A nice story.'

'You don't believe it?'

'There may be something in it, but he'd still have looked much the same as Yorick here—in time.'

'Time. Yes, that's it, Horatio, to think what time does to us, and what we all have to come to, in time. Let's take it a stage further— bear with me if you will. Can you imagine, for example, the dust of the great Alexander ending up plugging a bung-hole?'

'That sounds pretty far-fetched to me.'

'Not really. But not to exaggerate, listen. Alexander the Great dies, Alexander is buried, Alexander returns to dust. The dust is earth. Of earth we make loam, and out of that loam they could make a bung to plug a hole. A stopper, let's say to stop a beer-barrel. Are you with me? If not, listen again. Horatio, suddenly I'm inspired—I'm a poet. Here goes.'

Imperious Caesar, dead and turned to clay,
Might stop a hole to keep the wind away.
O, that that earth which kept the world in awe
Should patch a wall to expel the winter's flaw!

'Well rhymed, my lord—but I think you'd better rest on your laurels!'

'Ah, you're not impressed. Well, you may be right. But this brings death into a whole new perspective for me.'

'How so?'

'How so. Because for so long I've lived my life under death's shadow. Either I've longed for it, as a last release from—you know—the ills of the flesh, the troubles of the mind, all that stuff. Or it's been something to be shunned, because of the fear of what comes after, the dread of not knowing. But now—now I can see it steadily and I can see it whole, the sudden solving emptiness. The truth is, there's nothing comes after, so there's nothing to fear, is there?'

'Not unless nothingness is the very thing you do fear—you know, not to be here, not to be there, not to be anywhere, to be simply obliterated, extinct.'

'It's the common destiny, Horatio. You know what? I'd like to keep this skull.'

'Really? But why? What would you do with it? Keep it as a memento mori, you mean?'

'No, not just that, that's not it at all. Keep it for the laughter that was in it, all tucked away, all the fun and frolic. I expect my father's skull looks much the same by now. I've a hankering to have a look at it, you know, to break into that crypt and find out if it's still there. And if it is, to take it. It wouldn't be grave-robbing after all, would it? I mean how can you rob what nobody wants? I'm the only remembrancer. Morally it's mine.'

'And what would you do with it, the old king's skull?'

'It's my father's.'

'But wouldn't you rather be holding the new king's skull in your hands? Or placing your foot on it?'

'No. It wouldn't interest me. Nothing of any interest in there, nothing but schemes and shittiness. But my father's skull now—I think I'd have it at the window, on the window-sill, facing the ocean, sockets to the sea, those empty eyes, you know?'

'I know. And then?'

'And then—quiet then, shush, just listen awhile, and you'll hear, just like in a shell, that soft sough, you know that sighing sound that the sea makes, and maybe even deaf wars, none of the loud blood and thunder that used to surround him, and even deaf seas, no more noisy, lousy crossings, you know, only the tides' slow flow, the ebb's assiduous patience, where the brains once were, the heroes of the corps.'

I was wondering what to say to all of that, when Hamlet stopped me, with a hand on my shoulder. He was ahead of me.

'But wait—look! Here comes the king, and the queen, the courtiers, a whole cortege. It's a funeral. Let's take cover, lie low and see what's happening.'

The procession entered the graveyard, with a doctor of divinity following in cassock and gown. But what struck us was the absence of music, no singing, no chanting of prayers, the usual rites had been curtailed. And with royalty present, why was so ostensibly important a funeral so limited and so subdued? Hamlet made the connection.

'It looks like whoever is being buried was of some importance but may have been a suicide. That's what the two diggers were arguing about. Let's wait and watch.'

I didn't have to wait or watch. It hit me like a hammer and I didn't dare tell him. It had to be Ophelia. And my fears were confirmed when Laertes stepped forward and confronted the churchman.

'And now? What comes next?'

The priest was hard-faced, sullen.

'Next she faces her maker.'

'As do we all. As will you. I mean the funeral rites. What ceremony are you going to perform?'

'None. I am not authorised to carry out any further commemoration. She died in circumstances dubious to say the least—highly suspicious in fact, and had it not been for the royal command, overruling the order for the burial of such dead, she would have been buried outside these walls, in unconsecrated ground, which is where she ought to be, and where she'd remain, until the last trumpet summoned her to meet her maker and face her punishment.'

Laertes looked ready to spit in the harsh doctrinal face, but he spat out words instead.

'Punishment! Have you ever heard of prayer? Won't you say at least one? Of your charity? If you have any?'

'Not one. For charitable prayers she should have flints and stones thrown on her instead, and the shards that Job used to scrape off his boils when he sat in the hands of Satan. And here she is with garlands and flowers to be strewn over her, and the bringing home of bell and burial. There was a time she could have been buried at a crossroads, with a stake through her heart.'

'God almighty, do you hear this? Is there nothing more you can do?'

'Nothing more? What else do you expect? I've made the church's position clear to you. It would be blasphemous to do more. A prayer would profane the service of the dead, as would a requiem, even more so, to sing her to rest. She has not earned the rest granted to peacefully-parted souls.'

'Her soul was troubled!'

'That is not my affair.'

'And forgiveness?'

'That's God's affair. Her troubles were her own affair.'

Laertes turned his face up to the sky and closed his streaming eyes.

'Forgive her, Lord! Lay her in the earth. And may violets spring from her chaste and unpolluted flesh.'

The open coffin was lowered into the grave.

'I'll say this much, you surly dog of a doctor, my sister will be an angel up above when you lie howling in hell!'

The words struck Hamlet like lightning.

'Ophelia! Ophelia?'

Gertrude came up to the graveside with an armful of flowers, which she scattered sadly, gently, over the corpse.

'Sweet flowers for a sweet girl, sweets to the sweet, adieu. I'd hoped you might have been my Hamlet's wife. I thought I would have one day decked your bridal bed with blossoms. I little thought I'd be strewing your grave instead.'

It was too much for Laertes.

'Oh, God in heaven! Punish him, I beg you! Bring down all your wrath on that execrable head of his! And curse him to hell! Your madness, your shattered mind, this shambles of a service, your whole life before you cut short—this is his work!'

The sexton came up to throw his first spadeful of earth over the corpse but Laertes stopped him and stood looking down into the grave.

'No! Not yet! Hold on! Keep the earth off her for a little longer! Let me take her once more in my arms—for the last time!'

He leapt into the grave and lifted the corpse out of the coffin, hugging it hard to his chest. The dead Ophelia's hands had been clasped across her bosom, intertwined with flowers. Now her arms swung down and dangled awkwardly as her brother's tears wetted the cold white face.

'Now! Now, sexton! Now pile on your dirt! Hurl it on and bury me alive with her! I'll lie here in the earth with my sister and go hand in hand with her to heaven, in spite of this uncharitable priest!'

The gathering was aghast. Some buried their faces in their hands, unable to bear the emotion of the moment, and Laertes' naked grief. It was all too raw. But there was another shock awaiting them. I tried to prevent him but Hamlet suddenly stood up and revealed himself. He strode over to the grave, shouting loudly, angrily. The mourners stood like mutes, open-mouthed.

'Who's this grief-stricken god of tears and sighs? Do you think your blubbering stops the stars in their courses? Who do you think you are? Feast your eyes, my friend—Hamlet the Dane is here. I have returned!'

He sprang into the grave. Laertes dropped his sister's corpse and grabbed Hamlet by the throat. The arena was the dead-hole, the space was limited, but they struggled over the body as if for possession of it. Claudius barked an order and attendants ran up on either side of the pit and pulled them apart and out of the grave. Hamlet was hysterical.

'Does he want a fight? I'll fight with him on this matter until I'm a corpse myself—and even then I'll fight on!'

Gertrude tried to bring the thing into the realm of reason.

'What matter is that, my son?'

'What matter? What else is there? What could matter more? I loved Ophelia! Forty thousand brothers couldn't compete with what I felt for her!'

Laertes tried to break free of the attendants. Claudius held up his hand.

'Leave it, Laertes! Leave it alone! Don't you see? He's mad.'

You couldn't argue with it, not in the light of what followed: a mad rant even by Hamlet standards.

'All right then, what are you going to do? What else are you up for? Weeping? Fighting? Fasting? Self-laceration, perhaps? Tearing your hair? Rending your clothes? Why don't you light a pyre—and leap onto it like Dido? Or just swallow down goblets of vinegar! Suppose you eat a crocodile instead? Tough and terrible creatures, but they shed copious tears, you know, and every one a hypocrite! Do you think your whining counts for anything here? You want to be buried alive with her? I'll tell you what, so will I, and they can chuck millions of acres on us, and make the mountains of old look like warts! Go on, go on, keep on with your grimacing and your raving, don't stop, I can do better than that! I'll make funnier faces than you! I'll make you a pygmy to the pain I've known! What is it about you anyway? Why do you treat me like this? I always respected you. I never intended you any harm. But it doesn't matter. My turn will come, and even Hercules won't stop me, though if Hercules himself didn't silence dogs, how can I? They keep yapping, and fawning. But every dog has his day…'

His passion spent, Hamlet stormed off. Claudius called to me.

'Go after him, Horatio. Try to calm him down.'

I followed—but overheard Claudius whisper something to Laertes about their last night's conversation, and the need to put it to the test. Naturally at the time I had no idea what he meant. It was only later, after Osric had sung under interrogation, that I understood the nature of the arrangement. Meanwhile, with increasing typicality, Claudius urged Gertrude to 'set some watch over *your* son.'

'As for this grave,' he said, indicating Ophelia's last resting place, 'it will have its own memorial, soon enough.'

It was only afterwards that I gave his words a sinister twist in my mind. They were ambiguously innocent, but if intended as a message to the knowing ears of Laertes, may have meant that Hamlet's murder would serve as an avenging headstone of sorts to Ophelia. His death would be her memorial, and things would go on from there.

After everyone had left, Hamlet asked me to come back with him to the graveyard. Only the sexton was still there, his work of filling in the grave almost complete. Hamlet still seemed drawn to him as a symbol of the ambience of the place, as if all that mattered to him now had something to do with death.

'I'll tell you what, master delver, if you'll finish singing that song for me, I'll ask my friend here to go down to Yohan's for that flagon you fancied. Looks like your digger friend got settled in there and forgot all about you. So—to lubricate your larynx—what do you say?'

'I say yes, sir—to a flagon of his very best bitter beer!'

I went off, leaving Hamlet sitting by the grave, listening to the song.

Low lies the skinless skull
By whose bald sign I know:
That stooping age away shall pull
What youthful years did sow.

For beauty with her band
These crooked cares has wrought:
And shipped me into the land
From where I first was brought.

And ye that bide behind
Have ye no other trust:
As ye of clay were cast by kind
So shall ye waste to dust.

When I came back with the beer, Hamlet was still sitting there beside the thirsty sexton.

'Yes, Horatio,' he said, somehow reading my thoughts. 'It's got something to do with death. Everything does.'

Sound and Silence

It wasn't until after the events in the graveyard that Hamlet let me have a full account of what had happened on the aborted voyage. On the first night he lay in his cabin, tossing and turning and struggling to sleep, like the bilge-rat mutineers in their fetters down below, so he said. Something was telling him not to fall into the arms of Morpheus—if he did, he might fall into the hands of a fate that had been written for him by another arm, a hand and a fate which only he could un-write. What was it? There are times when you can't plan ahead wittingly and with forethought, but you follow instead some sort of gut instinct, and always there's the feeling that no matter what you do to shape your destiny, there's that guiding hand at work, doing it for you. You could call it providence, you could call it God, or the intervention of some unknown power, a divinity that shapes your ends, rough-hew them how you may. Whatever it was, it made Hamlet rise from his bunk and listen, as if expecting some kind of call or command. It never came. All he heard was the creaking of the ship's timbers as it dipped and pitched on a gently rolling sea, under the stars.

He knew he had to act. He came up from his cabin, his sea-gown scarfed about him in the dark, and went up on deck. The helmsman had his back to him, no-one else there. And again there was that great sea of troubles, billowing between him and England. Now came the crafty part, requiring stealth, the furtiveness of the fox, and the backbone of the sea-wolf. Boldness be my friend, he told himself—there are no other friends on board. And he thought he heard his father's voice again, in that wordless slow breathing of the sea, the sough of the waves, whose sound is an endless adieu. At this point I, Horatio, must reiterate: I am no great story-teller, I am a humble slave to fact and circumstance, and therefore, as has been my practice so far in presenting these letters. I pass on the task into the hands of those involved in these events, or rather I put it into their own mouths. In this case Hamlet's…

I groped my way about the swaying ship in the dark and found their cabin. I eased open the heavy door. There they lay together, snoring their two heads off. The dribbling wineskins were littered about them, rolling to and fro across the floor as the ship heaved and sighed just like them, only without the snores. I stood and looked and listened. Even their snores came out together, in perfect harmony. If one of them woke and needed to piss, I thought to myself, the other would be sure to follow, even in sleep. But they were out for the count. I stood on for some time. Then I saw what I knew I must be looking for—a locked casket. How easy was that? I stole it, stole back to my cabin with it, picked it with my dagger, took out their commission, and broke the seal.

And what do you suppose I found? What did I read there, do you think? You can think, but you'd never credit it. A secret order, written and signed by the king of knaves himself, unbelievably devious. The English king was commanded, with all sorts of dire threats, and various terrors to be faced if he failed to carry out the royal order, to allow me on my arrival no respite of time whatever, not one single minute, but to lead me chained and bound to the block, to look the masked axe-man in the eye. Not a moment should be wasted, not even time taken to sharpen the axe before my head should be struck off. Even if the blade were blunt, the grinding was proscribed, the beheading to be dispatched as a matter of great gravity and extreme speed!

Yes? Yes, I know, Horatio! But even then, at that moment, even knowing the knavery of this unscrupulous usurper, even knowing it all ahead, his criminality, still I was shocked and stunned. I'd been sent to England supposedly to collect tribute money for the crown. That was the pretext. And instead I was to have been put down like a dog. No fiend of hell could compete. For some time I sat there in a daze, staring at the order. It was difficult to take in. It felt like a wild dream. But I surprised myself—my brain had already unconsciously gone to work on the solution before I went into action. I held this diabolical piece of parchment in the swinging ship's lantern until it was ash at my feet. Then out of my sea-trunk I took new parchment, quill and ink—I had intended to write letters from England and was well equipped—and I devised an entirely new commission, ordering that its bearers should without debate be put to sudden death, not to be granted time even for confession and absolution from sin. They were to go damned and headless to hell. And to seal up the new order—even then providence was in control. I still have my father's signet ring, and I had it in my purse among my possessions. It matched exactly the Danish seal that had been used to secure the order for my execution. The stratagem would never be detected. I signed it with a fair version of the Claudius hand, sealed it, and locked it back in the casket, which I took down to the cabin of the still snoring pair. It was their last sleep before the big sleep, because the next day was the sea-fight with the heaven-sent pirates, and what happened after that, my friend, you know already...

'My God!'

I couldn't help myself saying it.

'So you've sent Rosencrantz and Guildenstern to their deaths.'

Hamlet gave me a hard glance.

'What does that mean?'

'I mean that they may not have known what was in that casket, what exactly their commission consisted of. Claudius could have been using them, deceiving them as well. You can't be certain that they were privy to the king's plot.'

A cold grin from Hamlet.

'Well, they may not have been privy, but they were his privates—or they made love to his privates! Or his posterior. They were arse-lickers. And now they've gone to lick the dust of England.'

'Still—'

'Still nothing, Horatio. They courted this whole business, and now their wedding-day has come. Some people shouldn't meddle in some matters. Not if they're too small for it. They were nobodies. And they came between two mighty opposites and got crushed.'

'Mighty opposites. I never thought of Claudius as mighty.'

'Nor do I. It's the King I'm talking about. I mean the real king, my father, the powerful piece. I'm nothing in comparison, but these two pawns were less than nothing. They got in the way. End of story. End at least of their story. It's over. And they don't deserve a drop of my compunction. My conscience is clear.'

As Hamlet spoke, that feeling grew stronger in me that something had changed in him since his return, something uncertain yet essential. There was an indifference, an absence of concern. And the madness had gone out of him. But I was in no doubt about Claudius.

'A king without a conscience. He's utterly ruthless.'

'Exactly. He murdered my father and whored my mother, he buttered-up the back-scratchers and came between me and the election, he stole the throne. And on top of all that he used these two pawns in the game-play to have me beheaded—well away from his own doorstep. So, if we're talking about conscience, wouldn't it be on my conscience if I didn't pay him back? And in his own coin too, to the death, the cancerous bastard. He's an ulcer on the arse of the state. He's an ulcer in my life. It's time to lance it.'

'And talking of time, it's only a matter of time till he finds out what you've done. He'll hear the news from England any day now.'

Hamlet shrugged.

'No matter. For the time being the day is mine at least, though a man's life be merely as brief as the time it takes to count to one.'

'That's too true. There's no second chance.'

'Not unless life's a rehearsal. What do you think?

'You mean for the next life? Eternal life?'

'I don't know about eternal life. Not any more. But I know I regret my behaviour to Laertes. I should have seen better into his situation, and seen my own reflected. We both have murdered fathers. It was just that he overdid it, all that ostentation. We all have our griefs to bear.'

'Or maybe in a way he was stealing your thunder, don't you think?'

It was a gibe. If Hamlet had an answer to it, he never had time to give it. We were interrupted by the arrival of Osric, of whom up to that time, apart from the gossip already referred to, I had no knowledge beyond the purely visual, having seen him fluttering about the court. He was overdressed as usual and wearing a fantastically large plumed hat of the latest fashion. As soon as he saw Hamlet he doffed the hat and bowed so low his brow almost touched the floor, and he forgot to come up again. Hamlet winked at me.'

'Do rise, sir.'

'My lord?'

'I'm sorry, let me address you in your own language. Do re-attain the perpendicular.'

'Oh, thank you, your lordship, and if I may say so, your lordship is most welcome back to Denmark.'

'You may, you may. And am I indeed? I'm so glad. And it's exceedingly kind of you to say so. But apart from your most gracious welcome, is there anything I can do for you? In particular?'

Osric bowed low again, with an exaggerated flourish of the hat.

'Only if your lordship is at leisure?'

'I am. But not if you keep waving that hat at me. And what's that little bit of lace in your other paw?'

'It's my handkerchief, my lord.'

He brought it airily to his nose, glanced at it, and gave it a flutter. Hamlet winked again.

'Ah, now far be it from me to instruct a courtier like yourself how to unclog his snout, but you ought to give it a good blow. Nor should you, once you have snorted, open your handkerchief and gaze into it, however briefly, as though pearls and rubies must have descended from your brain. It is but snot. And now tell me what it is that you would most earnestly wish to impart to me.'

Osric failed to detect the mockery in Hamlet's tone.

'Something from His Majesty, your lordship.'

'His Majesty. Your lordship. These are elevated circles we move in. But why don't you put your bonnet back on? It's meant for the head.'

'Thank you, your lordship, but it's so hot, you see.'

'Hot? Hot, sir? No, no, sir, believe me, it's turned suddenly cold. The wind is northerly today, wouldn't you say?'

'Well, yes, of course, it is rather cold, as you say.'

'But you've just said it's hot. And it is indeed on the hot side, for my own constitution at least, how about yours? Shall we make up our minds, then? Hot or cold—which is it?'

Osric was left at a loss.

'Your lordship, I really can't tell.'

He fanned himself furiously with the hat.

'But I can tell you the king's message.'

'At last.'

'Well, my lord, if I can first say that we have newly come to court—from France—Laertes the son of our much-missed late Lord Chamberlain.'

'Much-missed. Yes, I knew the Lord Chamberlain. And I didn't miss him. I know his son too. We've met. Quite recently in fact. In his sister's grave. So much for Laertes. And what about him?'

'My lord?'

'Oh, I beg your pardon. Am I being too blunt? Permit me to rephrase. What imports the nomination of this gentleman? What of him?'

'Of him I have to tell you, from His Majesty, that in his particular field he is by reputation unparalleled—without a peer. *Absolument!*'

'Really? And what's his absolute field? In particular?'

'In particular, in respect of his weapon.'

'And what's his weapon?'

'Rapier and dagger.'

'That's two of his weapons. Good for him. And what does any of this have to do with me? In particular?'

'Simply, my lord, that the king has offered to lay a bet, to put it bluntly, that if you were willing to cross swords with Laertes, purely in play, you understand, a friendly bout, let's say that in a series of twelve rounds, Laertes' total number of hits would not exceed yours by three or more—or let's say twelve for nine. What do you say?'

'What do I say? Twelve bouts, and twelve for nine is what *you* are saying is it?'

'It's what His Majesty is saying, my lord, if you are willing to answer the challenge.'

'I see. Well, it's a fair challenge, and it's a fairly good time of day for me, for a spot of exercise. So what I say is—bring it on. And I'll see if I can win for the king.'

Osric bowed himself out with a dozen flourishes. But the decision disturbed me, the willingness to submit to the whim of the minute, as if he'd somehow lost direction, and drive.

I said nothing on this front, but I spoke my mind.

'You'll lose this wager, you know.'

He didn't object to my honest opinion.

'I don't think so, Horatio. I've had plenty of practice since he went to France. I imagine I can come off the better man. And yet, you know…'

'What is it?'

'I don't know. A sudden bad feeling, that's all. But that's all it is—it's nothing.'

'But if it's troubling you—'

'As much as an old wife's tale would trouble me, which is not at all.'

'No, that's not right. If your instinct is against it, say so, and I'll have it cancelled. I'll say you're not well.'

Hamlet waved me away.

'Good grief, no, Horatio, let's not get credulous in our old age. We're young enough yet for superstition.'

'Yes, but if you have a gut feeling—'

'I do have a gut feeling. But it's got nothing to do with fencing.'

'With what, then?'

'How to put it? It's clear to me now. What's to come is to come, yes? If it's now, it's not to come, if it's not to come it'll be now, if it's not now, it's still to come. And what does it matter when it comes? The readiness is all that matters, you know what I'm saying? It's like what they say about your possessions. What does it matter what you own? You can't take any of it with you when you go, can you? And even if you live longer, you don't know what living longer will benefit you, if anything at all. So why be loath to leave a little earlier? Why be afraid? An early death might even save you from a lot more misery, don't you think? You know the old adage—they whom the gods love die young. And that other one—call no man happy until he is dead. So what does it matter, any of it? Nothing matters. And what will be, will be, you've heard that often enough before.'

There was something in his voice, the words he used, and the way he spoke them, that conveyed to me an even stronger awareness of the change that had come over my friend, what I had come to call the sea-change, in the Hamlet who had come back from the sea, the Hamlet who had glimpsed what he had previously failed to find, some dim design in the workings of the universe, beyond his comprehension, but which lent him a new calm, a sense of peace. And I had the feeling that he'd said all that he wanted to say, not merely in respect of that particular moment and the circumstances surrounding it, but about everything, absolutely everything. I was perturbed by it, the grey fatalism which had taken hold of him, and it made me anxious and uneasy on account of the event that lay ahead. It had been planned by the king, who had already tried to take his life.

There was no time to dwell on it, however. Our quiet talk was loudly interrupted by the sound of drums and trumpets. A line of attendants entered the hall first, carrying cushions and chairs, and setting out tables and benches for the spectators. Claudius clearly intended to make a spectacle out of it. The attendants were followed by the trumpeters and kettle-drummers, and by the king and queen and all the court. Osric and another courtier, as the two appointed judges, brought in the foils and daggers, which they placed on a table against one of the walls, and last of all Laertes came in, ready for the fence. Claudius took him by the hand and led him over to us.

'Will you take his hand, Hamlet?'

'Gladly. I've done you wrong, and all I can do is to ask you to pardon me. For some time now I fear I have not always been in my right mind, and the Hamlet who wronged you was not me. I was not myself. It was some other Hamlet who behaved so badly, not the Hamlet I would want to be, and whom I know myself to be. I hereby disown that Hamlet. The madness that took hold of me—it possessed me—was as much my enemy as yours, and I'm left feeling as if I've shot an arrow at random, over the rooftops, and accidentally harmed my own brother. Will you believe this? And will you accept my apology?'

Laertes stood coldly aloof.

'I accept your apology, sir, and will not dishonour it, even though, as a bereaved son and brother, I have good cause for revenge. But I won't be reconciled to you, and I will keep my distance, until or unless a truce can be declared between us, an official one that will keep my good name intact.'

Hamlet shook his hand warmly.

'That's good enough for me, my friend. Come on then, give us the foils. I'll be your foil, Laertes. You'll shine like a bright star, and show me up as the dim lamp I am by comparison.'

'Ah, you're mocking me now.'

'Not at all, Laertes. I've heard how well your skills went down in Paris—and they know a thing or two over there.'

Claudius clapped his hands.

'Well then, we're ready. Osric, give them the foils.'

Laertes took one from him and tried it out with a couple of passes. Hamlet was about to do the same when Claudius held him back.

'You understand the wager, Hamlet?'

'Perfectly well. You've backed me to win. But I'm afraid you've laid the odds on the weaker side.'

'Not at all. I have absolute confidence in you. But since your opponent is considered to be the better man, the odds give us the advantage.'

I didn't know it at the time, but those few seconds of talk were sufficient. They gave Laertes time to put the poison plot into practice, unbeknown to anyone in the hall other than Claudius and Laertes, and Osric the accomplice.

'This one's too heavy for me. Let me try another.'

Laertes returned the supposedly over-heavy foil to Osric and went over to the table where he knew Osric would have placed the unblunted and poisoned rapier, hidden among the others. A moment's scrutiny.

'This is better.'

He now had the fatal weapon in his hand. Hamlet, just as Claudius had predicted, was casual in his choice, and hardly glanced at the first foil he took from Osric.

'This one suits me well enough. They're all the same length, presumably?'

Osric nodded, and Hamlet took his confirmation for granted. Everything was now in place, except for the fatal fail-safe, the poisoned chalice. The king gave the order and servants came in carrying flagons of wine along with cups. Claudius gave the address before the play began.

'Friends, witness the wine—here on the table. I declare that if Hamlet wins the first or second hit, or draws the third bout, the battlements of Elsinore will discharge their fire. The king will drink to the prince's performance. And into this cup I now drop a precious pearl—more priceless than any worn in the crown by the last *four* kings of Denmark! Give me the cups. And let the drums speak to the trumpets, the trumpets to the cannoneers, the cannons to the heavens, the heavens to the earth, echoing his success! Now the king will drink to Hamlet! Players—begin!'

The pair swiped the air for exercise, getting the feel of the foils, and themselves ready for action, like competing swimmers taking a few deep breaths before the plunge. Then they turned to face one another, approached each other formally, so that their weapons touched, and they held them there for a few seconds, motionless, till Osric brought up his blade from below and struck, breaking the contact. The match was under way.

A moment's pause before they approached each other again, but this time almost like dancers, light-footed and elegant, about to engage. Only the long foils, levelled intently, like unfired arrows, quickly dispelled the dancing image. The swords were all that separated them, and they hissed like snakes as they swept the space between the two men, poised to strike. Then a sudden flurry of action and Hamlet turned to the spectators and held up both arms, rapier and dagger, in a gesture of triumph. It was a hit. He shouted for confirmation.

'One!'

Laertes shouted back.

'No! Never!'

Hamlet turned to the arbiters, arms spread out wide in appeal.

'Judgement?'

Osric gave it.

'A hit! A very palpable hit!'

The king signalled, the drums and trumpets sounded, and from up above us the battlements boomed and the spectators applauded. Laertes listened impatiently.

'All right, let's go again!'

Claudius raised an arm.

'Hold on, there! First, give me drink!'

A servant filled a goblet and passed it to him with a bow. Claudius held his hand up high, displaying the jewel.

'Hamlet, this pearl is yours. You've earned it. Here's to your health.'

He drank from the goblet and dropped the pearl into the cup. Or what appeared to be a pearl. Or only a pearl.

'Give him the drink.'

Hamlet waved it away.

'No, not now, not yet. I'll play the next bout first. Set it down.'

What was now a poisoned chalice was placed on the table and the second bout began. But now the pace of play had accelerated and the body language had changed. Hamlet was invigorated by his first hit and Laertes attacked with less grace and greater determination. It made no difference. Hamlet made a feint followed by a sudden lunge and got through his guard.

'Another hit! Judgement?'

Laertes swung his sword in a gesture of frustration and fury.

'No need! A touch—I admit it!'

Loud applause again. And Gertrude smiled strangely at her husband.

'You betted well, it seems.'

'That I did. Our son shall win, I think.'

Hamlet was back, it seemed, as his 'son.' I asked myself at the time what it meant, if anything. It was said unsmilingly. It wouldn't be long now before I knew why. And Gertrude was just about to spoil a plot she knew nothing of. She left her place and went over to Hamlet.

'You're perspiring, my love. Here, take my handkerchief and rub your forehead. You don't want sweat in your eyes, not when you're doing so well and looking likely to win. I'm going to drink to your victory—from that precious cup of yours.'

She left him with her handkerchief and crossed over to the table. She lifted the goblet and raised it high in the air.

'The queen carouses to your success, my son!'

Claudius made a feeble attempt to dissuade her.

'Gertrude, my dear, don't drink—not yet.'

She smiled faintly.

'With your permission, I will.'

And he did nothing to stop her as she took a sip and went over to Hamlet again to offer him the cup.

'No, not yet, I'd sweat all the more.'

'Then I'll wipe your face again—like I did when you were a little boy.'

Hamlet was in high spirits now.

'Come on, Laertes, show us what you're made of! You're holding back, aren't you? You're toying with me, you're letting me win, you're indulging me, you're taking pity on me because I'm not cut out to be your opponent, I'm just not worthy of you, that's it, isn't it? I mean it's obvious, everyone can see how superior you are, the pride of all France—if not of Denmark!'

The mockery was impossible to miss. Laertes sprang at Hamlet and attacked savagely. Hamlet lashed back like lightning and they clashed without a hit. Osric made his judgement.

'Nothing neither way.'

The third bout over, Hamlet broke off and came across to where I stood. We were exchanging a few words while he took a breather when I was aware of a grim-faced Laertes striding intently up to us. Hamlet had his back to him. I thought he wanted to say something. Instead he yelled out.

'Taunt me, would you? Take this, then!' He swung the rapier and slashed Hamlet's upper arm, the sword-arm. His shirt sleeve tore open and blood spurted out. We looked at the slight wound and stared at each other in disbelief. Then Hamlet went berserk.

He ripped away the sleeveless protective top, and stripped down to his shirt now, he pitched into Laertes like a wrestler ready to close. All ceremony and elegance evaporated, the pair were no longer opponents, they were enemies, and deadly ones, swiping and slicing, and swinging their swords high and bringing them down on each other like executioners' axes. Then weapons and bodies got locked together and Osric called the end of the bout, instead of which Laertes stabbed at Hamlet with his dagger and Hamlet smashed at his wrist and the dagger spun high across the hall, narrowly missing some of the spectators. They were no longer applauding. Hamlet aimed a kick at the other wrist and the sword sailed through the air, following the dagger, and skidded along the floor. Laertes chased after it but Hamlet got there first, slammed a foot on the sword, picked it up, examined the point, and with infinite mock courtesy and a deep bow, handed Laertes his own blunted weapon and faced him for the fourth challenge. Osric glanced at the king.

'No! Part them! They're out of control! Stop the match!'

It was too late. Hamlet battered at his man so savagely that Laertes' defence was down in what seemed less than a second, and in that same second, as Hamlet stabbed him deeply in the chest, the queen keeled over. The spectators screamed.

'The Queen! The Queen!'

Osric ran over to Laertes, where he lay bleeding on the floor. 'How bad is it?'

'You know how bad it is, Osric. As bad as it can be. I'm killed by my own treachery.'

All the spectators now stood on their feet, shocked and terrified, looking at the king. Hamlet shouted above the uproar.

'What's wrong with her? What's happening?'

Claudius was still attempting his grinning act.

'It's all right, friends, don't worry, it's the blood, she can't stand the sight of blood, it makes her feel faint!'

Gertrude half raised herself on one arm from the floor as the attendants gathered round her.

'No, no—it's the drink! Oh God, my dear son Hamlet, it's the drink, the drink! It's, it's—I'm poisoned…'

They were her last words.

'Lock the doors!' roared Hamlet. 'Nobody leaves! It's treachery!'

'It's here, Hamlet! Right here!

Laertes lay in a pool of blood, spreading across the floor. He was unable to lift his head. Osric raised him slightly.

'No need—no need to look further. Hamlet, you're a dead man. Nothing can help you. There's not half an hour of life left in you. You're holding it in your hand, what killed you. It's not only unblunted, it's poisoned, a deadly venom, there's no antidote for it, we're both done for, and your mother too. The pearl that went into the cup she drank from, that wasn't all that went in, and it was meant for you. It was the plot… it was the king… the king's to blame!'

Hamlet stared again at the point of the sword.

'Invisible. Like all his crimes. And it's poison again, poison to the last, to the very end. Then poison—go to work!'

He threw himself at Claudius and toppled him to the floor, stabbing him repeatedly. Shrieks from the spectators.

'Treason! Where are the guards? Unlock the doors!'

Claudius gasped out his last words.

'Help me, friends! Call for my guards! I'm only wounded!'

Hamlet reached out for the poisoned cup and kneeled astride the bleeding, pleading king.

'Only wounded are we? The blade not enough for you, no? Here, you incestuous, murderous, damnable dog of a Dane, have a swig of this!'

He forced the goblet between the teeth. The wine welled up as he tried to spit it out, dribbling blood-red over his beard, and he choked and hacked and gasped as half the contents of the cup went down his gullet.

'Is your precious pearl here? No? No, she's gone too! Better go after her, then. A pearl without price—so my father thought. Follow her. Follow my mother!'

Laertes was only just alive. His last words were barely audible.

'Is the king dead?'

Hamlet knelt down.

'Dead—and destined for hell.'

'It's the place for him. He's murdered both of us. Forgive me if you can, Hamlet. Forgive me your death and I forgive you my father's. We were fools of fate, and we were preyed on by a killer, a killer without a conscience.'

Laertes never lived to hear Hamlet's acceptance of his plea. The prince, who was now the king, fell to his knees.

'So there it is, friend, Horatio, just as we spoke about that short time ago. The time has come.'

He looked over at his mother, dead on the flood, if dead she was. None of us could have known the exact moment of her passing.

'And for her too, that poor wretch of a queen. And I'm being taken into custody, it seems. A stern officer, this Death chap, stern in his arrest, doesn't give you much time, does he? No time to tell all these good people what happened here. I leave that to you, Horatio.'

'No you don't!'

That's when I grabbed the goblet and made to drink the dregs, and Hamlet dashed it from my hand, begging me to defer death's felicity for a little while longer yet, and tell his story.

'And do one last thing for me, my friend, while I'm still here.'

He begged me to instruct the court to wait there in the hall for a short time until he returned.

'Returned. Returned from where?'

'I want you to help me up to the ramparts, if you can. I want to look out to sea for one last time.'

He stood up with difficulty, breathing hard, and I supported him up the stairway and onto the battlements. I had my arms round him, partly for the support, partly too because it was our last living embrace. Knowing it himself, he placed his hand on my chest and pushed me ever so gently away, as if to say we had to prepare for the separation that was shortly to come, the one that never ends. That's what his quiet eyes were saying as they gazed into mine. There was the ghost of a sad smile on his lips. Then he looked out from the ramparts, across the water for that one last time.'

'There it is, Horatio—the sea of troubles. It's still there, and always will be. But see how calm it is today, and so infinitely quiet. No more troubles, eh, old friend? The troubles are over.'

We went back down into the hall.

It was in a deathly hush. As we came through the door the whole court sank quietly to its knees, acknowledging King Hamlet, as he had to be, a king for a matter of minutes. There was no-one left to elect. He looked at the kneeling audience and shook his head. Suddenly he slipped to the floor, out of my arms. The court gasped. I laid his back to the wall, to keep him half propped up, and thought that that story of his, so important to him, was almost over. But in the sudden hush that had fallen on Elsinore, we heard something, from a distance, the unmistakable sound of soldiers on the march, coming closer, followed by a volley of shots.

'What is it?' asked Hamlet. 'These sounds of war?'

Osric was sent out. Hamlet's breathing was becoming increasingly laboured and his eyes were dimming.

'Hurry!' I shouted.

Hamlet smiled. But Osric returned almost at once, having met the sentries.

'It's young Fortinbras and his army, newly come from Poland—in conquest.'

'And why the gunfire?' I asked.

'A salute—to the English ambassadors, also just arrived.'

Hamlet tried to rise but fell back again against the wall.

'Too late, Horatio. I won't live to hear the news from England. But before I die I declare my wishes for the election of my successor. It should be Fortinbras, the conquering hero. He has my dying voice. Tell him what has happened, and what has prompted me—if you can read my heart—to give him what would have been my kingdom. He will be a worthy successor to my father. I could never have held a candle to him in that respect. Or to my father. Fortinbras is Denmark's man. And he will blot out all that came between. And for the rest, for the rest... the rest is silence.'

His heart stopped. Hamlet was dead. Good night, sweet prince? Easy to say so. Easy to announce the flights of angels, ushered in to sing him to rest. I spoke some such words. But as I knelt there beside my dead friend, I thought that the silence he had spoken of, the last word he breathed, would have been his best friend in the end, the most welcome and most gracious of friends—if nothing else as sheer relief to an action-wearied soul, freedom from conflicting motives, endless leisure for probing into all life's' worries, vexations and enigmas, release at last from the labour or even love of fitting words to thoughts; and silence as the one sole language of eternity, the only true utterance of the infinite. High-sounding words, I know, but they were my pedant's thoughts—which that gathering would not have wanted to hear, even if they could have understood. The choirs of angels were a simpler proposition, though not one that Hamlet in his last frame of mind would have expected or even wished to be implemented. And in any event—silence preferred. Much more relaxing.

I was turning over these totally immaterial ideas in my admittedly dazed brain, when practical reality intervened—in the form of Fortinbras and a number of his soldiers, together with the English ambassadors. Fortinbras had been warned that there had been a bloodbath. Young as he was, he was already a hardened soldier, but even he was taken aback by what he saw—the dead bodies strewn about the hall: the king, the queen, Laertes, and the young king of minutes, all lying there, two of them in dark pools of their own blood. He didn't mince his words.

'Bloody hell! What in God's name happened here? It's a court carnage!'

The first English ambassador nodded gravely.

'A dreadful sight indeed. And we've come too late, it so appears, with our affairs from England. The royal ears are deaf, it seems, that should receive our news, to tell him that his order is fulfilled: that Rosencrantz and Guildenstern are dead. And so—how to render our report?'

'Not to him,' I said, indicating the corpse of Claudius. 'Not that he would thank you for it, had he the life left in him to do so. He never gave the order for their execution. That came from another hand. But now that you are here, newly come from England, and you, young Fortinbras, from your Polish wars, I ask you to take charge of what's to come, to place these bodies high on a stage for all to see, after which I shall do all I can to spell out the reasons for their deaths, and unravel a tangle of tales that will beggar all belief.'

Fortinbras nodded briefly.

'I'm not one for talk. But by all means let's hear what you have to say. It needs to be said. As for me, I believe I have some claim here to this kingdom—certain rights, if you like, which should not be forgotten, and of which I intend to take advantage.'

'I don't know about your rights, as you call them,' I said, 'but I do know that this is what young Hamlet intended, and I too have intentions—to make his intentions clear. But for this moment, let's do as we have said, explain events, and give these bodies—not all of them the dignity—but for now at least the display we have agreed upon.'

'Agreed,' echoed Fortinbras, 'but first'—he was making it clear that he was now in control—'first Hamlet. The others will follow. Hamlet was a prince, all too briefly a king. I'll have four of my captains carry him like a soldier up to the stage, for he was most likely, had he been elected to the throne, to have proved a great king, worthy to follow his warlike father. And to mark his passing out of this life, and into the country of the dead, where no kings rule, I'll have the soldiers' music and all military rites speak loudly for him. I'll have it no other way. And I'm certain he would have had it no other way. He would have been a hero. And so—take up the bodies. They befit the battlefield—where I've seen a thousand times worse—but here they offend the eye. Carry on, then, and give the order. Tell the soldiers—shoot!'

Epilogue
A Gallery Of Ghosts

Enter the Ghost of Hamlet

Somebody once said that my tragedy was the tragedy of a man who could not make up his mind. A slick abridgement and a neat summation, and almost plausible. But what does it mean? Make up my mind about what? About killing Claudius, I suppose. And that too sounds almost plausible—on the face of it at least. I killed him in the end not because I'd made up my mind to do it, but because I had only minutes left to live and so I had nothing to lose—it was a reflex action, if you like, triggered by his own actions against me, not mine against him. Everyone else that mattered was dead anyway, except Horatio, so what the hell? My revenge, to put it another way, was never a deliberate decision, it was just something that happened, and could quite conceivably never have happened, but for Claudius, and his poison plot. My mind was always foot-loose. It milled thought like the sea mills salt, and like the sea always awake, always anxious, always busy.

And so: the inability to arrive at a decision—yes, it's an interpretation of sorts, and one that seems to suit the facts, or some of them. Here was a man who just could not make up his mind—and there you have me, explained, if not entirely exonerated. That's me catalogued and classified: the thinker who thought so much he couldn't actually decide what he *did* think—about anything. Call me a dreamer, then, an abstracted introvert, unsuited to the cut and thrust of action, preferring instead the realm of speculation, meditation—and words. But no, that's a simplistic image and a fake portrait of me, a superficial one at any rate, specious and glib. A man who could not make up his mind. Nine words—and all is clear? Not to me. Clear to an actor perhaps, who wants his man tailored to a formula that will suit the role he wants to play. But I wasn't playing a role. I was, to put it rather grandly, struggling with the meaning of life, not exactly helped by a dose of good old melancholia.

All right then, you will ask me, what *was* the truth? What was it that held me back? I was cynical, of course, bitterly cynical about life, the sweat and stench of the flesh and its decay after death. I was disillusioned by human beings: the corrupt quintessence of dust, food for worms, meat for maggots, and long before that a dishonest and despicable lot, even the ones you loved or wanted to love, and even your dear mother a feeder on fornication and adultery, sold body and soul to a grinning hypocrite, a slippery politician, a softie and a heavy drinker and an incestuous libertine and usurper—not to mention a murderer.

Can you wonder that I asked myself that ultimate question of philosophy: is life worth living? Not particularly, considering the evidence to the contrary: the slings and arrows, the whips and scorns, the thousand shocks—you know how it goes on—the burdens under which you grunt and sweat like an ass, until death unpacks you, and you go you've no idea where, perhaps to face the terrors of an afterlife, not even knowing what they are or what that is: the undiscovered country and its bad dreams. I used to worry myself sick about all that, when I believed in an afterlife, and when the present life disturbed me, when that sea of troubles broke on Elsinore's shore; and contemplating it as I did, I was left unable to kill either my enemy or even myself, to end the heartache.

Some men would have found it easy. Thought and action: a marriage for them, for others a divorce. An easy wedding for men like old Odysseus, for example, wrestling with wars and women, and all the time thinking one step ahead, and making every single point of the compass his ingle-nook, his home. But it was always war. And it was the same with my father: he was at home when wandering, while still straining for home. And when at home he was always fighting the wanderlust. So there was no real rest. 'I'll rest when I'm dead,' he liked to say. But death had other ideas…

One other thing, and I've thought about it over and over. I was an only child, *the* only child, when kings were busy scattering their maker's image through the land, legit and illegit. Why? And what if? What if I'd had a brother to confide in? Or a sister? Was I enough? I suppose I know the answer to that, of course. He had other offspring. They were the stories he told, tales of kings and princes who were heroes, not like me, stories the mind makes up to combat death. Other men tell them over and over at nights, burning out the hours, spinning out the fantasies for the faces in the firelight, and the old remembering mouths, and ears. Amleth was one of these stories.

But I know what you'll be thinking, and you'll be right. I'm avoiding the issue. Very well then, let's face it. Why didn't I act at once to avenge my father? Not because I was afraid to—I was no coward, and had no fear of the consequences. Not because I had an aversion to bloodshed as such. Not even because I had doubts about the authenticity of the ghost—when I said so I was coming up with an excuse. I was trying to rationalise my inaction. No, the ghost was real enough, even if it had been nothing more than a projection of my own loathing and suspicion and need for hitting back at him, at her, at all of them. Yes, my wit was diseased, my will was broken, I hated myself for my failure, and I hated myself all the more for my self-hatred. It all felt futile.

But then so did revenge. What was the *use* of killing Claudius? What would it achieve? Would it save my mother's honour, undo her dishonour? Would it bring my father's mouldering body back to life? His suffering spirit back from purgatory? And on from there—would it resurrect the drowned and dead Ophelia? Would it open up the prison doors and free Denmark, when Denmark after all was merely a single cell in an open prison—a world-wide clink? Would it alter the universal scheme of things, purge the foul and pestilent gases, make the stars meaningful and the man in the moon mad no more?

Once you start thinking like that—and I couldn't stop thinking like that—you end up asking yourself: what's the use of anything? What's the point? The point was, I'd looked into the abyss. I'd seen that action, any action, is absurd, futile, momentary, the movement of a muscle this way or that. Suffering, on the other hand, is long, obscure, and infinite. And all that's got nothing to do with making up your mind. The man you see in Horatio's letters is not a man who thinks too much—that's the soft approach. No, he is a man who thinks that the universe stinks, it smells of mortality. And his soul is sick with it. And sick of it. This prince is not pining, he's passed on, he's a spiritual stiff. I saw all that so much more clearly when I came back to Elsinore after the aborted voyage. I saw myself so much more clearly. Horatio was right about that too. He called it a sea-change. But not into something rich and strange; quite the reverse. Bones don't turn to coral when you sink them in the sea, and they don't turn to gold when you lay them in the earth. And eyes don't turn to pearls either. Yorick's eyes told me that much—or rather his eyelessness. By that time I could hear it loud and clear: that dumb hush in the skull's distracted globe, the actor's ultimate horror—no applause after the play of life, only the dreamless theatre of the dead head. No angels either, only annihilation. It was the big silence.

And I was ready for it. I was more than ready for it. I wanted nothing else, other than to expel the woman trouble, the double-trouble, my mother—and Ophelia. The girl I never had. No, I never did it with her, though once I dreamed I did, dreamed I slept with her, in the sea-grass it was, on the dunes, when I fucked her brains out, and woke to the scent of blood, salt and nausea, and the kirkyard mould stopping up my mouth, after which came the gravediggers, heaping earth on the two of us. A nightmare. It *was* a nightmare, my sperm inside her, and that sadness after a shag, the sadness all creatures taste. I tasted it often enough in Wittenberg, but I couldn't transfer the taste to Elsinore, couldn't erase the images, the privates at their pumping, the tongue's prick kittling the cunt of her mouth, and my whanger drilling her to mid-point, where my dead heir spurts in starch, Ophelia's blown egg…

Tears then? And sorry smiles perchance, at that awkward tender moment? Then fish-guff, cunt-funk, and the slimy withdrawals… oh, fuck! Oh, fuck, no! no! The body's a stinking gutter-hole, a sewer. I just couldn't do it with her…

But you could, mother, with him, lying with him as easy as you lied to your husband, his brother. Don't blench then, I beg you, from what you two practised without conscience in my father's bed, where his goat's tot got stuck in, and the semen clots blotted the sheets. Entered and exited, in and out, over and over, repeat performances, a long-running play, each orgasm a round of applause. Oh, well fucked, you two! Now do it again! And again! And make the wet fur of her fud as slippery as your prick.

Only don't ask me why I let Ophelia die. I don't know why. I told myself I loved her more than that death it was my life's sudden work to avenge. But I didn't prove it. I clowned instead, to counter an ingrained ennui. And now it's too late. It's finished. Leave my brain to the doctor's dissection, whatever he'll make of it, what troubles he'll find written there, what rooted sorrows, what disease. My cloak, let Horatio have it, to warm him when his heart grows cold to me, as it must. My sword, poems, treatises, I bequeath to the city—not Elsinore, but Wittenberg. No stone either. Place me over Ophelia, in the coition position. Our dusts shall couple till time stops, and so on into eternity. There's no fire, though. It doesn't matter. Perhaps… perhaps death the apple will round us into ripeness, or into rot. Ripeness and readiness, rotting, silence, rest. I'll say it again. I was ready for it. I wanted nothing else.

Exit

Enter the Ghost of Claudius

I didn't want silence, I wanted dancing and drinking and the battlements booming out—and so did everyone else, except him. Denmark was no prison, as he claimed, nor was the world one—it's the mind that imprisons you, if you let it, or if that's your choice. I offered Elsinore an alternative universe: a free one, a healthy one, filled with life, good nature, eating and drinking, celebrating, getting on with people, meeting them halfway, cutting them some slack, bending over for them, waving them on with a cheery smile, keeping the state machine ticking over and its enemies smoothed into complaisance, averting hostilities—see how I handled the Fortinbras problem—and the threat of war, using courtesy and consideration and tact—all this along with healthy sex and, like I said, the cannons sounding out for fun each time you bend your elbow and take a swig. What's wrong with any of that, with living the good life?

That's what I wanted and I went for it. No smiting the sledded Polacks on the ice for me, no bloody noses and cracked crowns, and drinking toasts out of the skulls of your enemies. Keep them appeased instead and drink their healths out of golden goblets—they don't have to be poisoned ones, not if the enemies are conversable and ready to settle for life, not death.

Death. Death, you see, was my brother's trade, and death was what I gave him, though not the kind of death he would have chosen. It was murder and I tried to hate myself for it but couldn't, not quite enough to make a good confession. Still it was only one murder and I put it behind me and smiled on life and on the world. I was happy to be of the world with all its crassness and shallowness and criminality and glitter, and my court was happy to follow me. I was a life-force. We got on well together. We belonged to corrupt humanity with all its failings. We were warm and weak and well contented. We wanted life and—I'll say it again—not death.

That was the trouble with Hamlet. Death was his thing. He'd been inspired by the spirit of a rotting corpse. *He* was what was rotten in the state of Denmark. He was not inhuman but he was anti-human, anti-life. He believed in nothing, not even in himself, nothing but the memory of this ghost, and at times he didn't even believe in that. But his strength was ghost-begotten, and everything he stood for tended towards annihilation. He'd seen through humankind and he'd written off the world. Good for him, and good for his philosophy. But he was static and negative and the only hindrance to a good life and a healthy Elsinore. Look at the number of deaths he caused, directly and indirectly. They'd all have remained alive but for him. Even Fortinbras was shocked by the havoc he'd caused. I used ambassadors to good purpose. He was the ambassador of extinction. Death was his embassy, and he got on well with death. It was the muddle of life that troubled him. By the end he'd lost interest in it. He never really wanted to live. That was his choice. If only he'd let us choose for ourselves. But he chose for us. And dragged us all along with him. Into the dark.

Exit

Enter the Ghost of Gertrude

I didn't want the dark either, I wanted the sun. And it seemed so easy, at first, so comfortably, unthinkingly easy. Easy? Easy to call me easy? Yes, why not, call me easy—easy under a crown, easy under a man, easy in bed, especially an adulterous one, easy between incestuous sheets, legs spread for my husband's brother, yes, that's me, if that's how you care to call me. I've been called a sheep in the sun too. But even a sheep needs more than the sun, as a woman needs more than a son. A sheep needs to feed. A sheep needs grass. All flesh is grass, they say. And I needed the grass, the flesh. So you can add that to the roll-call. You can call me the sullied flesh as well. And you can call my second marriage a double defilement—it sullied my flesh because man and wife are one flesh, and so it stained my lean and hungry first husband by corrupting his heroic spirit with the grossness of the bloated second. Only God could have sundered me from the first, and God didn't—poison did, but failed to kill the spirit, so I remained married to my first husband in the eye of God and married to the second in the eye of hell.

And in the eye of Hamlet. For him it was even worse than incest, because of the one-flesh law. In his mind's eye he watched the three of us in bed together, the bloated brother between my legs in the first husband's indissoluble presence: a threesome, and a kind of cannibalism too, a manner of self-eating. I know that's how he saw it—his tirades left nothing to my imagination, it all came spilling out of him, the loathing, the bitterness, and at times I thought the poison of jealousy. Oh yes, Hamlet too used poison. But the king to him was the only poisoner. His uncle, he said, had a gut for garbage, and had reduced life at Elsinore to a process of appetite and excretion long before I stole from my celestial bed to prey on garbage too. Worse still, I copulated with a snake, a goat—I was guilty of bestiality.

Enough of that. You will want to know if I was an accomplice to the murder, though Horatio's letters have exonerated me from any complicity in that crime. Adultery, not murder, was my sin. You may also wish to know if I too committed suicide, like Ophelia. Did I suspect the cup prepared for my son to be a poisoned chalice? Did I doubt the complexion of the popped-in pearl, or did I think the pearl had a companion, and did I drink from the cup as a desperate test? Surely if it really was a poisoned chalice my husband would never allow me to drink from it innocently? So by drinking I was ensuring my son's safety.

No—none of that happened. It was never in my mind for a moment, I had no suspicions. It was only afterwards, after I had drunk, and had begun to feel the fatal effects, that the words came flooding back to me. *Good Gertrude, do not drink!... As kill a king!... A second time I kill my husband dead... Poison in jest... He poisons him in the garden for his estate...!* And suddenly I understood. And oh, God! What an agony of horror and regret was there! But the terrible truth had come too late. In my dying moments I knew that my son too had been poisoned. Nobody even marked the exact moment of my last breath. That came just a little after my last words. And I lived long enough to learn the truth, while the death I died was the same death my cheated husband died.

I was not surprised by my son's coldness to me at our last meeting, but I still loved him and was hurt by it. He made no effort to contact me after coming home from the sea. He ignored me at Ophelia's graveside, though I spoke some sweet words to that sweet girl. I wiped his face during the fencing. I even caroused to him coquettishly with my not yet faded charms, and wished him success. Cold courtesy was all I got. I was 'madam', not mother. I was the wretched queen. Hardly a fond farewell. And I lived and breathed long enough to hear his contemptuous adieu to the king he'd just killed: *Follow my mother*. As if I too were destined for hell.

What was my fault, adultery apart? I wanted sex, that was my sin. My first husband got his rocks off—you know by now how it goes—smiting the sledded Polacks on the ice. He never gave much thought to smiting me, where I wanted to be smitten—between the legs, in bed. I longed for it. I was smitten enough by him when we were young. We were both smitten. But as soon as he'd impregnated me, as soon as he'd begotten his son, he was offski to Polonski. What more can I say? He loved me, yes. But he didn't love my needs. My needs were in bed, his were in the field. And so I succumbed to his brother. That was my crime.

Also I clung to my youth, refusing to grow old. I still had my charms. Call me names, again, call me shallow, lymphatic, an amiable adulteress. Yet I wept like Niobe when my deceived husband died. I used to hang on him, after all. It was the obvious way of deceiving him. Were my tears false, then? Not altogether. They were real precisely because I had been false to him. So there was some shame and guilt. But the shame was shallow and the guilt easy to shed, like tears; no real remorse. Maybe I was immune to the thorns that would prick and sting more precious people. I suffered from a kind of blindness of the spirit, which was why I couldn't see *his* spirit, not even when it appeared in our old bedchamber, remembering the nights perhaps, the nights we had when we were young and I was faithful. It was only later that it hit me, the shame and the self-reproach. I was so guilt-sick by then that I couldn't even bear to see Ophelia, that poor deserted girl. I wished I could blot her out. Her sorrow, her lost innocence, they seemed to symbolise everything that had gone wrong. It was only when I stood over her grave that I felt a bond of sorts, a motherly feeling for a motherless child—a long way from home.

Exit

Enter the Ghost of Ophelia

A long way from home? You could say that—except that there never was a home, not really. There was a busy father and an absent brother. And yes, there was a motherless child, who did sometimes feel that her hopes were in vain… until he came along.

Did he love me, then? You've read the letters, Horatio's notes. What do you think? He importuned me with love, as they say, oh yes. But lots of men importune ladies whom they don't really love—it's what men do. He whispered sweet nothings to a sweet nothing—the sweet nothing he wanted me to be. Later he talked about the sweet zero between my legs. And that's all he did, all he ever did—talk about it. He never filled it, that sweet nothing, never came into it, never acted on it, all talk and no action. The idea mattered to him, always the idea, not the thing itself.

He sent me letters, though, as you know, and he wrote me poems. Doubt thou the stars are fire. I didn't doubt that the stars were fire. I didn't doubt that they weren't. I never even thought about the stars, or cared about them. I cared about him, I cared for him. How much did he care about me? He cared more for Horatio, I think, his best friend, his only friend. Why was he so friendless? When you have that sort of special friend, you share things, don't you? Intimate things that you wouldn't share with anyone else.

Intimate. So I asked Horatio—did he ever allude to me in their talk? Horatio was truthful. Not once. Not one mention. And did you notice, he never once referred to me in his last moments on earth, by which time I'd been long blotted out of his life, airbrushed from his emotions. And the country matters? All that was just more talk. Mine was the undiscovered cuntrie. Was there any cuntrie he cared for? If I may sound so crude? Maybe his mother's. As for me, the long purples were as close as I got to penetration—and they were dead men's fingers. Let's face it, apart from a few murmured pleasantries to Horatio, the only real words of love he ever uttered were spoken to a skull. Alas, poor Yorick. Why alas? Yorick was fortunate, he was favoured. Here hung those lips that I have kissed... how many times did he say? He'd lost count. He never kissed me once, never mind country matters. But he got it right when he likened my dad to old Jephthah. Sacrifice your daughter to the system, whatever that may be, and let her go out and bewail her virginity. She died a damsel, virgo intacta. I had plenty of that to bewail. He even advised me to become the bride of Christ. And if not the living death of nunnification—or nullification—then the hell of the brothel. As I was such a little whore. A virgin whore. Either way a negation of life. And a prison door to procreation. A fitting sentence for the gone girl of Elsinore. Nobody even missed me at the end. Follow my mother... Wretched queen, adieu... The rest is silence...Rosencrantz and Guildenstern are dead... Go, bid the soldiers shoot! Not a word about the gone girl.

And yet there could have been a time, even if I'd died thereafter, there could have been a time for such a word. There was time enough at my graveside, all eternity. Instead, he sent Horatio down to old Yohan's—a stoup of ale, if you will, old friend, for my new friend, the grave-digger—to toast the jester, another old friend, long lost now, lost in earth.

But not to toast his old lover, though—notice that, did you? Not to toast his sweet Ophelia, lying fresh and forgotten in her grave. Oh yes, he could have twisted me into the song he never sang for me. He could have gone down to Yohan's, himself, gone down and got drunk for the love of me, for the loss of me. Or better still, he could have gone down to Jake's place, down at the Black Swan, down past the graveyard, where the rafters rang with laughter, so I've heard…

I've heard. I was never actually there, you see. How could I be? I was never out of Elsinore. The first time I left Elsinore was when they took me to my grave; rather too late, you might say, to learn a little about life outside the castle walls. But I can sing it for you now, if you like, and you will like it, I promise you, it's sad and soulful, bitter-sweet, and right up your street, time-wise at least—well, almost. I know who you are, you see, I know exactly who's listening. I can play with the centuries, now that I'm freed from time. I'm freer than I ever was. And I suspect Jake would have loved to hear me sing this one. He was a bit like the sweet prince himself, you know, melancholy, mournful, witty, profound, but without the cruelty that made the sweet prince so cold. I'm stepping outside my ghost's role now, I know, like one of those off-duty Naiads, having a cigarette in the bath, a sneaky smoke between watery seductions. I've had enough of water. I'm enjoying the elbow-room, the unconstraint, the sheer irrelevance. Except Jake is not, you see, so irrelevant. He was the prince of the taverns and the taverners. Hamlet spoke of him, I remember, in the good days, the early days. He called him Jakes, his joke for a place to piss in, Jake's place. In another time and place we could have gone there together, the prince and I, and got drunk. It would have been nice, a little tipple and a titter. Princes have been known to haunt taverns, haven't they? Ah yes, but Elsinore was a long way from Wittenberg, the sweet Ophelia was no bar-stool slut, and the prince's drinking days were over. Mine never got started. But I could always sing. And I'll sing again now—not from the heart, that's not possible, my heart's withered, and turned to dust in that graveyard, long ago—but from the soul, which is what I am. The spirit sings, if you like, and this is my swan-song, my black swan-song. It's the song he should have sung for me, the song he would have sung for me, if he had really loved me. As usual, I'm having to sing it myself. Are you all ears? You should fill a glass for this one—it's made for it. How would it go, now? Like this. Of course—how else?

> Down at the Black Swan
> I'll drink till I'm half gone -
> I'm back from the bilboes,
> I'm bending both elbows,
> And I'll quaff to forget
> That once she was mine.
>
> Down at old Jake's place
> I'll tank up at piss-pace,
> I'll swill and I'll souse,
> And bib and carouse,
> With a skinful forget
> That she was so divine.
>
> Down at Jake's boozer
> I'll booze like a loser,
> I'll sup up and swig
> And drink like a pig,
> And I'll slug to forget
> She was sweeter than wine.
>
> She came to her lover -
> The watery cover,
> Slipped into the bed,
> Ungendered, unwed,
> And sang to forget
> How she'd pined to be mine.
>
> Go to your grave, girl,
> Lie like a lost pearl
> Under the green sheets,

While the rude priest bleats
We mustn't forget
That you crushed the true vine.

So landlord pour a generous measure,
Drinking's now mine only pleasure,
Life is woeful on the wagon,
Fill me up another flagon,
Drown my sorrows till I'm tender,
Here I'm on an all-night bender
Now that she's gone...
Now she's gone

Only he'd never have noticed that I'd gone, if it hadn't been for my blasted brother, making such a song and dance about it. You were right, Horatio—brotheroo was stealing his thunder, making himself the man of the moment, and Hamlet couldn't stand that, it turned the sweet prince sour. Upstaged. And angry. Me? My life was never my own, and I did lose it all. I was just some bony beauty, dying of the greensickness called love, though maybe in his heart of hearts—I mean in one of his hart-panting-after-the-water-brooks moments—he pictured me as one of those round-buttocked goddesses, their dresses bursting with their fructifying flesh. Unlikely. He probably had nightmares of me instead, menstruating by the moon, for five days a month displaying a dramatic womanliness with which he was unfitted to cope. The red flag's flying, the Red Sea's in, full tide, bloody hell, she's bleeding between the legs again, real goddesses don't shed blood, they exude ichor, ethereal juice, that defines their divinity. And in his bad dreams he withdrew one sticky little finger from the mouth of the fussy little pussy that squirmed and purred and lived excitedly between my legs. It didn't matter. I was a flicker of lightning, no more. I could have lasted longer than a flash. He could have strung me out longer, just a little longer. Could have, could have. But no, he couldn't. Because he wasn't a Black Swan man, he was nobody's man. And at one time

I really thought we had something. I could have had children. Do you remember, once he had even promised to teach me to read…

Exit

Enter the Ghost of Polonius

There was no need for her to read. Read what? His letters were affected anyway, and his poems mere posturings. Oh, yes, I know, don't tell me, I know what you're about to say—here he comes again, sneaking out from behind the arras of eternity, death's screening curtains, to speak his piece, safe from stabbing maniacs. No more of that, now that I'm laid in earth. And in his grave rained many a tear… So sang Ophelia. And did it? Did it rain hard for me? Apart from my son and daughter I didn't see that much rain, and not a drop from His Majesty, whom I served so well. It was only old Polonius, the platitudinous old Polonius, the garrulous old git, worldly wise but morally shallow, the spouter of the utilitarian ethic, nothing too deep, nothing much to rain for. Well, if I may beg to excuse myself, my job was not to see too deep—and I didn't. My duty was to oil the established order. To which I was a time-server, and a faithful one. I did well by the new king. I never suspected he was a murderer. An adulterer? I may have seen a thing or two. I had my spies. And I may have had my qualms. But murder—no. So I got on with the job, and without thinking too hard about it. Was that so bad? I could name a man who did the opposite. Now he was a deep thinker. And where did that get him? Where did it get Denmark? Straight into the hands of Fortinbras, the young whizz-kid and the old enemy. He was no deep thinker either. Sometimes it pays not to think too much. And now, if you will excuse me, as brevity is the soul of wit, it's back behind the arras for me. I won't be out again…

Exit

Enter the Ghost of Laertes

What can I say in my defence? They all seem to be excusing themselves. Hamlet had lost a father—and a mother too, as he saw it. I had no mother, and I lost a father—and a sister. Talkers are no good doers. While he talked about revenge, I acted. Do you see how easy it was? To storm Elsinore and have the king at my mercy? I could have killed him on the spot and had the people on my side too. I could have been king. I could have been somebody. I could have been a contender! How much easier would it have been for the people's hero? But he wasn't made of that stern stuff.

Not that I was that much of a success in the end. I tried to be the effective revenger and I ended up, I admit it, it's been said, an irresolute bungler. Like my father, I didn't think too much. Had I done so… but I was wax in craftier hands and I became the easiest of dupes. Still, I had no scruples. I went along with the trap the king had set and I added my own device to help it along, and I died of it. I should have looked after her better, I should have been more careful. I should have been more kind. But I was hardly alone in that. Was Hamlet kind? Was there even a grain of kindness in him? All of us should have been kinder. All of us should have taken greater care…

Exit

Enter the Ghost of Fortinbras

I was never a man of words and I shall waste none now, except to indicate an irony of sorts. Three men lost fathers and I was one of them. The other two took their revenge. I didn't. But I took something bigger: the crown and the kingdom of Denmark, including on another front the territories, lost by my father to old

King Hamlet. So it worked out neatly for me as it happened, and it was a form of requital. The whirligig of time, as has been said, brings in his revenges. Normally I was not accustomed to leaving it to time—there was little enough to waste, with wars to be fought and territories to be won. But on this occasion my hands were full. And the whirligig did it for me.

Exit

Enter the Ghosts of Rosencrantz and Guildenstern

We liked a whirligig, so we did. But not the one that did for us. That was cruel. And he was cruel when he wanted to be. Anyway, here we are, together. And you wouldn't expect us to enter separately, now would you? Not after all that's been said and done. And we'll exit together too. After all, we died together on the same block. That pleased Hamlet, in the single second he took even to register our shared death. We were false friends to him, there's no denying it. He had a true friend, one who was content to be poor, un-self-seeking. We weren't content to be poor, we were in the pay and pocket of the king. We were snakes on the make. But we were drawn into it, we didn't know what exactly was wanted of us when we arrived at Elsinore. And we didn't know for sure what was in that packet. So as things turned out, we were pawns on the chequerboard of politics. We were characterless characters, nobodies, nonentities. But as nonentities we were hardly worth the killing, were we? He took out his failure on us innocents and he let the murderer live—until things went the other way. When he came back to Elsinore he showed no intention of acting against him, none. We were a side-show. We were a vicarious revenge, and a mistaken one, just like Polonius. Admit it. We were an excuse…

Exeunt

Enter the Ghost of Osric

I admit everything. And I admitted everything. Under interrogation. There was no need for torture. I was happy to talk my head off, in order to keep it on. I was always happy to serve. And now I must take my leave—after what flourish my nature will, and indeed must, if you will excuse me…

Exit

Enter the Ghost of the Gravedigger

Excuse me. *First* gravedigger, if you don't mind. You may say there should be no hierarchies in the graveyard, whether above or below its equalising dirt. But somebody has to dig that dirt, and I did all the digging for that girl's grave—and up came Yorick's skull. Would you believe it?—cap and bells and all. It's been said already—the dead just won't stay dead, will they? That's one thing this story teaches you. Even bloody Yorick! He was the bugger who emptied a flagon over my head once, as you know, the mad bastard. What a waste of wine! And now there he was, back up out of his pit, a nothing, a double nothing—two holes where there had once been two sparkling eyes. That hit Hamlet in the eye, all right.

Hamlet. Yes, I remember the Prince of Denmark, looking eye to eyelessness at that skull. He was a book man, was Hamlet, used to eying up whole volumes in folio, they said, unlike me. I never read a book in my life. How could I? I couldn't read. But I eyed up many's the skull. And a skull isn't hard to read. You don't even have to be clever to read it. You don't need to know Latin, or any language, come to that. And it's a damned good read.

Think of it now. The skull has a message, same as a book. But the skull's message is non-lingual—if a little gravedigger can use a big word. Or you could say it's multi-lingual—there's a bigger word—or universal, unambiguous—bigger still—not like a book, which must have all sorts of different readings, I suppose, different layers. A skull doesn't have layers—it's lost all of them, skin, flesh, everything, just as it's lost all it had on the inside too, all that grey matter. Just think of the brainy worms that must come crawling out of that lot, after a damned good feed. Well-read worms, eh? And all those intellectually juicy slugs.

That appealed to Hamlet. I can still see him staring at that skull, and I remember the look in his eye. He was thinking—I've read all them books, but here's a book now that makes you want to put down all the others, this is the number one best-seller, and after this one you don't want to read any more. You don't need to. You've looked death in the face and now you're ready to face your own death. The readiness comes once you'd held that skull and looked into its gone-out eyes. It doesn't have to be the skull of a jester, it could be anybody's, but all the better if it's someone's you once knew, someone who once had a face that you knew. That's the kind of skull that gives you the best read of all. I found that out for myself a long time ago. At one time I was the best-read man in Denmark.

Exit

Enter the Ghost of Yorick

And I was the ghost of laughter. I got dug up by accident, so it appears. Nobody was looking for me—who'd look for an old clown? And but for the fool's cap, nobody would have even known it was me. How could they? We all look the same in the earth: jesters, generals, kings, comedians. The breath of kings and clowns, eh? Makes you think. I heard somebody here say something about a fellow jester, just like me, who sang for death to come and take him away, as he'd failed in love. Do you remember that one? It was only a song, of course, but that's how it went. He asked to be laid in sad cypress, and for his white shroud to be stuck with yew. Not a flower, though—not a flower to be strewn on the black coffin, and not a friend, not a solitary friend to greet his corpse, and weep for it there. Just chuck the bones into the ground, old chaps, and forget the thousand sighs—they're not needed.

Was that how it went with me? Not at all. I had a good life at Elsinore, entertaining the women mostly, when the old king was off on his campaigns, which was most of the time, and his wife was finding her own entertainment, mostly in her brother-in-law's bed. I was father and mother to that boy, I can tell you, and we had our fun. He had wit, plenty of it. Doric Yorick he once called me, he was hardly any age at all at the time, and I said, hey, little halfling Hamlet, that's enough of that, I'm the jester here, I'll do the jokes! A clever little prick.

And so he came face to facelessness with me after twenty-three years, his dear dead jester friend and second mum and dad. That gave him quite a turn. Yes, my own face had gone, and so had the laughter. The cap was all that was left. But just for a moment there, the laughter came back to him, or an echo of it at least, when he remembered charging about the castle on the back of an old clown.

That laughter was there, though, at Elsinore, never forget it. Once there had been laughter...
Exit

Enter the Ghost of Sigmund Freud

Laughter? Yes, I know, that's not my field. And there aren't many laughs in my field, I know that too, just as I know I don't belong here, and I shouldn't be poking my psychiatric nose in. It's a faulty stage direction, I suspect, that's brought me here, but still my field does happen to be human nature, same as Shakespeare's. He'd never heard of Freud, but he had heard of human nature, and knew a thing or two about it, so if I can just chuck in my tuppenceworth, now that I'm here...

First penny of the tuppenceworth—the Oedipus Complex. Hamlet couldn't kill his uncle because like all boys he'd had fantasies about killing his father and marrying his mother, and so he identified with Claudius, who, in killing the old king, had done what Hamlet once wanted to do himself. All of that deep in the subconscious part of himself, of course, but it meant that his uncle therefore incorporated the deepest and most buried part of his own personality, so that he couldn't kill him without killing himself. And he just couldn't get his mother's bed out of his head. That's where he most wanted to be.

Second penny—the Orestes Complex. Many men develop a hatred of their mothers, a hatred which can be built up to a matricidal intensity because of the frustration they experience when their mothers, as they must, eventually cease to provide them with exclusive and all-embracing maternal care. So Gertrude's infidelity turned Hamlet's excessive attachment to his mother into bitter hostility—hostility suffered because of her attachment to his uncle, which was a betrayal both of himself and his father. You may find this persuasive. I'm an Oedipus man myself. And I'm a man who knows men well enough to know that some men will make bitter-sweet use of the thing they hate, while their lust learns to play with what it loathes for that which is far away. I trust I make myself sufficiently obscure?

Either way one thing is clear: the relationship with Ophelia was doomed from the start. The mother had got there first. He couldn't get out of his mother's bed to get himself into Ophelia's. When he spoke to her about country matters it was another country he had in mind—so deep in his mind he couldn't work out exactly which country he wanted to get to, death or sex. Not that it made any difference. Both to him were the undiscovered countries. As for death, he got there eventually, as we all do. But he just couldn't get into the cunt.

Exit

Enter the Ghost of Old King Hamlet

Yes, I know it, I hear it, I can catch what you're thinking before you even say it: I'm the ghost of a ghost, the hint of a spirit. I'm a memo, nothing more, not worth as much as a double-entendre, let alone a double entry. And why not double that, in the interest of accuracy, and make it four? Begone, bell-wether, troublemaker, who can't even count. Avaunt and quit my sight! Thy bones are marrowless and thy blood is cold! And so on. Yes, yes, I've heard all that before.

And you're right. But we all lose our marrow, and all our bloods run cold. That's what blood does in the end, that's what bones do. Except that they don't, not quite. Snoring bones, remember? And the dead won't stay dead, remember? I was the first of them to make that point, and they've all said their piece. I can't be seen by the wet sentry. Cold iron rails and wave-worn spiral steps don't bother me, though centuries of footfalls have turned them to a stone sea. No need to open doors either, not even the marble walls of the crypt. I can glide through. And the time is right. The sea lies soot and silver under the moon, and I arrive like the music of experience, sudden, intense, entire. Yes, you can guess I love this sort of thing, the whole scenario.

But why come again? Why the second run? Didn't I do enough first time round? I wasn't content to be a corpse you'll say. Eight other corpses had to follow. I had to make it nine, so that even young Fortinbras was staggered by what he saw: a blood-bath in a hall. And he was no pansy, he was leader of the pack, the top dog of the dogs of war. So: guilty as charged, yes?

Well, no, actually, now that you ask—if you're asking. I wasn't the one who fucked it up. He was given a perfectly simple job to do: to chop the fucker down and leave his mother out of it. What could have been simpler? But no, he had to complicate it, had to get in the way of it, to interpose his intellectual self, his ego, turn it into a Wittenberg philosophy class, a fucking debating chamber. Where would Denmark have been if I'd been a debater, if I'd played that game? We'd have been a catspaw for Norway, that's where we'd have been. But I acted differently. I acted. I was no king of councillors and conferences and court-talk. I once broke up a conference to split the skulls of the angry prattlers. I left prattle to the politicians. My slick-shit brother was good at that, him and his yes-men with their bent backs and subservience and their tongues dripping liquorice—lick-your-arse allies, the followers in the rear, the crawlers up the bum. Fuck them.

Me now? These wheeler-dealers never knew me, not the real me. They never stood at the sterns of ships and watched the stars, nailed to the winking armour of the nights, and the long dawns. That was the real me. I was kith and kin to earth and ocean. I gave my mind to the skies, to the Hyades, the Pleiades. I sat beneath the camp-fires of the constellations, me and my men. I gaped away the moon with them. I sold myself to those twinklers. A foul and pestilent congregation of vapours? No, they weren't, not if your own mind wasn't poisoned against them. No, the stars were old friends, familiar faces, fellow-watchmen, stolid sentries, navigators. They saw me through my campaigns, which was enough for me. I never looked to them for answers, never hankered after certainties, never among all the shifting skylines of my days. Somebody said it before me: the stars? They kept quiet, the buggers, stayed silent on those sorts of questions, outside the compass. And quite right too. There's only one certainty in the end: an axe-blade or a swordpoint. Beyond that I never troubled. I was an earth-stepper and a sea-gangrel, simple. The earth a sterile promontory? The sea a sea of troubles? The sea never troubled me, nor the earth neither. Why would they? How could they? Hot dust and cold salt had scoured my thoughts of everything—wife, son, queen, throne, Elsinore. What thoughts remained were mainly for my men, those soldiers who stood with me and took the ghost-road to eternity, and like young Fortinbras's men, went to their graves like beds.

And so: I supped from the full bowl of my senses, that's all. It's all I needed—that and the clouds' glower over my head, and the blue ploughlands of the sea that Gertrude hated, because they took me away from her hungry haunches. I didn't do too much ploughing there, it's true. It was wine in the mouth instead in the dew-drenched dawns, the salt stink seeping from whatever alien armpits you found yourself nuzzling naked at daybreak, blindly after battle—it didn't matter, it didn't mean I didn't love her dearly, it was the stuff of war, that's all. And I lived by it, but didn't die by it. I was cut off instead, stung sleeping by a snake. He didn't even have the decency to use a dagger, the cunt. Nor did my son, come to that, not until it was too late. The catastrophe was in full swing by then. Proved most royally? Had he been put on? Do me a favour. Young Fortinbras got that one wrong. Approximately one hundred per cent. He couldn't see a man as anything other than a soldier—cannon fodder, food for powder. And yet the people liked my son, he hit it off with them, because he had the common touch. But King of Denmark? No. He wasn't cut out for it.

I told him. I ordered him: don't taint your mind. He was kneeling at the time, when I said it, and I laid my hand on his head, and I could see it in his eyes, that he thought the gesture threatening, as if I was tainting it for him, as perhaps I was, by the contact, ghostly as it was, or all the more so, perhaps. At any rate I did see it at the time, the tainted mind. I saw it in his face. I knew exactly what was coming.

And now? Now I know that hell isn't a lake of fire, it's simply separation from God. And Purgatory? The fasting in fires is a metaphor. It's fasting all right—it's deprivation of what you miss most. I wish I could say it was her. Or him. Wife or son. I've said it, I did love them. But what I miss most is being in the field—that's why I showed myself in full fake armour, coming home again afterwards, to Elsinore, just as I always came, to a nice afternoon nap and a long sweet sleep, snake-free.

Exit

Enter the Ghost of Horatio

So what did you learn from my letters? That I loved Hamlet? Yes, I loved him, for all his failure. What else do you think? Would I have wanted him to succeed? Would I have wanted him to be a Fortinbras, or a Laertes—a killing-machine, or a grubby little plotter? No, I was content to listen to him talking about Caesar and Alexander, both brought down and wrecked by the wrangles of time, both turned to the same dust as the dead jester, and one re-moulded in Hamlet's mind to block a hole in a barrel of booze. It was trite talk, and unhealthy talk too, if you like, but I was happy to hear it. Had it been otherwise, had he been healthy, he could have taken an instant revenge and restored a rotten Denmark to health and happiness—and life. But the truth was he loathed life. He preferred pretend life—a play, a book, ideas, talk. And he lived on memories: I think I see my father... Yes, she would hang on him... Here hung those lips. Ideas. Images. Memories. It was always the same with Hamlet. A player's speech, a sexton's song, a gravedigger's ramblings—he was at home with fictive and frivolous things, preferring the unreal to the real, and finding forgetfulness and fun in the things that didn't matter. The things that did matter turned out to be a burden.

Until he came back from the sea, scrubbed clean of love, purged of all urges, needs and desires, a changed man: cool, calm, contemplative, un-suicidal, almost indifferent—and without either the mask or the madness. Claudius was right about that. The sea did expel the something-settled matter in his mind, in his heart. And he could no longer accept that the lawful use of his God-given reason was simply to chop a man down, as a butcher topples a pig. He'd already had that chance and he didn't take it. A common soldier could have done it, a hired hit-man, the local butcher. Why stoop to it? It didn't need a Fortinbras.

And they never met: the man of action and the man of thought. One of destiny's ironic omissions, you could say. And yet I have to say I was glad of that too. If they'd met, what could they have said to each other? Fortinbras marched in and announced that Hamlet would have made a great king, just like his father! No, he wouldn't. What did Fortinbras know? He treated Hamlet like a dead soldier. Wrong. But it was all a man like Fortinbras could understand. It was a kindness of fate, I thought, that when the two men finally came together, one of them was dead, and what would have been a pointless conversation never took place.

So: my beloved friend, Hamlet, was something of a failure as a friend. I was there for him only when needed, but ultimately, he needed to feel alone. He was a failure as a lover too. I loved Ophelia! Oh, please! There it was the prince who protested too much. Even the way he phrased it, over her grave, had the effect of putting her into the past. That wasn't love. It was shame, perhaps, that love wasn't there, and most likely never had been. He fondly remembered kissing the lips of the dead Yorick. He never remembered kissing the lips of his lover. But then she never was his lover, was she? Not really.

What's left to say? If you ask me, I'd say this: this was not the tragedy of Hamlet. He lost his life, yes. But all of us lose our lives. That's not tragedy. What then? His best qualities counted against him, unfitted him for life, or for the life-circumstances in which he found himself—that's closer. But closer still is that he never really wanted life. He'd lost the taste for it. He wasn't on for it. He got what he wanted instead: oblivion, silence, rest. Ophelia didn't want that. She wanted life. And all of them acted against her in some way. I tried to show it, in the letters I left behind me, and in penning them as I did, I left myself out of it as best I could. I let everybody have their say except myself. I wasn't asked to play a part, other than that of the neutral narrator, which I suppose suited my punctilious personality, if I had a personality at all. But now that my worldly task is done, I'll say it now and I'll say it once only—Ophelia had my heart. How else could a poor pedant put it? She had my heart and never knew it because I could never reveal the secret gift. I barely confessed it to myself, let alone to her. But I loved her—the longing in her eyes, her lips, the deep sweet spirit that got crushed at court, a butterfly between millstones. I think I was the only one who ever truly loved her. Hamlet never could, never did. And she was the one and only innocent at Elsinore. This was her tragedy.

Exit

Re-enter the Ghost of Ophelia

Good Horatio, dear good Horatio, sweet old chap—no, I didn't love you, not in the way I loved your friend. But I could have loved you, another time, another place. I could have loved anybody if he'd let me. I could have made men love me, fall down at my feet and die for me in the good old style. I could have startled all of them. Amazing Ophelia could have spoken Latin and Greek and written them too, could have written letters with fantastic calligraphic loops and flourishes, could have composed pieces for court musicians. I could have asserted myself. Disobedient Ophelia: stop your fussing, old man, and let me live! You've had your time. Or imperious Ophelia: get off your high horse, Hamlet, and come down to earth! Or even abrasive Ophelia: begone, big brother, mind your own affairs! Get back to your French floosies! And leave me to my life.

Ah yes, my life. But what was my life? It wasn't mine. I wasn't me. There was no me. I was a version of me. I wasn't even my own version. I was their version, his especially. I was the version of me that he'd invented for himself. I was the girl without a vagina. That was the first version. Then he came up with the second version—I was all vagina. I was a virgin forest with no one to plant a standard. I was a whole cuntrie and there was nobody in it, not even me. I didn't exist.

I didn't exist—and there was a sense in which I didn't even want to exist, I wanted to wrap myself around him instead, to be oblivious to all but him, oblivious as the weed that roots and rots in ease, remember? You know how it goes. I wanted to be that clinging weed, mindless even for an afternoon, if not an all-night session, I wanted him to root himself in me, to start a growth. I wanted him to be oblivious too—oblivious to everything but me, oblivious to Elsinore and all its irrelevance. When you really love someone after all, everything else is irrelevant, isn't it? Instead of which I knew all too well that I was the irrelevant one.

And yet, he told me he loved me. It was a lie. He didn't love me, he loved the girl who didn't exist, the dream-girl with the excellent white bosom, not the bared breasts which he never touched, or even saw. God forbid. Even my lips would have been a start. But they were all figments of his imagination. I had no such attributes.

I was a non-girl even before I became the gone-girl, in spite of the poetic protestations. Oh, my Ophelia, never doubt that I love you! But never doubt that my love-poem will stay where it belongs—on the page. It won't leap up and deflower you, never fear It's an affair of words: words, words, words.

Of course it was. It was never a love affair, it was a conspiracy of sorts, a well-woven lie. He was never going to rescue me, to sweep me up with him onto his white charger and carry me off and out of Denmark and change my life. And so my life stayed as it was, and what it was, a needlework of mediocrities that he wasn't going to unpick. It was a stich-up of shortcomings: the motherless child, the dutiful daughter, the innocent little sister, the wrong choice, the forbidden choice, the decoy, the bribe, the bait, the cow loosed to the bull, the whore in the convent, the nun in the brothel. Let's face it, I was a mistake, the courtly love that was all court and no love, the prince's intellectual indiscretion, to be corrected, cancelled, regretted—oh yes, greatly regretted, all too late. But all the same he whored me in his mind, he took me without penetration, and in the end he was unkind, he was cold, he was a bloodless butcher. And he killed my heart, he killed my soul. He was Elsinore's executioner. He was just like his uncle. He was a murderer.

A little harsh? Is that what you're thinking? Remember now I can hear what you're thinking. You're wondering if the grieving ghost is going to give way to the angry one. But no, I left anger to the others—to Hamlet mainly. And he had enough anger for all of Elsinore. As for me, it was sorrow that I felt, not anger, call it self-pity if you will. I used to cry sometimes in my closet, in my cold bed, especially at nights, between the snow-sheets. I cried because I wanted to be warm with someone. I cried because I could never imagine meeting someone I could love, apart from him. I was sick with the sorrow of not knowing what things would be like, what they could have been like, what might have been, who I could have been with, what they might have been to me, or who I'd ever be with, if anyone. I was just so hopelessly lonely and alone. Sometimes I cried in my sleep. Or sometimes I dreamed of it—you know, spending the night with a man, an entire night, and begging the horses of the night to ride slowly for us, so that our love-journey could last longer, longer than the dawn. I wanted to watch him eat me with his eyes, unable to get enough of me, to share the same glass, lip to rim, rim to lip, and lip to lip, to let him lean in on me and brush the dried wine-stain from my open mouth, so as to taste me, so as to be me, to let him break into my bodice and bring out the buried longings there, the suppressed needs, before searching deeper, all the way to the forbidden me, the real me, the immaculate misconception, the essential Ophelia...

There were times too, other times, when I could feel a baby beginning in my belly, a tiny little raindrop, a lentil of love that would grow into a pod, a sweet pea, a dish fit for a prince to have put there. But he didn't, as you know, and he couldn't. Everyone at Elsinore was cursed with genitals—except him. So he never put it there, and never would. I put it there myself, and woke up crying in my sleep, bereft of my dream. It was a wish-baby, that's all, a bit of wishful thinking, nothing more.

And then—then it was too late. On came the cortege—and I was the guest of honour, right up there at the head of the procession, the first time I hadn't been bundled away out of sight and safe from harm, so that the gone girl was suddenly the belle of the ball, I was the belle of the passing-bell, you might say, the garlanded girl, with wreaths of the wrong sort, all done up in my box. And what did he say? What did he say when it hit him that I was the grave-girl? He said—the fair Ophelia. Hear it again—the fair Ophelia. Yes, that was me, safe in my box, just as I was when I was at my orisons, or my needle-work, or sewing in my closet, when I could have been undressing instead, or in the privy...

Would it have mattered? Would it have made any difference? No. And yes, ah yes, there she is and there she isn't, the fair Ophelia. Don't go too close to her, though, no closer than those three words, not too near the nub, the rub, no, keep her at a distance, safely sanitised, generalised, impersonalised by the article, *the*, not *she*, no, not *her*, but *the*, *the* fair Ophelia, drained of self by that same article, definite yes, but definitively indefinite, most definitely a non-person, the fair Ophelia, the girl with nothing between her maid's legs…

Will that suffice? If not, it doesn't matter any more, not now. I'm so much happier now, now that I've left all that behind me, all the obligations, the entrances and exits. One: dance to your daddy and his strict political tune, even if it's duping your true-love and selling him out to the skulking king. Two: sit quiet and let yourself be degraded by the same true love, let the whole court picture him picturing your private parts. Three: get all done up in black, for he is dead and gone, lady, murdered by the said true-love when he too was dead and gone, dead to reason and dead to you. Four: gather herbs and flowers, culled for careful distribution, assign significances, ticking the boxes of the mind and heart. Five: go mad, so easy to do, appear in public with said herbs, and hand them out correctly labelled, while singing obscene and soulful songs—Oh, sweet Ophelia!—and expressing your unfulfilled longing, your deep desires. Six: crack up and exit from Elsinore. Seven: drown yourself in style, sing-a-long-a-willow-tree and play with long purples to make the clowns cackle, toss them off in a last fling, the only fling and the final fraud, for he never got a purple up for all his talk, he was so frigid. Eight; make sure you go under, still singing your melodious lay, for they'll all pity a trilling virgin, and they'll all love the dead girl and go mad over her grave—even him, forty thousand times madder than the bereaved brother, so he ranted, and so I once believed, when I was a little innocent, long time passing now, and that did not last long.

Anything else? Left undone perchance? Oh yes. Last stage of all: get buried—easiest of exits, not my problem, not my job, to be laid in earth, the only bed I was ever laid in, cold clay, and put me back, back on my back, where you could have had me, any night you cared, had you cared enough. Too late now, death's my lover now, the Grim Rapist, and worms will welcome the woman, and try that long-preserved virginity. See, here they come now, quietly up the thighs, to the portals of the hymen, and there you have me—ravished at last. I'm undone. And nothing's left to do— unless to do it all again, eternally, and haunt them from my grave?

Too late for that, my friends. They're in their graves already, all of them, even you, Horatio, even you. And you, with a headful of ghosts, were the only one among them that least deserved a haunting. But I'll say it again—I could have loved you. Love was all I wanted. And love denied where it was so desperately needed, it was a kind of haunting too, and more than mere pathos. I think you said it once—it was tragedy. The rest were just deaths. Death's all right. Nothing better. Nothing tragic about death, not if you deserve it, or if you want it, if it's what you live for, if life's lost its meaning for you and the urge to exist has gone. But who am I in the end? The nonentity of Elsinore—what does she know? Not much. I never pretended to know much. I wasn't given the chance. I do know one thing, though, and I know it now for sure, surer than before. That gravedigger—he got it right in his own muddy way. At least he wasn't far from the truth when he said it: she killed herself in self-defence.

Re-enter the Ghost of Horatio

Rest, rest, perturbéd spirit.

Exeunt together

A note on anachronism and language

The Great Cham once said of Shakespeare that a pun was the fatal Cleopatra for which he lost the world. Not everyone would agree that things were quite that bad. What is indisputable is that the Bard's many anachronisms do not detract from his plays, which are, in the end, about people, and not about what they wore, whether knickers were invented or clocks ticked in the sixteenth century.

In writing this novelisation of Hamlet I have followed the same principle and allowed the anachronism to boldly go wherever it led me. This relates to language. The Elizabethans did not think they were speaking 'Elizabethan', and so, while lacing the narrative liberally with Shakespeare's own lines and with sixteenth century mannerisms, I have also tried to impart a modern feel to the language, allowing the narrator to speak directly to the third millennium reader, who will not, hopefully, come away from the book thinking. 'All very realistic, I'm sure – but why are they talking so funny?' It was a matter of balance and I hope I got it right.

Acknowledgements

In December 1959, in my sixteenth year, having just failed all my exams, I was preparing to leave school early and go to sea, and happened to be sitting glumly in front of a twelve-inch black-and-white Bush tv set, which just happened to be switched on. Next thing I knew I was listening to a voice-over telling me that 'this is the tragedy of a man who could not make up his mind'. It was the 1948 Olivier film of Hamlet. I was riveted, transfixed, and begged my mother to let me stay on at school and repeat my 4th Form year, assuring her that her boy could do better. The boy did do better. And the boy, now an old man, never lost his feeling of gratitude to Olivier, and to the life-changing influence on me of that film.

I soon came to realise just how severely it had been cut, and how it had been filmed on a shoestring. Luckily I have lived long enough to see many more memorable Hamlets on both stage and screen, most memorably of all Sir Ian Mckellen and Sir Ben Kingsley on stage, and Innokentii Smoktunovsky on screen. Too many Ophelias have suffered from her traditional stage and screen portrayal as a doll without intellect, 'sweet, not lasting'. Helena Bonham Carter, to whom this book is dedicated, put paid to that tradition with her performance in the 1990 Zeffirelli film, in which she championed Ophelia, playing her, with spirit and character, and not as a wimpy, passive thing without any sexual feelings.

This old git ain't no googler, I'm afraid. I still write with pencil and paper, and, I still slope my writing towards the door, fearfully, as I was ordered to do in 1949 by Miss Sangster, in St Monans primary School. But some time after finishing this book and preparing it for the press, I asked my wife Anna to look up Helena Bonham Carter, and I was delighted to read what she had to say. In particular: 'It would be great to re-write the play from Ophelia's point of view.' Great, I thought, that's part of what I have just done. But I couldn't have done it without the loving support of Anna and my daughter Jenny doing the typing for her old dad, not to mention the research and digital skills of Rachel Brown.

As for scholars and critics, I'm old enough and ugly enough to have been inspired by the old stagers: A. C. Bradley, Granville-Barker, Wilson Knight, L. C. Knights, G. B. Harrison, A. L. Rowse, Dover Wilson – and George Ian Duthie, who taught me Shakespeare in the sixties at Aberdeen University I have since learned a lot from more recent scholars such as Frank Kermode, James Shapiro, Stephen Greenblatt, René Weiss, Jonathan Bate—and from Dominic Dromgoole's and the Globe's astonishing round-the-world journey with Hamlet to mark the 400th anniversary of Shakespeare's death: a monumental and uplifting excursion and account.

Special thanks to Richard Proudfoot, General Editor of the Arden Shakespeare, for valuable information and words of wisdom and experience.

Hamlet is the greatest drama ever written. For that very reason you might well ask: so why turn it into a novel? Why do we even need it? This is where my ultimate thanks must be paid – to Lesley Affrossman and her team at Sparsile Books, who work for love, not money, and whose faith in my take on an old story means that readers can now decide for themselves if they have learned anything new from this version of the most performed play of all time. Look into it, reader, one more time, and if you can, grant me absolution.

Books by the same author

Fiction:

Peace Comes Dropping Slow
Two Christmas Stories
Into the Ebb
Venus Peter Saves the Whale
Last Lesson of The Afternoon Will
Penelope's Web

Non-fiction:

A Twelvemonth And A Day
With Sharp Compassion
Where the Clock Stands Still
To Travel Hopefully: Journal of a Death Not Foretold
Hellfire and Herring
Sex, Lies and Shakespeare
Aunt Epp's Guide for Life: A Victorian Notebook

Translations (with A. Kurkina Rush):

Yuri Tynianov, Young Pushkin
Yuri Tynianov, The Death of Vazir-Mukhtar
Yuri Tynianov Küchlya

Editorial:

New Words in Classic Guise: The Poetry of Felix Dennis
Alastair Mackie: Collected Poems 1954-1994
Alastair Mackie: Discontinuities, Journals and Poems in 2 vols.

Poetry:

A Resurrection of A Kind

Screenplay:

Venus Peter